Tom was born in 1960 and grew up in the suburbs of Los Angeles in a conservative family. He found his niche in the LGBTQ+ community in his early 20s but faced the rejection of his church and much of his family. One of his joys in life is meeting people from different cultures, religions, and lifestyles, and his goal is to be a positive influence to everyone he meets. Although he didn't start writing until his mid-50s, it has become his passion and a major outlet for many of his personal struggles as well as pleasures.

Dedicated to my mom, who encouraged me to write from the heart.

Tom Bither

Moye Schast'ye

My Happiness

Austin Macauley Publishers™

London * Cambridge * New York * Sharjah

A CIP catalogue record for this title is available from the British Library.

ISBN 9781528989497 (Paperback)
ISBN 9781528989503 (Hardback)
ISBN 9781528989510 (ePub e-book)

www.austinmacauley.com

First Published 2023
Austin Macauley Publishers Ltd®
1 Canada Square
Canary Wharf
London
E14 5AA

Special thanks to Irina Ghazaryan, who helped me with the Russian words and phrases and continued to encourage me through the entire process of writing, proofing, and waiting for publication; and to Alejandro Parra, who gave me valuable and critical feedback and never let me give up.

Moye Schast'ye[1]

Part 1

Schast'ye Zhdet[2]

1 *Moye Schast'ye*: My happiness, my joy

2 *Schast'ye Zhdet*: Happiness waits

Chapter 1
The Autumn Encounter

It was a typical Siberian autumn in 1710. The leaves on the trees had turned from green to orange and then to brown and had finally fallen to the ground several weeks ago, before the first snowfall. The bare oak and larch trees looked naked standing above the blanket of snow, but the abundance of fir and spruce trees held the snow in their branches 50 to 100 feet above ground. *Pyatidesyatnik*[3] Alexeev Kondurov was marching his troops across the countryside near the Vychegda River. The snow was six feet deep and the temperature was well below freezing. The river had already frozen over and the water beneath the ice had an eerie dark look as it flowed past the riverbank. The large dark masses of sturgeon could be seen herding beneath the ice, reminding onlookers of the great prize the river held. On the banks of the river, herds of reindeer knelt boldly to drink, unaware of any danger or threat.

Lieutenant Kondurov had already lost four of his thirty-five *streltsy*[4] to the bitter cold, and he was determined not to lose even one more. The troops were exhausted though, and the company was low on food and still had many miles to march before they would reach their destination. The lieutenant was 29 years old, six feet tall and weighed 190 pounds. His shoulders were broad and strong. His arms, chest and legs were thick with muscle and his waist was tapered and well-defined. He had light brown hair that he kept trimmed to just below his ears and he always maintained a well-shaven face. His eyes were green with flecks of gold and brown and they were shaded by his long, light brown eyelashes. He had fair and smooth skin that would have given him a boyish look, except for his square chin and a furrowed brow that had a noticeable cleft separating the brows

---

[3] *Pyatidesyatnik*: Lieutenant

[4] *streltsy*: Soldiers

like a great ridge. Alexeev had been in the Tsar's army since he was 18. His assignment brought him and his troops to Pechora, in the northeast, to retrieve sensitive documents and valuables necessary for an upcoming peace treaty with the Turks, and they were now returning to Moscow after nearly eight months in the rough and frigid terrain. As they neared the river, they snagged and killed a stag and caught three large sturgeon. It was a good feeding for a few days and nights, but the meat didn't last long and the wildlife kept their distance after the kill. They followed the river for the next week hoping to catch more fish, but their resources were again running low and the ice covering the river was too thick to break through.

As they crossed over the river to the northwest, they entered the little town of Storozhevsk, a rural farming community of about 1,000 families. The lieutenant had heard good things about some of the homes in this area and the hospitality of the townsfolk: how they welcomed the military anytime they happened to be travelling through the area. They were also known for their lavish kindnesses. He saw candlelight glowing in a nearby home, so he led his troops up the path to the large white cottage with green trim. The yard was well-maintained and all the pathways were shovelled, exposing the pristine cobblestone walkways leading here and there from the road to the house, encompassing the building and extending into the backyard and beyond. As he approached the home, the front door opened and a man in his early fifties walked out onto the porch. He was slightly bent with age and the top of his balding head was covered with a knitted cap that looked like it had also seen many winters. The gentleman was a little shorter than average but appeared distinguished and healthy, though a little chunky but not heavyset. He was obviously doing well and not lacking in material things, and the fireplace in the living room radiated a warm glow behind him. The stained-glass windows on either side of the front door gave off a multi-coloured welcoming array as well.

"What can I do for you?" the man called out. "Have you lost your way?"

"My troops need food and shelter for the night. We have been traveling for several months now and still have a long journey in front of us. Several of my men have taken ill and we are nearly out of food. Can you help us?"

"Yes, of course. Take your men around back. There are stables and a large outbuilding with plenty of room for them to bed down for the night. There are also several large fireplaces inside with enough wood to last the night and for several more days. I will have my servants bring them food and drink for the evening. When you have settled them in, please join me in my home and you and I will have food, drink and a good long talk."

Alexeev bowed gracefully and motioned his men to follow him. There was something about this gentleman that made the lieutenant feel warm and welcomed. Maybe it was his soft smile, or the twinkle in his eyes, or perhaps his distinguished grey temples, moustache, and chin beard. Whatever it was, Alexeev was anxious to get to know this man better. There was also an unfamiliar feeling in his gut, a flutter or quiver, that made him feel both nervous and full of deep pleasure at the same time. It was difficult for him to think about his men, but he managed to get them settled in their temporary accommodations. One of the servants met them in the back by the outbuilding and led them inside.

"Good afternoon, I am Pavel," he said as he reached out his hand and smiled. Pavel was several years younger than Alexeev but spoke with the authority of his master. He was well-dressed, well-groomed and had a Slavic accent. "I am available to you and your men for any of your needs. I will arrange for the evening meal and breakfast. There is a large room on the left side of the building where they can bathe, and if there are any clothes in need of cleaning, one of the other servants will gather them and clean them while you are here. The master also has a storage room in the back where he keeps the cots and bedding for guests. How many men do you have in your company?"

"There are thirty-one now," he replied.

"Very good. While they are washing up, I will have supper prepared for them. One of the servants is heating the water in the upper tanks for the showers, but it should be ready within the hour. Meanwhile, if you could have them set up the cots in the back room and separate their clothes for washing, we will do the rest. There are large baskets in the back room for their clothes. If there are any clothes that need mending, have the men separate those from the others. We have a tailor that will mend those while you are here." Just then, Kirill and Anton entered and started guiding the troops to the storage room. They looked more like boys than men. Alexeev guessed they were probably 15 or 16 at best. But they looked strong and healthy, and obviously knew what they were doing.

Each of Alexeev's men retrieved a cot and set them up in the designated area. Then Anton brought out the bedding and began distributing the sheets and blankets for each cot, while Kirill started gathering the clothes that needed washing and mending. Then Kirill led them to the bathing area and showed them how to use the heated water tank for the showers. The bathing room floor was completely tiled, and there were benches on three sides of the room with shelves above them stacked with clean towels. The far wall was lined with showers, each one having a niche with new bars of scented soaps.

After the men showered, they changed into fresh, clean robes that were hanging on poles on either side of the benches, so they could have the rest of their clothes washed. This was a special treat they appreciated very much. Usually, their missions did not give them much opportunity to clean their clothes, and often they would have to make use of river water and rocks along the banks, and sometimes without the advantage of proper soaps. It was the first proper shower or bath they had since the start of their mission eight months ago, so their spirits were uplifted and everyone was laughing and joking and enjoying the moment. They were all looking forward to a good meal and a pleasant, restful night's sleep.

Foka and Ivan, two other servants, started bringing in the food for supper and laying it out on the long wooden table in the centre of the main room. Soon, the men were banqueting on a lavish meal of various hot and cold meats of pork and deer, cooked, pickled and fresh vegetables, a variety of fruit compotes, braided breads and rye breads, pastries, vodka and wine from the master's cellar. While the men ate, Alexeev went with Kirill to make sure all the clothes were gathered. He also inspected the sleeping area to ensure every cot had sufficient bedding for the night, and he and Kirill built a fire in the large fireplace to warm the building for the night. Alexeev was impressed there were so many cots and blankets available and they were provided such a wonderful meal. It looked as if somehow the master had anticipated the lieutenant and his troops would stop by for a visit. Kirill explained this was a military-friendly farmhouse, and the master opened his home quite often to travellers of every sort: the occasional foreigner, families crossing the wilderness in search of a resting place and more often, military troops in need of basic comforts and accommodations for a night or two. The master believed in always being prepared for anyone who might need assistance.

When the men finished eating and were settled in for the night, Alexeev walked up to the back door of the cottage and knocked. The gentleman opened the door and smiled, "Welcome to my humble home. I am Tomas Pedorov, but my friends call me Tomi. I was a soldier once myself when I was a young lad like you." Alexeev felt relieved and walked in, removing his hat with respect. "Have a seat, my young comrade."

"Thank you for your hospitality, *Dvoryanin*[5]. You have been very generous to my men, and most kind," said the lieutenant. "How can we repay you?"

"No need for that, my boy. Your company is more than sufficient, and please call me Tomi. I am neither noble nor part of the aristocracy." Tomi led Alexeev into the dining area where a table was set, and a fine dinner was prepared just for Alexeev. There was roasted chicken, green beans with pickled onions and carrots, *borscht*[6], rye bread with cheese and honey, candied apricots and peaches and homemade blackberry wine. The home was warm from the fire, and occasionally, Tomi would walk over to the fireplace and place a small log on the fire, or prod the burning logs with the iron poker, or fan the flames with the bellows. He sat Alexeev at the head of the table and served him each dish, explaining in detail the spices he used for each dish, or the cooking preparation, and he was especially proud and talkative about his blackberry wine.

"I can't tell you enough how grateful I am that you took us in and provided us a meal and a place to stay for the night," said the lieutenant.

"It is a miracle you found your way to my home at all…or possibly, the fates have allowed you to find me," answered Tomi. "But I want you to consider staying here for a few more days. Pavel told me several of your men have fever, and at least half of your company looks like they are suffering from malnutrition. Let them rest here for a while so they can regain their strength."

"That is too much to ask of you," Alexeev said.

"Let me be the judge of that. I have the resources, the space, and the time to spend as I see fit, and it would please me if you and your men would be my guests." Tomi started to clear the table.

"But I insist we repay you in some way. Perhaps my men and I could chop wood or make repairs—"

Tomi interrupted, "We can talk about that in the morning. For now, you need a hot bath and a good night's sleep. I have hot water all ready for your bath, and there is a spare bedroom at the top of the stairs for you to sleep." Tomi led the lieutenant to a room on the side of the kitchen. There was a large tub, clean towels, scented soaps and washcloths. Tomi went over to the tub and turned the valve to let the hot water fill the tub. "While you are bathing, I'll get your bed ready."

---

[5] *Dvoryanin* – nobleman

[6] *Borscht*: A popular soup in Eastern Europe, usual made with beets, cabbage and potatoes.

Alexeev bowed graciously and thanked him. Then he started to get undressed. Meanwhile, Tomi went up to the spare bedroom and lit the matching blue lamps that were hand-painted with yellow and orange daisies, put clean sheets and blankets on the bed, lit the fire and left a bottle of scented oils on the nightstand next to the bed. Then he went into his own bedroom and found a long robe for Alexeev to wear. He took it down to the bathing room where Alexeev was nearly asleep in the bathtub.

"You look like you are exhausted," said Tomi.

A little startled, Alexeev sat up and started rinsing his hair, then took a washcloth and finished scrubbing his arms and face. "It was very relaxing," he said as he stood up and took the towel from the rack and started drying himself off.

"I have a few teas I've used to reduce fevers," said Tomi. Alexeev's naked body was a marvellous sight to behold. Tomi lost his train of thought for a moment. "…your body will be firm and dry in no time…I mean, their fevers should be gone in no time." Tomi dropped the robe and blushed, then quickly walked out of the bathing room.

Alexeev finished drying himself off, then put on the robe and gathered his clothes together. He followed the yellow-orange glows and flickers of the fireplace out to the parlour where Tomi was just getting ready to smoke his pipe. He leaned in, not wanting to interrupt Tomi's privacy. "May I join you?" he asked.

"Of course, of course," he replied. "I have an extra pipe…do you smoke?" He held out a beautiful cherrywood pipe.

Alexeev took the pipe and looked it over, "Yes I do, but I don't get the opportunity very often."

Tomi handed him the tobacco pouch. "This is a blend from Turkey. I have a customer who smuggles the tobacco leaves back for me in exchange for some of my bottles of wine."

"The Tsar is also fond of smoking," Alexeev commented. He didn't want Tomi to think he would turn him in for possession of tobacco. "He thinks it is a very civilised practice."

Tomi just smiled and lit his pipe. He didn't like to get into political discussions or debates. "Would you care for a cup of *Krupnik*[7]?"

---

[7] *Krupnik*: (Polish) Hot honey-spiced vodka drink

"That would be wonderful. I haven't had *Krupnik* since I left Moscow in March."

Tomi poured him a cupful and handed it to him. Alexeev inhaled the steam, then took a sip. "Wonderful!" He took another sip, then lit his pipe. The two of them sat for a while in silence, enjoying the peace and warm glow of the fireplace while the hot blend of spices, vodka, and honey warmed the insides of their bodies. "Do you live here alone?"

"I had a companion several years ago, but no more. Now it is only me, Pavel, and my servants." Tomi wasn't completely sure how much of his private life and feelings he wanted to reveal to the lieutenant. Alexeev leaned back on the settee and set his cup down on the end table. He held his pipe in one hand and stretched his other arm behind Tomi across the back of the settee. Tomi quickly stood up, a little unsure of the lieutenant's intentions, and put another log on the fire even though it was already going strong. The robe was opened above Alexeev's waist, exposing his muscular chest. Tomi had a difficult time concentrating and found himself focussing on the well-defined chest muscles. They were covered with a moderate layer of light-brown hair that perfectly embraced the curves and lines of his body. Tomi was mesmerised by his beauty and masculinity. He still had images in his mind of Alexeev's naked wet body in the bathtub. He visualised how the soap suds clung to his skin and how the water flowed down Alexeev's chest like a majestic waterfall caressing a glorious mountain of solid granite. He imagined those muscles pressing up against him, and how it would feel if Alexeev's weight was on top of him, forcing him to the ground, holding him in place—

"I said, may I have another cup?" The sound of Alexeev's voice brought Tomi out of his trance.

"Of course." He quickly poured another cup. "I'm feeling very tired, Lieutenant. I hope you won't think badly of me if I excuse myself."

"Not at all. I'm feeling tired myself," he said as he stood up and took his cup with him. Tomi led the way to the bedrooms up the stairs.

"Your room is here on the right," he said. "Don't worry about your men. Pavel will make sure they are all well-fed in the morning. My room is here on the left. Let me know if you need anything." As Tomi turned towards his bedroom, he nearly ran himself into the wall, but abruptly stopped just in time.

Alexeev bowed and held back a laugh. “Thank you for everything. Have a pleasant sleep.” Then Tomi quickly backed himself into his bedroom and nodded, embarrassed and flustered.

The next morning was at least as cold as the days had been for the past week. Tomi got up early to start breakfast for Alexeev and to make sure Pavel had everything under control for the troops. He never doubted the abilities or loyalty of his servants, especially Pavel, but he always wanted to make sure they knew he was around if they needed him. Pavel was well-trained in household management, was knowledgeable of accounting and had a good understanding of civil law. Tomi had ensured Pavel’s education and had personally trained Pavel in the wine business, and now it was his job to make sure the profits increased each year. His education enabled him to advise Tomi on matters of investment, supply purchases and charitable giving, and the two were like-minded on giving to the poor, assisting the down-trodden and helping the military. Tomi had served several years in the army, so he was very aware of the struggles they encountered every day.

The kitchen in the house had a large oven to accommodate Tomi’s love of baking, and another kitchen in the outbuilding. Foka and Ivan were already busy preparing breakfast for the men. They had baked several dozen loaves of bread in Tomi’s oven before anyone else was awake and were now using the facilities in the outbuilding to finish making breakfast for the troops. There were jars of pickled cabbage and *ikra*[8], several trays of sausages ready to be heated, pots of water heating on the stovetop for tea, jars of honey, plates of cheeses and butter, a variety of fruit compotes and two large bowls of *chalka*[9] dough ready to be formed and baked. Kirill had finished a few batches of clothes and had hung them in the warming room to dry. He was getting ready to wash the last few batches. Anton was tending the animals and had already milked the cows and given them their feed, and now he was gathering the eggs. Pavel was diligently overseeing each task and giving his men the proper encouragement each one needed and deserved. Tomi had a good group of men and boys who worked hard for their pay and were rewarded handsomely for well-done jobs.

The smells of breakfast sausages, eggs, fresh baked bread, and *chalka* soon filled the outbuilding. Tomi was busy making breakfast for Alexeev in the kitchen in the house and soon the aromas from Tomi’s kitchen drifted to the

---

[8] *Ikra*: Caviar

[9] *Chalka* – A soft, sweet Polish bread

upstairs bedroom. Alexeev was soon awake and feeling very hungry. He made his way to the kitchen where Tomi was getting ready to pour the hot water into the teapot.

"Here, let me do that for you," he said. He carefully poured the hot water over the tea leaves then returned the pot to the stove. Tomi took the pan of sausages out of the oven where they had been heating and transferred them to his china platter with the scarlet rim and pinecone designs. Then he transferred the eggs and *blini*[10] as well. He had already set the table and placed a honeypot, a dish of fruit compote and a small tray of *tvorog*[11] near the head of the table where Alexeev would be sitting.

"I think everything is ready. If you could take the teapot and the platter of sausages, I can get the rest." Alexeev picked them up and raised them above Tomi's head, barely missing him as Tomi fumbled his way past him. Then he followed Tomi into the dining room.

They sat together and had their fill of the eggs and sausages and Alexeev raved about how good everything tasted, especially the *blini*. They talked a lot about the men's health situation and Tomi insisted the troops stay for at least a few more days so they could get over their fevers. He assured Alexeev he had plenty of food and supplies, and not to worry about any kind of repayment. But Alexeev didn't want to take without giving back. Most of his men were still strong and healthy and there was no reason why they could not work while the others were recuperating.

A few years ago, Tomi had drawn up plans to expand his cellar but he didn't have the manpower to complete the job, so he explained to Alexeev what the job entailed. The cellar was accessible by a stairwell just off the kitchen next to the hallway, and by a trap door that opened into the backyard about 20 feet from the house near the woodshed. The cellar covered an area of about thirty by forty feet, and Tomi wanted to double its area. He had the lumber for bracing the walls and ceiling, and several beams already cut to size for bracing and support. Tomi explained he could never find the time or the manpower to get past the planning stage. After the cellar is expanded, Tomi could increase his storage capacity, thus increasing the potential of his business.

Alexeev looked over the plans and agreed to have his men complete the cellar for Tomi. They would start immediately after breakfast. Alexeev estimated the

---

[10] *Blini*: Russian pancakes that are thin and flat like crepes

[11] *Tvorog*: A traditional Russian cheese, similar to farmer's or cottage cheese

job would be finished in about three days, possibly four, and by then the rest of his men should be well enough to travel again. Tomi was glad for the help and was especially pleased Alexeev would be around for a few more days. After breakfast, he took Alexeev down to the cellar to assess the situation, then out to the storage building where Tomi had all the lumber and supplies. By then, his men were finishing up breakfast. He separated the healthy men into shifts, since the cellar was particularly cold this time of year. While one shift shovelled and cleared the space, the other shift would prepare then shore up the side walls and ceiling with the lumber and bracings.

While the men worked, it gave Alexeev and Tomi a chance to get to know each other better. Tomi had Pavel take the carriage into town to fetch the doctor so he could examine the men, and by noon, the doctor had examined all the men who were exhibiting symptoms: fever, nausea and diarrhoea. His diagnosis was *bilious fever*[12]. The doctor's first order was to confine the sick men and keep them isolated as much as possible. They were prescribed honey with cinnamon and lemon four times a day and would need to take steam baths every day until their fevers were gone. He also had a few potions that could be mixed with tea and drunk several times a day. Pavel was placed in charge of administering the treatments, since he had the same fever the previous year and was not likely to fall sick again. The outbuilding had a second floor, so the men who were ill could easily be confined and treated in privacy without exposing the healthy men any further. Fortunately, no one else came down with the fever, so Pavel would only be treating and tending to six of the thirty-one men. Foka would make sure everyone had plenty of nutritious food to eat and drink to build up their strength.

Alexeev oversaw his men in the cellar for a few hours that afternoon but decided they could work better without him. So, he joined Tomi and they talked all afternoon. The men decided two-hour shifts would be long enough, so they scheduled their breaks accordingly. This ensured each of them had time to warm themselves, rest from the strenuous labour and have time to get something to eat throughout the afternoon. By evening, they reported one-quarter of the way done with the digging and bracing, so it was likely they would finish by the fourth day.

---

[12] *Bilious fever*: A medical diagnosis often used for any fever that exhibited the symptom of nausea or vomiting in addition to an increase in internal body temperature and strong diarrhea.

They had been away from home for several months though and many were getting restless. Even though the respite was a welcome change, they still needed a fun activity to help keep their minds off home and their families. During the summer months, the lieutenant would get them involved in competitions, like races and relays, wrestling, *tablier or draughts*[13], *babki or knucklebones*[14] and *svaika or quoits*[15]. But most of those games were best played outdoors and in warmer weather. He decided to start an arm-wrestling tournament to fill the evenings for the next three nights. He even convinced Tomi and his servants to join in the fun. Several of the men were very strong and sure to be the best of the group, but a few of Tomi's servants looked like they would do well, at least they could give competition to some of the troops. He talked over the competition with *Desyatnik*[16] Sergey who was very enthusiastic, especially when Tomi announced he had four bottles of his best blackberry wine he would give to the four top winners of the competition. Sergey relayed the information to the rest of the men.

So, the men sat down for dinner and planned out the competition. Everyone was paired up for the first round, then they would rotate through each other until everyone had the opportunity to challenge for the first round. Pavel drew up a schedule for the competition on a slate board and had chalk so he could mark each of the winners of the first round. The men were ready for the competition to begin.

The competition would start with the shortest and smallest men in the first round. Since Tomi was shorter than all except one of Alexeev's men, and only one of his servants was shorter than him, namely Anton, Tomi would be competing in the first round. He was very relieved, because he knew he was not a very strong man compared to the rest of the men present, and he had no qualms about admitting his weakness. The men lined up all the tables after dinner and had the first round of contenders sit in their places, ready to begin. Each pair was assigned a third man to be the judge over the round, ensure rules were followed and especially to see that no one got hurt.

For the first match, Tomi was paired with Fedya, who was one of Alexeev's youngest men. He was seventeen and about an inch taller than Tomi, but he

---

[13] *Tablier or draughts* – Traditional Russian board game similar to parcheesi

[14] *Babki or knucklebones* – A traditional Russian game played with the leg bones of cattle

[15] *Svaika or quoits* – A traditional Russian folk game played with iron pegs

[16] *Desyatnik* – Sargent

looked like he was one of the ones Pavel said might be malnourished. They put their arms together and grasped hands. Five other pairs did the same. Alexeev stood over Tomi and Fedya and counted down, "three…two…one…go!" They struggled for a few moments and their arms wavered back and forth slowly. Fedya looked into Tomi's eyes and it looked like he was gaining the lead, but Tomi surprised him and himself and pinned Fedya's arm to the table. About the same time, each of the other five pairs finished their matches. Alexeev congratulated Tomi and patted him on the back.

Then they stood up and rotated to their next match. This time Tomi was paired with Dmitry, who was about twenty-five, well-built and about three inches taller than Tomi. They locked arms and hands and again, Alexeev counted down, "Three…two…one…go!" This time, Tomi knew he had been beaten before the countdown was done. He struggled to keep his arm upright even for a few moments, then submitted it down to the table. The next two matches went on much the same way, with Modya, eighteen years old, and Alik, the youngest member of the company at sixteen years old. Tomi's only win was with Fedya and he had a feeling Alexeev set it up for Fedya to let Tomi win his first match. But it wasn't important to Tomi. He realised the whole idea of this tournament was to engage the men in an activity to get their minds off of the stress and loneliness of their mission.

The next set of matches for the first night was amongst the biggest and strongest of the group. Although Alexeev was among the strongest, he was not the largest or tallest in his company. The tallest was Ivan, who was about four inches taller than Alexeev, then Afanas and Dem who were three inches taller, then Slava, Stefan and Zakhar, who were just an inch taller. Toma and Yegor were also taller than Alexeev but they were excluded from the competition because of the fever. Then there was Aramazd who was the same height, yet thinner, and Taras and Stas who were also the same height and roughly the same build as Alexeev. His real competition would be with Sergey and Viktor. They were both as tall as Alexeev, but they were stockier and more muscular.

They were paired off as follows:

Viktor and Stas
Stefan and Zakhar
Slava and Dem
Taras and Ivan

Sergey and Aramazd
Afanas and Alexeev

Tomi was nervous about the pairing of this first round, because it looked like Afanas could beat Alexeev, perhaps not easily, but he wanted Alexeev to win. After looking at the rest of the men, Tomi wondered if Alexeev could even make it to third or fourth place. So many of them were very muscular and tall. He hadn't noticed before, but it looked as if the entire company was made up of men who were nearly perfect physically, like well-built, well-chiselled statues, at least when they were compared to Tomi, whose physical appearance was anything but staggering. Even when he was a younger lad, in his twenties and thirties, he could not compete physically with very many of his peers. He was usually the shortest and nearly always the weakest in his company when he was in the army. He always had duties related to brainwork rather than physical prowess or expertise. But army men always protect each other. Rarely did they pick on the weakest, but rather, they would come to the defence when any of their own were in danger.

He watched as the men sat down across from each other. Several of them had taken off their shirts, no doubt to create as much freedom of movement as possible, but likely also to posture their masculinity and strength. Alexeev hadn't removed his shirt but he had unbuttoned it down to his trousers. Tomi could see the chiselled muscles on each of the men and he wished he could see more of Alexeev's glorious body. Was it more than he imagined and remembered? He could see the light brown hair covering his pectorals and he could see the deep cleavage between the muscles, but he dared not stare lest anyone suspect his curiosity. He was especially fearful of how Alexeev would react if he knew Tomi was enamoured by his beauty and entranced by his manliness and charisma.

Alexeev and Afanas latched arms and grasped hands. Afanas had a tattoo on his forearm that made his muscles look even more intimidating. The hairs on his arms and wrists were jet black and the veins on his arms were pumped with blood. He was one who had removed his shirt. Tomi could see his pumped-up chest and deep grooves around each muscle, accentuating his great strength. As he grasped Alexeev's hand, his chest twitched and bounced. It had nearly a hypnotic effect on Tomi. He could barely concentrate on anything else. He saw the valleys between Afanas' muscles on his torso leading down to his navel and the thin lines of black hair trailing down to the top of his trousers. Tomi laid his hands over the top of the two clutched hands of the wrestlers. He heard voices yelling in the background, but he couldn't make out the words. He looked down at Alexeev, who smiled back at him and winked. Tomi could hear himself say, "Three…two…one…go!"

Suddenly, he was out of his trance. The two men were struggling with all their might. Alexeev was obviously exerting a lot of strength, but he seemed rather calm and composed. Afanas was tense and his muscles were flexed tight. The match went on for several minutes. Both men were sweating and their arms were glistening in the lights of the many candles throughout the building. Afanas' face started to grimace and Alexeev knew the time was right for him to make his move. He exerted the reserve strength he had been holding back and slowly pinned his opponent's arm to the table. Afanas looked Alexeev squarely in the eyes, then smiled, grabbed the back of Alexeev's head with his free arm, then they stood up and shook hands and the first match was over.

Tomi congratulated Alexeev and gave him a kiss on the cheek. Then he looked into his eyes and smiled. He hoped Alexeev understood his smile meant more than just a laud for his victory, but he quickly turned around and began congratulating the other winners. He asked Pavel to bring in several bottles of vodka and all the men toasted to the successes of the day and to the victors of the tournament. As the men finished the bottles, Tomi and Alexeev excused themselves and walked back to the house. It had been a long day and a long evening. The clock struck twelve when they got inside, so they decided it was too late to stay up any longer, even for good conversation. They walked up the stairs and Tomi opened the door to his room. There was a cold draft and he shivered.

"You're cold," said Alexeev. "Let me come in and start the fire in your fireplace while you get ready for bed."

"That's not necessary—"

"I insist," he said as he took Tomi by the arm and guided him into the bedroom. "Now you just get yourself ready for bed while I build the fire." He quickly threw some twigs and logs into the fireplace, then lit the wood. "That should warm you up now."

Tomi had taken off his clothes and had put on his nightshirt and woollen cap. Alexeev held back a laugh. He was not used to seeing anyone wear a cap to bed, and he never wore any clothes to bed at all as a general practice. It always felt unnatural to him to confine his body with clothing when he slept. His cousin Orlov, who had raised him, asked him one time why he wasn't ashamed to go to bed naked. Alexeev's reply was very simple, "If the gods created us in their image, like the sacred books claim, then they would not want us to cover their works of art with manmade clothes. We only wear clothes in public because of our shame, not their shame of us. So, when we sleep, and they are the only ones who see us, we should be more than willing to show them how beautiful their creation is."

"Thank you for lighting the fire, Alexeev." He pulled back the covers and slipped his legs between the sheets. "I always have a hard time lighting a fire very quickly."

Alexeev walked over to the bed and tucked the blankets around Tomi's legs. "I don't want you getting a chill. We don't need Pavel looking after you along with my men." Then he sat on the bed. "I want you to know how much I am indebted to you for your hospitality. Not only have you given us shelter and food, but you are helping me keep my men entertained while the rest of them recover." He put his hand on top of Tomi's hand. "Thank you…tomorrow I will get up with you and build the fire in your kitchen. I think you are working much too hard on my account." He squeezed Tomi's hand, then got up and walked towards the door. "Have a good rest tonight, Tomi."

"Good night, Alexeev." After he left the room, Tomi turned over towards the fireplace and watched the flames dance behind the iron lattice screen. He had a difficult time falling asleep with everything that happened that night. He thought about the possibility of Alexeev staying on but couldn't think of a good reason why he should stay, other than his own selfish desires. He fantasised about Alexeev coming to bed with him and resting his muscular body on top of him. He imagined the hot air of Alexeev's breath on his neck, and their moist lips drinking in each other's passion. He felt his cock getting hard underneath the covers. He took a deep breath and felt a tear forming in the corner of his eye. He wiped it away, then turned himself onto his stomach and clutched the pillow and fell asleep.

Chapter 2
Winning and Losing

The men's spirits were soaring the next morning. They were light-hearted and jovial, and anxious to get their duties of the day completed so they could carry on with the arm-wrestling competition after dinner. Alexeev knew his men well and he also knew human nature. When his men have something to look forward to, they perform better on their jobs, even if the job at hand is very difficult. But he also wanted to make sure he didn't cast a shadow on those who wouldn't perform well in the competition, so he made sure they all received due praise, even if they lost, as long as they gave it their best effort.

Tomi got up early to start making breakfast, but to his surprise, Alexeev was already in the kitchen firing up the stove and getting a pot of water ready for the tea. "Good morning, *sonya*![17] It looked like you might sleep all winter, so I thought I'd help you get things started," said the lieutenant with a smile.

"Thank you, *moy general*[18]*,"* replied Tomi as he bowed to Alexeev. He reached up into the cupboard and retrieved two cups and saucers. Then opened the pantry and found the jar of honey for the tea. He scooped out a generous amount of tea from the tea tin on the table and poured it into the teapot.

"May I add a few mint leaves?" asked Alexeev, as he opened a small pouch he had in his pocket.

"Certainly."

Alexeev dropped a few of the mint leaves into the pot, then poured the boiling water over the tea leaves. The smells of the tea and mint soon filled the air. Then Alexeev leaned over to Tomi and kissed his forehead.

"What's that for?"

---

[17] *Sonya*!: Sleepyhead! (literally, dormouse)

[18] *Moy general*: My leader, my master

"I checked in on my men this morning. I've never seen them sleep so soundly. And last night, several of them told me how well your servants are treating them and how excellent the food is."

Tomi wasn't used to compliments. "I enjoy helping people, that's all."

"You've done more than just helped them…we were running out of food, and I wasn't sure we would be able to find enough to keep us going, especially since some of them were getting sick." Alexeev got a little choked up. "I'm not used to having to rely on others…not for survival."

"Maybe it's time you start," Tomi said softly. He wanted to say more. He wanted to ask Alexeev to stay and consider settling down. He wanted to tell him it's all right to be vulnerable and it's all right to need others in your life…but Tomi wasn't sure of himself. He lacked self-confidence and the boldness it takes to confront others or even speak his mind, even when it is for their own good…so he kept quiet.

While Tomi made breakfast, Alexeev went out to the woodshed and brought in a wheelbarrow full of wood for the house. Foka and Ivan were busy preparing breakfast for the troops, but Alexeev decided to let the men sleep a little while longer. He wanted them to get as much rest as they could while they were here because they still had a long journey ahead of them going back to Moscow. He also checked in with Pavel, who told him a few of the men in isolation were feeling better last night and he thought their fevers were going down. That was wonderful news. He had feared the men might be so tired and worn out that recovery could take several weeks.

By the time he brought the wood inside the house Tomi had breakfast ready. So, the two of them sat down at the table and ate together. Tomi had made *blini* with *tvorog* and blackberry jam, and sausages with pickled onions and carrots. When Alexeev was at home in Moscow, his cousin Orlov would cook for him. These were the kinds of meals Alexeev was used to, but only at home, and Tomi was almost as good a cook as his cousin. But when he and his troops were on missions they had to eat whatever they could find, or forage, or kill, which wasn't always very easy. Many of their missions were in winter, when hunting was more difficult because of the extreme weather conditions and the scarcity of wildlife. Fishing was sometimes a better option, but their missions didn't always take them by the rivers, and in winter many of the rivers were frozen over.

After breakfast, Tomi needed to ride into town to take care of some business with the mayor and a few merchants so he left Pavel in charge. "Anything you need before I return, just ask Pavel. I may not be back until late this afternoon, but I'll try to be back in time for the competition!"

Once the men finished their breakfast, Alexeev got them started on their shifts in the cellar. He wanted to get two-thirds of the way done before dinner. Of course, he made sure everyone took their breaks and had a good lunch as well. Alexeev even took his turn with a shovel. His ulterior motive was to check in on the progress of his men. Although he knew they wouldn't let him down, and they always did superior work, he still wanted this job to be done with exceptional mastery. He thought about Tomi all day long. He remembered his smile and the way he would bow his head when he was uncomfortable or embarrassed. He remembered the soft skin on the back of his hand and he even remembered his smell: it reminded him of lavender and vanilla. He didn't know just why he couldn't get the thought out of his mind, of being around Tomi, but he wasn't disturbed by the thoughts either. He discovered the more he thought about Tomi, the happier it made him. *I need to find out more about him*, he thought. *I wonder if he feels the same way about me? But I don't even know what I feel about him, and I don't know why I can't stop thinking about him*. He decided he would take the time to get to know him better after the competition. Maybe they could sit in the parlour for a while and talk just as they had started to do that first night.

The men made good progress all day. By the time they were ready to take a dinner break, the job was nearly two-thirds done. Alexeev was very proud of their accomplishment, especially since they had uncovered a massive stone just after lunch and had to break it into pieces in order to remove it. Tomi had not yet returned from town, so Alexeev had dinner with his men. He reviewed the schedule for the competition with the men and then they began with the winners of the first rounds facing some of the men who had not yet competed. Tonight even a few of Tomi's servants would rotate into the competition, including Pavel and Ivan. Pavel would compete against Naum and Ivan would vie off against Vlasiy.

The men who were sick with fevers were feeling better so they snuck down to watch the competition, even though they were not yet strong enough to join in. To Alexeev's surprise the six men were cheering for Pavel to win. They were all indebted to him for taking such good care of them. He would come upstairs several times each day to make sure they had plenty of food and tea, along with administering their regular routine of medicines, and he personally bathed each one of them and made sure they had clean clothes and bedding each day. Yegor, the youngest of the six, developed the shakes earlier in the day after breakfast, and Pavel held him in his arms until he calmed down and fell asleep. Pavel also kept the fireplace going all day and all night to keep them all warm. It was no wonder Tomi praised Pavel so much and paid him such a high salary. He was well worth his pay, and Tomi knew it.

So, Pavel won against Naum, then he won against Metvei and also against Vlasiy. But then he lost to Yevgeny, Aleksandr and finally to Igor. The rules of the competition were that three losses took you out of the rotation, so Pavel bowed out gracefully, though his six patients protested with much exuberance. Tomi arrived back from town just in time to see Pavel's last match. The younger men had a few more matches to complete before the older, stronger men began their matches for the evening. Ivan did a little better than Pavel. He won against Vlasiy, Metvei, Naum and Aleksandr, but lost to Yevgeny and Igor. He would advance to the third night's rounds.

Tonight, Alexeev would be up against Stefan, Taras, Viktor and Stava, and he would win all four matches. By the end of the night, there were only two that were yet undefeated: Alexeev and Sergey. After the matches were over, Pavel brought out several more bottles of vodka for the men, and while they all drank to each other's health and good fortune, Tomi and Alexeev excused themselves for the evening and went inside the house.

"You were wonderful tonight," whispered Tomi. "I think you must be the strongest in the group!" He put his hands around Alexeev's sweaty bicep and squeezed. Alexeev flexed his arm, reacting to Tomi's comment.

"You think so?" he said. "I don't know if I can beat Sergey though. The men are always saying he is the biggest…and strongest."

"I'll bet you could take him down easily." Tomi hung onto Alexeev's arm as they walked up to the house. Alexeev didn't seem to mind, in fact, he smiled as if he was enjoying the attention. "I still have some *Krupnik* from yesterday. Would you like me to heat some up?"

"That would be wonderful," he said. "I'll start the fire in the stove for you."

Tomi brought out a large covered two-handled pot and set it on the stove. Then he got out a loaf of bread and some cheese and set them on a tray. "We can sit for a while and talk if you like."

While they waited for the *Krupnik* to heat, Alexeev told Tomi about the progress on the cellar and how they would probably only need one more day to finish the job. Tomi was a little disappointed, not that he was disappointed in the progress, but because he had hoped the job would take at least a week. When he had originally told Alexeev about the excavation, he was thinking it would be a task difficult enough to keep Alexeev around for a while so they could get to know each other better. He wasn't counting on Alexeev and his men being so proficient in their skills.

Finally, the *Krupnik* was hot, so Alexeev poured a good portion of it into an earthen pitcher. They brought food and drink into the parlour and sat down and made themselves comfortable. Tomi took off his shoes and untucked his shirt, then Alexeev did the same. They poured themselves a cup of the spicy elixir and served themselves some bread and cheese. The two men talked for hours. They found they had more in common than either of them realised at first. They were both unmarried, both grew up in farming communities, both enjoyed the same appreciation of musical composers, of *partesny*[19] singing and traditional chants, especially Nikolay Diletsky and Simeon Pekalitskiy. Both had the same favourite writers: William Shakespeare, Miguel de Cervantes, Andres Gryphius and the German poet, Walther von der Vogelweide. And both had an appreciation for hot spiced vodka. Hours passed, and their conversation became more intimate and personal. They shared stories of their army experiences, their home lives growing up, a few of their past accomplishments and failures and their hopes and dreams and fears.

As they talked about their past lives and experiences, the conversation began to unveil secrets hidden inside their thoughts, behind their words. They both knew they wanted each other, but both held back. Alexeev had been alone his entire life and had never experienced the intimate company of a lover, wife or partner. Throughout his life, he had been told how handsome he was, how charming and how charismatic. But he was not convinced these attributes were an advantage. Women had always adored him, flirted with him and tried their best to woo him into matrimony, but he always knew his desires were not for the feminine, but for the masculine gender. But because of his military vocation, the expression of male-to-male love was not accepted or condoned, especially among officers. So, he kept his feelings secret and was resigned to endure in his abstinence. Therefore, he never really understood how those desires could be

---

[19] *Partesny* (Partesny singing): A style of polyphonic singing, based on the Western European system of harmony and counterpoint, which arose in the early 17th century in the Ukraine and in the mid-17th century, spread to Muscovite Russia.

fulfilled by anyone. In just a few months he would turn thirty, and he was still a virgin.

Tomi, on the other hand, had a male companion when he was in his late teens and early twenties, but it was a very secretive affair as they were both enlisted in the army. After his companion died in battle, Tomi never found anyone else he could be as close to. Although he surrounded himself with younger, attractive male servants, he was always respectful of their individual desires and their needs to live their own separate lives. He respected them too much to try to force his own desires on their young innocent lives. But he was always looking for a man who would fill the hole in his heart, an individual who would love him with dignity and respect. There were a few men who were temporary companions: drifters, handymen, the occasional out-of-town merchant or young men dissatisfied with the confinements of marriage. But there were none who ever truly loved him. He recognised a quality in Alexeev. He radiated dominance, forcefulness, masculinity and authority, yet was tempered with kindness, tenderness, meekness and passion.

Alexeev wanted nothing more than to be close to Tomi. Perhaps it was in part, due to the *Krupnik*, but he found himself touching Tomi's hand, brushing his hand against Tomi's cheek, then he set his hand on Tomi's thigh and gave it a gentle squeeze. Tomi smiled, then blushed and stood up to cut the tension. Alexeev stood up as well. Then Tomi reached his hands behind Alexeev's neck, pulled his head down to him and kissed him on the lips.

"I'm sorry, I shouldn't have—" Tomi stopped mid-sentence. "I should go to bed. This vodka is getting me drunk." As he spoke, his foot got caught on the leg of the settee. He stumbled into Alexeev's arms.

"I'd better help you up to bed," said Alexeev as he put his arm around him and steadied him to his feet. He walked Tomi up the stairs and into the bedroom. Then he guided him onto the bed and started to light the fire. "Would you like me to help you with your clothes?"

"No, I'll be fine." He laid back on the bed and fumbled with the sash around his trousers. He had too much to drink and now could barely control his movements. Alexeev finished building the fire, then came over and took off Tomi's trousers, then helped him remove his shirt.

"Where is your nightshirt?" he asked. Tomi just mumbled and pointed in the general direction of the dresser. Alexeev opened a few of the dresser drawers until he found the nightshirt. Then he helped Tomi put it on. He helped him get under the covers then he leaned down and kissed Tomi's forehead. "Goodnight, *schast'ye moye*[20]."

It was not easy for Alexeev to get to sleep that night. He kept thinking about Tomi and the kiss. He wondered if Tomi knew what he was doing, or if it really was the *Krupnik* that had caused his passionate advance. He wondered if Tomi would even remember what happened in the morning. Alexeev felt his cock getting hard. He wondered if they could ever have a relationship that would be meaningful, caring and loving. He wanted to love someone who could love him back. He didn't want a passing or fleeting romance, and he didn't want a physical relationship separated from the passion of the heart and the connection of the mind. He wondered if Tomi was the one he could spend the rest of his life with.

The next day, the men finished the cellar just a few hours after their lunch break. Alexeev and Tomi went down to inspect the finished room and to see if Tomi was satisfied with their work. He walked around the perimeter of the cellar and they showed him the beams and braces. Two of the men, Stas and Viktor, had built a lattice shelf on one wall of the cellar, specifically for storing wine, and on another wall, Stefan and Dmitri had installed shelving for preserves, cheeses and any other foods requiring cold storage. Tomi was very pleased with their work and Alexeev was very proud of his men.

During the morning hours, Tomi had spent much of his time preparing several *blini cakes*[21] and berry syrup to celebrate. Plus, when he had gone to town the day before, he purchased woollen travelling coats for each of the men and new woollen stockings and scarves. He wanted to make sure they were well protected while travelling back to Moscow. So, he invited all the men to join him in the outbuilding dinner hall. He thanked them for their splendid work, then presented each of them with their new travel clothes. After they thanked Tomi for his generosity, Foka and Ivan brought in the *blini cakes* covered in berry syrup, along with an ample supply of vodka. They all enjoyed the sweet treats and libations while they took some time to rest and relax before the final competition.

Alexeev got things started and set up the pairs of the younger competitors for their final matches, while the stronger and larger men got ready for their turns. Much to everyone's surprise, Alik made it to the final rounds in his group. His

---

[20] *Schast'ye moye*: My sweetheart

[21] *Blini cakes*: Stacked *blini* with custard or cream filling separating each layer. Topped with custard cream sauce and fresh fruit.

final match would be with Karp who was twelve years older, and about thirty pounds heavier. Karp was the odds-on favourite, but Alik had proved to be a very scrappy competitor. The two locked arms and grasped hands. Sergey counted them down, "Three…two…one…go!" Both men struggled back and forth, each with sturdy determination, healthy fortitude and lean muscle. The match seemed to last for hours by the perception of Alik and Karp, but in reality, it was only a matter of minutes. Alik had learned from watching the method used by his mentor, Alexeev: he held back at first, just enough to make Karp expend his energy continuously, then gave it his all when he felt Karp's strength diminish. That was enough, and at the right moment, he forced Karp's arm all the way to the table. Karp was astonished, but probably no more so than Alik. He knew he was strong, but he never imagined he would be able to beat Karp. Alik jumped up to his feet and waved his arms in the air, then leapt into Alexeev's arms, wrapping his legs around Alexeev's waist. Alexeev hugged him back and congratulated him, then Tomi presented him with the prize of his best blackberry wine. All the men gathered round and congratulated him and patted him on the back. Even Karp stood up and shook his hand in recognition of his win.

Now it was time for the final matches, for the strongest and largest. Both Sergey and Alexeev were tied for the lead and were both undefeated. They would compete with each other until one of them had lost three times, then the other would be declared the winner. They both got ready for their matches. Sergey removed his shirt and started stretching and flexing. His arms were huge and his biceps looked like there were round rocks the size of melons beneath his skin. His shoulders looked like they had been carved from granite and his neck muscles jutted up from his shoulders like thick towers. In fact, all of his muscles looked like they were carefully and meticulously carved, then covered with veins and skin. His eyes were piercing blue, the colour of lake water in the springtime, and his hair was black, accented by a few strands of grey on his temples. His face always looked a little scruffy because he only shaved about once every two to three weeks, and he wasn't caught smiling very often. As one of the leaders in the group, he felt it was his duty to scowl in order to keep the men in line.

Alexeev, on the other hand, kept his shirt on, although he did unbutton it down to the trousers and he rolled up his sleeves. His opened shirt revealed to everyone that he also had large, bulging chest and arm muscles and his forearms looked particularly intimidating. He stretched and flexed and cocked his head from one side to the other. Tomi found his eyes wandering down to Alexeev's chest, trying to get a glimpse of the impressive pectorals. He could see Alexeev's muscles glistening with a thin layer of sweat as he prepared for battle.

Tomi imagined him defending the city against the evil giants of mythology, grappling in hand-to-hand combat, striking his enemies with lethal blows. His mind conjured up naked opponents with bulging muscles, unkempt beards and long, matted hair. They were wild and savage but doomed to be conquered by the magnificent Alexeev Kondurov. He pictured himself as one who had been taken captive, tied and bound and unable to defend himself. Then the mighty warrior appears in the middle of the battlefield: clean-shaven, muscles glowing in the sunlight, fists clenched, and ready to defeat the savages. One by one, he wrestles them to the ground and pounds them until they are unconscious, battered and bleeding. Four, five, six, then ten of them—

"You need to say, 'three…two…one'," said Afanas, as he tapped Tomi on the shoulder.

Alexeev and Sergey were seated in front of Tomi at the table, staring at each other. "Sorry," said Tomi. He placed his hands over the top of the two men's clenched hands. "Three…two…one…go!" All the men howled and yelled as Alexeev and Sergey struggled for victory. Their powerful muscles warred against each other, first one advancing, then the other. Each of the two men were passionate in their efforts. Sergey's pectorals were flexed and firm, and Tomi could see the deep chiselled valley between Alexeev's pecs as well. Then slowly, but with great difficulty, Sergey overtook the lead and finally pinned Alexeev's arm to the table. There was a hush in the room, and then a roar and cheer for Sergey for his first win with Alexeev.

Tomi was overwhelmed with excitement and for a moment nearly lost his balance. He asked Afanas to start the rest of the matches. Then he sat down next to Alexeev where he could watch. Pavel poured him a glass of vodka, of which Tomi immediately took a sip. Then Pavel filled the competitors' glasses and invited the rest of the men to join in. Alexeev took a sip and swished it in his mouth before swallowing. Then he held up his other arm in challenge for the next round. The men roared as they clasped hands once again. Afanas counted them down and the second round began. This round seemed to be more intense than the first. The arms seemed to swing back and forth like a pendulum in slow motion. Tomi felt his own arms flexing and his muscles getting tense.

Then he saw Alexeev start to get the upper hand, Sergey was on his way down. "You can do it, *Davay! Davay!*[22] You can beat him!" Tomi yelled and stood to his feet.

Alexeev heard Tomi's exclamation of encouragement. He looked at Sergey, smiled and finished the job. The men roared and shouted just as much for Alexeev's win as they had for Sergey's win after the first round. Alexeev looked over at Tomi and winked, then he picked up his glass, raised it towards Tomi and emptied it down his throat. Pavel immediately filled his glass again.

The next two rounds took longer and were obviously taking their toll on both Alexeev and Sergey. Tomi could see Sergey's arm muscles were red from strain, and Alexeev's shirt was soaked with sweat, and there was a rip on the shirt sleeve where the bicep had torn through. He rolled his sleeves past his biceps and he rubbed his forearms. Each of them had won another round, so they were tied: two and two. This last round would decide which one was the champion. Tomi could see the peaks of Alexeev's nipples pressing against his sweat-soaked shirt. He wanted to lick the sweat from his chest and latch his lips onto the nipples and suck the immortal juices from this god-like specimen of perfect manliness. Even Alexeev's face looked muscular: his square jaw and prominent cheekbones, the ridge above his eyes covered by his thick, light-brown eyebrows and his straight narrow nose that accented his firm upper lip perfectly. Alexeev wiped his brow with a handkerchief he had in his pocket, then he wiped his hands dry and set the cloth down on the table.

Tomi watched as the two men prepared for the last round. Sergey brought up his massive arm to the table, then Alexeev did the same. They clenched arms and grasped hands for the last time. He heard Afanas count them down, "Three…two…one…go!" The sweat poured down from each man's face and their knuckles were white from the intense grip. Tomi couldn't imagine what strength one would have to possess to defeat either one of these two gladiators. He could smell the musky scent of their sweat in the air, and it was arousing. He reached out slowly and took hold of the sweat-soaked handkerchief and slid it into his pocket. He couldn't concentrate on the competition, he could only think of Alexeev holding him down, pinning him to the floor…and kissing him. He wanted to feel the weight of Alexeev on top of him, he wanted to feel Alexeev's tongue inside his mouth, he wanted to feel those hard nipples brush against his

---

[22] *Davay! Davay!:* Come on! Come on! (an enthusiastic interjection)

own nipples. And he dared to imagine Alexeev's hard thick cock pressing between his legs searching for somewhere to penetrate.

Suddenly, he heard the roar and shouts of the men. *But who won?* he thought. Then he saw Sergey smiling and grasping the back of Alexeev's head. Alexeev bowed his head in submission.

"Congratulations, Sergey," said Alexeev. "You are officially the strongest in our company…until next time!" He smiled and shook his hand, then offered up a toast to everyone's health and happiness, to the Tsar and finally to the victor! Tomi presented Sergey with his finest bottle of blackberry wine and Sergey gave him a tight bear-hug that nearly made Tomi pass out. Then Tomi let everyone know he was also sending several cases of wine and vodka with them for their trip home as a further reward for their excellent company. The men roared and shouted in appreciation.

While the competition had been going, Foka and Ivan had been preparing dinner for the men, so they brought in the trays of food and the table settings. Soon everyone was settling down and satisfying their hungers and talking about the competitions and the last few days' events. The men who were recovering were almost back to normal: their fevers were gone and they had gained most of their strength back. Pavel let them know they could rejoin the group in all their activities. Kirill and Anton had already moved their cots to the main room where the rest of the men were staying, so all thirty-one men were present for their last dinner together at Tomi's cottage, even young Yegor.

Tomi and Alexeev stayed and joined the men for dinner, but then excused themselves after they had finished and went inside the house. Alexeev sat at the dining room table while Tomi heated the last of the *Krupnik*. Pavel started the fire in the fireplace in the parlour and stove earlier so the house was warming up. Tomi complimented Alexeev on his fine mastery and strength and told him he was sure he would beat Sergey the next time. He also told Alexeev he was welcome to come back whenever he came through the area and that there would always be an extra bed waiting for him. He handed Alexeev a cup of the hot brew and they drank a few glasses while they talked. The strain of the match, the warmth of the house and the alcohol from the heated vodka was making Alexeev very warm and uncomfortable, especially since he was also starting to have sensual feelings for Tomi. They both had finished their drinks, so Tomi got up to pour them some more from the pot on the stove.

Finally, Alexeev slipped off his shirt and revealed his strong, muscular, hairy chest. His nipples were hard and his cock throbbed beneath his tight-fitting trousers. Tomi came up behind him and ran his fingers through the hair on Alexeev's chest. Alexeev breathed in deep and flexed his muscles. Tomi licked his finger and rubbed one of the hardened nipples, then grabbed Alexeev's massive chest muscle. It felt so good to feel a man's body again. He bent his head down and kissed Alexeev. His tongue explored the inside of Alexeev's mouth, then he kissed the rough stubble on his chin and neck. Alexeev leaned his head back and breathed in deep then moaned in excitement.

Alexeev placed his hand on the bulge in Tomi's trousers and felt the hardened cock underneath. Then Tomi unfastened his trousers and pulled out his cock, offering it to Alexeev. They both smiled and knew exactly what was about to happen. Alexeev grabbed Tomi's circumcised cock and wrapped his lips around it. His strong rough hands aroused Tomi even more and the cock got harder and harder with each pass over Alexeev's lips. Alexeev reached up and pulled Tomi's face towards his and kissed him on the mouth, then inserted his forefinger into Tomi's mouth as he sucked on his earlobe. Tomi sucked on Alexeev's finger, then licked and sucked his rough, strong hand. They both embraced each other and fell into a passionate surge of ecstasy. Alexeev forced Tomi to the floor and turned him over, face down. He pulled out his hard, thick, uncut cock, now throbbing and swollen, its veins coursing with blood. He pulled Tomi's trousers off, spat on his hand, then rubbed the spit on his cock and gently slipped it into Tomi's receptive ass. Tomi reached back to spread his buttocks. "Push it in deep, lieutenant. Give me all you have!"

Alexeev pumped his cock in and out, in and out, in and out, in and out, gently at first, then faster and harder. In and out, in and out, in and out, while his cock got harder and more blood pumped into the muscle to make it swell larger and larger. In and out, in and out, in and out, sweat dripped from his chest onto Tomi's back that was now bare: their clothes were strewn here and there around the living room. The moisture of the sweat between them made their bodies slide back and forth as steam rose from their hot, conjoined encounter.

Tomi turned over onto his back and raised his feet to the air as Alexeev slid his cock back inside the moist hole. They were one with each other. As Alexeev pumped more vigorously, Tomi reached down to his own cock and stroked it with each pump from Alexeev. Their cocks were pumping in unison, one in penetration and one by masturbation, both creating a harmonic resonance between them. As Alexeev pumped harder and harder, deeper and deeper, his chest flexed and hardened. He raised his arms above his head and flexed his biceps, then licked the sweat from the muscles on his biceps. As Tomi gazed at this perfect specimen of masculinity above him, the excitement caused him to clench his fists and punch Alexeev's chest. The excitement was mutual, and Alexeev encouraged Tomi to continue punching. His chest turned pink from the pounding and his muscles flexed back and forth with each blow.

As they continued, their energy turned to passionate wrestling and although Alexeev would have no problem overcoming Tomi, he held back and was careful not to inflict any pain on his submissive partner. He laid on his back, allowing Tomi to take the aggressive position. Tomi grabbed Alexeev's wrists and held them to the floor. "You see, even though I am older, I am still stronger than you," he said in jest. Alexeev played as if Tomi were overpowering him and he begged for mercy. "But I cannot let you up until I have had my way with you." Of course, Tomi was very aware Alexeev could overpower him at any time, but this role play seemed very passionate to Tomi. It stimulated him and made him feel roguish.

Then Alexeev flexed his muscles and raised Tomi up with no difficulty and brought him back down to rest on his chest. He wrapped his great arms around Tomi and kissed him. He rolled over on top of him and held his arms down, just as he had let Tomi do to him moments before. He smiled down at Tomi, "Now who will be the master?" He winked at Tomi, then buried his head in Tomi's chest and sucked his nipples. "Shall I make you beg for mercy? Or perhaps you will beg me for more."

After hours of passionate wrestling, they wrapped their arms around each other's sweaty bodies and kissed and groped each other. Their hard cocks slipping between them as their legs encircled each other's waists. Alexeev hooked his arms around Tomi's legs and once again inserted his cock into Tomi. His chest widened as he forced himself deep into Tomi and his nipples hardened and extended themselves as they dripped with sweat. Tomi reached up and grabbed the nipples and pulled them. Alexeev moaned with pleasure. Then Tomi moaned in ecstasy as the weight of Alexeev's torso and abdomen pushed against his cock. He could feel his body reaching the limits of its passion as an anticipated orgasm grew closer. Finally, they climaxed together. Alexeev shot his load inside Tomi, and the flood inside him immediately compelled Tomi's ejaculate. His thick cum shot onto both their chests. It looked like milky rain drops on Alexeev's chest hair. Tomi wrapped his arms around Alexeev and sucked his nipples, licking off the sweat and cum mixture from his chest.

Alexeev continued to pump his cock into Tomi for several more strokes, then reached down and slowly removed it from Tomi's ass. Tomi panted and threw his arms above his head, still pulsating in satisfaction. Then Alexeev reached down and placed his hands gently under Tomi's head and drew it up to his. He kissed him gently on the lips, then caressed his neck with his tongue. He could taste the salt from their combined sweat. His kisses travelled down Tomi's chest. Each nipple was gently kissed then sucked. Tomi arched his back in delight. The kisses continued down Tomi's ribcage to his naval, then followed the trail of hair down to his cock. He gently kissed the tip of the cock, licking off the cloudy liquid, then tenderly licking the length of Tomi's cock and caressing it between his fingers.

"I have never met anyone like you, Alexeev. You are strong and forceful, yet you hold me gently and tenderly." Alexeev continued to fondle Tomi's cock, then sucked his balls. Tomi's cock was limp and soft, but his ball sack was tight and dark pink. Alexeev licked his finger and drove it into Tomi's ass, then thrust two fingers in at the same time. Tomi reached down and grabbed his legs to spread them wider. The sweat on his face was rolling into his ears and down onto his neck, and he felt a sudden chill come over him. Alexeev noticed this slight change in Tomi's demeanour and he slowly removed his fingers. Then arching himself over Tomi, he wiped the sweat from Tomi's face, neck, and ears. Placing his hands behind Tomi's head, he gently lifted him up and kissed him. He sensed Tomi's energy was spent, though he wanted to wrestle in passion for much longer.

"We should get some rest," he whispered. He sat up and brushed the hair from his forehead, then stood up. Tomi looked a little pale, but Alexeev wasn't sure if it was because the only light in the room was from the fireplace and the moonlight coming through the window. "Let me help you up," he said as he reached down and held on to both of Tomi's hands and slowly pulled him up to a standing position. Tomi wavered slightly, as if he were a little dizzy. "Are you all right?"

Tomi was a little embarrassed. "Yes, I'll be fine. I just haven't done this for quite some time and I am a little out of shape."

Alexeev put his strong arm around Tomi to help steady him. "Let me take you up to the bedroom, then I'll come back and get our clothes."

"I think I need to sit for a few minutes…"

Before Tomi could finish his sentence, Alexeev picked him up in his arms and walked to the fireplace, "If you can hold the candle, I'll carry you up to the bedroom." Tomi reached out and lit the candle, then held it in front of Alexeev to light the way. Almost effortlessly, Alexeev carried Tomi up the flight of stairs, taking two steps at a time to the second floor. Tomi's bedroom door was slightly opened so Alexeev backed in with Tomi in his arms. He set Tomi down on the bed, then took the candle and set it on the nightstand. Tomi shivered and quickly pulled the bedcovers back and tucked himself underneath. Alexeev pulled the covers up to Tomi's chin and tucked them around him to keep him warm. He saw the fireplace hadn't yet been lit. "I'll light the fire before I go back downstairs for our clothes." Soon he had a roaring fire warming the bedroom. "I'll be right back," he said as he picked up another candle and lit it.

When Alexeev got downstairs, he gathered their clothes together and noticed the grandfather clock in the parlour said it was fifteen minutes after one o'clock. Then he went into the kitchen and cut a few slices of *chyorniy khleb*[23] and cheese, took a few pieces of the candied fruit from the shelf and filled the carafe with the remaining *Krupnik*. He put the food and a goblet on a platter, flung the clothes over his shoulder and carried the plate of food and the carafe upstairs to the bedroom.

Tomi was still awake and sitting up in bed leaning on a pillow he had propped behind his back against the headboard. "I'm glad you are still awake. I brought some food from the kitchen I want you to eat. I didn't see you eat more than two bites of food while we ate with the men." Alexeev set the plate on the nightstand and poured some of the hot brew into the goblet.

"Oh, I'm not really very hungry."

"Tomi, all through dinner, you served me food, waited on me and my men like you were our servant, and all the time I was eating, you didn't sit down for more than a moment. You looked like you were going to faint when we were downstairs and you didn't even have enough energy to walk up the stairs to the bedroom. Now, I am going to watch you eat everything on this platter, and I won't let you go to sleep until you have finished." He sat on the edge of the bed next to Tomi and handed him the platter of food, then smiled. "Make me happy, *dorogoy*[24]," he pleaded.

---

[23] *Chyorniy khleb*: Russian rye bread

[24] *Dorogoy*: Dear, darling, sweetheart

Tomi picked up a slice of bread and took a bite. He raised his eyebrows. "This is good!" he said a little surprised. "It usually doesn't turn out this well." He continued eating and took a few more bites of the bread and cheese then handed the second slice to Alexeev. "Please have this one. I can't possibly eat all of this."

"You really are a very fine cook. Everything you've made these last few days was delicious." Alexeev took the slice of bread with cheese and took a bite, then took a sip from the goblet and handed it back to Tomi. "I love your wine, too. Alik opened his bottle at dinner and poured me a glass. I don't think I have ever had blackberry wine that tasted so good."

"You are kind." Tomi kept eating, but also kept looking at Alexeev. There was something about this man that made Tomi feel safe and secure, and he kept remembering the conversations they had and how many things they could relate to together. "You even like my wine." Alexeev chuckled and took another sip from the goblet. "I don't want you to leave me, Alexeev. I want you to stay here with me forever."

"I feel the same way, Tomi, but you know I can't stay, not now." He hesitated to continue, "I would be honoured to stay here with you…but I only wish the timing was right. I still have several more years before the Tsar will approve my leave."

"I shouldn't have said anything. I don't want to make you feel badly, but I wanted you to know how I feel." Tomi finished the last bit of food then set the plate back on the nightstand. "Maybe I could come to Moscow and visit you sometime? I do have a nephew who lives just outside the city."

"Moscow is more than 1,300 kilometres away, more than a month's journey in good weather," he said, trying to make Tomi see their situation realistically. "Besides, I will be on missions for the Tsar for the next several years, so I don't know when I will be in Moscow or when I will be away."

Tomi dropped his head a bit, realising this night was probably the only memory he would ever have of Alexeev and the harmony they experienced. Once again, he would be alone. Once again, he would live a life of separation and isolation from the things he loved so dearly. Once again, he would have to face the reality he may never be able to give his love to anyone else.

Alexeev sensed Tomi's unsettled demeanour. He took the other pillow and set in up against the headboard and sat next to Tomi, then put his arm around him. Tomi rested his head on Alexeev's strong chest. "I know what you're feeling, my dear," Alexeev whispered. "Maybe someday we will be together again." After a long passionate embrace and a few tears, the two finally laid down and slept for the few remaining hours until morning.

The wind whistled through the bare trees in the early morning hours and the thumping of hooves from a herd of reindeer made a curious vibration on the wood floors as they passed through the fields and across the road in front of the Pedorov cottage. The sounds and vibrations woke Alexeev. Tomi's head was resting comfortably on Alexeev's muscular chest, and the thought of leaving him in a few hours still seemed unbearable.

"*Dobroye utro*[25]*, schast'ye moye*," he whispered in Tomi's ear. A small tear rolled down his cheek as he thought of what his life would be like when he returned home to Moscow at the end of this assignment. Home was a small bedroom above the boarding house kitchen behind his cousin's house on the outskirts of Moscow. His belongings consisted of a few changes of clothes and uniforms, an old mantel clock he had inherited from his father and a silver brooch with two one-carat emeralds left to him by his mother. Her last words to him were, "*Ne khorosho byt' cheloveku odnomu*[26]." Alexeev was only eight when his parents both died of influenza, but he knew his mum wanted him to be married and to seek out a wife when he was old enough. But in his heart, he wondered about his future. Even at such an early age, he knew he was not like the other boys. He always imagined his road would be a solitary journey, one devoid of the company of a woman. When he matured and grew into his manhood, he could have had his pick of any of the women in Moscow. He developed into a handsome, masculine, charming, polite and well-educated man. He had a fine career in the army and was making a name for himself among his fellow military leaders and he even gained the trust of the Tsar himself. But he also knew he could not be happy with a woman, and he knew the military did not provide him with the necessary challenges he needed to feel complete and fulfilled.

"I've been listening to you breathe," whispered Tomi. "It was a comfort to me during the night. I laid here with my ear to your chest and counted your breaths, and then listened to the beating of your heart. It has been many years since I have had a companion in my bed, and you have been a strong and magnificent one for me." He stroked Alexeev's chest and sucked his hard nipple. Then he reached down under the covers and felt Alexeev's cock, now getting

---

[25] *Dobroye utro*: Good morning

[26] *Ne khorosho byt' cheloveku odnomu*: It is not good for a man to be alone

harder from excitement. "Come down on me this morning. Let me be your lover until you have to leave." Then Tomi turned on his stomach and raised his buttocks to receive Alexeev's entrance and penetration for the last time. Alexeev gently placed his arms around Tomi in a full embrace. He grabbed Tomi's chest with both of his calloused hands and squeezed his breasts. He slowly slipped his moist cock into Tomi's ass and began to pump in and out, in and out, in and out.

The heat of their bodies seemed to create an ethereal steam that surrounded them. The air in the house was cold: the fire in the fireplace had gone out an hour before and the warming effects had now diminished significantly. Alexeev's muscles tensed and tightened as he pumped Tomi. He felt Tomi's nipples hardening, so he pinched them with his forefingers and thumbs, pulling them and milking them with every thrust of his cock. Tomi moaned in a rapture of delight and begged for more, "Take it slower, but get it in deeper. I want this feeling to last forever." Alexeev slowed his thrusts to prolong the moment and he licked the sweat from Tomi's back. Wrapping his arms under Tomi's, he pulled him to an upright position. He grabbed Tomi's chin and turned his head around to face him. Alexeev plunged his lips around Tomi's mouth while his tongue explored the inside of Tomi's throat. He took hold of one of Tomi's ankles and drew the leg up on top of his shoulder and rested it there, still pumping and thrusting. Tomi's ass could feel every inch of Alexeev's cock as it penetrated deeper and deeper, slowly in, then slowly out. The pressure of Alexeev's cock inside Tomi felt wondrous. It was an incredible, delightful feeling of pressure and heat.

Tomi had never felt a hard, muscular body like Alexeev's before. His last relationship was with a spindly young farmhand who only stayed for a few months, then left suddenly to avoid the possible shame and shunning from the community. No one knew of their affair, but they were both fearful of what could have happened if they were found out. Tomi also had a longer relationship with an army sergeant shortly after he enlisted. The sergeant was several years older, burly and very hairy. Tomi wasn't particularly attracted to him physically, but they had a few common interests and both needed companionship. The sergeant was killed in battle a few years later and died in Tomi's arms, bleeding to death from his wounds. The experience marred Tomi's spirit and kept him from entering into any relationships until after he left the army. It wasn't until he settled in Storozhevsk that he sought out the companionship of others, including the farmhand, but those relationships proved to be fruitless and unfulfilling ventures. Tomi wanted with all his heart to make a safe and secure home for

Alexeev, but he believed there would be a sacrifice of freedom to interact with the rest of the community, and he feared their union would end in a few hours. Though his mind was distracted and occupied with the reality of eventual loneliness and despair, Tomi's body was finding new heights of ecstasy and pleasure.

Alexeev was pumping more vigorously now and Tomi was on the verge of ejaculation. Just then, Alexeev pumped deep and Tomi thought he felt the cock exploded inside him. At the same moment, Tomi sprayed a few drops of sperm onto the bed underneath him. But Alexeev continued to pump in and out, in and out, in and out. Tomi was amazed Alexeev was still hard because he thought he felt the warm liquid surge inside him. He turned over onto his back and grabbed his legs. "Give it to me again, *moy general*, get it in as deep as you can go." His request sounded almost desperate. Alexeev pumped harder and more forcefully. The sound of their bodies slapping together startled them both, but their faces were smiling with pleasure and excitement. Tomi's buttocks were bruising from the rough impact, but he didn't want him to stop. The pain was too good, and it aroused a sensation of extreme, carnal pleasure. The moment was intoxicating. Alexeev grabbed Tomi's hands and intertwining their fingers, he held Tomi's arms onto the bed in a wrestler's position of forced surrender. Tomi grinned and struggled, as if he wanted to get away but he spread his legs wider to allow for a deeper penetration. Alexeev smiled, relishing the idea of conquering his prey, this manly flesh. Now with each thrust, he held it in to maximise the feeling, then pulled his cock out slowly, then forced it in deep and held it in even longer. He repeated this over and over; his sweat poured onto Tomi's body. Then he slowed and entered only the head of his cock into Tomi's ass. In and out, in and out, in and out, rapidly in short bursts. His control was masterful and his precision caused Tomi to gasp in excitement as he struggled to catch his breath. The suction of Alexeev's cock head exiting Tomi's ass was a skilful act that prompted a sensation Tomi had never experienced before.

Tomi imagined the explosion inside him for the second time as Alexeev's body tensed and pushed deeper and longer, but still the pumping did not stop. He wrapped his lips around Tomi's right nipple and began to suck, then pinched the left nipple and began to pull. Then Tomi grabbed Alexeev's hair with both hands and pulled his face up to his lips. He was shaking as he kissed Alexeev. He sucked Alexeev's neck and licked the sweat from his neck and shoulders. "Give me no mercy! Pound me with everything you have and make me beg for more!"

He was gasping for air. Alexeev's cock was still as hard as it had been from the beginning. He pulled it out and quickly wiped it off, then he grabbed Tomi's head and forced his lips down onto his massive cock.

Tomi's mouth opened and received the impressive morsel. Alexeev forced Tomi's head down to take the cock deeper into his throat. Tomi sucked and gasped, sucked and gasped. It was all pleasure, and an emotional charge of frenzy. He lapped the balls with vigour and delight, putting one in his mouth, then the other, then both. He licked his finger and thrust it into Alexeev's ass. Alexeev took a deep breath, then arched his back as he stood straight up on his knees. He interlocked his hands behind his neck and stretched out his arms, showing his enormous biceps and pectorals. He flexed as Tomi sucked his cock. Then Tomi stopped sucking and held Alexeev's massive cock with one hand, stroking it vigorously, while fingering Alexeev's ass with the other hand.

Alexeev yelled with excitement, "I'm going to come, I'm going to come!" Tomi kept stroking and pulled back the foreskin as he licked the tip of the cock, then slipped his tongue down the length of the cock. Just then, the cock exploded with a stream of sperm onto Tomi's face and neck.

"You are so amazing, *moy general*," he said, still gasping for breath. "How did you become such an exquisite lover?"

"It's because you are so receptive. But why do you question what makes us both happy, my love?" He scooped some of the cum from Tomi's face onto his finger and placed it in Tomi's mouth. Tomi licked the finger until it was clean. Then Alexeev scooped the cum from Tomi's neck and stuck his finger into his own mouth. He smiled at Tomi, then kissed him. Alexeev relaxed and laid down next to Tomi, exhausted from the sexual workout. "My men would not understand our encounter, so you must be discreet for my sake."

Tomi sat up partway, leaning on his elbow and rubbing his hand over Alexeev's hairy chest. "No one will know…but I will remember you for the rest of my life, and I will take our secret to my grave." Then he kissed Alexeev's chest and laid back down. There they rested in silence while they recovered from the labour of their encounter. Both were satisfied beyond their wildest dreams and hopes.

As the morning light shone dimly onto the hardwood floors of the cottage, they heard the birds chirping in the trees in the courtyard between the cottage and the outbuilding. After a short time, Tomi got up from the bed, cleaned himself and got dressed, but left Alexeev to sleep a while longer. He walked out to the servant's quarters and made sure Foka and Ivan had everything under control to prepare breakfast for the men. They had already gathered eggs to make fresh *syrniki*[27] and *blini* and would use their own *tvorog*. They also milked the cows for fresh milk and cream, brought in fresh sausages from the larder, fruit and preserves from the cellar and prepared turnips and vegetables grown on the farm. Then Tomi went to the laundry room to ensure there were no more clothes from the company in need of cleaning. All had been dried, folded and given back to the men. As he passed back through the kitchen in the outbuilding he could smell the wonderful spices Foka used in his recipes and it made him hungry.

Tomi was going to prepare a special breakfast for Alexeev too. He would make *vatrushka*[28], sausage and eggs with onion and turnips, and a special Chinese tea he had brought back from one of his trips to the East. The rich smells of breakfast cooking persuaded Alexeev to get out of bed and get dressed. The house was still cold, as Tomi had not yet had a chance to build a fire anywhere but in the stove, so the kitchen was warming.

"What can I do to help?" asked Alexeev.

"Could you build a fire in the parlour to take the chill off the house? I think there is still some wood just outside the back door." He forgot for a moment Alexeev was still his guest and should not be expected to work for accommodations. But Alexeev was by no means insulted. In fact, he was pleased and felt honoured to repay the kindnesses Tomi had lavished on him and his troops.

Within a few minutes, Alexeev had a roaring fire warming the home. He walked to the outbuilding to make sure all was well with his men and found them well cared for by Pavel and the rest of the servants. They were all dressed in fresh, clean garments, and were seated at the long wooden tables bedecked with elaborately adorned tablecloths, light blue needlepoint napkins and expensive china and silverware. Each place setting had a silver goblet for their drink. There were homemade candles in silver candleholders arranged and lit down the centre of the table giving the whole presentation a warm, family atmosphere. Even the men who had been sick were cheery and full of energy as if they had never been sick at all. Everyone was smiling, laughing and exchanging stories. When they noticed the lieutenant enter the room, they all stood up and raised their glasses

---

[27] *Syrniki*: Fried cheese cakes

[28] *Vatrushka*: Sweet rolls with a creamy cheese filling

to toast him, and also to toast Tomi's hospitality. Alexeev promised to send their host out after breakfast so they could thank him personally.

Then he returned to the cottage, knowing his men were well taken care of. Tomi opened the door. "Are your men having a good feast? Did my Pavel take care of them?"

"You have been more than hospitable to me and my men. I can never repay your kindnesses," Alexeev answered. "You must be sure to go out to see them after breakfast, so they can thank you properly."

"Repayment is not necessary, it was my pleasure. Besides, I got a larger cellar in exchange! Now let us sit and eat one last time together before you leave." A tear rolled down Tomi's cheek and he began to choke on his words, but he brushed the tear away before Alexeev could see. "We may never see each other again, and I want to savour every moment we have together." They talked of their hopes and dreams all through breakfast. They laughed about the futures they dreamed about and cried about the realities of their situations. Alexeev wondered if they would ever chance to see each other again, but realised they were from two different worlds and another meeting was not likely. His heart was breaking inside and he fought back the tears. He wanted to be strong and brave and face his fate without despair, but the more he thought about Tomi and the life they could not share, the more he trembled inside.

The morning ended too soon. The lieutenant and his men would need to continue their journey to Moscow so the documents they retrieved could be delivered to the Tsar on time. Tomi knew there were no words he could say to convince Alexeev to stay and he didn't want to break his heart by begging. He knew Alexeev's duty was to his country, and his duty had to take priority over these new-found feelings. Alexeev wondered if the pain from this parting would ever end or even diminish. He held back the tears because he didn't want Tomi to know how much he regretted leaving. He thought it might be kinder if Tomi didn't see his pain and anguish. But Tomi could see the silent lamentation on Alexeev's face, and Alexeev could hear the despondency in Tomi's voice.

They walked to the outbuilding together. They managed to keep their composure while Tomi addressed the troops. "I was so happy to be able to host such a fine group of men. I hope you have all been well-fed and well-rested, and I want you all to know the tournaments were as much a pleasure to me as they were to you. Please accept the sacks of apples and sausages Pavel has prepared, along with several baskets of *buterbrody*[29] prepared for your trip. You are all welcomed back here whenever you are passing through." Tomi also had several cases of blackberry wine and vodka, and several jugs of cider brought up from the cellars for the men.

Afanas stood up. "I have been elected to speak for the group. We thank you for your kindness, your hospitality and your generosity. We have all had our fill of your fine foods and wines and we thank you most humbly for offering up your warm accommodations, and especially for hosting and participating in the competition! But most of all, we thank you for caring for our comrades who were sick." He bowed to Tomi as the rest of the men cheered and waved. Tomi smiled and blushed and nodded to Alexeev.

Parting was full of cheek-kissing, tears and hugs. Each of the men came up to Tomi and kissed and hugged him as they passed by into the courtyard. While the goodbyes were being said, the servants prepared and brought out the food for their travels along with the cases of Tomi's blackberry wine. Tomi waved to Lieutenant Alexeev and his men as they marched away. Tears flooded his face and he felt a knot in his stomach. He knew it was very unlikely he would ever see this man again and the sorrow was overwhelming.

As the last man disappeared from view, Pavel and the rest of the servants returned to the house and to their normal duties. But as Tomi stood outside and wept, there was a sudden feeling in his gut like he had been punched. He let out a scream and doubled over then fell to his knees and vomited. He continued convulsing for several minutes and couldn't help screaming in agony. Pavel heard his cries and ran out to see if he could help him. He knelt down next to him and put his arm on Tomi's shoulder.

"Is there anything I can do, Master? Was it something you ate? Are you sick?"

"No, Pavel, no!" he exclaimed. "I loved him and now he's gone!" Tomi turned towards him and continued to cry as he rested his head on Pavel's shoulder. "He's gone! He's gone! What am I going to do?"

Pavel didn't answer but held him close and patted his back to try to comfort him. After several minutes, Pavel helped Tomi to his feet. "It is too cold out here for you, master. Let me take you inside and I'll prepare some tea with honey." Tomi stood up and walked back into the house leaning on Pavel and still crying.

---

[29] *Buterbrody*: Sandwiches or bread served with butter

He could barely make it up the steps to the front door without collapsing, but Pavel steadied him all the way. Once inside, Pavel led Tomi to the parlour where he could sit down for a while. "Are you going to be all right while I make your tea?" Tomi nodded in response, so Pavel gently released him and went to the kitchen to prepare the tea and honey.

But Tomi soon collapsed on the floor in front of the fireplace and continued to weep. He felt despair and an overwhelming gloom. He could still smell Alexeev's scent on his clothes and he could still remember every word that was spoken between them. His fingers remembered every muscle he caressed and his tongue could still taste the sweat and cum from their morning love-making. Though the fire had gone out, the room still held the aroma from the fireplace: a mixture of cedar, pine, and larch woods. The tears choked out his vision until his eyes were red and swollen shut. As he wept, his body convulsed and his belly shuddered but there was nothing left in his stomach, and there was nothing to comfort him, nothing to fill the emptiness that was left, like a void in his heart and life. Pavel brought the tea and honey and left it on the end table, but Tomi continued in his remorse.

Several hours went by. Pavel sent Anton to check on him, but he saw his master was still weeping on the floor. He approached him and tried to get him to his feet, but Tomi screamed in agony, wrapped his arms around his knees, and fell back to the floor still weeping uncontrollably. Anton left quickly, not knowing what else to do. Pavel and Anton kept the house and business going and talked among themselves about what to do. They discussed fetching Tomi's doctor to make a visit, but Pavel knew this was not a sickness of the body, but a grieving of the spirit and heart. He considered asking the priest to stop by, but knew Tomi was not on good terms with the church. It was three days before Tomi got up from the floor, and it would be weeks before he was able to return to his normal life again. Tomi was not a large man, he was only five feet six inches tall and weighed only 165 pounds, but this experience had caused him to lose twenty pounds. He looked pale and drawn and weak. It would be more than a year before he would gain back his strength, and his health would suffer for several years to come. His heart would take a long time to mend as well, for he missed Alexeev and did not know how to fill the tremendous feeling of emptiness.

Chapter 3

Alexeev's Dream

In the summer of 1716, six years after his rendezvous with Tomi Pedorov, Alexeev could still remember every moment and every detail of their encounter as clearly as if it had happened yesterday. He thought about Tomi every day and often wondered what happened to that fine gentleman who was so generous to him and his men years earlier. He hoped, possibly beyond all reasonable expectation, that Tomi still thought of him as well. He remembered their time together and their amatory exploits of those few days and nights. When he left Tomi, he vowed he would never be with anyone else. But the loneliness was becoming unbearable. Several of his close friends and comrades had gotten married in the last five years and he felt more alone than ever before. He longed to feel Tomi's touch again, the warmth of someone sleeping next to him and that dear, sweet head rimmed with brown and grey hair resting on his chest as it did that night long ago in the green and white cottage in Storozhevsk near the banks of the Vychegda River.

The depression often felt crushing, like a great weight pressing down on his shoulders. He was unable to concentrate on his work, and sleepless nights became more frequent. Alexeev started visiting the local *kabak*[30] more frequently to try to drown his sorrows and forget about his loneliness. Although there was no permanent solace in the bottom of the bottle, some of the nights seemed to go by a little quicker when they were numbed with liquor. His waking hours were no more tolerable though. He saw Tomi's face in every stranger and heard Tomi's voice in every dim and distant conversation. Strange dreams became more frequent, though they never seemed to be complete and were often interrupted by night sweats and restlessness. The dream stories would always

[30] *Kabak*: A public ale house, bar or tavern

begin the same way and then abruptly end, and he would awaken suddenly in a frenzy, unsettled and confused.

The summer was very hot and humid that year. July temperatures were blistering with high humidity for the last seven days. Each day tempers flared and patience grew thin. There were nightly altercations in the *kabak* and injuries were commonplace, especially among the military men. Fist fights resulted in bloody and broken noses, blackened and bruised eyes, torn uniforms, bruised and broken ribs, not to mention broken chairs, stools, tables, lamps, and windows, as well as frayed nerves.

Tonight, Alexeev was very depressed and thought constantly about Tomi. The *kabak* he frequented was on the banks of the Neglinnaya River. The rushing water could be heard beating against the riverbanks from the windows overlooking the river. The building was nearly 300 years old: a rustic wooden tavern with a narrow hall of tables and benches. It was close to the men's barracks and served meals daily, as well as beer, ale, wine and various vodkas and other liquors. Alexeev preferred the spiced vodkas. They helped him remember those long talks with Tomi while sipping a cup of hot *Krupnik.* Tonight, Alexeev was accompanied by his cousin Orlov at whose boarding house he was staying and where he called home whenever he was in Moscow. Most nights they would talk of childhood stories, or military adventures, or talk about the family business. On this occasion though, Alexeev was especially distraught and had far too much to drink. Orlov was a good friend as well as his cousin, and he tried repeatedly to get him to stop drinking. Alexeev could be a gentle soul when he was sober, but he was often very aggressive when intoxicated. Even though Orlov knew he would never intentionally harm him, he feared Alexeev may not be fully aware of his actions and knew his cousin could easily overpower him.

"Cousin, you need to stop drinking. We need to get home and I need to get you to bed," he begged.

"No, I don't want to go to bed…bad dreams."

"At least stop drinking then and we'll talk…would you like that?" Orlov said, trying to settle him.

"I shall never see my love again, Orlov."

"Who is your love, Alexeev? Did you meet her today?"

Alexeev's eyes swayed back and forth as he tried to focus on Orlov. "The years have cheated us out of our happiness…*moy drug*[31]…and I am ruined. Why must life be so cruel and unforgiving?" He clenched his fists and pounded the table, then he grabbed the lapel on Orlov's coat.

"Now, don't get upset, my friend. Maybe we can find her again and the two of you can be together."

"Tell me, Orlov, why must I be alone and unhappy?" Alexeev released his grip on Orlov's coat and held his drooping head in his hands and wept.

"You have had too much to drink, my friend. Just tell me who she is so I can find her," said Orlov, as he patted Alexeev's shoulder in half-hearted recognition of what he thought was probably a drunken fantasy.

Alexeev shoved Orlov's hand away from his shoulder and nearly knocked him from his chair. Then he shouted, "My love is in Storo…Storozhevsk."

"But, cousin, you haven't been there for many years."

Alexeev continued shouting with slurred speech, "We met six winters ago…when I was bringing the troops home from…Pechora." As he finished his thought, he imagined he was back in Tomi's cottage. He gazed out the window. The rushing river sounded like the wind in the trees in the courtyard between Tomi's cottage and the outbuilding. Suddenly, he stood up. "I should chop wood for the fire. You will need plenty of wood to last this winter since the snow is so high."

Orlov stood with him and cautiously set his hand back on Alexeev's shoulder. "But it's the middle of summer, my friend. There has not been snow for several months, and if there were, it would surely melt in this heat." Orlov could tell the vodka was putting Alexeev into a drunken dream-state.

Alexeev turned towards Orlov and grabbed his arms. "Tomi, my love, I worry you will not be able to cut enough wood. You are not strong enough…I should stay with you. You are not well…" He paused for a moment, then touched his hand to Orlov's cheek. "Your bed is so warm…I miss your head on my chest." With the last word, Alexeev dropped his sweaty head on Orlov's shoulder and continued mumbling incoherently. He was taller and heavier than Orlov, and when his body started to go limp, it was like manoeuvring a 190-pound sack of flour.

---

[31] *Moy drug*: My friend

Orlov carefully steered him out of the *kabak* and managed to manoeuvre him into his carriage, then drove him home. He held onto him and helped him get out of the carriage, then guided him to a cot in the storage room just off the kitchen and said nothing to anyone about the conversation they had. Orlov was not sure what to think. Whether Alexeev was just intoxicated and talking foolishness, or if the words were truth coming from the heart. Alexeev had talked about Tomi on several occasions, but never inferred they were anything more than acquaintances who had a chance meeting six years ago on one of Alexeev's military missions. He always spoke highly of his hospitality to his troops and the wonderful food and wine they had while they were there. But Orlov always imagined Alexeev would eventually settle down and marry one of the most beautiful young ladies in town. He could have his pick of nearly every single lady in the city because of his manly nature and handsome build, not to mention his charm and magnetic personality. He was the desire of every unmarried woman, and the envy of every man, both married and unmarried.

The incident that night, however, made Orlov start to wonder and it concerned him greatly. He thought about his relationship with Alexeev since childhood. There were never any girls he would talk about and only on rare occasions did Alexeev take a girl with him to any functions or events. In fact, the few times he remembered Alexeev with any women had been with their female cousins. He only had male friends and acquaintances both in the army and in his personal life around the boarding house, and he avoided social settings altogether. Orlov pondered these things and wondered what he could do to ease the pain Alexeev was going through. He was fond of Alexeev and considered him as close as a brother and even as his best friend. He wanted him to be happy and fulfilled. So, he made up his mind. In the morning, he would have a candid talk with him and let him know he could confide in him anytime he wanted. After a few hours of worrying, pacing and studying his thoughts, Orlov finally went to sleep.

That night, Alexeev had a dream…

I woke up on top of a stove. Not like the ones you see where you cook with pans on the top, but the kind your great grandmother used to bake breads. It had a large opening in the front to slide the bread in on a large flat tray attached to a pole. Underneath was another opening where you would place the wood or coal for burning to heat the stove. And at the very top of the stove, above a normal man's height, was a flat space large enough for a grown man to recline comfortably. There was also a stepladder on the side for him to get up and down. The heat from the stove made the area on top a very comfortable place to rest and a most desirable place to be in a cold house, especially in winter.

I could not move my legs though and my arms were weak. I was wrapped in a blanket yet I was not a child, I was an adult as I am now. The room was dark except for the glow emanating from the stove. I could feel the warmth but I appeared to be helpless and unable to move from on top of the stove. I was somewhat comfortable but I did not know where I was. There was a window across from me looking out onto the farmland outside. It seemed to be a pleasant, sunny day and I could see an old man working in the field. Through another window there was a view of a path that led from a nearby road up to the house I was in. The path was lined with a variety of flowers: white chamomile, pink azaleas and yellow lilies. There may have been more, but those were the only ones I recognised.

Then I heard a woman's voice coming from the other room. She was singing and her voice sounded frail but sweet, and there was something very familiar about her. The song was familiar too, perhaps it was from my childhood. "*Kotya, koten'ka, kotok*[32]..." She sang for several minutes.

It was a comfort to listen to her singing and I wished the song would go on forever. "*Dam kusok piroga, Da kuvshin moloka*[33]..." Then, just as the song ended, she came into the room. She was a short, elderly woman, perhaps in her sixties. She was a little bent over and I could see that her hands were gnarled with age. She held a cane with one hand and a basket in the other hand. The basket was filled with the same flowers I had seen out the window.

"Good morning, Ilya," she said. "I have brought you some flowers from the garden to brighten the room."

Was she speaking to me? I wondered. *Am I Ilya?* I remembered the story of *Ilya Muromets*[34]...yes, in this dream I am Ilya, the cripple, and this was my mother. Yes...I have had this dream before.

"Thank you, Mum," I said instinctively. But she was not really my mother. Not the woman who raised me. My parents had died when I was a child. I did not understand how she could be my mother, yet she was. Is this how my mother

---

[32] *Kotya, koten'ka, kotok*: Kitty, kitten, little cat

[33] *Dam kusok piroga, Da kuvshin moloka*: I will give you a piece of cake, and a jug of milk.

[34] *Ilya Muromets*: A folk hero of ancient Kievan Rus', a knight errant

would have looked if she had lived? "Are you going to market this morning?" I asked.

"Yes, my son. We need a few things and I'm trading some fresh eggs and radishes. Papa had a good crop and the hens laid more than a dozen of eggs this morning." She reached up and patted my head. "While I am gone, Father Jonas and a few of the visiting priests will be stopping by to pray with you. Papa might still be in the field so they will let themselves in when they arrive. I will leave water in the kettle on the stove for their tea and there are biscuits on the table. Invite them to help themselves. I will be back before sundown." She kissed me on the cheek and continued to arrange the flowers.

"Thank you, Mum. I will try to make them feel at home."

The hours seemed to pass by slowly after mama left for market. I was not sure, but it seemed like being left alone was a regular occurrence, and it bothered me. Was I really crippled? Maybe this wasn't a dream. And was this my bed? It must be a dream. I could not remember this place, yet it seemed so familiar. The blanket was old and warm like an old dear friend and there was a faint smell of lavender and vanilla. The room was cozy and there were objects on the shelves that I recognised: a silver candlestick, a blue lamp with orange daisies, a large red-rimmed platter next to a pine branch and embroidered blue napkins dangling over the edge of the shelves. There was the clock that my father left me, and Mum was wearing that silver broach with the two emeralds. Many things reminded me of my childhood, but some things were familiar and I didn't know why. It was like a familiar person you see on the street in a city you have never been to before. But I felt like I belonged here.

Then I heard a knock at the door and it opened. "Ilya, do not be alarmed. It is me, Father Jonas. I have brought a few of my fellow priests from the neighbouring parish." The man's voice was deep and scratchy like it belonged to a life-long pipe smoker. I seemed to recognise Father Jonas but not the other three priests. The four of them entered the home and gathered around me. Their presence was almost mystical. I could feel a spiritual cloud fill the kitchen and it seemed there was a warm mist filling the room. "We have come to pray for you so you will be healed!" I could not speak even though I wanted to. My breath felt like it was nearly gone. I gasped for air. I felt a tingling in my whole body as they prayed. They circled the stove many times while they prayed. I could smell incense burning and it stung my eyes and made it harder to breathe. There was a glare of candles moving past me, a fuzzy blur in the darkness, and I felt faint. As

Father Jonas continued to pray the other three priests began to chant. I didn't recognise the language or the chants but they sounded so beautiful, like an unearthly trio of angels resounding through a warm canopy of damp, fragrant incense. My lungs stung and it became increasingly difficult to breathe.

I must have passed out. When I regained consciousness, I was lying on the floor staring at the ceiling. It startled me because I knew I could not get back on top of the stove by myself, and Mum and Papa were not in the room with me. I was frightened. Then I looked down at my legs: they appeared to be straight underneath the blanket, not bent and gnarled like they had been moments before. And my arms felt strong. I raised one arm and flexed my bicep as I felt the muscle with my other hand. The muscle was large and hard and it ripped through the sleeve at the peak! I pulled the blanket off my legs. I was naked but I could see my legs were muscular and healthy. As I stood to my feet, I realised I was no longer crippled. It was an exciting event and I danced around the kitchen and hopped up on top of the table in one jump, then jumped down to the floor, then back up on top of the table, then down again: over, and over again. I was elated! My legs were strong! My arms and chest were powerful and muscular and I felt rejuvenated. I could feel the blood coursing through my veins and the air filling my lungs. It was invigorating!

I looked around the room but the priests had all gone. No one was around. There was no one to share my joy. I ran outside and shouted, "I am healed! I am healed!" But no one could hear me. I looked out into the field. I could see Papa in the distance, so I ran to him and shouted as I ran, "Papa, I am healed! I am healed!" It felt so good to run like I had never felt before. I could feel the air as it satiated my lungs. The stinging sensation was gone and I felt like I could inhale enormous amounts of air and still not be satisfied. It was refreshing! The cool breeze lapped against my strong, muscular legs as I ran and I could feel the brisk air cooling my genitals as they swung freely between my legs. I realised I was not wearing any trousers but it didn't matter. I ran up to papa and grabbed him and lifted him over my head. I threw him high into the air and then caught him in my arms. "Papa, I am healed! The priests came and prayed for me and I am healed!" We both cried as we embraced each other.

Papa laughed and cried. "You must repay this debt by serving them," he said. "Go into town to the church. Find them and ask what it is you should do for them; how can you repay such a kindness…but first, we must get you some trousers!"

Just then everything changed. I was on top of a mighty, white steed. I was on my way to battle. Father Jonas had instructed me to go to the village of *Shoynaty*[35] and save the villagers from the attacking Tatars and from Solovey, the evil highwayman from the woodlands of Bryansk. I felt strong and sure of myself. I had a sword and shield by my side and I was ready for battle. I was not afraid but was determined to defeat my enemy. My muscles were strong and pumped and ready to flex. I felt the rush of blood through my body and it felt strangely sensual and arousing. My cock felt hard against the saddle.

I crossed over the Vychegda River as the sun rose over the horizon. I could see several houses burning in Shoynaty. I recognised the landscape, the river and the valley. This was Storozhevsk. I rode forward, faster and faster. I could see the Tatars approaching a small green and white cottage. They were led by Solovey. He was dressed in black and looked menacing. I came at them from behind and wielded a sword in both hands through the army of Tatars, slaying them two by two from either side of my mighty stallion. They fell to the ground leaving a bloody path behind me, with many more of them fleeing into the woods in terror of my strong and sure weapons. When I rode through to the front of the ranks, I could see Solovey.

As my horse turned to flank him, I jumped off and knocked Solovey's sword to the ground. We fought in hand-to-hand combat, wrestling each other with all our strength. His blows to my chest and side targeted my thick muscles, but I was not hurt or slowed by his feeble moves. We exchanged blow after blow, fist to flesh. I returned every hit with mighty counterblows to his sides, hammerings to his back, and pummelling to his chest. His body was bruising, and with each strike, his sweat mingled with blood would spray into the air. I was mighty and courageous and full of passionate aggression. I threw him to the ground and forced my knee into his lower back while I stretched his arms backward. He screamed in agony. Then I locked my arms around his neck from behind and tightened my grip until he weakened. At first, he struggled and tried to reach behind to loosen my grip, but after a few minutes his arms went limp and then he passed out. I released my grip and let his wretched body fall to the ground, helpless and defeated.

Then I saw an older man lying on the steps of the cottage. He was bruised and beaten. I ran to him and lifted him into my arms, it was Tomi. "Oh Tomi,

---

[35] *Shoynaty* (also known as Storozhevsk) is a small village about 96 kilometres northeast of Syktyvkar in the Komi Republic, Russia, on the banks of the Vychedga River.

what has he done to you?" I kissed his cheek and wiped the blood from his forehead. I brushed his hair back and could see that one of his eyes was bruised and blackened. His shirt was torn open and I could see the bruises and gashes on his chest and stomach. I carried him into the cottage and laid him down on the floor in front of the fireplace. I removed his shirt and started to dress his wounds. "My darling, do not die, please do not die, *schast'ye moye*." Tears started rolling down my face and they dripped on Tomi's chest.

Just then, Tomi opened his eyes and gazed at my face. "Alexeev, is it really you. Oh, how I have missed your gentle touch, *moy general*." Yes…yes, my name was Alexeev, not Ilya, though the character whom I inhabited in this dream seemed to resemble Ilya Muromets. *Oh, how much I too have missed my Tomi.*

It seemed like the next few days happened in a flash, but I must have nursed Tomi back to health and I remembered making love to him. "Come back with me so you can meet my parents," I said. "I can work the farm and you can take care of the home with Mum." I was naked in his bed. There we were once again together in each other's arms, making passionate love. Tomi's naked body was underneath me. I felt his cock rub against my stomach and he wrapped his legs around my waist and pulled his body up to mine. Like a twenty-year-old, he ravaged my chest with his lips. I could feel him sucking my hard nipples and biting my chest. Then he sucked on my neck and shoulders. As I rolled onto my back with Tomi now on top of me, I raised my arms above my head. He started licking the sweat from my armpits. It was a sensual feeling like I had never felt before, but I wanted the feeling to continue forever. As he continued licking my pits, he reached down and grabbed my hard cock. We were both drenched in sweat and my cock was slippery with pre-cum. He began to stroke my cock with one hand while he grabbed my hair with the other hand. Just then I realised he was stroking both our cocks with one hand. It was an amazing feeling. Suddenly, we both ejaculated at the same time and I felt the hot cum shoot up onto my chest. Our milky white liquids mixed together as they shot through the air onto my chest. It was carnal and fleshly. It was erotic and it was love.

We laid on his bed for hours, simply enjoying each other's bodies and the warmth we were making together. His caress was tender at times, then savage and animalistic. He worshipped my muscular body, then bound my hands and feet and teased me by tickling my hard body and sliding his tongue over my muscles. He squeezed and pulled my testicles, drew back my foreskin, and licked the tip of my cock. Then clamped my nipples and wrapped my chest with rough chords. He beat my chest with a rod and slapped my stomach with a wide flat stick. Then he raised my legs and spanked my buttocks until it turned red and burned with stinging pain. I never knew that such acts of bondage and pain could make me feel so hot with primal sensuality and uninhibited pleasure. Finally, we embraced in a deep kiss. I felt his tongue caress the back of my mouth, as mine also perused his mouth. I remembered this taste, the taste of my lover from six years ago. I missed him so much. My life without him had been so lonely and empty.

As we rode back to my parents' farm, I held Tomi in front of me. I wrapped my strong arms around him and caressed his waist, reaching down to feel the bulge of his cock beneath his trousers. I pressed my chest tightly against his back. My nipples were hard as they rubbed against his shoulder blades. My cock was hard and I could feel it pressing against his buttocks. As he turned his head towards mine, we kissed passionately…

Alexeev woke up suddenly. He was drenched in sweat and his arms were wrapped around his pillow. The sheet and blanket from his bed were tangled around his legs and waist. After he untangled himself, he went over to the wash basin and wiped the cum from his cock, waist and chest, then washed the sweat from his face and neck. He wasn't sure what time it was but thought it must be late and past his usual time for breakfast. He could smell the aroma coming from the kitchen so he knew breakfast was already being served. *Mmm, Orlov must have outdone himself this morning*, he thought. *I smell eggs, sausage, and onions…mmm…and syrniki! My favourite*. So, he got dressed and was ready to start his day.

Chapter 4
Morning Tea and Confession

Orlov woke up early. It had been a very restless night because he could not stop thinking of the things Alexeev said to him at the *kabak*. He knew Alexeev was drinking heavily, but he never knew him to talk nonsense like that before. *Why would he talk of another man in that way? The ladies adore him. Maybe he's sick*, he thought, *or maybe he was hallucinating, or under a spell of some kind.* He hurried into the kitchen. His tenants would be waking up soon and as the boarding house master, he was responsible for preparing the meals.

The boarding house accommodated about 50 guests and he also welcomed some of the neighbours who paid a nominal fee for their meals: often, these neighbours were elderly and their children had either died in the wars or were serving in the military, leaving them to struggle on their own. It was common that these aged patrons could not afford proper meals very often and Orlov's good heart and good nature, along with his good fortune, gave him the opportunity to provide this service for far less than it was worth. And even when breakfast was ended, he would send much of the leftover food home with these unfortunates so they would at least have some food later in the day. Many of them were neighbours he had known since his childhood, so they were more like aunts and uncles to him. They taught him how to fish and hunt. They bandaged his skinned knees, removed splinters from his fingers, and shared cookies and cakes with him. In recent decades, they even did these same kinds of things for his many children. Many of them had attended his wedding. They were his extended family and he could not turn his back on them or ignore their misfortunes.

Orlov owned a large parcel of land beyond the boarding house where he built the house for his own family. Although he originally built a home with three bedrooms, a large kitchen and dining area and a second-floor attic with two spare rooms, he was continually expanding or adding on rooms to accommodate his growing family. He had seven children, four of whom were now married with children of their own. When Alexeev was eight and his parents died, Orlov's parents took him in and cared for him as their own son. Although Orlov was nine years older than Alexeev, they immediately bonded because Orlov only had sisters. They became an inseparable duo and the bond grew stronger as they grew older. Alexeev became his personal shadow and spent most of his early years by Orlov's side. Orlov was a handsome man, not tall, but well built. He kept himself in good shape by working the farm with his father and always paid close attention to his grooming. He was always clean-shaven, had relatively short blond hair, and clean, pressed clothes to sufficiently attract the ladies. Alexeev admired him and tried to be like him in every way.

Orlov married Kira the day before his 19th birthday, and by the end of the first year, their first son was born. They continued to live with his parents for ten years. But when his father gave him a large portion of his land in Moscow, Orlov decided to build a house for his family and a boarding house for his business. The land was strategically located near a military camp and within a short walk to one of the city's major marketplaces so it seemed the ideal place to attract tenants. He learned how to cook from his mother and grandmother, so he also offered meals as an added benefit for his tenants. He and his father farmed the land behind the two houses and boarding house so food was plentiful. They also raised chickens, cows, horses, goats, and occasionally a few pigs. Alexeev helped Orlov build the structures and continued to stay with Orlov and Kira and their family of seven children. Over the next 12 years, they built four additional houses on the property to accommodate the marriages and families of Orlov's children. Alexeev's service in the army allowed him to spend several months each year in Moscow as an advisor to the Tsar whenever he was not retrieving and delivering critical documents or valuables. Together, Alexeev and Orlov created a thriving business.

This morning, Orlov was preparing *deruny, kartoshnik*[36], *syrniki*, ham, eggs and sausage, along with sweet breads and rye breads, fruit compote and his own special blackberry-rhubarb jam. Boarders would also be served tea, vodka or milk, and a special *cheremsha*[37] prepared by his wife. Orlov had four sons (Andrei, Kostya, Vladimir and Oleg) and three daughters (Nastya, Klara and

---

[36] *Kartoshnik*: Potato cakes

[37] *Cheremsha*: Pickled wild garlic

Inna) who all worked either on the farm tending the vegetable gardens and fruit orchards, or in the barn feeding and caring for the animals, or in the boarding house cleaning and maintaining the grounds. Even some of the older grandchildren would help out in the gardens or in the kitchen. It was a fine and prosperous family business but Orlov's generosity always kept him from becoming a wealthy man. He would rather see the needs of his loved ones and neighbours met, than obtain riches and status. Orlov believed he had a good life: he loved his family and enjoyed the company of his many friends and neighbours. And he especially loved to cook. He made it a point to prepare a different set of meals for every day of the week and was always collecting recipes from friends and neighbours. He even had recipes from other countries, so occasionally he would have a Tuscany day, or Bavarian day, or Cathay, or Swedish, or French. He loved to experiment with food and the children were always his best critics. They were quick to tell him when they didn't like one of the foreign dishes, like the French *escargot*[38] or Cathay's thousand-year-old duck eggs but were also very quick to ask for seconds when he made something they thought was delicious, like Tuscan lasagne or Bavarian *kirschenmichel*[39].

As the smell of breakfast foods permeated the boarding house, Orlov could hear the stirring of activity throughout the building, both upstairs and downstairs. The residents would soon make their way down the halls and stairs into the dining area, where they would partake of their morning meal and share the news of the week and the current gossip that made its way from one family to the next. Their meals were included in their monthly rents, and for the neighbours Orlov kept a wooden box with a slot on top near the front door where they could drop in a coin or two for their meals. Orlov never tracked what they would put in, but always trusted them to pay as they could. For a few of them who were particularly hard off, Orlov would stand by the box and cover the slot with his hand and simply smile and say, "Someone paid for yours already", but he never seemed to be able to remember or identify who that generous individual was when they would ask. All his neighbours appreciated his generosity and always paid what they could, and many of them even brought recipes handed down from several generations to share with Orlov as an alternative payment. Orlov cherished every recipe as if it were made of gold.

---

[38] *Escargot* (French): A French delicacy, cooked land snails.

[39] *Kirschenmichel* (German): A traditional bread pudding made with cherries, cinnamon, almonds and chocolate

The first customer of the morning was little Anna. She was always happy and was either smiling or giggling, or both. This morning, she came skipping down the hall. Occasionally, she would stop to examine a pebble, or feather, or some other object she happened to see that caught her eye. She was a four-year-old bundle of smiles and curiosity from the top of her curly blonde hair to her pudgy bare feet. Sometimes she would wear little blue, or pink, or white socks, or little brown shoes if it was Sunday, but most often, her feet were bare. She had little rosy, dimpled cheeks and short, stubby, little fingers that held her cloth doll in a tight grip. Her doll, which she had named Roza, was made of leftover material from dresses and shirts her mum had sewn together, and it had brown button eyes, a pink button nose and a braided piece of red cord sewn into a smile where a mouth would be. It was also wearing a small bonnet made of the same material as her dress and there were several strands of yellow yarn resembling hair trailing from beneath the bonnet, neatly tied into a ponytail with a red ribbon. Anna was wearing her favourite white dress with little blue embroidered flowers encircling the hem below her knees with the same flowers bordering her collar.

"Ah, *dushen'ka*[40] Anna, come in my dear. And how are you this fine morning and how is Roza? Is your mum coming down soon?" Orlov asked as he pinched the little one's cheeks, then pinched the cheek of the doll as well.

Anna giggled. "Hehe, yes. But Mum is swatting Makar and Shura for smoking. She caught them out back this morning with Papa's pipe." Makar and Shura were the two older boys (7 and 10) who were always getting into mischief. "What smells so good, Uncle Orlov?" Most of the younger children called him uncle even though he was not related to them.

"Oh, I am glad you asked," he said, with a look of deep concern. "I need a taster to make sure this jam belongs on this toast. You know I am no good at that sort of thing." He slapped the side of his head and smiled, then handed Anna a small piece of rye bread covered with blackberry-rhubarb jam. "Have a seat while I get the rest of the food ready." Anna was grinning from ear to ear and had her fingers covered in jam before her first bite. Knowing the routine, Orlov handed her a glass of milk and a damp cloth as he chuckled to himself.

Anna sat quietly in her chair as she happily ate the piece of jammed bread. She swung her legs quickly and joyously as she sat and she would occasionally put the piece of bread up to Roza's braided mouth as if to give her a bite of the

---

[40] *Dushen'ka*: Darling

delicious morsel as well. When she finished the bread and milk, Orlov wiped her hands with the damp cloth, then handed her a book with many drawings of animals, birds, plants, trees and flowers.

When Orlov was a young adult, he would often take walks in the meadows or woods with Alexeev and draw pictures of the things he would see. He had a talent for drawing but he was never able to nurture his talent into anything other than a hobby. He managed to save and collect his drawings though and had bound them together so he could share them with the little ones for their amusement. When he was younger, Alexeev would stare with wonder and wide eyes at the pictures, and later all Orlov's children had their turns going through the pages and learning about the world around them. He used to take them on family picnics or hikes so they could see the animals up close, then he would make up stories for their bedtime amusement and relate them to the pictures he had drawn. Now he was sharing the pictures and stories with his grandchildren and the occasional neighbourhood or boarding house child. So, Anna now took her turn going through the drawings. She was fascinated with the animals she had never seen before: mountain lions, great bears, eagles, gulls and swans, as well as beetles, crickets, bees, wasps, flies, ticks and spiders. Then there were many pages of flowers of every kind. He stopped by where she was seated every once in a while, telling her about his adventures in the woods where he saw these fascinating creatures and Anna would open her eyes wide in wonderment, or smile and giggle in amusement.

Over the next three hours, the boarders came in gradually for breakfast in their family groups, and the neighbours joined anxiously as well. Most of them were very used to the routine. They would pass by the kitchen counter and pick up a plate, then walk by the long serving table where Orlov had placed trays, bowls and dishes with all the various breakfast items. Everyone could take what they wanted and Orlov was quick to refill dishes as they ran low. The parents would help serve the younger children and two of Orlov's daughters would stand by to help serve the elderly and clear the dishes from the tables as the patrons finished their meals. All of them were satisfied and well-fed, and each in turn started their separate daily routines once they had their fill.

Just as the last guest was leaving, Alexeev entered the dining room from the kitchen door, nibbling on *syrniki* in one hand and alternating with sips from a cup of chamomile tea in the other hand.

"Sorry I did not come in earlier to help you," Alexeev said between nibbles. He was still wearing the clothes from last night, but on him they still looked good even though they were creased in all the wrong places from being slept on. Alexeev had the kind of physique anyone would lust over. He was tall and well built. He had wavy hair that looked great even before it was combed. He had high cheekbones and a cleft between his eyebrows. His broad chest, shoulders and strong arms were intimidating enough to ward off any attackers, though the gentle expressions from his face made everyone feel welcomed in his presence. This piece of masculinity was who Orlov needed to confront this morning. He felt compelled to ask questions about what he heard Alexeev say during his drunken stupor the night before. But he needed to be tactful and discreet. He wasn't sure how Alexeev would react and didn't want to chance being punched in the gut or shoved to the ground. He knew, however, that Alexeev was a gentle giant by nature and no more dangerous than a kitten after finishing a bowl of warm milk.

"So, you are sleeping with men now?" he blurted out. Orlov was well known in the town for not being able to keep secrets and certainly not being tactful about anything. Although he was a dear man, loved by almost all and very generous, he had the tact of a bull moose in heat. In fact, the town had a saying about Orlov, "If you want everyone to know something in a hurry, just tell Orlov it is a secret."

As Alexeev's jaw dropped, so did his cup of tea. "What did you say?" he gulped. "How did you know? Have you told anyone?" He was dumbfounded. A sudden fear came over him and his face suddenly went pale. His legs got weak and wobbly. "I need to sit down." He started to sweat and he felt weak all over.

"No, I have not told anyone," Orlov said quickly to reassure him, "and I am not going to. Besides, who would believe me. But what are you going to do and why have you never told me? I am your closest relative and your best friend. I raised you as my little brother and you never said anything about this to me before." He put his hand on Alexeev's shoulder. "Don't you know what hurts you also hurts me?"

"I was afraid of what you might think...and afraid of what everyone else would do if they ever found out." He wiped his forehead. "I met someone six years ago, when I was bringing my troops through the Storozhevsk township in the Komi region. We only spent a few days together but I knew he was the one for me. Tomi was kind and warm and he made me feel comfortable and complete.

But I am afraid I will never see him again, Orlov." He buried his face in his hands and began to weep. "I didn't want to say goodbye to him but I couldn't stay."

Orlov spoke softly, "Alexeev, if you love him that much you need to go to him and tell him how you feel. You cannot hold something like this inside you. It will tear you apart. It is already tearing you apart."

Alexeev wept a while longer. He knew Orlov was right. He could not think of anything but Tomi. It seemed like every minute of every day was filled with memories of Tomi. Every cottage reminded him of that green and white cottage where they made love on the parlour floor. Every time he saw a man who was slightly bent over or someone who was balding, he thought it was Tomi. And every time he ate *blini* or tasted blackberry jam it reminded him of those mornings when Tomi had made breakfast for him. When he smelled cedar or pine it reminded him of when he built up the fire in Tomi's fireplace. He could never put that encounter in Storozhevsk behind him. Tomi was everything Alexeev had been dreaming of all his life. Orlov was right, he would have to find Tomi again no matter how long it would take him. Before he could make that journey, though, he needed to obtain permission from the Tsar to resign his commission with the military. He served the Tsar well though and was confident his many successful and secretive missions would gain him favour. But he would need to find a replacement before he could leave.

He felt a little better now that Orlov knew his secret but also worried it would only be a matter of time before the entire town knew. This would be the one secret Orlov would never tell though because of his deep devotion to Alexeev. Over the next few weeks, he gave notice to his superiors in the army, sent his plea to the Tsar and prepared to leave. The Tsar immediately sent back approval, pending his replacement. There were several good candidates to replace him so it looked like the way was clear for him to leave. Although many were sad to see him go, they also wanted the best for him and knew it was time for him to start a family and settle down. Everyone assumed Alexeev had marriage and family in mind, and he never said otherwise.

His nights grew increasingly restless though. Alexeev knew if he stayed in Moscow he would be miserable and alone. He thought of Tomi often and would toss and turn every night before finally falling asleep. He would ponder over the mental images of their night together and imagine their future together in each other's arms. He was desperate to get on the road and start his journey but wanted to wait until after the new year so he could earn a little more travelling money.

That would also give Orlov time to find someone else to work in the boarding house. Alexeev only worked weekends for Orlov but his duties usually involved replenishing the inventories and supplies. The job involved a lot of heavy lifting so whoever Orlov hired would have to be in great shape and preferably a young man in his teens or early twenties. Perhaps one of Orlov's younger sons might be interested in taking the job. Both Kostya or Oleg were strong enough and might also need the extra cash.

Over the next few months, Alexeev built a few more rooms onto the boarding house so Orlov could accommodate a few more families as renters. The extra rooms would let Orlov take in a little more rent and help offset his expense and frequent generosities. It was good hard work and it kept him busy. Orlov paid him generously but Alexeev's thoughts would always bring him back to Tomi. He was hoping to earn enough money to purchase a horse for his travels and possibly a few extra changes of clothes as well. He was a resourceful young man and knew how to live off the land. He could hunt and fish and was familiar with the edible foliage of the region, so he was confident he would have plenty to eat along the way. But he worried perhaps Tomi had found someone else to make him happy, someone who would share his life and share his bed. The possibility of the object of his affection loving someone other than him made him sad and angry. He swore to himself he would fight for Tomi's love if it came down to that. He thought to himself, *I will beat the man who would touch my Tomi. I will crush him with my bare hands and make him regret ever—* He had to force himself to think of other things so the anger would not overtake his life. *Oh, how I miss that man. Oh, how I love you,* schast'ye moye.

Chapter 5
Town Meeting

Winter seemed at first like it was coming early to Moscow. It was only October and already the newly cobbled streets had frozen over. The women had their children bundled up in their long coats, mittens and fur caps, and the men talked about how soon they thought the rivers would freeze over. It rained hard yesterday evening and late into the night, and the temperatures had fallen overnight to below freezing. Alexeev was ready to head off to the market early in the morning, ready to pick up some supplies for Orlov. Walking would be a challenge on the icy road through the centre of town, but having lived in these conditions for many years, not to mention his military training to work under icy conditions all over the country, gave Alexeev a great advantage over the typical residents. He didn't appreciate crowds though, so he usually tried to go to market on slower days or at least before the crowds started to gather. There were not nearly as many people in the courtyards now as in earlier years though. Many people were migrating to *Sankt Piter-Burkh*[41] where the Tsar was hoping to relocate the capital within the next few years. The move already had a major effect on many of the surrounding cities since most of the stone masons were commissioned solely for the new buildings ordered by the Tsar for *Sankt Piter-Burkh*.

Alexeev had not been summoned to the new capital but had received a special letter with his schedule for decommission within the next day or so. He had no more assignments to fulfil, so all that was left was the final paperwork in Moscow. This morning he hoped to pick up those release papers. He anticipated his supervisors would also give him the remainder of the year off as a courtesy for all his years of exemplary service, at least that was a common practice.

---

[41] *Sankt Piter-Burkh*: Fromer name of St. Petersburg

Alexeev was not planning to continue to work with his cousin Orlov, but instead would make his way back to Storozhevsk as soon as possible so he could find Tomi even though their amorous happenstance only lasted a few days. "It is time for me to settle down and find a life for myself," he would say. "I am not getting any younger and keeping myself busy in the boarding house will only keep me from my true love and my true destiny." Orlov knew he was talking about his love for Tomi but he would simply smile and nod his head. He wanted to tell Alexeev to get on with his life and search for Tomi, but Alexeev kept postponing his departure, saying the venture was a hopeless one. "I do not even know if he is still in Storozhevsk, and he might even be with someone else by now. I have already fought my battles for the country, I do not want to start a war of the heart." Then he would quickly turn his head away to hide the fact that his eyes were welling up with tears. Deep inside, he imagined Tomi had either forgotten about him, or had become involved with someone else, someone closer to his own age, and those thoughts deeply troubled him.

"Do as you wish, my friend. But you will always be welcome in my home and in my business. I can always use a man with a good head on his shoulders. I will wish you well no matter what you decide." On that note, the conversation was quickly put to an end with no real resolution. Alexeev didn't usually share his feelings and Orlov rarely pressed for more information, at least not on this subject.

"I will try to be back before noon," Alexeev said as he cautiously ventured out onto the glistening and slippery streets.

At first it seemed he was the only one on the boulevard, but before too long he was joined by one, two, four, eight and then twelve others, all on their way to the centre of town. Soon the thoroughfares were crowded and bustling with men, women and children. The marketplaces were busy but Alexeev managed to greet the usual familiar faces of neighbours and fellow soldiers going about their business for the morning. His first stop was army headquarters. It was just a formality but the paperwork he received provided proof he had fulfilled all his obligations and could now live his life as a civilian. There was no regret in leaving, no misgivings, and no shame, but still there were many strong feelings involved. Alexeev loved his troops and always enjoyed his missions and assignments even though they were often difficult and strenuous. The army allowed him to see much of the country and gave him the opportunity to visit other kingdoms, nations, and cultures. Most of his military experience involved the safe delivery and retrieval of strategic papers and critical documents, so his combat experience was minimal. He was well trained in hand-to-hand combat though, and in the use of the sword, musket and the new bayonets. But he would end his military career without receiving any injuries, other than the few bruises he received from settling skirmishes between his own men, and he had never killed anyone, enemy or otherwise. That fact was a relief to his conscience, as he generally believed peaceful negotiations were preferable to physical aggression. He always felt it was a personal loss every time any of his men were injured or died due to the circumstances of their missions.

After concluding his business at headquarters, he continued into the town square to complete the rest of his chores. He stopped in at the candy shop and bought the regular supply of hard candies for the children: number one on Orlov's list. He always made sure he had enough candy on hand to put smiles on the faces of the little ones, especially little Anna, and he also made sure he had a good supply of powdered cocoa on hand in the winter so he could mix it with hot milk, cinnamon and a little sugar, and sip it in front of the fireplace: number two on Orlov's list. It was a good alternative for tea and it also made his wife, Kira, a little more accommodating when it came to bedroom activities.

After the candy store, he was off to the spice trader for nutmeg, cinnamon bark, cloves, salt, sugar, ginger root, garlic, tarragon, mace and especially white pepper. Alexeev loved a little white pepper in his tea. He said it warmed him from the inside out. So, the pouch of white pepper would be packed away for his trip. His final stop was in the food court where he would purchase 50 pounds of wheat flour, 50 pounds of rye flour and an ample supply of yeast for baking breads.

Now any ordinary man would be over-burdened by the sheer weight of these purchases. The weight would be overwhelming to the average, healthy, young man, let alone the added difficulty of trekking over the ice-covered cobblestones. But Alexeev was an exceptionally strong man, built and trained for endurance through extreme conditions. He could surpass the abilities of most men of his size or age. His military background had given him a definite advantage he might not have obtained otherwise. This combined with his exceptional good looks made him the catch of the day every time he went to market. Women, both young and old, flocked to him like moths to a flame. Smiling and winking, batting their eye lashes, offering to assist him in finding the things he needed, inviting him to dinner or dances, or begging to introduce him to their unwed daughters or sisters.

He would simply tip his hat, smile, and thank them, but would always have official business to take care of on the day or night in question. He had become an expert at making up polite excuses.

On this morning, the ladies were attentive as usual. There was an occasional smile or nod, a brief touch to the shoulder, or the bold gesture of grabbing his buttocks. His reaction varied from a polite tip of his hat to a full blush of his cheeks but the attention merely added to his determination to leave Moscow and begin his search for Tomi. As he continued through the marketplace, he stopped at the tobacco shop and purchased a few pouches of tobacco for his pipe, then he went into the cutlery shop and examined some of the knives. But he decided they were too expensive and his old hunting knife had served him well for many years, so it would probably be good for at least a few more seasons. He enjoyed the conversation though, so every detour was worth it and it gave him the opportunity to see some of his friends, perhaps for the last time.

As he passed by the bakery, the baker's daughter Nina, rushed out to greet him. "Don't pass by so quickly, Lieutenant," she said as she grabbed his arm and pulled him inside. Nina had been pining over him for the last decade, ever since she turned 15 and her papa told her she needed to find a husband before it was too late. She simply could not understand why Alexeev never paid her any attention and never responded to any of her overtures, but she wasn't about to give up. "Papa just made some fresh *syrniki*. You must try some," she said as she shoved a fresh one into his mouth.

Nearly choking on the hot cheesecake, he almost dropped his packages, but managed to balance them while trying to recover from being force-fed. "Umm, hummm," he managed to mumble past the mouthful of food. He nodded politely as he backed out of the bakery. Nina just shook her head and put her hands on her hips, then tossed her head back as if she had been insulted. Then she turned sharply, went back in the store and got back to work.

Finally, Alexeev wandered by the jeweller's shop. For years, Alexeev had watched old *Dedushka*[42] Abram created beautiful jewellery from pieces of scrap silver. He admired Abram's workmanship and especially his attention to detail and intricacies. Abram even boasted, "For you, my boy, I would make the finest jewellery you have ever seen." But he probably said the same thing to most of his potential customers. He had known Alexeev's parents for many years before

---

[42] *Dedushka*: Grandpa

they died, though, and he had known Alexeev all his life. After spending some time looking over the treasures in the display cases, Alexeev bid Abram good day and promised he would come back to him if he ever needed a special piece of jewellery made.

So, he continued his walk through the town. The last shop on Alexeev's route was the flower shop. Now, it wasn't very often Alexeev would have an occasion to purchase flowers and it wasn't on his list of things to do today. Orlov's daughters grew flowers of their own to display throughout the boarding house and Alexeev never had any girlfriends, so it was a rare occurrence for him to go into the shop. But as he walked by, he was enticed by the fragrant aroma of the flowers in the shop. There was a remarkable and familiar scent reminiscent of something from a dream, or perhaps a deep, hidden desire: he remembered chamomile, azaleas and lilies. He set down his goods outside next to the door and looked in. He saw white chamomile, pink azaleas and yellow lilies. He took a deep breath as he entered the shop. The shopkeeper was a little old lady, bent over with age. Her white hair was drawn up in a bun and she had dim greyish-blue eyes. She wore a beautiful long green dress lined with black ribbon and embroidered with lacy dark-green grape leaves and little purple beads that were clustered every inch or so, resembling bunches of grapes.

"I noticed you have lilies, azaleas and white chamomile? That is unusual for this time of year," he said with a nervous smile on his face.

"Yes, they certainly are an unusual treasure for winter. They were brought up from the southern valley late last night. My nephew has a covered garden to protect the flowers from the cold. Would you like some for your wife...or girlfriend, perhaps? It would be a shame for them to freeze or wither before they can be appreciated."

Alexeev gently caressed one of the delicate blooms in his rough and calloused hand. "They are certainly beautiful and so fragrant," he said as he took another deep breath.

Just then another patron walked into view from behind the flower baskets in the centre of the store behind Alexeev. "I think your wife would be overjoyed to receive such a wonderful gift," said the stranger.

Alexeev heard the comment but was still gazing at the marvellous display. The stranger's voice was vaguely familiar though, as if from a pleasant childhood memory or perhaps a dream. He bent down to the lilies to get a more sufficient volume of the aroma into his nostrils. Their fragrance was so sweet, his smile broadened as he inhaled. "No, I have no wife or girlfriend. But they are beautiful just the same."

The stranger walked up behind Alexeev and gently rested his hand on Alexeev's shoulder. Just then a sudden chill came over Alexeev and the hair on his arms and neck stood up. Then the stranger leaned over and whispered in Alexeev's ear, "Then buy them for the man you love."

Startled by the comment, Alexeev stood up straight and turned around towards the voice. It was Tomi Pedorov! There was a twinkle in his eye and a wry smile on his face. Oh, what a beautiful sight for Alexeev to behold! Tomi held his arms open wide to embrace Alexeev. As the two engaged in a warm, tight hug, Alexeev burst into tears and wept on Tomi's shoulder. "Oh, *schast'ye moye*, I thought I would never see you again." He kissed Tomi full on the lips with no care of the shopkeeper's presence. "But what are you doing here in Moscow?"

"I am only here for a little while longer. I am visiting my nephew and his family. But I need to start on my journey home within a few weeks, before the weather gets too bad to travel." His voice faltered as he ended his sentence. There was a certain dismay in his voice and possibly a slight hint to acknowledge a glimmer of hope.

"We have so much to talk about, Tomi," said Alexeev. "But I have some supplies I need to deliver. I live with my cousin just on the edge of town."

"Are you on foot?" Tomi asked, surprised anyone would be walking on the icy roads. "My carriage is out in front. We can drop off your supplies and then you can accompany me to my nephew's home where I am staying…if you like." He looked up at Alexeev and smiled.

Alexeev burst into laughter, wrapped his arms around Tomi and twirled him around lifting him off his feet. "All right, all right, but first I need to complete a transaction." He turned to the shopkeeper. "Wrap up these lilies, azaleas and white chamomile. My handsome young man here needs to be surrounded by the beauties of nature." Tomi handed the shopkeeper several silver coins in payment, then he took one of the pink azaleas from his bundle and tucked it over her ear and kissed her on the cheek, "For the most beautiful shopkeeper in town." She smiled and touched her cheek in mid-blush.

She looked at the coins, smiled and said, "Thank you, kind sir, you are most generous. And I hope the two of you have a wonderful day." She wrapped up the flowers while the boys continued to chat and embrace.

Alexeev loaded his cargo into Tomi's carriage and then helped Tomi with his packages as well. The shopkeeper brought out the flowers all wrapped up carefully and securely and handed them to Alexeev. Then she bid them '*Dobroye utro*' and returned to her shop. Alexeev carefully put the flowers in the back on top of the packages. The boys could hardly keep from embracing each other and almost every move they made was arm in arm. "I don't want to lose you again, Tomi." His eyes were still flooded with tears.

Alexeev pointed the way to Orlov's boarding house but Tomi handed the reigns to him. "I'd rather have you lead me, *moy drug*."

"*Moy drug? Moy druuug?* Last time we were together it was *moy general!*" Alexeev sat up straight, stuck out his chest and acted a little indignant. "Have you replaced me with some other *general*?" As he spoke those words, he gulped and hoped that was not the case. His heart still belonged to Tomi and he still had a hole the size of the Caspian Sea in his life. It would be devastating if Tomi had found someone else, and the thought of Tomi being intimate with another man made him jealous and stirred up an anger deep within him.

"There has never been anyone but you since the night we made love, *moy general*," he said, trying to reassure him. "I have been waiting for you to find me again." Then he put his hand on Alexeev's knee. "I did not know you were here in Moscow."

"I'm never sure when I'll be here or for how long. But I have a room here at my cousin's boarding house."

"Are you still a lieutenant?"

Alexeev reached into his coat pocket and pulled out a rolled-up paper tied with a red ribbon. He handed it to Tomi. "As of this morning, I am a civilian."

Tomi took the paper, then looked at Alexeev. His eyes started to well up with tears and he threw his arms around him, "Oh, Alexeev, you truly are *moy general*!"

"Now, don't make me lose control of the horses." He put his arm around Tomi. "I love you, my dear, and I always have." They both held back the tears but continued their embrace until they were in sight of the boarding house. "There it is, Tomi. My cousin Orlov owns and runs this place. He has been very good to me. He is like an older brother."

"Such a big place! There must be 10 or 12 rooms at least, how many can it accommodate?"

"I just added on two more rooms, now there are 22, not including the rooms and houses for his own family and my room above the kitchen. I think he could take in close to 60 tenants now. Orlov does all the cooking for the guests and his family takes care of everything else: the farm, the orchards, the gardens and the upkeep of the building. He has seven children and they all help with the business."

Tomi didn't want to let go of Alexeev. He clasped Alexeev's hand and intertwined their fingers. Then Alexeev brought their hands up to his face. He noticed the tenderness of Tomi's hand and his long slender fingers. He kissed the back of his hand and it made Tomi smile.

Alexeev drove the carriage to the side of the boarding house and up to the entry door to the kitchen. They both stepped down and Alexeev began unloading his supplies. Tomi reached into the back of the carriage and separated out half of the flowers and followed Alexeev into the kitchen. He found a large earthen vase by the water basin, filled it with water, then arranged the flowers and set them on the kitchen table. Meanwhile, Alexeev unloaded the rest of his purchases from the carriage. Tomi went to the back door and held it open for Alexeev as he carried in the two large sacks of flour as if they were feather pillows. Tomi loved to watch Alexeev use his muscles. It was exhilarating and brought back memories of their encounter in his parlour six years ago when Alexeev removed his shirt to reveal his strong, sculpted chest. Tomi had dreamt of Alexeev's sensual and masculine body many times over the years and he remembered how tender and caring Alexeev was. He was the picture of power and energy kept under control.

As Alexeev passed through the back door he leaned over and gave Tomi a kiss. "The flowers look wonderful, Tomi. There are some spruce bushes on the other side of the carriage. Would you like me to cut a few branches to intermingle with the arrangement?"

"Great idea. But I can do that while you finish putting the purchases away. Do you have a knife I can use?"

"Use mine. It's in my front pocket."

Tomi reached into Alexeev's pocket and pulled out the knife then stood up on his tiptoes and kissed Alexeev. Just then, Orlov came in from the other end of the kitchen. Tomi blushed a little and bowed his head a little embarrassed.

"Orlov, this is my good friend, Tomi," Alexeev said.

Orlov hurried over and grabbed Tomi's hand. "Oh, I am so glad to finally meet you, Mister Pedorov. Alexeev has told me much about you. Welcome to our home." He shook Tomi's hand then kissed him on the cheek.

"I'm pleased to meet you too, Orlov. And please call me Tomi. I was just going out to cut a few sprigs from your spruce bush to complete the flower arrangement."

"That is a beautiful bouquet. Here, let me go out with you and we'll cut them together."

As the two of them walked across the driveway, Alexeev called out, "Don't mind me, I'll just be a few more minutes unloading all these supplies!" Then he winked at Tomi and kept unloading.

"Now, Tomi, I don't want you to feel uncomfortable at all while you are here. I know all about your affair with my cousin six years ago, and all I want is for him to be happy. He has been so miserable lately, especially the last five or six months. He's been getting drunk, getting into fights in the *kabak*, and he has been spending far too much time alone, if you know what I mean. Did he tell you he has even stopped going to church services on Sunday? Tsk, tsk, tsk…and my wife says he isn't eating like he should. Usually, Alexeev eats more than his share of food, and of course I don't mind. After all, he's still a growing boy…well, a growing young man. Not that he is too young for you. But as far as I know he has never been with any other man…of course, he hasn't been with any other woman either. But you probably already knew that. And now that you're here he doesn't need to be alone anymore, not that he was ever really alone, because he and I practically grew up together.

"We went to school together…well, not the same class because I am nine years older than him, but my parents took him in when his mama and papa died. He was only eight, but he stuck to me like a little shadow. We even shared a bedroom and shared a bed until I got married. So, we were very close. Not that he and I ever did anything together except sleep. You know he's my cousin. Well, of course you already knew that. I remember thinking how wonderful it would be if he got married and brought up his family with mine. Our kids would play together and he and I would take our wives strolling in the meadow in the summertime. But, of course, that didn't happen. No, he has been alone since he was a child, no women and certainly no men either. Not that he couldn't have had any one of them…women, I mean…hmm…I hope I haven't said too much."

“I think that’s just about enough…” said Tomi, “spruce branches, I mean.” While cousin Orlov was reciting his soliloquy, Tomi had cut several beautiful sprigs of spruce for the bouquet.

“Yes, those should be fine. Oh, Mister Pedorov, I can’t tell you how much it means to Alexeev to finally have you here. Now you can be with him…well, together…at night…uhhh…not that it is any of my business…” So, the two of them walked back into the kitchen and together they arranged the sprigs of spruce among the flowers in the vase. Orlov continued to stumble over his words and Tomi continued to arrange the sprigs, hoping Alexeev would realise his predicament and rescue him.

Alexeev was unpacking the box of spices onto the kitchen counter and overheard some of the awkward conversation. “Tomi, did Orlov tell you all about my love life, my childhood, my education, my ancestry, the birthmark between my shoulder blades and the blister I had on my foot a few weeks ago—”

“Oh, come now, I’m not that bad!” interrupted Orlov. “…Well, maybe I am.” He smiled sheepishly and looked at Tomi a little embarrassed by his own talkative nature. “I am sorry if I talked your ear off.”

Tomi patted Orlov’s shoulder, “Nothing to be sorry about. You made me feel like family.”

Then Alexeev stepped over to Tomi and put his arm around him. “Orlov, my friend, I am going to spend the night with Tomi and his nephew and I think we may be leaving for Storozhevsk sometime in the next few weeks.”

“That’s so sudden…but…there is nothing keeping you here anymore, is there. No need to wait around here when you can be getting on with your life. But I will miss you, my friend.” Orlov gave Alexeev a hug, then he hugged Tomi and gave him a kiss on the cheek. “Now don’t worry about anything. I will make sure my daughters start packing up your things so you can leave whenever the two of you are ready. Is that all right?”

“That would be wonderful. I’m going to get a few things from my room that I’ll need for tonight, and then we’ll be back tomorrow around noon.” He quickly went out the door and up to his room above the kitchen.

“Orlov, I want to thank you for all you have done for Alexeev. I promise to take good care of him.” They hugged again and then Orlov walked Tomi out to the carriage and helped him up into the seat. Then Alexeev came out with a small bag. He gave Orlov a quick hug and kiss on the cheek and jumped up into the carriage. He grabbed the reigns and off they went to Tomi’s nephew’s house.

The house was just a few kilometres past the boarding house, but they talked about how much they missed each other over the last six years the entire way. They also caught each other up on a few things each of them had done over the years. Tomi developed a new blackberry wine recipe, which included a hint of cinnamon. His wine and cordial sales were one of his major sources of income along with his berry jams, compotes and relishes. Alexeev kept himself busy in the military. He had made several trips to *Sankt Piter-Burkh*, helping the Tsar prepare to move the capital. It was Alexeev's job to organise and facilitate the move of many of the sensitive documents and national treasures from Moscow to *Sankt Piter-Burkh*. He had a good group of men to help accomplish his tasks but the time they spent together on the road made him understand his loneliness better. His experience with Tomi made him crave their physical connection more over their six-year separation.

Their hands were clasped with their fingers tightly intertwined the entire way. Every now and then one of them would raise their entwined hands to their lips and gently kiss the union, then there would be a long gaze into each other's eyes and an understanding smile. Now and then a tear would wander down a cheek, sometimes accompanied by a vocal flutter that would break up a word or two. But Alexeev was getting increasingly aroused as he anticipated their physical union and could feel his cock swelling and hardening beneath his trousers. Tomi loved the smell of Alexeev. He had an alluring and erotic scent he had never sensed from anyone else before. He remembered their encounter when their sweat mingled as they made love. It was that musky smell of Alexeev's sweat that made Tomi lose his concentration as it awakened that animal magnetism enabling him to be the willing and grateful recipient of Alexeev's advances. The two of them were well-matched but they would have to postpone their excitement and repress the stimulation for at least a few more hours while they socialised with Tomi's relatives. As his nephew's home came into view they slowly released their grasp and began to compose themselves.

"I don't want to give my nephew any cause to ask unneeded questions just yet," said Tomi.

Alexeev looked into Tomi's eyes. "As long as you will be mine tonight."

Chapter 6

Dyadya Medved'

As they rounded the last bend in the road, Alexeev could make out the beautiful two-storey cottage. There were several apple trees in the front yard and a cobblestone walkway and drive from the dirt country road to the front door. The first floor of the cottage was made of block stone and mortar: dark grey basalt rock offset by white marble. Six stone pillars supported the balcony, three on either side of the front door and the covered porch area was a magnificent blend of birch and walnut inlays bordering the huge picture windows that dominated the front-facing wall, deck floor, and the double-door entrance. Red rose bushes graced the lower portions of the cottage and surrounded the home in the springtime like a crimson velvet wreath. During the winter though, they were cut back to only a few bare twigs poking up from beneath the snow with their bases covered in straw to protect the roots from freezing. To the untrained eye they looked like large mounds of cotton or wool.

"My nephew, Vanya, and his wife, Sveta, have spent the better part of the last decade building this home," he said in an almost boastful tone. "I am very proud of the two of them." He paused for a moment. "The last time I was here was when my brother Stas passed away seven years ago, he was Vanya's father. Let's see…that was about a year before you and I met. He was eight years older than me."

Alexeev could see Tomi's eyes starting to water. He gently wrapped his arm around Tomi's shoulder. "You miss him very much, my dear. I am glad I am here to at least meet his son."

Vanya was a master carpenter by trade and a very lavish and artistic one. His designs were well-known in Moscow and his woodwork was sought after by many well-to-do families in the region and as far away as *Sankt Piter-Burkh*. His artistry and expertise were gaining notoriety in the provinces surrounding

Moscow too. He was most famous for his wood inlays and intricate wood carving designs on bedroom furniture and dining room tables. He designed all the woodwork in his house and it had quickly become the envy of the neighbourhood. He was never without work and could afford many luxuries for his wife and family. But he was also a generous young man. He believed he had an obligation to give back to those who had helped him in the early stages of his career and had a responsibility to pass on his good fortune to those who were in need. Tomi admired him for his charity and for his kindness to everyone he encountered. His nephew frequently donated to community charities and was always quick to provide food or clothing to those who were less fortunate.

His wife Sveta was a gracious hostess, housewife and mother of three girls: Faina aged 12, Filippa aged 9 and Feodora aged 7. Vanya's father, Stas, had died a few days before Feodora was born. Stas had contracted measles the prior year, and even though he recovered, he remained weak for several months. Vanya sent a message to Tomi during Stas' bout with the measles illness, but by the time Tomi arrived, Stas had contracted influenza due in part to his already weakened physical state. He was unconscious with a high fever when Tomi arrived and died a few days later. The death devastated Tomi and he blamed himself for not arriving sooner. But when Feodora was born two days after the funeral, Tomi's heart melted and his love poured out to his third grand-niece. As he held her for the first time, he hoped that Stas was looking down on all of them and sharing the joy of his new granddaughter. But Moscow was almost 900 miles away and Tomi was unable to make such a long trip through the wilderness very often, even though he missed Vanya and his family very much. But he would write frequently and send packages of jams, dried fruits, and blackberry wine as often as he could. It was Vanya's idea to add a touch of cinnamon to the blackberry wine.

Vanya had heard the carriage before it came around the bend. He was stepping out of the house as Tomi and Alexeev pulled off the road and in between the house and the outbuilding. The door to the outbuilding was propped open and Vanya directed Alexeev to pull the carriage in through the door. As Alexeev hopped out of the carriage Vanya rushed in to greet them. "Welcome back, *Dyadya Medved'*[43], did you have a productive day in the city? And who is this handsome stranger?"

---

[43] *Dyadya Medved'*: Uncle Bear

"*Medved'*?" Alexeev whispered in Tomi's ear as he helped him down from the carriage.

"I will explain later," Tomi whispered back, a little embarrassed. "Alexeev, this is my nephew, Ivan." Alexeev dipped his head towards Ivan at Tomi's introduction.

"So, this is the famous Alexeev you've been writing to us about for so many years…and talking about, especially this last month, ehh *Dyadya.*" He nudged his uncle. "Alexeev this and Alexeev that…you are part of our family now. And please call me Vanya." He put his hands over Alexeev's shoulders and kissed him on each cheek. "Can I help you unload anything?"

"I think let's go in and have some tea first. It has been a long day," said Tomi as he instinctively took hold of Alexeev's hand.

"Oh, we should bring in the flowers you bought. If we leave them out here the blooms will freeze." Alexeev opened the back of the carriage and gently gathered the flowers together.

"What beautiful azaleas and chamomile…and wherever did you find lilies this time of year? Sveta will be overjoyed. She's been urging me to go to the florist so she can liven up the house with blooms." Vanya took a big whiff.

"Tomi and I met while we were in the flower shop in town and he couldn't resist buying the whole lot of them. I think he would have bought out the store if we had stayed any longer." Alexeev gave Tomi a gentle tug on his chin.

"Let's get inside, Vanya. I'm feeling a chill." Tomi wrapped his arms tightly around himself.

Then Alexeev removed his coat and put it around Tomi. "Yes, we'd better go inside before my love turns blue."

"Yes, yes, of course. I am so glad to finally meet you. Uncle talks about you like you are the Tsar's first cousin," he said as he winked back at Alexeev who was following a few paces behind. "Sveta has just made some Almond *Kulich*[44]. Her recipe is the best in the country." There was a chill breeze blowing so they hurried inside. "Sveta, my dear. Uncle *Medved'* has brought home a visitor!" He turned to Tomi and smiled as he called out. The young and pretty Sveta came out from the kitchen still wearing her apron. Sveta was a young, vibrant, strawberry-blonde with rosy cheeks, crisp blue eyes, a dainty nose and full red lips. She wiped some flour from her face with the back of her hand and extended her other

[44] *Kulich*: A traditional Russian and Ukrainian Easter cake

hand towards Alexeev. "Lieutenant, this is my beautiful bride, Sveta. This is our uncle's…uh…this is Alexeev."

"Oh, very pleased to meet you, Lieutenant," she said as she continued to fuss with her face and hair and pulled on her dress to straighten out the wrinkles her mind had imagined were there.

"The pleasure is mine," said Alexeev as he bent forwards and gently held and kissed the back of her floured hand. She smiled and blushed and continued to tidy her appearance.

"Uncle, you said he was handsome but you didn't tell the half of it!" Just as the words came out, Sveta realised she was talking out loud and promptly waived her hands in the air as if to take back the statement that might make Alexeev feel uncomfortable. "Never mind me, I talk foolishly sometimes. Come in out of the cold and sit, sit…please make yourself at home. Vanya, show them to the parlour while I bring in the tea and *Kulich*. Oh, my goodness, I need a few more cups!" She rushed back into the kitchen to gather the afternoon refreshments.

Vanya led the way to the parlour and invited them to sit down. Alexeev could not get over how beautiful the home was: ornate woodwork and carvings on all the bannisters and pillars; fine hand-painted oil lamps; beautiful woven rugs and tapestries; the woodwork on the furniture was exquisite. Then as Sveta brought in the tray of *Kulich* and tea, he noticed the intricate pink pattern of lilacs on the bone china and the raised pattern of roses on the silver tea set. Sveta poured the tea and handed a cup to Alexeev, then Tomi and finally Vanya. Then she served them each a slice of *Kulich*. As she cut each slice, they could see the steam rising from the freshly baked bread and the wonderful aroma of the sweet yeast bread and the almonds made each of the boys smile with delight. As they each took a bite, the bread nearly melted in their mouths as the glorious flavour caressed their taste buds. It was truly a work of wonder, a culinary masterpiece, and no one doubted the recipe must surely be the best in the country.

"Where are the girls, Sveta?" Tomi asked as he licked a few wayward crumbs from his fingers.

"Oh, they're next door with the Melnikovs, celebrating their son, Viktor's, 13th birthday," said Vanya.

Sveta promptly leaned in towards Tomi and whispered, "I think Faina has a crush on him! She follows him around and takes him little gifts. And she always wears her best dress when she knows he'll be around." Tomi just smiled and took another bite of his *Kulich*.

"So, Vanya, Tomi told me you are the best carpenter here in Moscow. Well, actually, he said you are the best carpenter in the world!" As Alexeev continued, he stood up and admired the work. He ran his hand along the banister to feel the intricate carved patterns. "Did you carve these banisters and all this lovely furniture?" Then he ran his hands over the table and leaned down to examine the inlays.

"Yes, I was apprentice to the best carpenter there ever was, my father Stas. He was Tomi's older brother. That banister was one of his designs. He had carved a table with the same design around the edge and I made a drawing of the design before he sold it."

Tomi jumped into the conversation, "Vanya, you are too modest. Although I am the first to admit your father's woodwork was very masterful, you have added your own flair to his designs. I think you have surpassed the master in every way. Vanya has brought back some of the designs from our ancestors. Stas had drawings that have been handed down for many generations in our family. His great-great-grandfather was also a carpenter and designer. But Vanya also has designs that are his own originals."

"You have a very fine talent. So intricate…it is no wonder Tomi speaks so highly of you." Alexeev seemed a little mesmerised by the carvings.

"He was asked to go to *Sankt Piter-Burkh* to design some furniture for the Tsar," Sveta chimed in.

"Now Sveta dear, you know I would have to be away for too long." Vanya then turned and spoke to Alexeev, "The Tsar wanted to commission me for a two-year engagement, which would take me away from home for that long, or I'd have to move the family to *Sankt Piter-Burkh*. But I like it here, and there is plenty of work for me here in Moscow now that so many other craftsmen have been called to *Sankt Piter-Burkh*. But I haven't given a final answer yet."

Alexeev nodded in agreement. "It is a good opportunity but I think you have a good thing going on here as well. Besides, if things change here, I am sure the Tsar would welcome you if you changed your mind later. I've been transporting many of the country's documents and valuables to *Sankt Piter-Burkh* over the last few years. They will still be working on the new capital for a few more years… Have you ever thought of doing the work here and having it shipped to *Sankt Piter-Burkh*? You might be able to travel there and stay only a few weeks to show him some of your work, draw up the designs and get them approved, then return here to do the work."

Sveta leaned over to Tomi and whispered, "Maybe I can convince him to take me and the girls with him…I'd love to take a trip to the coast!" Tomi smiled and nodded.

"That's a possibility, I suppose. I appreciate your advice, especially since you have worked for him before."

After they each had second helpings of the *Kulich* and Alexeev had his third, and they had consumed the last drop of tea, Sveta gathered the china and silver and excused herself. "So, what are your plans for the rest of the day, Alexeev?" Vanya asked.

Tomi spoke up, "I was hoping…he might be able to spend the night here instead of going all the way back to the city." He looked at Alexeev then glanced at Vanya for approval.

"Of course, you are welcome to stay," Vanya said immediately to eliminate any doubt of acceptance. "Uncle *Medved'*, show him to your room so he can start getting settled. We will get the fire going down here and get things ready for dinner."

After Vanya left the room, Alexeev turned to Tomi with deep concern. "Are you sure you want me here tonight, Tomi? I do not want to make anyone feel uncomfortable."

"You heard Vanya. And you are part of the family now. And family is always welcome." He grabbed Alexeev's hand and pulled him along behind him and guided him upstairs to the room where he was staying.

The bedroom was large and spacious. It had a small fireplace near the large oak bed, and a stack of wood in the woodbin to the left of the mantle. There was a beautiful quilt with rich hues of blue and purple over the bed, and a knitted blanket of the same colours folded neatly on the cedar chest at the foot of the bed. The room smelled of orange blossoms and pine. The dresser was a masterpiece of carved oak and it matched the headboard and footboard of the bed set. The design theme on the furniture was a forest scene with deer, squirrels, and flying eagles. On top of the dresser was a vase of freshly picked and fragrant Daphne flowers. The vase was ceramic: a light peach colour with dark blue and purple flowers painted in clusters. There were also two matching night stands on either side of the bed and a wash table with a beautifully polished black marble basin and a ceramic pitcher that matched the vase on the dresser. The towels that hung from the wash table were a deeper blue and purple than the quilt and blanket, but their hues were well-coordinated all the same.

"I have made up my mind, Tomi. I will stay." Alexeev flung his strong arms around Tomi and lifted him up off the floor and kissed him. He tightened his grip and let his tongue rediscover the inside of Tomi's mouth. Then he released his grip and unbuttoned Tomi's shirt and pulled it back to reveal his black and silver curly chest hair. "So, that is where the bear has been hiding! *Dyadya Medved'.*" His lips made their way down to Tomi's chest and latched onto his right nipple. Then he grabbed the left nipple with his forefinger and thumb and began to twist and pull the left one as he sucked the one on the right. Tomi tilted his head back and took a deep breath.

"Oh, how I have missed you, *moy general*." He fell back onto the bed and pulled Alexeev onto him. The warmth and weight of Alexeev's body pressing against Tomi was amazingly wonderful. He smelled that old familiar scent again and he could barely contain his joy. The strong, rough hands grasping his flesh, manipulating his nipples and stroking his chest was a memory Tomi had tried to repress during their separation. But the memory was too strong, too potent, too compelling. Tomi had hoped, almost in desperation, he and Alexeev would someday be together again, but the dream of that reunion seemed nearly futile and almost hopeless up until today. Now it was a reality. He was in Alexeev's arms again. *I will never let him go, not again*, he thought. *I made that mistake six years ago. I should have followed him to the ends of the earth so we could be together*. The feeling of loneliness had been too much for Tomi to bear.

Alexeev was overwhelmed by Tomi's presence as well. He wanted to pin him to the bed and kiss every inch of his glorious body. He felt his thick cock throbbing in his trousers and he wanted to pull it out and thrust it into Tomi's receptive ass. Then Alexeev gathered his composure. After all, he was a guest in Vanya's house and there was a certain way a guest should act. He restrained his desire and slowly, gently, calmed his action with Tomi. "I love you, Tomi, but I think we should wait until later." He pulled himself back and began to rebutton Tomi's shirt. "Don't think I will not have you later, though," he smiled and gave Tomi a tender kiss on his chest before he fastened the last button. "Now, I must redirect my energy for a while. After I bring your packages in, I want to help with some chores. Show me where is Vanya's woodshed and I will chop some wood for him while you help him prepare dinner."

Tomi gave a little chuckle. "Vanya does not cook! He would burn water if you let him near the stove. I'll send him out with you to the woodshed. Sveta and I will take care of dinner."

"Your wish is my command," said Alexeev, as he bowed endearingly.

Tomi passed by and swatted him on the buttocks. "Follow me, knave!"

The two scampered down the stairs with youthful energy. The thought and anticipation of a later encounter had made the interim duties much more pleasant and they welcomed the challenge. They felt renewed and an inner strength had returned to both of them.

As they scurried into the living room, Vanya watched with an inner awareness of the spark and excitement between them. He was keenly aware of the energy between two lovers, as he was still passionately in love with Sveta and would often scamper through the halls on her heels, racing to the bedroom for a quick afternoon romp between the sheets. "What's this? Back so soon? I thought maybe you would be napping for a while…to recuperate from your long day in the city, of course." He winked knowingly at Alexeev who simply cleared his throat and glanced with raised eyebrows towards Tomi.

"Alexeev would like to chop your wood," Tomi said, trying to ignore Vanya's insinuation.

"Oh, certainly. Let me show you the way. We have much to talk about." He wrapped his arm around Alexeev and guided him out the door.

As the two of them walked off, Tomi called out to Vanya, "Now you be careful what you talk about young man…or I'll put you over my knee!" He wondered what questions Vanya would ask. *What could they possibly have to talk about? I hope he doesn't ask him embarrassing things about our private lives.* He went into the kitchen with some hesitation, still wondering what could be transpiring between his lover and his nephew, who had apparently become fast friends. He looked back a few times trying to catch a word or two, but dinner would need to be made and Tomi didn't want Sveta to get all the credit.

"Well, Sveta, I am taking over your kitchen. I want this dinner to be special for Alexeev so I am going to make a few dishes that are my specialties," Tomi spoke with confidence and conviction. Sveta was a little stunned but she knew Tomi wanted to impress his friend, so she waited for his instructions. "I want you to make your famous Black bread. You made that last week and it was wonderful with Vanya's goat cheese. If I remember right, that took about three and a half hours to prepare and bake. That will give me enough time for my *Halupki*[45]. Alexeev lives alone and I don't think he gets the finer meals from the

[45] *Halupki*: Stuffed cabbage

boarding house very often. I will also make mushroom and turnip soup. He likes mushrooms…I remember he commented on that when we had breakfast together." Knowing that comment might beg the question of what they were doing having breakfast together, Tomi quickly added, "…and I also want you to make those cranberry-orange cookies. You know, the ones with the orange zest in the icing. I think I saw some candied orange zest in the cellar."

"Yes Uncle, anything else?" Sveta inquired. "Will we be having tea or wine with the meal?"

"Does Vanya still have a bottle of his raspberry wine? I think it would go well with the stuffed cabbage."

"Yes, I think so. I will go down to the cellar and bring up a few bottles. What else can I bring up? Do you need pork or chicken for the cabbage?"

"Bring both…and the apple vinegar," he added.

Off she went to fetch the needed ingredients from the cellar. Meanwhile, Tomi hurried himself in the kitchen, pulling spices from the cupboard and oils from the shelf. Then he filled the stove and oven with wood and got the fire started. The cold air was coming down from the mountains early this afternoon so a fire in the stove would take the chill off the room. He needed a large pot for the mushroom stew and the one he wanted was on a high shelf, too high for him to reach. He found a stool in the pantry and stood on top of it to reach the pot. Just as he pulled the pot from the shelf, he felt dizzy, then the room seemed to spin. The next thing Tomi knew, he was flat on his back on the kitchen floor and the pot was on the other side of the room. There was a twinge in his side, but he got up, straightened himself out, brushed off his trousers and shirt and picked up the pot.

A few minutes later, Sveta came up from the cellar with the requested items and set them on the counter. "I heard a noise. Did you drop something?" she asked.

"Yes, I was getting the pot from the shelf and it slipped out of my hands." He picked up the stool from the floor while she was turned towards the counter arranging the food. As he set the stool upright, he noticed a sharp pain in his side, but there was much that still needed to be done.

While Tomi and Sveta worked diligently in the kitchen with dinner preparations, Vanya and Alexeev were out in the woodshed chopping logs down to size for the fireplaces and for the stove.

"Tomi told us you are a lieutenant in the Tsar's army. Will you return to the army after the new year?" asked Vanya.

"I will admit the thought had crossed my mind before. It is not a bad life, working in the military, but I am not getting any younger," he said as he thought about all the years he had already served. "And now that Tomi and I have found each other again…well, I want to settle down and enjoy life. I want to start my own business…the Tsar has known for some time I wanted to leave at some point. He and I have often talked about it and he approved my discharge once he received my formal request earlier this week. I picked up my final papers for retirement just this morning before I met Tomi in town. I had already planned to go and find Tomi no matter how long it would take and no matter where it would take me. I am very much in love with your uncle."

"That's good. I'm glad for both of you." He reached out and placed his hand on Alexeev's shoulder. "You know, I have never seen Tomi so happy as he was this afternoon when he returned with you. When he showed up three weeks ago he was very depressed, but whenever he would talk about you his eyes would light up. All he could talk about was, 'Alexeev is so handsome, he is so witty, he is so strong, he could make me laugh and smile'. But then he would say he didn't think he could find you, and he didn't know where you were or even if you were still alive. I think he thought maybe you had gone to Europe with the Tsar." Vanya squeezed Alexeev's shoulder a little tighter. "But you are here now. Be good to him, Alexeev. He needs you, and I think you need him too." He smiled and the two of them exchanged a knowing glance.

After a few hours of chopping wood, the two men were hot and sweaty. They had stripped down to their shorts and were ready for a bath. Sveta had anticipated their need, and while her bread was baking, she had heated enough water to fill the bathtub. "Vanya!" she called from the back door. "The tub is full and the towels are next to the basin. After you and Alexeev get cleaned up, dinner will be ready."

"Thank you, my dear. We will be in shortly," he called back. "Come follow me. There is a shorter way to the bathtub through the back porch."

The two men stripped off their shorts and bathed together in the large copper tub. Afterwards, Vanya handed Alexeev a small vial of cologne. "This is Tomi's favourite," he whispered. "Put a little on now, and then again before you go to bed."

Alexeev placed it in his coat pocket after dabbing a few drops on his neck and chest then he rubbed some on his hands and applied it to his armpits. It was the familiar scent of lavender and vanilla. He also took this opportunity to trim the hair around his cock and shave the stubble from his face and neck. He wanted to make sure that his encounter with Tomi tonight would be a most pleasant and memorable one. Vanya had a large mirror in the bathing room, the largest one Alexeev had ever seen. He examined himself in the mirror inspecting his torso, flexing his muscles, then lifting his cock and testicles to ensure they were clean and smooth to provide a comfortable experience for his lover. Then he trimmed his fingernails and toenails, took a brush to his hair and rinsed his mouth with mint and clove tea.

Finally, he dressed himself: pulling his white linen shirt over his head and buttoning the sleeves around his wrists instead of rolling them up past his elbows like they usually were. Then he carefully tied his Croatian tie. He took a damp rag and wiped the dust from his boots then brushed the dust and lint from his coat. He cleaned up well and was fairly pleased with his appearance. He wanted to impress Tomi and show him that he cared enough to look his best for him, so he found Vanya in his room and asked him if he could borrow a hat for dinner.

"I have just the one that will match your coat. It is one I often wear when I attend mass on Sundays." Vanya pulled a black hat from his wardrobe. The colour of the hat matched his coat perfectly, and it was a good fit for his head. After he put it on his head, Vanya helped straighten it and then he formed the brim slightly to match the contour of Alexeev's face. As he leaned in to adjust the tie, he noticed the faint hint of cologne on Alexeev's neck. Vanya smiled then turned and broke off a Daphne flower from the bouquet on his dresser and pinned it to Alexeev's coat. Vanya smiled and whispered, "Tomi will be very pleased…and I am happy I have a new uncle!" Then he kissed Alexeev on the cheek and they walked to the dining room together.

Chapter 7
Midnight Ecstasy

Dinner was wonderful. Tomi couldn't stop staring at Alexeev, all dressed up in his coat, tie and hat, and he also noticed the sweet scent of lavender and vanilla cologne emanating from his neck. It almost brought tears to his eyes to think Alexeev had done all this to please him and to look like a gentleman for his relatives. Alexeev was equally impressed with the *Halupki* and he raved about the mushroom soup. The bread and cheese were a good complement to the meal and Alexeev made sure he praised Sveta for her delicious cranberry-orange cookies. Then the chamomile tea and raspberry wine rounded off the evening meal very well as they all adjourned to the parlour.

The four of them sat and conversed for several hours, talking about music and poetry, and their mutual appreciations of operas and ballets. Alexeev shared humorous stories about his troops that made both Vanya and Sveta laugh, but Tomi was lost in a dream world as he stared deep into Alexeev's bright green eyes. He couldn't hear a word that was said. All he knew was the one he loved was sitting close to him and it made his blood run hot. Perhaps it was just as much the effects of the overabundance of wine he had consumed but the feeling was taking over his senses, and for a while his attentiveness to Alexeev took his mind off the pain in his side. As they talked about their interests, Alexeev mentioned his great interest in poets and poetry.

"Oh Vanya, read to them a sonnet from Shakespeare. You do that so well." Sveta said enthusiastically as she hung tightly onto Vanya's arm.

"My dear, they don't want to hear sonnets tonight," said Vanya. There was a little shyness in his voice, though he knew Tomi loved to listen to him read from Shakespeare's plays.

Alexeev perked up and chimed in with encouragement, "Please do, Vanya. I love the English poet and I rarely get to hear his sonnets."

Vanya walked over to his bookshelf and brought down one of his volumes of Shakespeare. "Well, let me read you one of my favourites. It is sonnet number 18, *Shall I Compare Thee to a Summer's Day*[46]."

"Oh Tomi, you will love this one. Vanya reads it to me often," whispered Sveta.

Sonnet 18: Shall I Compare Thee to a Summer's Day?

Shall I compare thee to a summer's day?
Thou art more lovely and more temperate.
Rough winds do shake the darling buds of May,
And summer's lease hath all too short a date.
Sometime too hot the eye of heaven shines,
And often is his gold complexion dimmed;
And every fair from fair sometime declines,
By chance, or nature's changing course untrimmed.
But thy eternal summer shall not fade
Nor lose possession of that fair thou ow'st;
Nor shall death brag thou wand'rest in his shade,
When in eternal lines to time thou grow'st,
So long as men can breathe or eyes can see,
So long lives this, and this gives life to thee.

"Beautiful, beautiful," said Alexeev. His arm had made its way around Tomi during the reading, and Alexeev pulled him closer at the end of the sonnet. "Perhaps I can share a poem with you now." Alexeev was especially fond of some of the English poets as well. One of his favourites was Christopher Marlowe. He had collected a few poetry books over the years and had taken it upon himself to memorise many of his most cherished poems. He decided to recite one of his favourite poems to the group, and especially to Tomi.

"We would be most honoured," Vanya said as he placed the volume back on the shelf.

---

[46]*Shall I Compare Thee to a Summer's Day*: William Shakespeare (1564-1616) English poet and playwright, Sonnet #18 (*Public Domain*)

Tomi sat back on the settee as Alexeev stood up. "Now let me see, this poem is called *The Passionate Shepherd to His Love*[47], by Christopher Marlowe…"

The Passionate Shepherd to His Love by Christopher Marlowe

Come live with me, and be my love,
And we will all the pleasures prove,
That hills and valleys, dales and fields,
And all the craggy mountain yields.

There we will sit upon the rocks,
And see the shepherds feed their flocks
By shallow rivers, to whose falls
Melodious birds sing madrigals.

And I will make thee beds of roses,
With a thousand fragrant posies,
A cap of flowers and a kirtle
Embroidered all with leaves of myrtle;

A gown made of the finest wool,
Which from our pretty lambs we pull;
Fair lined slippers for the cold,
With buckles of the purest gold;

A belt of straw and ivy buds,
With coral clasps and amber studs;
And if these pleasures may thee move,
Come live with me, and be my love.

The shepherd swains shall dance and sing
For thy delight each May morning:
If these delights thy mind may move,
Then live with me, and be my love.

---

[47] *The Passionate Shepherd to His Love*: By Christopher Marlowe (1564-93) English poet and playwright (*Public Domain*)

Then Alexeev took Tomi's hand and gently kissed it. He sat back down beside Tomi and again wrapped his arm around him. The couples talked for a while about the love that was expressed in these poems and each of their passions for poetry and prose that was written abroad.

"Oh, how I love poetry," said Sveta. "I also like to study artwork. Vanya and I went to Rome and Venice a few years ago. Oh, the paintings there were so beautiful. I was in heaven." Her eyes rolled back in her head while she imagined all the beauty. "I wish we had artists like Michelangelo here in Russia."

"You do know we have many beautiful treasures in this country too, though," Tomi added, "and many wonderful artists. When my family moved from Prague to *Nyen*[48], we stayed in Veliky Novgorod at the North end of Lake Ilmen for several months. While we were there, we went to the Church of the Transfiguration and saw the most beautiful frescos. They were painted by the Byzantine artist, Theophanes." No one noticed that Tomi was short of breath because of the lingering pain in his side.

"Yes, I've heard of those but have never had the chance to visit," said Alexeev.

As the fire in the parlour fireplace died down, Alexeev noticed that Sveta shivered when she pulled her knitted shawl over her shoulders. Then Tomi shivered as well. "Here, let me make myself useful and put another log on the fire." Alexeev stood and removed his coat and wrapped it around Tomi. Then he picked up a large log with one hand and laid it on top of the coals. "There, that should warm you up again soon." He sat back down next to Tomi and put his arm around him. "I'll keep you warm, s*chast'ye moye.*" He kissed him on the forehead and Tomi leaned back onto Alexeev's chest, smiled and fell back into his dreamland thinking about the beauty of art and the wonderful imagery of poetry.

Sveta leaned in to Vanya and whispered, "They look so sweet together." Vanya smiled and nodded.

As the hours passed and the conversation began to lag a bit, both Vanya and Sveta started to feel the length of the day catching up with them. They both tried

---

48 *Nyen*: Current city of St. Petersburg. The town of Nyen was a wealthy Sweedish trading centre until 1702 when it was conquered by Peter the Great and renamed Sankt Piter-Burkh

to hold back their yawns but finally succumbed to their bodies' weaknesses and they had to excuse themselves.

"We must get to bed, my dear," said Vanya. Sveta nodded in agreement as she covered another uncontrollable yawn with her hand. "But you and uncle stay up as late as you want," he said to Alexeev as he stood and helped Sveta to her feet.

Sveta graciously excused herself and Vanya. "Yes, we simply must get to bed. And we will make breakfast in the morning so you can both sleep in." Off they went to their bedroom, arm in arm, up the dark hall then up the staircase with only a candle to light the way. The light from the fireplace glowed behind them but soon they disappeared altogether into the darkness.

Tomi and Alexeev had both enjoyed the wine a little too much and found themselves feeling very happy and relaxed as they positioned themselves closer together on the settee. When Alexeev could no longer see their hosts, he leaned into Tomi and kissed him passionately. "I have been waiting to do that since before dinner, my dear." Just then Vanya's pendulum clock chimed midnight. They reclined in each other's arms onto the settee and kissed and fondled each other for several minutes. Alexeev began massaging Tomi's chest and licking his hard nipples through his shirt. Tomi tried to mask the pain in his side by spreading his legs wide to draw attention away from the focal point of the pain. Though they were still clothed, they could feel their cocks rubbing against one another.

"Let's go up to the bedroom, love," Tomi whispered.

"Are you going to let the bear out tonight?" Alexeev said as he reached his hand up under Tomi's untucked shirt. "I want to see my bear again…please *Dyadya Medved'*, I want to hear you roar tonight. Arrrrrgh," he growled.

Tomi quickly put his hand over Alexeev's mouth. "Shhhh, not so loud." They both laughed and then embraced. Alexeev wrapped his coat a little tighter around Tomi's shoulders then grabbed a candle from the table next to the settee and lit it. He helped Tomi to his feet to steady him. Tomi was less accustomed to drinking than Alexeev. A glass of wine at dinner or a small shot of vodka after a meal was more his style. So, the five or six glasses of wine he had drunk this evening gave him a pronounced instability and weakness in his legs. He gladly leaned on Alexeev though and wrapped both his arms around his firm waist.

As the two made their way upstairs, they stumbled on a few steps, but Alexeev managed to keep Tomi from falling, holding him firmly to his side with one arm while steadying the candle with the other so he could see the way. Sveta had already lit one of the lamps in Tomi's bedroom before she and Vanya went to their own room down the hall. The room was glowing with a soft, pale light from the blue glass lamps on the dresser. Vanya had also started a fire in their bedroom fireplace. The room was getting warm and it smelled of burning pine and cedar. Alexeev removed his coat from Tomi's shoulders, walked over to the dresser and took the small vile of cologne from the coat pocket. He reapplied the cologne to his neck and chest, then set it on the dresser and walked back to Tomi who was now sitting on the edge of the bed. Alexeev knelt down on the floor in front of him.

Tomi unbuttoned Alexeev's shirt sleeves and undid the tie, then pulled it slowly from around Alexeev's neck. Then he untucked the shirt and slowly lifted it over Alexeev's torso. Alexeev smiled and raised his muscular arms above his head so Tomi could lift the shirt off the rest of the way. Tomi stood up to remove the shirt. As he stood up and exposed the chiselled chest he kissed the collarbone, then the neck. "Mmmm…my nephew gave you some of his cologne. That always gets me excited." He took a deep whiff and relished the moment. He ran his fingers over Alexeev's smooth and freshly shaved neck and chin, then put his hand behind Alexeev's head and gently pulled his head towards him and kissed him. Alexeev's tongue felt so good inside Tomi's mouth. It was a collective feeling of completeness and security. Alexeev's muscles were large and fit and firm, and Tomi could tell he had been flexing them and working them hard while he was chopping wood. His chest was solid like stone, his nipples were hard and extended and his stomach was carved and rippled with definition as if it had two columns of matching smooth river rocks beneath his skin. Then Alexeev stood and pulled Tomi's shirt off over his head in one stroke and reached down and unfastened Tomi's trousers and let them drop to the floor. He could feel Tomi's hard cock against his leg. Then he unfastened his own trousers as well and they dropped to the floor revealing his hard massive and thick cock between his bulging thighs.

They embraced and stroked each other. Alexeev clutched Tomi's chest hair and pulled it playfully. Tomi gasped with excitement: the tension was erotic and stimulating. Then he grabbed Tomi's hard nipples and pulled. Tomi fell against Alexeev, then pushed himself back. Alexeev pulled again and squeezed harder. Now their cocks were rubbing against each other as if they were engaged in a battle. Tomi took hold of Alexeev's chest muscles and clenched them with all his might. Alexeev touted a grin of pleasure and ecstasy as he leaned back to drive the intensity and increase the wonderful burning sensation. He held his arms out to the side and flexed his biceps for Tomi, showing him the full attributes of the great beast that was getting ready to dominate him. Tomi smiled with excitement, clenched his fists and pounded them against the massive pectorals. Then he wrapped both hands around one of the great biceps and squeezed as hard as he could but the bulging muscle did not give way. Alexeev bit his lower lip as he flexed and Tomi increased his grip on the muscle even tighter. His face made a grimace as he tried to force Alexeev to release his tension, but still the rock-hard mass was unaffected by the feeble attempt.

Finally releasing his grip, Tomi glided his tongue over the peak of the bicep, then sucked the salty sweat from Alexeev's arm and shoulder. He wrapped one arm around the back of Alexeev's neck, then clenched his fist and made several playful blows to Alexeev's rippled chest and stomach. Returning the playful bout, Alexeev suddenly buckled forward, as if one of the blows had hit a soft, vulnerable spot. Then he enveloped his large arms around Tomi and passionately kissed him, completely overpowering him and pinning him to the bed. As Tomi fell back onto the bed, he threw his arms back and stretched them out wide in complete submission to his captor. He laughed in reaction to the sudden assault from his domineering assailant, but then winced from the ever-increasing discomfort from his side. Alexeev's chest, now directly on top of Tomi's, with his weighty musculature pressing down on Tomi's weaker frame, made it difficult for Tomi to breathe.

Tomi didn't want Alexeev to know he had injured himself earlier, so he tried to endure the pain. Alexeev's tongue raced wildly over Tomi's chin and neck. It licked his shoulders and chest and the trail of his saliva dampened Tomi's chest hair. Little black ringlets of hair formed quickly as the tongue travelled over the chest and onto Tomi's nipples. Alexeev remembered that those nipples were very sensitive, so he concentrated his attention on the areolas to quickly stimulate Tomi's sexual energy. He circled the tip of his tongue around Tomi's hard nipple, then teased the hard protrusion with slight touches and flicks on the tip of the nipple. He clutched Tomi's breast in his hand and compressed the flesh, forcing the nipple to protrude even further, then he lightly bit it, drawing it gently with his teeth. Tomi gasped with hedonistic pleasure and grabbed the hair on Alexeev's head, pushing his head away, then pulling it back onto his chest again.

Alexeev opened his mouth wide and sucked in as much of Tomi's breast as he could, while his tongue continued to fondle the nipple.

"I haven't felt like this since the night we were together in your home," Alexeev said as he paused for a moment to look into Tomi's eyes. Tomi sat up on his elbows and smiled, then rocked his head back as if to ask for more. Alexeev continued to caress the breasts and nipples. It felt good to be close to someone, especially the one he loved. He licked Tomi's side, but as he did Tomi flinched and drew back. "Did that tickle?"

"No, my love, it's just a little tender."

"What happened? Did you hurt yourself?" Alexeev gently touched Tomi's side and tried to see if there was any visible injury.

Tomi quickly covered his side with his hand. "I guess I worked a little too hard in the kitchen tonight. I think I pulled a muscle trying to get one of the pots of from a high shelf." He winced again from the tenderness. "I'm sure it will be all right by morning." Tomi rolled over and opened the end table drawer and pulled out a bottle of ointment. He poured some on his hand, then spread it over Alexeev's hard cock. "I don't want that to stop us tonight." He rubbed Alexeev's cock, then sucked his large testicles: the right, then the left, then both. Alexeev could hardly contain his joy.

"*O, bog*![49]" Alexeev cried out with excitement. "*Akh, kak khorosho*![50]"

Tomi rubbed the enormous cock vigorously, then paused. He laid flat on his back on the bed and drew his legs up over Alexeev's shoulders. With one hand he guided the cock to his anal opening. "Put it in me, love." Alexeev grabbed Tomi's legs and inserted his cock into Tomi's hole, just an inch at first, then pulled it out slightly. Then back in for two inches, then slowly out again. Repeating this, in and out, in and out, in and out, until finally he forced his cock all the way in. Tomi screamed with pleasure, "That's it, *moy general*, go in as deep as you can!" Tomi grabbed his own limp cock and started pumping it, stroking it with each thrust of Alexeev's cock. Then he reached up and grabbed Alexeev's nipples. Alexeev flexed his strong muscles, showing off is large biceps and pectorals.

"Pull them harder, my love. I can take much more than that." Alexeev was completely involved in the action of pumping his cock into Tomi, while also experiencing the raw pleasure of the burning pain on his nipples. His legs slapped

---

[49] *O, bog!:* Oh god!

[50] *Akh, kak khorosho!*: Oh, how wonderful!

against Tomi's buttocks and his sweat dripped down from his strong, hard chest. Tomi grabbed his own cock again and continued to pump and massage his cock. But his cock wasn't getting hard so he clasped his hands behind his head. Alexeev continued to pump and thrust his cock into Tomi. "I'm going to pump you full of my cum, my love. You're going to have me inside you."

"Give it to me, Alexeev, give it to me, my love."

Alexeev continued for several more minutes. Then with a few forceful thrusts he pressed himself deep inside Tomi. He kept pumping, his cock was still hard and thick. He pulled it out and pumped it with his hand vigorously over Tomi. After another few minutes, he groaned and a wave of sperm shot out onto Tomi's chest. The look of pleasure on Alexeev's face was a look Tomi remembered from six years earlier in their first encounter. Alexeev laid down on top of Tomi. His full weight felt good to Tomi, but then for a moment he felt a sharp pain in his side. The cum mixed with their sweat between them. Alexeev kissed Tomi and wound his arms tightly around him. He rolled over so that Tomi was now on top. He wrapped his legs around Tomi and their cocks slid together as they held each other tightly. Their bodies had become one. Tomi held back the pain.

Their kisses were hot and deep as they drank each other's love and shared each other's souls. Tomi's chest heaved in and out in a deep trance as he inhaled Alexeev's scent, the scent he had so adored, and missed so much for so many years. But as he inhaled, the pain in his side grew more intense. Alexeev was in his own dream state, barely recognising the reality around him and nearly in a spell induced by his sexual desire for Tomi. He didn't realise how his weight was affecting Tomi along with the strength of his legs tightening around Tomi's waist. It was inflicting great pain and discomfort. But Tomi said nothing. He was too happy to express any words that would discourage Alexeev. That night they both decided they would always be together and no matter what, they would live together. No more loneliness, no more depression, only joy and happiness from now on.

Within a few minutes, Alexeev was fast asleep, his mind taking him into a dreamland of sexual pleasure, fond caresses, kisses, and love-making. His muscular arm rested across Tomi's chest and his warm and heavy breath was a welcomed sound in Tomi's ear. He gently moved Alexeev's arm off his chest and carefully rolled to the edge of the bed. As he sat up on the edge of the bed, he grabbed his side and began to cry. The pain was crushing him and it was making him nauseous. He knelt down and reached under the bed for the chamber pot and vomited. After a few moments he stood up, bent to one side, and made his way to the wash basin, then poured himself a glass of water and swished it in his mouth to get rid of the bitter taste. He put on his robe and picked up the candle that was still lit on the nightstand. Then he walked down the hall to Vanya's room nearly stumbling as he went, clutching his side in agony. He knocked gently on the closed door.

"Vanya," he whispered, "Vanya, can you come out for a moment?" He couldn't hold back the tears any longer.

Tomi could hear Vanya get out of bed. "Uncle, is something wrong?" When he opened the door, he saw the tears rolling down Tomi's face and he could see the pain in Tomi's eyes. "You're holding your side. What happened, Uncle?"

"I thought it was just a pulled muscle, but I think I may have broken a rib." Then he started to collapse.

Vanya quickly caught him and called out, "Sveta, come quickly. Tomi is hurt and I need your help." Within a moment, Sveta was by Tomi's side, helping keep him upright.

"Vanya, take him to the bed in the guest room. I'll go light some candles and get the ointment," she said as she rushed back into the bedroom. She quickly grabbed and lit a candle then led the way down the hall, but within a few steps Tomi buckled over in pain and fainted. Vanya caught him before he fell and picked him up and carried him the rest of the way. He laid him on the spare bed gently while Sveta lit a few more candles.

"Should I go tell Alexeev?" he asked.

"Not yet, *milyy*[51]. Let me take a look at him and get him wrapped up first." She pulled back the robe and examined the bruised area. "Oh my, Vanya, he never said anything to me. When do you think this happened?"

"I don't know, I just don't know," he said as he shook his head. "Uncle never wants to tell anyone when he is sick or hurt. He always tries to hide it."

"Well, I don't think the rib is broken but the bruise looks bad." She took a bandage wrap from the nightstand drawer. "I need to get the ointment before we bind his side. Stay with him so he doesn't fall off the bed." Sveta quickly went down the hall and returned promptly with the bottle of liniment oil. She poured some out onto the cloth, then placed it on Tomi's side that was starting to turn dark red.

---

[51] *Milyy*: Dear or sweetheart

"Lift him up a little so I can wrap this around him." As Vanya held him up, Tomi gasped in pain. He was barely conscious but he could still feel the sharp pain. "Gently, gently," she said as she reached under Tomi with the binding cloth. As quickly as she could, she wrapped the cloth around him a few more times, then tied it off to keep it in place. "I think that should do it. Now lay him back down. I'll stay with him while you go wake Alexeev. I think he should be here now."

Vanya walked quickly down the hall and opened the door to Tomi's room. Alexeev was sitting on the side of the bed, naked. "Oh, excuse me, Lieutenant. I didn't realise…I think you should come with me. Tomi is in the guest room. It looks like he may have a broken rib."

He quickly stood up and grabbed the robe from the foot of the bed. "When I woke up and didn't see him here, I thought something might be wrong," he said as he quickly wrapped himself in the robe. "Show me where he is."

As they raced down the hall, Vanya explained, "Sveta has already wrapped his side and put on some liniment. But I think we'll send for the doctor first thing tomorrow morning. If he can lie still, I think he should be able to sleep."

"We should have never…" Just then, they were at the guestroom. "Oh Tomi, my dear Tomi." Alexeev couldn't hold back the tears.

"Quiet, quiet, I think he's asleep again." Sveta had managed to get Tomi under the covers and had placed a pillow between his arm and the bruised side. "I think the wine is going to help him sleep through the night." She stepped aside as Alexeev approached. He bent down and kissed Tomi's forehead then stroked the top of his head gently. His hand trembled as he touched him. "Now don't you worry, young man, Tomi is going to be fine. But he needs to rest and let his body heal. Vanya can go for the doctor in the morning." Sveta patted him on the shoulder. "I think you should stay in here with him tonight. He shouldn't be moved until after the doctor sees him."

"I should build a fire so he stays warm." Alexeev got up and placed a few logs in the fireplace and got the fire going. "Thank you both. I'll stay by him and make sure he is comfortable." He shook Vanya's hand as the couple walked to the door.

Sveta placed her hand on Alexeev's forearm. "I'll bring him tea in the morning and breakfast if he wants it so you won't have to bring him downstairs." Alexeev smiled and nodded then closed the door after they left.

What have I done to my precious Tomi? he thought. *I should have known he was in pain. I should have stopped...why can't I control myself. Why did I squeeze him so hard with my legs? I should be gentler with him. My lyubimyy*[52] *is broken...* He continued to chastise and punish himself all night long. But he laid down next to Tomi and slid himself under the covers beside him. He was afraid to touch him for fear of waking him from his needed sleep. So, he stretched his arm above Tomi's head, resting it on the pillow then he placed his hand gently on Tomi's shoulder. Tomi slept flat on his back all night long and didn't wake up all night. Alexeev's attention remained fixed on Tomi. He watched over him and carefully got up every few hours to keep the fire going so Tomi could sleep in warmth and comfort. *Forgive me, schast'ye moye. I don't ever want you to be in pain again because of me*. He knew there was nothing more he could do until morning but he wondered what he could do to make Tomi feel better.

[52] *Lyubimyy*: Darling

Chapter 8

A New Day and a Slow Recovery

Tomi woke up in the morning to the sound of birds signing outside his bedroom window. They seemed to be singing in harmony with thc song in his heart. Last night was a love affair he would remember for the rest of his life, and hopefully, last night was the new beginning of a relationship that would never end. He could still taste Alexeev's sweet tongue in his mouth and he could still imagine the warmth of Alexeev's strong, protective arms wrapped around him. It was still dark outside but he heard the clock downstairs chime seven. There was a soft, orange glow from the embers in the fireplace and the room was still warm. Alexeev must have kept the fire going all night, he was such a dear man and so considerate. But as Tomi rolled over, he felt a sharp pain in his side and he vaguely remembered the ordeal that transpired in the middle of the night.

He recalled getting up and vomiting and he remembered walking down the hall in a blur to wake Vanya, but nothing else was clear. As his mind began to focus, he realised he was not in his own bedroom but in the guest room. Tomi laid in bed for a few moments longer trying to make sense of the images in his mind from the events that had transpired. Emotion flooded his mind as he wondered how he ever survived so many years on his own and how marvellous the rest of his life would be with Alexeev by his side.

He was wrapped in his long burgundy robe he had been using since his last visit to Moscow. It had belonged to his brother, Stas. Tomi remembered staying here in this very room when his brother was sick. But Stas never recovered, and a visit that should have been a joyous celebration turned into a dirge of sorrow, a funeral preparation, then mourning. Tomi had given this burgundy robe to Stas for Christmas several years earlier, just after Vanya and Sveta were married. The trim was embroidered with purple and lavender periwinkles Tomi had added, though he had never told Stas he had stitched them himself. When Stas opened the package, he commented how beautiful the embroidery was and how the woman who stitched it must be very talented. Tomi never forgave himself for not admitting to his own handiwork. He lifted his arm up to his face and thought he could still smell his brother's scent on the sleeve, then he wiped a tear of sorrow and remembrance from his face.

He wanted to get up but even the slightest movement was painful. He reached over to the other side of the bed but there was no one there. *I wonder where Alexeev is*? Just then, the door opened and Alexeev entered with his arms full of firewood. He turned and closed the door with his foot, then proceeded to the fireplace and set the pile of wood in the bin. Then he placed another log on the fire. As he stood, he turned towards the bed and noticed Tomi was awake and watching.

"I'm sorry, Tomi. Did I wake you?"

Tomi smiled. "No, I woke up a few minutes ago."

"How are you feeling? Are you in much pain this morning?"

"It hurts to move. But I need to pee. Can you help me get up?"

Alexeev came over to Tomi's side of the bed and reached under the bed for the chamber pot. "Don't strain yourself, let me lift you." Alexeev carefully placed his arm under Tomi's shoulder. "Put your arm around my neck."

When Tomi raised his arm, he felt the pain of the muscle stretching. "Oh, it hurts! It hurts!"

"Let me try something different." He got up and went over to the dresser and emptied the vase, then brought it over to the bed. He wedged a towel underneath Tomi's legs and buttocks, then placed the vase between his legs and guided his penis into the opening. Almost immediately, Tomi started to pee.

"That is so much better. I didn't know what I was going to do."

"Vanya is going to fetch the doctor after breakfast. He and Sveta bandaged you up last night." Alexeev removed the vase when Tomi had finished. "I should have been there for you. Instead, I was sleeping like an irresponsible—"

"I'll have none of that kind of talk," Tomi interrupted.

"But it was my fault you got hurt." He dipped a washcloth in the water basin, then wiped Tomi's penis and ball sack, then removed the towel.

"Whatever gave you that idea? When I was fixing dinner, I slipped off the stool and fell against the counter," he confessed. "I didn't realise until we were in bed and making love that the injury might be worse than a sprained muscle."

Then Tomi started coughing, gasping and holding his side. "Oh, that hurts so bad."

"I wish I could make the pain go away, *schast'ye moye*." Alexeev placed his hand on Tomi's forehead then kissed his cheek. "Do you think you can eat something for breakfast?"

"I think I can, but I'll need to sit up."

"Let me go downstairs and see if breakfast is ready yet, then I'll come back up with Vanya and we'll sit you up." Alexeev paused for a moment. "...but it's going to hurt to move you...I can put several pillows behind you for support and I'll bring a tray to set on your lap."

"I'll be brave, *moy general*." He reached out and squeezed Alexeev's hand. As Alexeev opened the bedroom door to go downstairs, Tomi could smell fresh bread baking. "Umm...I think I can smell Sveta's good sweetbread. I always like her breads." Regardless of what happened, he was glad he had come to visit his nephew, especially since he found Alexeev in the process. He thought of all the excuses he could have made to avoid coming to Moscow to visit, but they all seemed trivial and rather silly now. Even though he was flat on his back and in pain whenever he moved, he would rather be here than alone in his own bed in Storozhevsk. In fact, he had almost decided not to go into town yesterday. He wasn't really looking for anything specific, but Vanya convinced him to get out of the house and do something for a change. Truth be told, it was Sveta who asked Vanya to get him out from under her feet and out of her kitchen. So, actually it was thanks to Sveta and Vanya that Tomi and Alexeev got back together. Tomi pondered about how strange it was the way things happen. *The gods must be looking out for me...or maybe just fate*, he thought.

Alexeev left to go downstairs and wondered how long it would take for Tomi to recover. He knew a few soldiers who sustained similar injuries to their ribs on the battlefield. Sometimes when the rib was broken, it would cause lung infection, which frequently led to death. The possibility of losing Tomi made Alexeev uneasy. He stood for a moment outside the bedroom and trembled. *I must be strong for Tomi*, he thought. He knew from experience the patient needed to be encouraged to breathe normally even though it would be painful. Shallow breathing seemed to make infection more likely. He continued down the stairs. As he walked down the hall towards the kitchen, he heard activity in the parlour, so he poked his head in through the sliding door.

“Good morning, Uncle,” said Vanya. “Oh, may I call you that? I hope that doesn’t bother you.” He was building a fire in the parlour fireplace.

“Somehow, I don’t quite feel like your uncle. After all, I’m only a few years older than you. But I think Tomi would appreciate hearing you call me that.”

Vanya smiled. “Did the two of you sleep well? How is my *Dyadya Medved’* feeling this morning?”

“I think he had a good rest. I don’t think he woke up at all in the night. But he still had quite a bit of pain this morning. I was wondering if you could help me sit him up in the bed for breakfast?”

“Of course, anything you need, just ask. I’m going to call on the doctor after we finish breakfast.” He patted Alexeev on the shoulder. “Tomi will be fine. Doctor Leskov is one of the best doctors here in Moscow. He was educated at the Paris Lodron University in Saltsburg, and the University of Barcelona. He has even been called a few times to meet with the Tsar.”

Alexeev felt a little more reassured. “Thank you for getting the doctor. The only doctors I know are the ones who treat the troops, and they don’t have the best bedside manners. They tend to treat the wounds without regard for the patient’s feelings or pain tolerance.” Alexeev had seen quite a lot of agonising treatments during his tenure in the army. “I don’t know how much Tomi will eat this morning but he seemed to be hungry.”

Sveta prepared a tray for Tomi with a plate of bread, sausage and onions, tea and honey, and a small bowl of fruit compote. “Good morning, Lieutenant. How is Uncle feeling this morning?”

“He had a good rest, I think. But he is still quite sore.” Just then Alexeev saw the stool Tomi must have fallen from. He noticed one of the legs was slightly shorter than the others. “Vanya, if you don’t mind, I would like to use some of your woodworking tools later today.”

“Of course, anything you need. Is there something I might be able to help you with?”

“Perhaps. I will let you know.” Alexeev wasn’t sure what he wanted to do, but he knew he needed to make a stool that would be safer and more stable. The wabbly stool made him cringe inside and gave him a very uncomfortable feeling. He despised this object that had brought pain to his lover. It took all his strength of character to hold himself back from crushing the stool and tossing it into the fire.

"Here is Tomi's breakfast." She placed two sets of silverware and two napkins next to the plate on the tray. "And here is a plate for you too." Alexeev's plate had greater portions and included a hefty serving of steamed mushrooms.

"Everything looks so wonderful, Sveta. I hope Tomi is hungry." He picked up the tray and took a big sniff of the hot food.

"Now take it up quickly while everything is still hot," she said as she placed lids over the two plates and set a small vase with a sprig of Daphne on the tray.

"I'll be up in just a moment, Uncle." Vanya had stolen a slice of sweetbread from the table and was washing it down with a cup of tea.

"Go now, Vanya. You don't want to make our *Dyadya* wait for his breakfast." She took the cup of tea from Vanya's mouth. With a bewildered look on his face, Vanya reluctantly turned and walked out of the kitchen. "Then come back down so you can get the doctor."

Alexeev set the tray of food on the nightstand next to the bed. "Is that Sveta's bread I smell?" Tomi asked with a broad smile on his face. He was sometimes a little jealous his own breads never turned out as well as hers.

"Yes, she also made onions and sausage and some tea with honey. Vanya is coming up to help me get you to a seated position so you can eat." Alexeev pulled back the covers then pulled Tomi's robe around him to cover him up. Then he wrapped the robe's sash around Tomi's waist and tied it loosely.

"I've really made a mess of things, haven't I," he said. "I'm so clumsy."

Vanya stopped by Tomi's bedroom on his way to the guestroom to pick up a few more pillows. "I brought three pillows from your bed. Do you think that will be enough?" He set them down at the foot of the bed.

"I think so." Alexeev took one of the pillows and placed it against the headboard above Tomi's head, then he brought the other two and placed them next to Tomi. "Vanya, if you will stand over here on this side of the bed, I'll go around to the other side and raise him up. I want you to take hold of his robe down near his hips and slide him towards the headboard once I have him raised."

"Sounds good."

"Now Tomi, I don't want you to do anything, just relax. Let us do the work." Then Alexeev looked into Tomi's eyes. "I'm afraid it's going to hurt when I move you." The look on Alexeev's face was full of the pain he knew Tomi would be feeling.

Tomi pulled Alexeev's face towards his and kissed him. "It's all right, my love."

With that, Alexeev gently placed his arm beneath Tomi's shoulder and slowly raised him up. As soon as he was in a seated position, Vanya grabbed both sides of the robe and slid Tomi towards the headboard, then placed another pillow behind Tomi's head. Then he raised Tomi's legs and slipped the third pillow underneath his knees. Even though he felt great pain, Tomi didn't make a sound. Alexeev eased him back against the pillow, then slowly removed his arm.

"I'm proud of you, Tomi. I know that must have hurt," he said as he kissed him on the cheek.

"If you have everything you need, I'll go now and get the doctor," said Vanya. Alexeev picked up the tray and started to set it on Tomi's lap. "Oh, here, let me help you with that. The tray has legs underneath that fold down." Vanya carefully unfolded the legs while Alexeev steadied the tray. "Now it won't be easily disturbed if Uncle happens to move."

"Thank you, Vanya, I think we can manage now." Alexeev placed the tray over Tomi's lap, unfolded the napkin and placed it under Tomi's chin. Then he lifted his plate from the tray and centred Tomi's plate and handed him the cup of tea. "Here you are, *schast'ye moye.* Start with this."

"Doctor Leskov is only a short distance away. I should be back with him in about an hour." Vanya reached down and snatched two sausages from Alexeev's plate. "Payment for my services," he said as he waved them at Alexeev and pulled the door closed as he left.

"I'll have Tomi fed and cleaned up by the time you return," said Alexeev as he ruffled the top of Tomi's head. Then he walked around the bed and sat next to Tomi. "I hope you're hungry. Sveta made you a big breakfast so you can keep up your strength."

Tomi glanced at Alexeev's plate and just smiled. He ate rather slowly, as each swallow caused discomfort, but he managed to eat nearly everything on his plate. When he had finally eaten his fill, he set his fork down on the plate and pushed the tray away. "I can't eat any more," he said.

Alexeev set his own empty plate on the nightstand then he glanced over and saw that Tomi had left two sausages and a slice of sweetbread. "Are you sure? Maybe just one more sausage—"

"I'm sorry, I just can't eat anymore."

Alexeev picked up the tray and set it at the foot of the bed, then he picked up the plate and finished eating the two sausages and bread. "After we finish breakfast, I'll get you bathed and dressed for the doctor."

"I think I should stay in my robe. Doctor Leskov will ask me to get undressed so he can examine me and I think it will make it more difficult if I am fully dressed." Tomi wasn't sure he wanted to go through the difficulties of bathing either but knew it was probably necessary.

"I'll be back in a few minutes with a towel and some hot water." Alexeev gathered the tray and plates. "Would you like some more tea?"

"Maybe a cup after I bathe."

Alexeev nodded and took the tray downstairs to the kitchen.

Sveta was busy baking enough bread for the next few days. The kitchen smelled of yeast and there was a gentle aroma of cinnamon, nutmeg, and fruit compote in the air. The smells reminded Alexeev of Orlov's kitchen and the myriad of aromas that fill the room when they would talk together while Orlov prepared meals for his boarders. Alexeev would often sit for hours and watch Orlov bake, and Orlov would put him to work cracking nuts, or peeling apples, or chopping vegetables. He thought of Orlov as an older and wiser brother, someone in whom he could confide. While Orlov cooked and baked, and while Alexeev chopped and peeled, they would talk about their life situations, argue about politics or religion, and console each other in their griefs and sorrows. Alexeev would miss those valuable sessions.

He walked over to the water basin and washed and rinsed the plates and silverware, then dried them with the tea towel which hung from a hook next to the basin. As he watched Sveta knead the bread, for a moment he couldn't help but wonder what his life would be like without Orlov, without the wisdom of his mentor and dear friend. He surmised Tomi and Vanya had a very similar relationship.

"Is there a pail I could use for hot water? I want to bathe Tomi before the doctor gets here."

"Yes, there's one right there underneath the basin." She motioned with her elbow since her hands were occupied with kneading the dough. "There are washcloths and soaps in the pantry on the far right…and be sure to take the bottle of liniment as well," she added. "I'm sure the doctor will bring some of his own but I think you should have some handy."

"Thank you, Sveta." He placed the cleaned and dried dishes on the shelf and found the pail, soaps, washcloths and liniment in the pantry. There was a large pot of water boiling on the stove. "May I use some of this water?"

"Yes, yes. Use as much as you need," Sveta said as she continued kneading.

Alexeev filled the pail, then made his way back to the bedroom. Meanwhile, Tomi had nodded off. His head was tilted back and Alexeev could hear him softly snoring. He set the pail down next to the bed and placed the soap, washcloth and liniment on the nightstand. Then he went back out and down the hall to their bedroom where he collected a few towels. As he walked back in and closed the door, the creaking of the hinges woke Tomi.

"Are you ready for your bath, master?" Alexeev had laid the towel over his arm and he bowed to Tomi as a servant would.

Tomi smiled. "Yes, I guess I am ready for your next torturous activity."

"Shall I strap you to the bed or will you be a good and submissive subject?"

Tomi chuckled and shook his head. "I will cooperate. No straps this time, please." Even though it was only a slight chuckle, it caused a sharp pain in his side and Tomi grabbed his side and grimaced.

Alexeev immediately rushed towards him and apologised for making him laugh. Then he spread a few towels over the bed and tucked them under Tomi's legs. He carefully removed the bandage cloth from Tomi's torso and removed his robe, then soaked a few washcloths in the hot water and rubbed them with some soap. The soap smelled of sandalwood and pine oils. He handed one of the soapy cloths to Tomi, then he took the other cloth and started washing Tomi's back. In a few minutes, he took the two rags and rinsed them out, then soaped them up again. Tomi had washed his chest and arms, so now he started on his groin and legs. He managed to reach the area above his knees with little difficulty but he couldn't bend very easily to wash his lower legs and feet. Alexeev had finished washing his neck and ears. He took the cloths and rinsed them again and handed one back to Tomi to begin wiping the soap off. Alexeev went to the foot of the bed and finished Tomi's legs and feet.

"Do you think you can turn towards me and dangle your legs over the side of the bed?" Alexeev sat next to Tomi and let him wrap his arm around his neck. Then he placed his arm under Tomi's leg and helped him turn his body. "Here, just a little farther. Are you warm enough?" He didn't want Tomi to catch a chill.

"Yes, I'm fine. It's nice and warm in here," he said as he managed to move his other leg over the side of the bed.

Alexeev rinsed both cloths and continued to rinse the soap from Tomi's body. He handed one of the cloths to Tomi. "Here, do you want to rinse off your face?" The job was nearly done. Alexeev pulled one of the towels up over Tomi's back, and took the other towel and began drying the rest of Tomi's body. He couldn't resist kissing Tomi occasionally: a few times on his shoulder and arm, then on his chest and stomach, then caressing his legs and finishing with a few kisses on his toes. Tomi smiled and for a few moments, he forgot about the pain in his side. "I'm going to leave the bandage off until after the doctor examines you."

A tear started to form in Tomi's eye. "You treat me so well, Alexeev. I don't know how I survived these last years without you."

"I'm glad I'm here with you now." Alexeev leaned up and kissed Tomi on the lips. "Let me get you some of my mint and pepper powder, and a glass of water."

Tomi continued to pat himself dry with the towel while Alexeev walked down the hall to retrieve his pouch of tooth powder and a few spice balls. When he returned, Tomi was trying to stand, but his naked body looked like a pitiful wreck, trying to balance itself. He was bent towards one side clutching his injury, and desperately holding onto the bed with his other hand to maintain his balance.

Alexeev quickly lunged towards his crippled lover. "What are you doing, my dear? You should have waited for me to help you."

"I just wanted my robe. I thought I could take a few steps on my own." Tomi settled himself into Alexeev's arms and sat back down on the bed.

"I'm sorry, I should have left it closer to you. I shouldn't have left you without anything to cover yourself." He grabbed the robe from the foot of the bed and wrapped it around Tomi. "There now. Can I help you get situated back against the pillows? Just put your arm around my neck." He placed one arm around Tomi's back and the other underneath his legs, then lifted him into place against the pillows. Tomi looked a little startled that Alexeev could pick him up and move him so easily, but then he realised how fit and muscular was. He handed Tomi the pouch of tooth powders and then poured him a glass of fresh water from the pitcher. Tomi took a few pinches of powder and placed them in his mouth then took a sip of water and began swishing the mixture in his mouth. Alexeev handed him the bowl so Tomi could spit, then Tomi took another sip of water, rinsed his mouth and swallowed. "I'll set these spice balls on the nightstand for you. I think you'll like them. Orlov makes them himself and keeps them handy around the house."

Tomi sat back against the pillows and pulled his robe shut around his waist, then ran his fingers through his hair. Though he was balding and the hair he did have was always cut short, he went through the motions of straightening and smoothing his hair into place every morning. Even though this ritual seemed rather pointless and viewing the act in a mirror would often arouse a chuckle, he identified the action as quite necessary for beginning each day. Alexeev looked on and grinned to himself, then unconsciously ran his fingers through his own hair before becoming aware of his actions. He stopped himself abruptly and jerked his hand away from his head, hoping Tomi didn't see the action and think he was somehow mocking his lack of hair. Alexeev seemed to have an overabundance of hair and although he always kept it trimmed and neat, there was always a sufficient amount to ensure the necessity of a comb or brush. But he had already taken care of his personal hygiene earlier this morning.

Alexeev heard the front door open and muffled conversation from downstairs. "I think the doctor has arrived. Do you need anything before he comes up?"

Tomi shook his head. "I don't think so, but can you stay with me?"

"Of course, I will." He set his hand on Tomi's shoulder and kissed him on the cheek.

They could hear the patter of Vanya's and the doctor's footsteps coming up the beautiful oak stairs. Alexeev got up and opened the bedroom door, then moved a few chairs over next to Tomi's side of the bed. "Maybe I should put another log on the fire." He grabbed a log from the woodpile and set it on top of the dying embers.

Vanya knocked on the open door. "Good morning, Uncle, may we come in? I have brought the doctor with me."

Alexeev walked over to the two men to introduce himself. "Good morning, doctor. I am Tomas Pedorov's friend, Alexeev Kondurov." He shook the doctor's hand and motioned him to Tomi's bedside.

Vanya chimed in, "Alexeev, this is Doctor Leskov. Uncle, if you don't need me for anything else, I have some things I need to take care of. I'll send Sveta up a little later to see if you need anything."

Tomi nodded. "Thank you, Vanya." Then he reached out his hand to the doctor. "It's good to see you again, Doctor, but I was hoping it would be under different circumstances."

The doctor set his bag on one of the chairs and shook Tomi's hand and smiled. "You're not looking too well, and I think you've lost some weight." He felt Tomi's forehead then pulled down one of his eyelids to examine the colour. "Alexeev Kondurov, could you light a few more candles and open the curtain? I need more light in here." Alexeev immediately got up and followed the doctor's instructions. The doctor leaned in towards Tomi and whispered, "Is it all right for him to stay? I can ask him to leave if you want—"

Tomi interrupted, "Alexeev is my good friend and I've asked him to stay with me."

"Very well." The doctor pulled the chair a little closer to the bed and sat down. "So, tell me, Tomas, what have you done to yourself this time?"

Alexeev was still lighting candles and setting them on the nightstands but he felt the need to answer for Tomi. "He fell in the kitchen yesterday. I think he just bruised his side but we wanted to make sure the rib isn't broken. He's been in quite a bit of pain since last night." Then he dropped his head, a little ashamed and not altogether sure he should say any more. But honesty was one of his qualities…and faults. He felt the need to tell the truth, even if the truth could present himself in a negative light. "I think I may have worsened his condition last night when I embraced him around his waist. I didn't know he was injured and I think I hugged him too tightly."

"It's all right, Alexeev. The doctor knows I prefer the company of men," Tomi said, then he turned to the doctor. "He had his legs around my waist. I should have told him I was already in pain, but I didn't."

The doctor helped Tomi pull the robe back so he could examine his side. "Well, let's see how much damage there is." As he pulled back the robe, he and Alexeev could see the dark reddish-brown bruise that had already developed. The doctor had Tomi raise his arm. "Alexeev, could you bring the candle a little closer, please." As Alexeev got a better look at the bruise, his eyes began to well with tears but he held back his emotion for Tomi's sake. The doctor carefully touched and felt the bruise and rib. Tomi winced occasionally from the pain but the doctor had a very gentle and caring touch. "The rib is not broken. If it were, you would be in considerably more pain." He pressed his ear to Tomi's bare chest and listened to his heart for several minutes. "I'll need to listen to his lungs also. Can you take these pillows away for a few minutes?" Alexeev set the candle on the nightstand and removed the pillows from behind Tomi's back. "Now Tomas, I don't want you to hurt yourself, but I need you to lean forward." Tomi leaned forwards and braced himself on the bed with his arm, but his arm started to shake.

Alexeev noticed Tomi's arm quivering. "Are you cold?"

“No, he’s just weak from the injury,” said the doctor. “Sit next to him and let him rest his arm on your shoulder.” Alexeev moved close to Tomi and carefully lifted his arm and placed it over his shoulder. The shaking stopped. The doctor placed his ear against Tomi’s back and listened to his breathing. “I want you to take a few deep breaths. I know it will be a little painful, but I need to hear what’s going on in your lungs.” Tomi inhaled deeply then exhaled. It was painful, but he tolerated it. He breathed in deeply and exhaled a few more times. “That’s fine, now just breathe normally.” The doctor continued to listen, placing his ear in a few different positions on Tomi’s back. “Tell me about how you fell.”

“I was making supper last night,” said Tomi. “I needed the large pot for the mushroom stew. It was on one of the upper shelves. I remember getting up on the stool and reaching for it…next thing I knew, I was on the floor with the pot on the other side of the kitchen. Sveta must have heard me fall, because she came running in.”

“How was it that you fell?” he asked.

“I looked at the stool this morning, doctor,” Alexeev interjected. “One of the legs is a little short, so it wobbles.”

The doctor persisted with Tomi. “But did you lose your balance or could it be that you passed out?” The doctor looked deep into Tomi’s eyes. “Alexeev, bring the candle over here. I want to get a better look.” Alexeev brought the candle over to the doctor and held it out. The doctor guided Alexeev’s hand. “Hold it right there.” He covered one of Tomi’s eyes, then the other. “Now watch the candle but don’t move your head.” The doctor took the candle from Alexeev and moved it back and forth across Tomi’s line of sight. “Well, what do you remember? Did you pass out?”

“I’m not sure,” he said. “I…I don’t think so…but it all happened so fast. I don’t remember.”

“Have you had any dizzy spells recently, any more headaches?” The doctor handed the candle back to Alexeev and began feeling around Tomi’s head and neck.

Tomi’s eyes started watering. “The candle is a little bright.”

“You can set the candle back on the nightstand, thank you.” The doctor continued to feel, press and examine Tomi’s back, chest, stomach, and sides. Then he had Tomi lay down flat on his back with Alexeev’s assistance. He opened Tomi’s robe and examined his pelvis, groin, penis and testicles, then his legs, ankles and feet. “I seem to remember, when you were here for your brother's funeral, you came to me because you had severe headaches. How long ago was that?"

"More than six years ago," answered Tomi. "I saw my doctor in Storozhevsk after I returned home and he gave me a tea to drink whenever I feel the headaches coming on."

"How often do you drink the tea?" he asked.

"Oh, several times a week," said Tomi. "I keep a tin of the tea with me wherever I go."

"I can get the tin if you like. It's the one with the painted scene of the Great Wall, isn't it, Tomi?" Alexeev asked.

"Yes, that's the one." Alexeev got up and went down the hall to the bedroom. He found the tin on top of the dresser and brought it back for the doctor.

Once Alexeev was out of the room the doctor said to Tomi, "How much did your doctor tell you about your headaches? Has he been seeing you regularly?"

"He hasn't examined me for a few years, but I buy the tea from him about once a month."

"Hmm, I don't want to alarm you, but I think the headaches may be the cause of some other things that are going on with your physical health, including the fall yesterday." The doctor sat down and continued, "Do you want your friend to hear everything I have to say, or do you want me to tell you in private?"

"Let me take care of that." Tomi hesitated for a moment. "…I'll tell him later when he and I are alone." Alexeev came back in with the tin. He opened it and handed it to the doctor. The doctor examined the contents and sniffed the tea to determine some of its main ingredients. "Alexeev, could you make me a cup of this tea. Just put a few pinches of the powder in a cup of boiling water. I also like to add a little honey."

He took the tin back from the doctor and left the room to go down to the kitchen. He knew Tomi was trying to get him out of the room for a while, and now he was worried and suspected the worst. What could be so wrong he didn't want him to know about? Why didn't he want him to know? He respected Tomi too much to question him though. When he got down to the kitchen, he had to fill the kettle with water then wait for it to get hot again. Finally, he poured the tea into Tomi's cup and added a few pinches of tea powder and a teaspoon of honey. Then he brought it back up to the bedroom and handed the cup to Tomi. It appeared he had been crying but Alexeev kept silent and did not ask for an explanation. Tomi sat up with the help of the doctor, drank a few sips of tea, then set the cup on the nightstand and pulled the robe up over his shoulders. Alexeev helped Tomi get his arms through the sleeves, then pulled the covers up over Tomi's legs and waist and placed the pillows behind his back for support.

The doctor stood up and picked up his bag. "I want you to continue to drink the tea whenever you feel the headaches coming on. Keep the bruised area clean and continue to use liniment and binding while the bruise heals. I'll leave some binding cloths here for you. Alexeev, I want you to make sure he doesn't sit up here all day. I want him moving around, walking, stretching and light housework after a few more days so he doesn't get lazy."

"Yes, sir," Alexeev said, as if confirming his orders.

"Tomas, don't be afraid of the pain. You need to make sure you breathe deeply as often as you can. We don't want you getting winter fever." He started walking to the door then turned to Alexeev. "Make sure you keep him warm and get him up and walking as soon as he is able. I will be back in a week to look in on him." He shook his hand.

"May I walk you out?" Alexeev said, hoping the doctor might reveal something more about Tomi's condition.

"I know the way out, you just attend to Tomas."

Alexeev turned back around and sat next to Tomi on the bed. "How are you feeling, my love?"

"I'm a little tired. Would you mind if I slept for a while longer?"

"Of course not. But let me get the binding and liniment first." The doctor had left several swaths of binding cloth on the nightstand along with a full bottle of liniment. "Lift your arms." Alexeev tore off a square of cloth and poured out some of the salve on the cloth then held it to the bruise. He was careful not to press Tomi's side. "Here, reach down and hold this in place so I can wrap the cloth around." He wrapped the clean cloth around Tomi's torso a few times, then tore the cloth down the middle and tied it in place. "Is that too tight?"

"No, that seems fine." Tomi lowered his arms.

"Let me help you get more comfortable." Alexeev placed his arm around Tomi to support his back, then pulled out a few of the pillows and lowered him slowly down. "Now you can rest for a while. I'll close the curtain so the light doesn't keep you awake." He closed the curtains and blew out the candles so the glow from the fireplace was the only light in the room. "Rest well, my love." He kissed Tomi on the forehead. Tomi smiled and then shut his eyes.

Alexeev needed to take care of some business in town before he and Tomi could leave, and since it could be some time before Tomi recovered he knew he should get started right away. There was a small blanket on the dresser, so Alexeev unfolded it and positioned it across the covers on top of Tomi. He wanted to make sure Tomi was warm enough. He was already sound asleep and Alexeev could hear a soft snoring sound that reminded him of a cat purring. It was a quiet rumble that made Alexeev laugh to himself. He gave one last look around the room then slipped down the stairs quietly.

Vanya was just getting ready to go out to the barn and tend the animals when he saw Alexeev coming down the stairs. "Alexeev," he whispered, "what did the doctor say about Tomi?"

"Well, he told your uncle plenty, but I'm afraid they didn't share much of it with me," Alexeev said with a little reluctance. "Doctor Leskov did give some instruction to make sure he doesn't stay in bed all day, to keep the bruise clean and bound and keep applying the liniment. I think he'll sleep until lunchtime though."

"I know he didn't get much sleep last night, so I'm sure he must be very tired." Vanya patted Alexeev on the shoulder for comfort.

"I need to go into town and wanted to ask you if I may borrow one of your horses until later this afternoon?"

"Of course, you may. But let me give him some oats first. Do you mind waiting just a bit before you leave?" Vanya smiled and wrapped his arm around Alexeev's broad shoulders. "Come join me in the barn while I feed the rest of the animals. By then, Lightening will be fed and we'll saddle him up for you."

"Lightening?" asked Alexeev, wondering how spirited this horse might be.

"Don't worry, Lightening is the tamest horse we have. He is fast, but very gentle," Vanya reassured him. "So, what is your intention with *Dyadya*? You know he has been lonely all his life and he is not used to being properly courted." Vanya was very protective of his Uncle Tomi. When Vanya was a teenager, his father Stas would take him to Tomi's cottage every summer to stay while he would go south to the Mughal Empire, the Ottoman Empire or Cathay to purchase rare woods and other materials to bring back and use in his workshop. Stas' work was well-known in Moscow and much of his inlaid wood pieces were highly sought after. Vanya was very sensitive to the unconventional nature of his uncle and did not appreciate many of the male visitors who would try to spend time with Tomi, only to take advantage of him and disappoint him in the end. He had seen his uncle's heart break so many times over the years, often by younger men passing through Shoynaty. They would stay for a week, sometimes two, and flatter him. Then take money from him when he was vulnerable and leave, never to be heard from again. Tomi was too trusting and had a profound weakness for younger men. Even though he lived many miles away, Tomi would visit nearly every year after Vanya was older and write often when he wasn't able to visit.

Alexeev was not offended by the question and tried his best to convey his feelings without diminishing Tomi's character. "Years ago, when my troops and I visited Tomi's cottage, I fell in love with him. It broke my heart, not to be able to stay with him then, but I was not able to leave the service or move from Moscow. The gods and fates have been good to me though. This I realised when I met your uncle in town yesterday. From the very moment he set his hand on my shoulder in the flower shop, I knew I was still deeply in love with him. I think I have known it for the last six years. I want only to please him and make him happy so we can live together in happiness for the rest of our lives."

"I am glad to hear it, Alexeev. Uncle is very fond of you. He has been writing to me about you since he met you," Vanya's voice seemed a little desperate, "always vowing to search you out and declare his love for you. He has never written about anyone else quite like he writes about you. Whenever a young man takes advantage of him or leaves him with no explanation, Uncle always writes about how you would have never left if it hadn't been for the army. And since he's been here you are practically all he talks about."

Just then, Alexeev caught a tear trailing down his cheek. He wrapped his arms around Vanya. "Thank you for reassuring me, Vanya. I can see why you are Tomi's favourite nephew."

Vanya laughed. "Well, he only has two nephews, my friend! And knowing my uncle, he probably says the same thing when he talks about him." They both laughed for a while then continued to feed and water the animals. "Let's saddle up Lightening. He should be well-fed by now. Be careful as you ride to town though, there may still be some ice on the cobbled streets in the city."

"Before I go, I want to bring in more wood for you. I noticed you are almost out of wood in the kitchen and the parlour."

"Very good. I'll take Lightening around to the front for you."

"Could you also check in on Tomi after a while and make sure he gets a good meal for lunch?"

Vanya patted Alexeev on the shoulder, "Of course, of course. Don't you worry about a thing. I'll have Sveta prepare him a good meal."

Alexeev took hold of the wheelbarrow and started for the wood bin. After he loaded a good supply of wood into the kitchen and parlour bins he cut a few fresh sprigs of Daphne and left them in a vase on the kitchen table.

Alexeev rode to the boarding house first. He arrived just as Orlov finished preparing breakfast for the residents. When he walked into the kitchen, Orlov was putting the last batch of freshly raised rolls into the oven. "Come in, cousin, come in! Warm yourself by the oven and tell me what adventures you have been up to. Did you have a good time with Tomi last night?"

"Orlov, he has a wonderful nephew named Vanya, and his wife Sveta. They live just beyond the Vostryakovskiy road on the way to Bobrovo. He and his wife are very nice people. I know you would like them." Alexeev could hardly contain his excitement. "Tomi made dinner last night while Vanya and I chopped wood. Then we sat in the parlour and drank wine while we all talked."

"That is wonderful, Alexeev!" Orlov knew how important finding Tomi was to his cousin. "What will you do now?" Orlov knew Alexeev was preparing to leave the military and knew Alexeev was ready for a change in his life. Being separated from Tomi all these years was the main cause of his depression and drinking.

"Unfortunately, he fell and hurt his side last night. So, he'll be recovering for at least a few weeks. The doctor said his rib isn't broken, but he is not out of danger yet." Alexeev's face showed his deep concern. But then he smiled. "I want to live with him in his cottage in Storozhevsk. I want to work his farm. Orlov, I want to make him happy if I can." Alexeev poured himself a cup of tea then continued, "Do you remember that brooch Mama left me when she died?"

"Yes, the one with the two emeralds. When I was younger, I remember thinking how pretty that was. Oh, my boy, you're not going to sell it, are you?" said Orlov.

"No, don't be silly. I am taking it to Abram, the jeweller this morning. I want him to make it into something special, something I can give to Tomi as a token of my love for him." Alexeev did not want to risk bringing bad fortune to the relationship, so he stopped before revealing what he had in mind. "I want to see him when he opens his shop this morning, so I must be off. I need to be back by early afternoon so I can take care of Tomi."

"Nastya will be down soon. Leave me the key to your room and I will have her wash and pack your clothes. Then come by tomorrow if you like."

"That is very generous of you. Be sure to thank her for me." He suddenly started feeling very emotional. "I will miss you all very much, Orlov. You have been a good friend to me, and your family has always been like my very own." He gave Orlov a big hug. "I will try to come back tomorrow afternoon sometime. But I will make sure Tomi and I stop by before we leave town. It may not be for a few weeks yet." Orlov kissed him on the forehead and walked with him out to his horse. "Maybe we can all have a nice little dinner together before Tomi and I leave town. I'll talk it over with Tomi and Vanya and let you know."

"It would be my pleasure if you would allow me to host a dinner for the two of you." But Orlov had a banquet in mind rather than a small intimate dinner.

Then Alexeev rode off and headed towards town. It usually took him about an hour to walk from the boarding house to the town square where most of the businesses were located. Vanya and Sveta lived about the same distance from Orlov. Alexeev figured he could make it to the jeweller, then get back to Vanya's by noon, but he would have to ride the horse at a steady trot. Lightening was a good, strong horse so he should be up for the ride.

Alexeev arrived at the jeweller's just as Abram was opening for business. He tied the horse to the railing near the watering troth, then went inside to talk to the jeweller.

"Good morning, Mister Dvorkin, how are you today?" Alexeev reached out his hand to the aged jeweller. Abram Dvorkin had been a jeweller for more than 50 years in this same shop in Moscow. His parents moved to Moscow when he was only a toddler. They migrated from Poland in 1636, a few years before the king of Poland began restricting Jewish immigration into Russia. Although his family never practiced Judaism or its traditions, they were still Jews by birth and endured many of the prejudices of the day. Alexeev always valued the character of an individual above any other features or physical appearances. He treated every man with respect and welcomed differences as an opportunity to expand his knowledge and enhance his cultural experience.

"My dear Alexeev, it's good to see you, my son." Over the years he had made brooches and pins, bracelets, rings, earrings, and necklaces. Mister Dvorkin had even made the silver and emerald brooch many, many years ago. Alexeev's father had the broach made especially for his wife one year for her birthday, several years before Alexeev was born. Abram had told the story to Alexeev many times over the years, and he never tired hearing about it. He made jewellery for many of the families in Moscow over the years. "What brings you to my shop on this cold morning?"

With tears in his eyes, Alexeev removed the brooch from his coat pocket and placed it on the counter. "Do you remember making this brooch for my father many years ago? It was a birthday gift for my mother."

Abram picked up the brooch and examined it. Nodding his head, he turned it over and smiled. "Oh yes, these are my marks on the back. I do remember making this for your father. He brought in a silver ring and a silver teacup. The ring had these two emeralds that are in the brooch, and the silver was made from the ring and part of the teacup. I remember finding out later, the ring belonged to his father and had been passed down for a few generations. He didn't have much money at the time, so he asked me if I could take my payment out of the silver cup."

"You were very kind to accommodate him like that."

"Well, the excess silver from the cup was a generous payment and I knew how much the gift would mean to both him and your mother. Honestly, my son, I would have tried to talk him out of using the ring if I had known at the time about its sentimental value. But your father wouldn't have listened to me anyway." Abram handed the brooch back to Alexeev.

"This may sound a bit unconventional, but I have a favour to ask…" Alexeev handed the brooch back to Abram and explained his request to the jeweller.

"Where is Alexeev?" asked Tomi.

"He left a few hours ago. He brought in several loads of wood and asked to borrow a horse for the morning. He said he needed to go into town for a few hours but would be back in the afternoon for you…I'm sure Uncle Alexeev just didn't want to wake you," said Vanya. "Are you ready to get up and have something to eat?"

The pain in Tomi's side was making him feel a little nauseous. "I'm not very hungry," said Tomi.

"Oh, you need to have something. I promised him Sveta would give you a proper meal." Vanya helped Tomi sit up on the bed, then he swung his legs over the side of the bed. "Now, do you want me to help you get dressed?"

Tomi nodded his head. "I think my clothes must still be in the other bedroom."

"Yes, let me go get them. Now stay right here until I get back."

Tomi grabbed Vanya's wrist. "I am glad you are comfortable calling him 'uncle'. That makes me feel good." Tomi smiled at the thought of Vanya accepting his lover without hesitation.

Vanya kissed Tomi on the forehead and put his arm around him. "I knew he would be my uncle before you even introduced him to us. The sparkle in your eyes whenever you mentioned his name said it all."

Vanya retrieved Tomi's trousers, shirt, coat and shoes, then helped him get dressed. "I will have Sveta look at your side after you finish eating. Can you walk all right?"

"I think so," he said. "Don't get too far ahead of me though."

Vanya put his arm around Tomi and they walked down the stairs and into the kitchen together.

Alexeev had concluded his business with the jeweller and rode promptly back to Vanya's. Tomi was just sitting down for afternoon tea in the parlour when Alexeev arrived. "Good afternoon, Vanya, and good afternoon, *schast'ye moye*!" Alexeev leaned down to Tomi and kissed him. "You're looking much better."

"Well, how happy you look this afternoon," said Vanya. "You must have had a successful day."

"I have, my friend, thanks to you and Lightening." Alexeev poured himself a cup of tea and sat down beside Tomi. "My cousin is getting my belongings gathered together, so I will be able to pick them up tomorrow. That is, if I can borrow the horse again tomorrow afternoon?"

"That will be fine. I'm glad you had a productive morning."

Tomi set his hand on Alexeev's knee and rubbed back and forth. Then he put his hand on the side of Alexeev's head, turning it towards him, "And where else, may I ask, have you been today?"

"My dear Tomi, some things are better left unsaid until it is the right time," insisted Alexeev. "Be patient, my love." Then he kissed Tomi's forehead.

For the next three weeks, Tomi followed the doctor's orders and submitted to the daily routines Alexeev had planned out for him. He took deep breaths at least once every hour, stretched his arms above his head, leaned from one side to the other, and regularly walked everywhere he needed to go. And Alexeev made sure he needed to go to every room in the house several times each day. By the end of the second week he had Tomi walking outside, always by his side, then across the path to the neighbour's house for afternoon tea. By the middle of the third week Tomi was riding with Alexeev in the carriage into town. The carriage ride on the cobblestones was not the most comfortable ride, but it wasn't uncomfortable enough for Tomi to complain about…too much.

Doctor Leskov had seen him a few times during his recovery and was very impressed at the care and rehabilitation Alexeev had given him. At Tomi's age, recovery from a bruise to the side would ordinarily take several months, and the dangers associated with these types of injuries could, at times, be life threatening if the proper care was not given. Tomi was very fortunate to have a friend and lover like Alexeev who would take the time to ensure his full recovery.

At the end of the third week, and to celebrate Tomi's recovery, Alexeev arranged with Orlov to have Tomi, Vanya, Sveta and their daughters over for dinner. Orlov, his wife, Kiri, and all his children and grandchildren would be there, including the three babies born earlier in the year: seven children, four spouses and 20 grandchildren. There would be at least 40 in all, and probably several more when accounting for friends and beaus who often attended family gatherings without formal invitations. So Orlov planned a great feast, not only in honour of Tomi's recovery, but to welcome Tomi and his nephew's family into his own brood.

Orlov's daughters and granddaughters decorated the dining hall with paper flowers and scented candles. His sons bagged an elk and several wild pheasants for dinner. While some of the women and girls decorated, the rest were busy baking breads, pies, and cookies. Orlov's kitchen was very large and it had three ovens for baking. They also brought out many pickled vegetables and fruit preserves from the cellar, as well as a plentiful supply of wines, ales, and vodkas, and even though the holidays were still a month away, many insisted on having *sbiten*[53] as well. Orlov spent the better part of the previous day baking and decorating a special cake to celebrate Alexeev's retirement and his rekindled relationship with Tomi. He made his special 10-layer *Medovik*[54] honey cake, five of them in all. This was by far Alexeev's favourite dessert, but Orlov rarely made it because it took so much time and effort. For this occasion, however, Orlov didn't mind spending several hours on something that would make his dear friend happy. The five cakes would surround a three-foot iced sugar cone with gingerbread cookies and *pastila*[55] affixed to the outside.

---

[53] *Sbiten*: Hot drink made from spices and herbs with honey or sugar

[54] *Medovik*: Multi-layered Russian honey cake

[55] *Pastila:* (pastels) are a Russian candy similar to Turkish Delight

Vanya decided to take the family in his fancy carriage, kitted with two front-facing benches with deep blue cushions, and a back-facing bench with a tassel-lined shade, and they all dressed in their finest dresses and robes. He even had a red velvet robe with gold and silver braids that fit Alexeev, and Tomi had a dark purple velvet robe that used to belong to his brother Stas. They both wore black trousers and white silk shirts with black silk scarves, and they each had black hats provided by Vanya. They were a sight to behold, very stylish and elegant. Vanya wore his dark green velvet robe with the satin hem and silver stitched lining with a matching green hat and scarf, and Sveta wore a stunning light green dress with embroidered yellow daisies clustered in patches like bouquets along the waist. The three girls each wore matching white dresses with red and pink appliqué roses sewn around the sleeves, waist and hem. They also had matching red and pink woollen scarves. Vanya and Sveta rode in the front seat, the three girls rode in the centre seat, and Tomi and Alexeev rode in back. Vanya hitched up his four Northern Yakut horses for the ride to Orlov's place. Tomi enlisted the girls to gather pinecones earlier in the week. Then he taught them how to tie them together with string in a wreath, and decorate them with ribbons and beads. It would be the girls' gift to Orlov and Kiri. Tomi and Alexeev had gone into town earlier in the week and had picked up a crate of spiced vodka as a present, and Vanya and Sveta had picked out a beautifully carved jewellery box Vanya had made a few years back.

Orlov's family also wore their finest outfits for the occasion. Kiri wore a silk dress of various blue hues with a wide light blue sash tied like a ribbon around her waist, and Orlov wore his best robe: a light brown velvet, with yellow braids on the cuffs and around the collar. His three daughters and two daughters-in-law wore a host of colours as well. In fact, they covered the rest of the rainbow: Nastya wore a lovely red dress with pink satin trim, Klara wore a dark green dress with light blue periwinkles embroidered like stars around the hem and sleeves, Inna wore a lavender silk dress with a dark purple vest, Klava wore a peach-coloured dress with an orange sash around the waist and Ania wore a pale-yellow silk dress with a light blue vest and matching scarf.

Orlov had cooked the meats in the morning and had them sliced and prepared on platters with various cheeses, breads, sauces, and pickled vegetables, so everyone could help themselves. Everything was laid out on the long serving table, similar to the way he prepared for morning meals for his residents. There were also two large crystal punch bowls, one with hot *sbiten* for the children, and the other with *sbiten* and vodka for the adults. At the far end of the table were the desserts the women had prepared and the beautiful *Medovik* honey cakes and sugar cone combination. The ladies decorated all the tables with pine sprigs, pinecones and various paper flowers and ribbons, along with candles and scented oils. Throughout the dining hall, Orlov's sons had hung dozens of paper lanterns Orlov and his father had collected from Cathay over the years. Each one when lit, gave off a soft glow of colours and made the whole room feel very festive, cheery and alive. They also had candles and oil lamps down the centre of every table.

When Vanya's carriage pulled onto the side road leading up to the boarding house, they were greeted by most of Orlov's kin. The men had their youngest boys perched on their shoulders, the girls strolled out showing off their fancy dresses, while the young mothers carried the infants in their arms. Of course, Orlov and Kiri, proud *babulya i dedushka*[56], accompanied the group arm in arm. Vanya and Sveta couldn't hold back their smiles. They felt such warmth and love from the entire crowd. Oleg and Kostya led the carriage to a stop in front of the great hall, then helped Sveta and the girls down from the carriage. Alexeev immediately hopped down from the back and helped Tomi down as well. As Oleg prepared to draw the carriage away to the barn and stables, Alexeev enlisted Kostya's help with the crate of vodka, which he did gladly with a broad smile.

As the girls settled on the walkway, Orlov's granddaughters surrounded them and swept them away under a cloud of giggles into the great hall. Kiri smiled and kissed Sveta on both cheeks, welcoming her into their home, and Orlov hugged and kissed Vanya, then introduced them to his family one by one. He was proud he remembered all his children's names (and a little surprised) but had a little more difficulty remembering the names of each of his grandchildren. But Kiri managed to guide him and correct him on a few occasions. Compliments were exchanged for each other's dresses, and there was a mutual admiration for the other's good taste in fashion, then the ladies led the way into the hall while the men lagged and lingered behind. Several of them took advantage of the absence of the womenfolk to light their pipes and talk about the governmental changes taking place as a result of the Tsar's move to *Sankt Piter-Burkh*. Tomi had gotten to know each of Orlov's boys over the last two weeks and bonded successfully with each of them. They were getting used to calling him *Dyadya Medved'*,

---

[56] *Babulya i dedushka*: Granny and grandpa

which he had Alexeev to thank for giving away that little family nickname. But he loved being treated like part of this big, dear family. Tomi lived so far away from most of his family members, and he missed the communal nature of family gatherings. So, tonight was a treat both he and Alexeev would remember and cherish for the rest of their lives.

As the pipe smoke faded and diminished, the men gradually made their way inside. Tomi was glad they had not stayed out in the cold any longer as he was starting to take a chill. Alexeev saw him shiver a few times and removed his overcoat and wrapped it around Tomi. Once inside, the warmth from the fireplaces quickly brought comfort back to Tomi's cold bones, so Vladimir took the overcoats from Tomi and hung them on the hooks by the front door. Orlov had already put the final touches on the spread of food at the serving tables, and Kostya had just finished pouring the second bottle of vodka into the adult's punch bowl of *sbiten*.

Orlov stood up in the front of the dining hall and rang a large hand bell to get everyone's attention. "May I have everyone's attention, please." He held up his hands to motion everyone to come forward. "I am very proud this evening to announce my dear cousin Alexeev has completed his service in the army and has now retired." All the men cheered, hooted and whistled, and the ladies clapped. Tomi wrapped his arm around Alexeev's waist, laid his head against Alexeev's chest and gazed into his eyes with a huge smile on his face.

"But his life is not over…even though he is now out of a job." Everyone laughed. "We have already welcomed Tomi into our family. He and my cousin will be travelling east to Shoynaty-Storozhevsk in just a few days to start a new life together." There were more cheers and clapping. "But they leave behind a wonderful couple…Vanya and Sveta and their three beautiful and charming girls." He took Vanya's arm and pulled him closer. "Welcome these good people into our family." The whole family surrounded Vanya and Sveta and they all exchanged hugs and kisses again. "Now that we are all family, please help yourselves to the food."

For the next few hours, everyone ate and talked, ate and laughed, drank and talked, then drank and laughed. Once the eating slowed down, several of the children brought out their musical instruments and began to play folk songs. The boys quickly cleared the floor of the tables and chairs to make room for anyone who wanted to dance. Several of the men started clapping in rhythm to the music, then several of them joined and coaxed their partners out onto the dance floor, and the men and women separated to form two lines on the dance floor. They were getting ready to dance the *Khorovod*[57]. Tomi seemed a little shy, so Alexeev walked up to him, removed his hat and bowed to him. "Would you honour me with this dance, *schast'ye moye*?"

A gentleman would never turn down such a graceful request. He stood up, then bent towards Alexeev and reached out and took his hand and kissed it. "I would be most delighted, *moy sladkiy*[58]*.*" As they walked out onto the dance floor, the family clapped and cheered. Tomi grabbed a bright purple and blue silk shawl with gold fringes from one of the ladies who was not participating and draped it around his shoulders, then joined the line of women while Alexeev joined the line of men. They danced for quite a long time without any break, until finally Tomi felt the need to sit and rest. He kissed Alexeev on the cheek and whispered, "Thank you, *moy general*. I need to sit down for a while, but I want you to keep dancing as long as you want." Alexeev smiled, kissed him on the cheek, then he winked at Tomi and kept dancing with the group.

Tomi walked over to the tables and chairs that had been moved to the outer edges of the dining hall and sat next to Orlov. "You should get up and join your children in the dance," he urged.

"You know, Tomi, I think I will. I haven't done this since…since I don't know when." Orlov got up, took hold of Kiri on the way and rushed onto the floor to join Alexeev and the rest of the group. Vanya and Sveta had joined in several minutes earlier. Tomi sat by himself for the next hour. He felt a little embarrassed he couldn't keep up with the rest of them. It made him feel old. He also realised he was not a very handsome man, especially after seeing and meeting all of Alexeev's relatives. The men were all tall, fit, good-looking and masculine. Alexeev was definitely the best looking in the group, but there were none of them that didn't cause heads to turn. Tomi wondered why Alexeev loved him so much. It wasn't like he had any physical characteristics that made men, or even women, swoon. He wasn't particularly witty and he didn't have much of a sense of humour. When he worked as the city treasurer, the mayor once told him that his sense of humour was as dry as the desert sands of Egypt. And Tomi was not athletic, nor did he have any special or sought-after skills, although he did make a fine blackberry wine. But that wasn't enough to convince him he had

---

[57] *Khorovod*: Traditional Russian and Slavic dance. Derived from old Russian, *khorovod* means 'moving around the sun'

[58] *Moy sladkiy*: My sweetie, my sweet

anything special to offer Alexeev, or any man. He started to get depressed and a certain anxiety came over him like a profound lack of self-confidence. He wanted Alexeev to stop dancing and pay more attention to him. He wanted Alexeev to tell him why he loved him and what made him special. He desperately wanted to be convinced he was actually worth more than the dust he was made of.

Suddenly, he felt his eyes welling up with tears. He didn't want anyone to see how depressed he was so he quickly got up and went outside, then walked out to the barn and got into the carriage. He sat there and cried. These were uncontrollable tears and he didn't know for sure why he was crying. He had found Alexeev after six years of separation. He was finally with the one person he felt he could love forever and the one person who said he loved him back. Yet Tomi had convinced himself he was not worthy of anyone as perfect, as excellent in character, as lovingly devoted as Alexeev. He believed Alexeev deserved someone who was beautiful beyond words, someone who had a sharp wit and a creative mind, and someone who could keep up with him physically. Tomi blamed himself for his weaknesses and frailties. He imagined Alexeev would tire of the illnesses, injuries and weaknesses, and would eventually (and probably sooner rather than later) find the prince he so richly deserved.

Tomi heard the barn door open so he quickly dried his eyes on his sleeve. "Is someone there?" he called out.

"It is me, Alexeev," said the familiar voice. "What are you doing out here in the cold, Tomi? You should be inside where it is warm." Then Alexeev saw the sorrow in Tomi's eyes. His eyes were red and his eyelashes were still wet with tears. He was trembling. "Oh, my dear, what is wrong?" He quickly climbed up and held Tomi close to him. Tomi started weeping as soon as he felt those strong arms embrace him. "It's all right, you don't have to tell me anything. I love you and that's all that matters." He rubbed Tomi's back and kissed his neck, then he stroked Tomi's head and brushed his cheek with the back of his hand. Alexeev pulled a blanket from underneath the seat and wrapped it around the two of them.

He sat there and held him until finally he heard the soft rumble of Tomi's snore on his chest. The trembling had stopped and he was asleep. He sat there for a while longer holding his poor distraught lover and wondering what could be wrong, what could make him so upset that he needed to isolate himself from those who loved him. He didn't seem like he had been in any pain, although Alexeev knew Tomi didn't make it a habit of sharing that information with anyone. But he seemed to be in good spirits up until he left the dance floor. He saw him sitting alone, so he didn't think anyone could have said anything to him to upset him. And other than family, Tomi hadn't seen anyone else without Alexeev. *No*, he thought, *something must have happened that I didn't see. Maybe I embarrassed him when I asked him to dance...but he knows everyone here and he knows my family would never make fun of him*. He thought about the incident for a while. *Bozhe moy!*[59] *I made him dance in line with the women. That must be it. I humiliated him in front of his nephew and his nieces. How could I have been so stupid!* The more he thought about it, the angrier he became with himself.

Finally, he decided he needed to gather Vanya and Sveta and the girls and get everyone home so he could get Tomi into his warm comfortable bed. It would give them some privacy as well. So, he tucked the blanket around Tomi and wrapped the scarf around Tomi's neck to keep him warm, then he carefully stepped down from the carriage and went back into the dining hall to find Vanya. Sveta had already anticipated it was time to leave, so she was gathering the three girls together and making sure they were bundled up properly for the ride back.

Alexeev walked up to her. "I'm glad you're getting ready to leave. I think Tomi is very tired. He's out in the carriage sleeping." He smiled at the girls. He patted Feodora on the head and bent down to her. "You and your sisters look very pretty tonight. Did you have fun with the other girls here?"

Feodora giggled. "Hehe, yes uncle. Stasya and Sonya showed me their dolls, and *Dedushka* Orlov showed us his drawings."

"He did? Did you like all those wonderful animals? And did you like playing with all the beautiful dolls?"

Feodora nodded and giggled a little more, then she pulled on her scarf and managed to get her arm tangled up in the excess length of the fabric. Sveta jumped in and rescued her. "I don't know what I'm going to do with you, my little *tsvetok*[60]." Sveta wrapped the scarf around Feodora's neck once again.

"I'm going to find Vanya so we can go." Alexeev set Faina and Fillipa on the table near Sveta. "Now you girls stay right here with your mum while I find your papa." Sveta looked like she had things under control, so Alexeev walked around to try to find Vanya. He finally found him in the game room getting ready to play cards with the boys.

"Come join us, Uncle!" he said as he spotted Alexeev in the doorway.

---

[59] *Bozhe moy!* – Oh my God!

[60] *Tsvetok*: Flower

Andrei interrupted with a quick jab to Alexeev's shoulder, "So, we weren't good enough for you? You had to find a different nephew?"

Alexeev knew this was a joke, so he played along. He patted Andrei on the head., "I thought it was time we introduce some class and culture to this family...you're all so uncivilised." Andrei immediately lost his smile and the other boys let out cries of dismay. "Just kidding, just kidding. You know you've always been my favourite." With that, Alexeev kissed him gently on the cheek while he ran his hand through Andrei's hair. Andrei pulled away, but then laughed, realising the joke was on him. Then Alexeev walked up to Vanya. "Do you think we could leave now? I think Tomi has had a little too much excitement tonight. He's resting in the carriage."

"Oh yes, yes," he said without any hesitation. "Well men, I do believe it's time for me to go, but I promise you, we will do this again very soon." Vanya shook their hands and walked out with Alexeev.

"Sveta has already gathered the girls so I think we are ready to go."

"I want to say goodbye to Orlov before we go and thank him for such a wonderful celebration," he said. Then they walked over to Orlov and Kiri.

"Time to go, so soon?" asked Orlov.

"Yes, I'm afraid it's been a busy day. I think Tomi was especially tired this evening. I found him in the carriage nearly asleep, poor man," said Alexeev.

Vanya shook Orlov's hand, then kissed him on the cheek. "We had a wonderful time this evening. Thank you for having us all over. We feel just like a part of your family."

"You are welcome here anytime you are in the neighbourhood," he said with a big smile on his face. "Oh, don't leave yet!" He quickly ran over to the table where there was still much uneaten food. He set one of the uneaten cakes in a wooden box and covered the top with a cloth. "Take this with you..." Then he whispered, "It's Alexeev's favourite!" Then he called out to Alexeev, "Give my best to Tomi!"

Vanya smiled and took the box, then whispered back, "It's my favourite too! But I'll make sure he gets a piece!" Orlov roared with laughter and patted him on the back.

Alexeev had already made his way to Kiri to give her a hug and kiss, and then he and Vanya made their way through the family saying their goodbyes and giving hugs and kisses to each member of the family. They met up with Sveta and the girls and walked out to the carriage. Tomi was still asleep in the back seat. Alexeev hitched up the horses, then led the carriage out of the barn to the side of the boarding house where Sveta and the girls were waiting. He and Vanya helped the girls get up into the carriage, then Vanya helped Sveta step in and Alexeev took his place next to Tomi in the back. Vanya lit the two lanterns on either side of the carriage then proceeded onto the road home.

As they travelled down the road, Tomi awoke in Alexeev's arms. "How long have I been asleep?" he asked.

"Only a few years, *spyashchiy medved'*[61]," said Alexeev. Then he smiled. "Just an hour or so."

"I'm sorry I was not very good company. I hope Orlov didn't think I was ungrateful for the cerebration he hosted."

"Not at all, Tomi. I told him you were very tired." He stroked Tomi's back. "And he knows you've been ill."

"Yes, I thought I could do more than I should have," he said. "I'm not used to dancing." Then he smiled and kissed Alexeev's cheek. "But I liked watching you dance. You are so handsome and you're a very good dancer."

"Well, I'm not sure about that. I like to dance though…but I shouldn't have kept dancing when you wanted to stop. I shouldn't have left you by yourself."

"Nonsense! We don't have to do the same things all the time, or even like the same things. I just wish I could keep up with you so you don't get bored with me."

Alexeev put his hand on Tomi's face and turned it towards him. "I am never bored with you. Don't even think that way. I am excited when I'm with you and I miss you when we are apart, even for a short time. I can't imagine not having you in my life."

Tomi rested his head on Alexeev's chest. "I love you, Alexeev."

"I love you too, *schast'ye moye*." He wrapped both arms around Tomi and clasped his hands. "I love you dearly, Tomi."

They both looked back on the road as they passed though the outer edges of the city. It hadn't snowed for more than a week, so the roads were clear and drying out. There was a slight breeze in the air and the trees gently swayed their branches from side to side. There was a fresh scent of pine mingled with the occasional smoke from chimneys as they passed home after home. They could

---

[61] *Spyashchiy medved'*: Sleeping (hibernating) bear

see the stars clearly and a half-moon was almost directly overhead. As they both watched the night sky, they spotted a shooting star.

Tomi looked at Alexeev. "What did you wish for? Did you wish for riches, or fame, or power?"

Alexeev looked a little surprised by the question, but thought he needed to answer just the same, "I wished we would always be together."

Tomi looked deep into Alexeev's eyes. "You didn't need to wish for that, *moy general.* I won't ever leave you." He paused for a moment, then asked, "Do you want to know what I wished for?"

"If you want to tell me."

"I wished you would always be happy," he said.

"I will always be happy as long as I am with you."

For the rest of the trip, they watched the stars in the sky and pointed each time they saw another shooting star. They listened as they heard the wolves howling in the distance, or the owls hooting in the trees. They saw a few elk scamper through the groves on the side of the road and they could hear wood being chopped by farmers trying to catch up on their daily chores. Every now and then another carriage would pass by, headed towards the centre of Moscow and Vanya would call out a greeting. The other driver would call back and bid him a good evening or wish him well. They could hear the girls in the centre seat giggling, or playing word games, or telling stories, or talking about the cute boys at the party. And they caught bits and pieces of Sveta's conversation with Vanya about exchanging recipes with Kiri and her girls, or their plans to meet during the week for tea.

Things were getting back to normal for Tomi, and Alexeev was feeling more and more like he belonged by Tomi's side, and also like he was becoming more and more a part of his family. Tomi felt the same way about Orlov and Kiri. Even though Tomi's first encounter with Orlov had seemed a bit awkward, he found Orlov to be a loving and kind father figure for Alexeev, and he felt a brotherly love towards Orlov he had not felt since before his own brother, Stas, had passed away. Over the last few weeks, Tomi had the opportunity to get to know Orlov and his family. He had a few intimate talks with him when he opened up about some of the men he had been with before Alexeev, and Orlov seemed to empathise with some of the encounters Tomi had gone through. Orlov gave Tomi some insight on Alexeev's childhood that would help Tomi understand some of his peculiarities. Overall, it was a grand evening for both Tomi and Alexeev.

They both decided they would have to plan a trip back to Moscow once they got themselves settled in Storozhevsk. But this evening was nearly over and Tomi was getting tired as they rode on. He was scheduled to see the doctor in two days and hopefully, the doctor would tell him he had made a full recovery.

Tomi was getting anxious to start their trip home, and although he loved Vanya and Sveta dearly, he was feeling very homesick for his own cottage. It could take at least a month before they would reach Storozhevsk because of the weather and the cold, but Tomi didn't want to postpone their journey any longer than necessary. They made plans to pack up their things tomorrow, so they could leave as soon as the doctor cleared him for travel. But tonight, they would get some well-needed rest.

Chapter 9

The Long Journey Home – Getting Started

Tomi had finally recovered from his injury. The doctor gave him a full release to resume all his normal activities, including travel. The bruise had faded to a light pink and the pain had completely gone away. Doctor Leskov recommended he visit his own doctor once he returned home. He was a little concerned Tomi was experiencing headaches and his vision was still a little blurred at times. Tomi promised to see his doctor as soon as he could, though his true intentions were to avoid his doctor if possible, without raising Alexeev's suspicions.

Alexeev had made several trips to town on his own while Tomi rested in the afternoons, sometimes to finalise matters with the army, and a few times to help Orlov with miscellaneous chores. He also finished making a new folding step stool for the kitchen. It was a three-step stool that set firmly on the floor without rocking or wobbling and it could be folded when not in use for easy storage behind the kitchen counter. He came up with the idea from the folding tray Tomi used so he could eat in bed without having to balance the tray on his lap. Vanya's folding tray had legs that unfolded from the bottom to rest on either side of Tomi's legs, so the tray was lifted above his lap. Vanya was so impressed with the step stool's construction he offered to pay Alexeev a design fee so he could construct the same design and sell the step stools upon request. Alexeev was flattered at the compliment but gave permission without accepting any money since the idea came from something Vanya had originally designed.

"You're my family! How could I accept payment from my own nephew?" he explained. Vanya understood more and more why his *Dyadya Medved'* was so in love with this man. So instead, he made two folding chairs using the same folding technique and gave them to Tomi and Alexeev for use in the carriage for their trip home.

Alexeev had all his belongings packed in a trunk and he secretly tucked away the special gift he picked up at the jeweller. Sveta and Vanya helped Tomi pack his things. Tomi was getting anxious about taking the long trip across the wilderness back to his home. Fortunately, he knew several friends and relatives along the way where they could spend a night or two to rest the horses.

Finally, everything was packed and ready to go. Vanya handed a large basket to Alexeev to load into the carriage. "Sveta has packed a dozen *buterbrody* for the trip, and there are also berries, apples, dried meats and a few jugs of cider."

"Vanya, thank you for all your hospitality to me during my stay here. You can be sure, Tomi and I will return here as often as we can," he said as he hugged his new nephew.

"And you are invited out to my cottage as soon as you have some time to travel," said Tomi, leaving the invitation open.

Several hugs and kisses later and with tears covering their cheeks, the two set out to start their long journey home. Tomi's carriage was loaded with his own personal items, a few items he had inherited from Stas, Alexeev's trunk, as well as enough food to last a few weeks. They had several cases of wine and cider, a bag of beans and barley, a bag of tea leaves, a tin of cocoa and several pouches of tobacco.

Although the day started out sunny, the air was still cold and brisk. Tomi wrapped his long overcoat tightly around him and pulled his knitted cap over his ears. Alexeev was more accustomed to the cold weather and the icy roads so he took the reins. Then he wrapped his arm around Tomi and started the horses on the first stretch of their long journey. But Tomi and Alexeev were together and that was all that really mattered. They would never be alone again and their lives from now on would be side by side, hand in hand, and arm in arm. They both took a deep breath as the carriage pulled onto the road again. Alexeev tightened his arm around his cold partner, and Tomi looked up and smiled. He had all the warmth he needed inside his heart and on the seat next to him.

Klippity klop, klippity klop, klippity klop, the sound of the horses' hooves was a comforting sound to Alexeev. In a short time, they came to the boarding house to go through another round of goodbyes. They stopped by just long enough for Alexeev to pick up a few odds and ends he had collected that were memorable in some way but not of any great value. Orlov also packed food items for their trip: several loaves of fresh bread, a dozen jars of his blackberry-rhubarb jam, a sack of turnips, a few cabbages, a bundle of carrots, several onions, some spices and a few dozen pork sausages. Tomi promised to ship Orlov several cases of his blackberry wine and cordials as soon as he returned home as appreciation for the bounty they had been given.

Orlov was very well known for his generosity, especially towards his favourite cousin. "I will miss you very much, my friend. Be sure to come back and visit as often as you can. There will always be a bed ready and waiting for you and Tomi."

In good weather, the trip from Moscow to Storozhevsk could take up to a month, but this was winter and there was no telling what the next several weeks would bring. Tomi and Alexeev took their time travelling through the wilderness roads and planned to stay overnight at several strategic places along the way to refresh the horses. Alexeev was used to camping under these conditions but he was a little worried about Tomi, especially if it started snowing again. He wasn't sure Tomi was up for the harsh conditions of a trip this time of year, so he was determined to take the trip slowly, if necessary.

The first part of their journey would bring them to Nizhny Novgorod along the banks of the Volga River. Tomi's Aunt Galina Pavlovna, *Tetushka*[62] Gala as Tomi called her, lived in a large house along the river. She was his oldest living relative, aged 96 years last summer. She was his father's oldest sister and had been widowed nearly 65 years, since she was a young lady of 31 years old. Her husband was killed during the war with Persia in 1651 and she never remarried. She had four daughters though, all of whom were married and had left home many years ago, but she had made a good living for herself. She raised herds of pigs and sold them to the local butchers several times a year. Since the township was growing steadily over the years, the business paid enough for her to be well-off, and her knowledge of pigs she passed down to her workers made the business thrive. Of course, she no longer did the work or ran the business herself, but she had several workers who had been in her employ for many years and had managed the business for her for nearly twenty years now. They took care of the pigs and the farm. They also managed the household chores and did most of the cooking. Galina would occasionally make herself a pot of tea, but she was no longer able to manage much more than that. Each week the bookkeeper would review the business profits with her, but she trusted her workers implicitly and her review was more of a formality than a necessity.

[62] *Tetushka*: Auntie

The ride from Moscow to the Volga River would take seven or eight days, so the boys planned to stop each night along the road to bed down. The back of Tomi's carriage had an underboard floor Tomi outfitted with a cushioned pad and blankets. The sides were well insulated with a layer of straw between the outer and inner walls to keep out as much of the cold wind as possible. Tomi had equipped the carriage with many of the amenities from home to lend as much comfort as possible.

There were lanterns, towels and a small wash basin with a three-gallon barrel of water, scented incense sticks, wooden dishes, pots and pans, a case stocked with a variety of spices and the two folding wooden chairs Vanya made that fit securely onto hooks on the sides of the carriage walls to conserve space. Sveta had sewn together two matching cushions stuffed with soft down to add comfort to the chairs. Tomi had been using this same carriage for the past ten years, and each year, he added something to make the trips more enjoyable or a little more comfortable. This year Sveta also made cushions for the driver's bench for both the seat and back to match the cushions on the chairs. She made them from an old curtain with a burgundy fleur-de-lis pattern on a midnight blue background. These additions gave the carriage a regal and stunning look and made the long ride home much more comfortable.

The first stop came a little sooner than either of them anticipated when an unexpected snow flurry began around five o'clock in the afternoon. But the two took it in stride. Alexeev found an outcropping of trees for shelter and began to make camp. Once he secured the carriage, he immediately went out to gather wood for a fire while Tomi pulled out the tarp from one end of the carriage to shelter the horses from the snow. The tarp was rolled up on a pole along the length of the carriage. There were six other poles that hooked into eyelets along each side of the tarp, so it created a sheltered area large enough for the horses, a firepit and a sitting area for the two men. Then, there were four other tarps that hooked onto the tarp overhead. They rolled down like walls around the horses to keep them sheltered during the night. There were also a few taller poles that fit into the centre of the tarp to help any snow or rain to drain off more easily.

After he got the walls in place and the horses settled and covered with their blankets, he gave them each a bucket of oats and filled a troth with water for the evening. He unloaded some of the food for dinner and started to gather twigs to start a fire. By the time he was ready to start the fire, Alexeev was back with enough cut firewood to last through the night. Soon the campfire was roaring and the two men were warming themselves nicely in each other's arms in front of the fire. They feasted on *buterbrody*, berries and hot cider they warmed in a pot over the fire. Alexeev added a little cinnamon and cloves to the hot cider, which gave it a pleasant taste and made the two men smile a little bigger every time they took a sip of the brew. Later, Alexeev added a little vodka to the pot of hot cider, then filled their mugs again. They both felt the warming effects of the alcohol and Tomi started to feel a little more at ease as the evening progressed.

The glow of the moon shone through the clouds and made the snow on the ground glisten white as far as they could see. The snow-covered pines twinkled as the wind blew their boughs gently in the night air. The camp felt cosy and romantic, just the kind of atmosphere the lovers had dreamt of for their first night in the wilderness. Alexeev gently placed his hand on the side of Tomi's head, pulling it towards him, then kissed him. Tomi wrapped his arms around Alexeev's waist and was lost in the moment. He trembled in Alexeev's arms and realised it was due in part to the cold air. Alexeev took off his coat and covered Tomi, stood up and built up the fire with a few more logs, then he came back and resumed their embrace. He held Tomi tightly in his arms and kissed him.

"You're still shivering. Maybe we should go inside." Alexeev opened the shutter on the side of the carriage and angled it down so it would catch the warm air from the fire and let it flow into the carriage. Then he went back to hold Tomi. The heat of love between them was overwhelming and each of them could feel their cocks swelling and hardening in their trousers. They hadn't made love since the night of Tomi's injury, yet they had held each other close each night. Alexeev was a little apprehensive that his affections might injure Tomi again, but tonight Tomi was ready to be subdued once more by his lover. He placed his hand over the long hard cock beneath Alexeev's trousers, then smiled to let him know he was ready and willing. Alexeev leaned in and kissed him. They slowly stood up together still in a deep kiss as they walked towards the carriage. Stopping briefly, Tomi unlatched the rear opening of the carriage. They unfastened each other's shirts and trousers, disrobed and climbed into the padded sleeping area. It was a tight fit for two grown men, yet more than enough space for two lovers.

Their naked bodies were exposed to the bitter, cold air just long enough to make their nipples hard, but neither of them knew for sure whether it was due to the cold air or their passion. The fire was just outside the carriage. The flap Alexeev had angled down brought some warmth into their sleeping area, and it made the night under the tarp a little more comfortable for the horses as well.

The sleeping space in the carriage was quite a bit larger than Alexeev anticipated, and he was grateful for a flat, solid surface rather than the ground floor of tents he had for so long been forced to tolerate as a troop leader in the army, where roots, pebbles and stones kept one tossing and turning through the night. The cushioned floor and feather-filled quilt and pillows were a welcomed change from the army blankets he was accustomed to.

He laid himself carefully on top of Tomi, covering him like a shield, then he kissed him. Tomi's body sunk into the feather quilt so he was surrounded by a soft wall that held in the heat rather well. He also felt quite protected by the strong muscles flexing over him. The hair on their chests was soon moist with the heat and sweat of their passion. Alexeev's arms were thick and well-defined, and his veins were pumped full of blood. Tomi could feel the powerful biceps and triceps as Alexeev pushed himself up and down over his submissive body. And Alexeev's chest, though covered with a layer of light brown hair, was massive and strong: muscles pumped up over the rib cage, and a rippling stomach with a thicker trail of hair leading down to his well-trimmed genital area. His thick eight-inch cock was nearly twice the size of Tomi's, but it was gently resting and rubbing itself over Tomi's cock, not yet ready to penetrate. With each movement, each kiss, each flex of Alexeev's muscles, Tomi's cock got harder and harder. But Alexeev held back, waiting for the right moment.

As they made love that night, the two of them felt like they were consummating this new relationship, their new life together. So gentle and controlled was Alexeev's penetration, that Tomi obliged the passion to last longer than it ever had before, including their first night six years ago. They were still wrestling through this copulation in the early morning hours when the birds began their choruses.

By this time, Tomi had mounted Alexeev, turning him on his stomach, spreading Alexeev's firm buttocks with his hands, moistening the sphincter with his tongue and wedging his moderate cock into Alexeev's hole. Alexeev had never experienced anal penetration by a cock before, but gasped with pleasure and urged Tomi to go in as deep as he could. Tomi complied for as long as he could, but his stamina was not as enduring as Alexeev's, and it had already been a long night of passion. His cock released its cum into Alexeev. The heated liquid inside him made him feel alive and powerful. He turned himself over and pulled Tomi on top of him and kissed him roughly. Tomi felt the scrape of Alexeev's facial stubble as it scratched his cheeks and chin. He placed his hands on

Alexeev's chest and grabbed the powerful pectorals with all his remaining strength, reacting to the rough behaviour. Alexeev's cock exploded with a stream of cum between their bodies. Then Tomi took the cock with his hand and squeezed the rest of the cum out onto Alexeev's stomach, then licked the creamy liquid from his abdominal muscles.

Tomi had never seen Alexeev's face look so full of joy and happiness as he saw that morning, and Alexeev was never happier than he was when he was with Tomi. The two of them reclined for a few more hours in the carriage bed, resting and holding each other close, and each of them nodded off into their own separate dreamlands.

As mid-morning approached, they got themselves cleaned up and dressed. They were still tired, yet filled with delight from the closeness they had spent together. They ate a simple breakfast of bread, toasted on the campfire, blackberry-rhubarb jam and hot tea. Alexeev also heated a few sausages on a stick over the fire, but Tomi didn't want to eat anything more than the toast and jam and a small cup of tea.

Just before noon, they were all packed and ready to continue their journey. The snow had stopped sometime in the night and Alexeev was confident the roads would be fine for riding as long as it didn't snow again for a while. Tomi estimated they would arrive at *Tetushka* Gala's home in about five more travel days, weather permitting. As Tomi gathered together the uneaten food and packed up the utensils and dishes, Alexeev tended to the horses and got them situated in front of the carriage. Then he folded up their blankets and rolled up the tarps and poles and tied them in place. The snow was beginning to melt as the sun shone bright overhead, so it looked like they would be able to travel all day without interruption. But the night's grappling and sexual adventure had left Tomi drained and weak. Alexeev had him remain in the bedded carriage area for the better part of the next two days.

Alexeev stopped every two hours to rest the horses with two stops for their feeding. The route from Moscow to Nizhny Novgorod followed the Klyzama River most of the way, so they had plenty of water for the horses as well as for drink, washing, and bathing. Moscow was about 400 kilometres from Nizhny Novgorod and they averaged a little more than 50 kilometres a day after the first night. Alexeev made sure the rest of their nights by the side of the road were restful for the horses and for Tomi. There were only a few brief snow flurries on this first leg of their trip, so they didn't lose much time and the remaining nights were full of cuddling, kisses and snuggling by the fire, followed by sleep rather than love-making. Tomi hadn't yet gained all his strength back though he seemed to be improving with every day.

On their fifth evening, Alexeev stopped in Starodub-on-the-Klyzama, where Tomi's friend, Ludmil 'Ludi' Markov, lived. Ludi had taken Tomi in during his recovery from his injuries in the army nearly 20 years ago. Every trip to Moscow would include a stop at Ludi's on the way and also on the way back, and as a gratuity, Tomi would bring several bottles of his blackberry wine from his own cellars, and Sveta would pack tins of tea cakes or cookies she and Tomi would make together during his visits. The trade of libation and sweets for overnight accommodations was a welcomed part of the trip for both the traveller and the host. Tomi would also pick up a book or two from Moscow and gift those as well, since he knew Ludi didn't travel to large cities very often. For this trip, Tomi had a copy of Giovanni Domenica (Tommaso) Campanella's, *La Città del Sole*[63], that he purchased in Moscow. The book had not yet been translated into Russian, but Tomi knew Ludi had several friends from Italy who could help him with the translation.

Tomi perked up as soon as they approached the township and he started looking for familiar sites and road markers. Soon he directed Alexeev off the main road to a farmhouse surrounded by a metre-high stone wall. Alexeev drove the carriage alongside the barn and helped Tomi down. Within moments of their arrival, a tall, lanky, grey-haired man swaggered out of the house wearing a red velvet pelisse with gold embroidered trim, and a frogging fastened around the middle. Underneath, he was wearing a white silk shirt and a short white silk skirt. His shoes were white silk as well with gold chord lacing wrapped around his legs up to his knees. His hair was long with large curls and he wore several necklaces. Some were elegant gold chains and some were strings of pearls or beads. His fingers were adorned with rings of various metals and gems and his wrists and ankles each had many gold and silver bangles that made him jingle as he walked. His overall appearance reminded Alexeev of some of the princes and royalty he met on his journeys through the Asian kingdoms. Tomi hadn't forewarned Alexeev of Ludi's eccentricities in appearance, mannerism and his overall way of life, but Alexeev was accustomed to encountering all different types of

[63] *La Città del Sole*, written in 1602, a socialistic work by Tomasso Campanella (1568-1639) in which he attempts to reconcile humanism with Roman Catholic theology

individuals and he learned to observe, listen, inquire and accept without making judgments.

Ludi waved his hands high in the air as he walked quickly to the carriage. "Woohoo, Tomi, is that you?" he called out in his high-pitched, effeminate, yet scratchy voice. "I thought I recognised your lovely carriage. And who is this handsome young man you have escorting you across country." He was obviously a very vocal and very sociable individual. "Bless my house, the gods have favoured me with one of their own…oh, pardon me, they've favoured Tomi, and I just happen to be close enough to benefit from the overflow of their generosity!" Alexeev was slightly embarrassed and started to blush. He had heard similar compliments from the young single women in Moscow but never heard these sentiments expressed to him verbally by another man…other than Tomi.

"How wonderful to see you again, Ludi!" Tomi said as he leaned down from the carriage and embraced his dear friend. Alexeev quickly hopped down and lifted Tomi off the carriage. They kissed on the lips and embraced again. Then Tomi took Ludi's hand and turned towards Alexeev. "Ludi, this is my dear, dear friend—"

"Ahhh, Alexeev?" Ludi gasped as he interrupted.

"Yes, this is Alexeev, the love of my life."

Alexeev reached out his hand, but Ludi swung his arms around his torso and held him tight. "It's nice to meet you." Alexeev struggled to say as Ludi's hug forced the air from his lungs.

"And it is spectacular to finally meet you, Lieutenant." With that, Ludi put his hands on either side of Alexeev's head, pulled it towards him and kissed Alexeev on the lips, forcing his tongue in as deep as Alexeev would allow. Then he reached down and grabbed Alexeev's buttocks and gave it a squeeze. As he did, he turned his head towards Tomi and mouthed, "how glorious!" He wiped the sides of his mouth daintily with his finger. The startled look on Alexeev's face was eclipsed only by the surprised look on Tomi's face. "Well, come in, come in, dearies. It's cold out here and I'm sure you will want to warm yourselves by the fire."

"May I put the horses in the barn for the night? I don't think they should be standing out here in the open," asked Alexeev.

"Oh yes, of course. The back door to the barn is open, and there is a lantern hanging on the inside to the right of the door. Just come on in when you've finished, my dear." Ludi waved one hand at Alexeev and had his other arm around Tomi, leading him away into the house. Tomi looked back with concern at Alexeev, but Alexeev just waved him on and smiled to reassure him everything was all right.

It didn't take long to get the horses settled into a few of the empty stalls in the barn. Then he grabbed a bag from the back of the carriage Tomi had packed the night before with their overnight necessities and also a large tin of tea cakes. He noticed as he walked up to the house part of the stone wall had collapsed near the front porch. He set the bag down and examined the damage. Then picked up the bag again and went inside the house. There were candles lit in the long hallway that extended down the centre of the house, and Alexeev could see an orange glow flickering from a doorway towards the end of the hall. As he made his way down the hallway, he noticed several beautiful oil paintings. Many of them were nude men in various poses. They were men of all ages, races, shapes and sizes. Some were reclining, some sitting, some standing or strutting or flexing. There were men wrestling, kissing, embracing, and some were in positions Alexeev only imagined in his dreams. He had never seen artwork quite like this before, but was very intrigued and a little embarrassed. He examined one of the paintings more closely and noticed the artist's signature, *Ludi M.* He smiled and ran his hand through his hair contemplating the painting, then continued towards the glowing doorway. He could hear Tomi and Ludi laughing and talking as he approached the door. Alexeev gently knocked on the open door.

"Come in, Lexee, come in. Do you like that name? I think it suits you," said Ludi, still laughing.

Alexeev bashfully entered the room, not knowing what he had interrupted or how he should respond. He set the bag down, opened it and handed the tin to Tomi. "I brought our things in…and the tin."

Tomi sprang to his feet. "Oh, thank you, my love. What would I ever do without you?" As he handed the tin to Ludi, he opened it. "You simply must try these tea cakes. Sveta and I baked them just before we left Moscow." Alexeev noticed Tomi's manner of speaking had changed in some way, almost as if the eccentricity in Ludi's voice was infecting him in some way. He found it amusing and a little sexy.

Ludi gingerly retrieved one of the delicate, round, white tea cakes from the tin and took a bite. "How heavenly!" he exclaimed. "Tomi, you never cease to amaze me. Not only can you make wines and cordials, but you can bake as well." He circled around Tomi and offered one of the cakes to Alexeev. "You're going to have to watch what you eat, Lexee. Tomi's going to try to fatten you up, then you'll have to loosen your trousers." He patted Alexeev's flat stomach and held the tin back out to Tomi so he could join in the culinary sweet indulgence. Then he looked at Tomi slyly. "Or perhaps, that's the whole idea!" He burst out laughing while both Tomi and Alexeev nearly choked on the tea cakes.

Ludi's laugh was a high-pitched shriek that always seemed like it came out of nowhere, startling anyone within hearing distance. Alexeev imagined the distance was somewhere between the length of the house and the length of the property. Ludi was anything but shy, and he always said exactly what he meant and exactly what he was thinking. He had no filters for his words or actions. Alexeev soon realised he needed to toughen his sensitivity around Ludi and take no offence of the things he said…or did. He would eventually learn to appreciate Ludi's candour and even come to enjoy talking openly to Ludi and taking him into his confidence.

"You both must be starved and worn out. I can't imagine being on the road that long. Travelling from Shoynaty to Moscow, then back again in a matter of only a few months. Come join me in the dining room, Tomi. I'll have Yuri make us some supper." He took his arm and started leading him to the dining room. "Oh, Lexee, leave the bag here for now, but do bring the tin of cakes, my boy. *Voskhititel'no*![64]" He raved as he smacked his lips.

Alexeev left the bag and followed them into the dining room. In the centre of the room was a long, highly polished dark wood table surrounded by 18 ornate high-back chairs with white velvet cushions. There were four silver candelabras down the centre of the table and a beautiful white lace table runner. Alexeev imagined Ludi must entertain quite frequently and lavishly. The dining room, like the hallway, was lined with beautiful, erotic paintings all signed by Ludi. Alexeev found it curious how each painting seemed to be of a different man and he wondered how many more paintings there were throughout the house.

Ludi excused himself to arrange for supper while Tomi took Alexeev's hand and led him around the room to examine each painting. He explained how Ludi had known many of these young men personally, and each one had posed for him, sometimes in exchange for sexual favours and sometimes in exchange for food, lodging, or other necessities. Ludi and Tomi seemed like polar opposites in many ways, but very similar in others. Ludi was flamboyant and loud,

---

[64] *Voskhititel'no*!: Delectable, delicious

outspoken and liberal, while Tomi was reserved, quiet, and generally conservative. Ludi had been with many, many men over the years, and his relationships seemed rather trivial, or at least superficial. Tomi's relationships also seemed to be more than a few, sometimes fleeting and usually short-lived yet emotionally charged and generally disappointing.

"Don't worry, my love, you won't see my portrait anywhere in this house." He rested his head on Alexeev's shoulder. "I guess I was never his type, or at least he never asked. We were always close friends though."

"So, Ludi slept with all these men?" he asked, somewhat amazed and overwhelmed at the number of paintings in the dining room and hallway alone.

Just then, Ludi came back in. "Well, I didn't sleep with all of them at the same time, my dear!" The smile on his face let Alexeev know he was not offended by the inquiry. "And believe me, we didn't get much sleep either!" Ludi guided them around the room and told a story about each young man. He remembered each one clearly: their names, personalities, occupations, heights, weights, the length and girth of their cocks and particularly their fetishes and unique sexual desires. There were encounters with field workers, metal workers, carpenters, cooks, florists, merchants, politicians, tax collectors, priests, bankers, neighbours and even a few relatives. Some of the paintings included a depiction of the unique fetish of the individual: ropes, whips, feathers, clamps, phallic carvings, foods, water, mud, paddles and hot wax. Ludi had been painting for the last 30 years and said he had averaged about ten paintings each year, sometimes more if it had been a particularly warm summer. It was almost too much information for Alexeev to comprehend. His life had been a sexual desert compared to Ludi's, or even Tomi's. In fact, Alexeev had never been with anyone before Tomi.

As Ludi finished his discourse on the last painting in the room, Yuri rolled in a cart with all the necessities for supper. He had prepared *pelmeni*[65], roasted turnips and carrots, chicken broth with green onions, white wine and tea spiced with cinnamon, cloves and white pepper. Each course was served in beautiful white porcelain dishes with hand-painted pink and blue ribbons and trimmed in gold. The silverware was equally ornate with rose cluster patterns on each handle. Ludi had impeccable taste.

---

[65] *pelmeni*: Russian dumplings

After they were seated at the end of the table, Yuri served each dish and Ludi opened and poured the wine into crystal wine goblets. The three of them feasted on the bounty, and when they finished Yuri poured the hot tea into the dainty porcelain cups. The cinnamon and white pepper enhanced the warming effects of the tea and was especially appreciated in the cold weather. By the time they had finished supper, the clock in the hall struck ten o'clock.

"Well, I'm sure the two of you would like to get settled in for the night," said Ludi. "Tomi, you know the way. And Lexee, don't forget your bag in the other room. The bed has been made with fresh linens, and if you need anything else just let me know. I'll be in the parlour for a few more hours tonight. I'm finishing one of my paintings."

They thanked Ludi and Yuri for the wonderful meal and Tomi kissed Ludi on the cheek and wished him goodnight. He led Alexeev down the hall and up the stairs to one of the bedrooms. There were a few candles on the dresser that Alexeev lit from the one he had taken from the dining room. The dresser had a brown marble top and it had brass edges and handles. The bed was brass with a white mesh canopy and white blankets with yellow satin trim. Tomi poured some water into the basin next to the dresser, soaked a washcloth and washed his face.

Alexeev could tell Tomi was worn out. "You need to get to bed, Tomi," he said. He helped him off with his coat, then pulled a nightshirt out of the bag and set in on the bed.

They both undressed and Tomi got into the nightshirt. "Don't you have a nightshirt for yourself?" he asked his naked partner.

"No, I'll be fine." Alexeev took a few minutes to clean himself with the washcloth, then started a fire in the fireplace. "I don't want you getting cold tonight." Tomi snuggled underneath the covers. "There, now you should start to feel the warmth of the fire." Alexeev finished stoking the fire, then got into bed with Tomi. He wrapped his arm around him and kissed him on the back of the neck. "I love you, *schast'ye moye*."

"I love you too, Alexeev." He pulled Alexeev's hand up to his lips and kissed it, and within minutes they were both sound asleep in each other's arms.

Chapter 10
Ludi's Proposition

Alexeev woke up early and decided to take a walk around the property. He was particularly interested in taking another look at the collapsed stone wall. After he got dressed, he built up the fire in the bedroom then gave Tomi a kiss on the forehead. He lit a candle in the bedroom and brought it with him so he could wander around the house for a few minutes. When he got downstairs, he didn't find anyone awake yet. The clock in the hall struck six o'clock. He always started to get restless if he slept this long into the morning and usually got up early out of habit. He was curious as to how many more paintings he would find. They were thought-provoking and exhilarating and he was drawn more and more to their sensuality. The paintings stirred a deep and repressed carnal sensation he only allowed to surface when he was with Tomi, but since he had first walked through the hall the evening before, he found it difficult to think of anything else.

His imagination washed over each canvas as he contemplated who these men were and what they might have done in life. He caught himself posing and flexing, mimicking the men in the paintings. He was also intrigued by the many tools, props and toys many of the paintings included. He wondered what it would feel like to be tied down or to have feathers caress his muscles. He envisioned Tomi subduing him in the back of the carriage and tried to think of how it might feel to be paddled, or to have hot wax dripping onto his chest, or to have his arms and legs tied together behind him while Tomi teased him with the crack of a leather whip. Just then, he realised his cock was stiff and his nipples were hard, and his candle had burned down to a nub. The clock struck seven. *Have I really been looking at these paintings for an hour?* He composed himself, straightened his trousers and walked out the back door.

The eastern horizon was just starting to glow but sunrise was still about an hour away. The full moon had not yet set in the west so he could see well enough to take a walk around the property. There had only been a light dusting of snow here over the last few days but the ground was damp with an occasional patch of white on the north sides of hills or rocks or trees. The trees were lifeless except for the few pines that stood twice as tall as the rest, and there was a crisp, fresh scent in the air. The kind of scent that reminded Alexeev of the months he used to spend with his troops in the wilderness when he was on a mission. The stars in the sky were still brilliant and he could see the cloudy mist of stars spraying across the night sky like a blanket.

As he came around to the front of the house, he found the damaged area of the stone wall. He examined it carefully to see if the damage was minimal enough for him to attempt to repair it while he and Tomi stayed with Ludi. Everywhere Alexeev went, he tried to help out as much as possible to show his gratitude and appreciation for the hospitality of his host or hostess. He wanted to make sure his visits were never an imposition so his stays were at least mutually beneficial to both parties. The wall was built very simply. It was less than a half metre wide and the stones were originally stacked to a height of a little more than a metre. It looked as if a carriage may have backed up into the wall to dislodge a small section. He determined it would be easy enough to repair and the job might take the better part of one day, or a few hours a day for three or four days. He finished his evaluation then walked around to the back door again. The sun was ready to rise so he started a fire in the oven.

There were already candles lit in the kitchen so he knew someone was awake. Yuri soon came through the door carrying a basket of food items for breakfast.

"Good morning, Yuri. I started the fire in the oven for you."

"Thank you, sir. I can manage the rest," he said as he set the basket on the kitchen table. "Have you been out for a walk?"

"Yes, it's a nice crisp morning."

"Breakfast will be ready in about an hour, sir. Ludi doesn't usually get up this early, but he told me to make sure breakfast was ready by nine o'clock for you and Mister Tomi." Yuri looked as though his routine had been interrupted by the unexpected guests. But he was always gracious, humble and polite.

Alexeev nodded as he left to go upstairs. "Tomi and I will be down on time for breakfast."

Tomi was already awake but hadn't gotten out of bed yet. He was still tired from the previous few days on the road. His back hurt from the rough roads and he felt a headache coming on. It felt like the start of a rough day.

"Good morning, my love," said Alexeev. "Did you sleep well?"

Tomi sat up a little too fast and it made his head pound more. "Ooo, I have a bit if a headache this morning."

"I'm sorry you're not feeling well," Alexeev sat on the bed next to Tomi and put his arm around him. "I should make you some of that tea your doctor gave you." Tomi nodded and shaded his eyes. The sunlight was just coming through the window. "I want you to take it easy today. Just rest and lie down whenever you need to." Alexeev placed his hands over Tomi's neck and shoulders and started to massage him. "After breakfast, I think I'll give you a thorough massage to get you relaxed."

"That feels wonderful." Tomi was already feeling the tranquil effects of the massage. "Mmm, do we have to go down to breakfast?" He turned his head towards Alexeev and kissed him. "I'd better get dressed."

"I think we left the tea in the carriage. I'll go down and bring it in." Alexeev kissed him once more then went down to fetch the tea. He passed through the kitchen on the way out and let Yuri know he would be making a special tea for Tomi.

Yuri had breakfast ready for Tomi and Alexeev when they came down to the dining room. There was *blini* and fruit compote, fried eggs and *tvorog*. Alexeev fixed Tomi's special tea. Ludi didn't join them for breakfast and Yuri let them know he usually started his day around noon. Tomi was feeling much better after he ate and decided a walk might be beneficial. So, he and Alexeev agreed they would take a walk into town. Starodub had been a prominent municipality for many centuries but was burnt down and levelled in 1609 during the Polish conflict, nearly one hundred years ago. The township had not recovered well over the last century, yet several of the prominent families stayed to re-establish the community. The town could be crossed on foot in a little more than an hour, and the town centre was a little more than halfway across town, so Tomi felt it would be a reasonable bit of exercise for him to accomplish.

Alexeev made sure Tomi was bundled up for the walk since the days were already cold and getting colder as winter approached. Yuri pointed out a footpath through the fields behind Ludi's property that was a shortcut into town. The path was wide enough for two or three to walk comfortably side by side but not wide enough for a horse-drawn carriage. There was a bakery in town (nearly the only business along with a small market), so they decided to bring something back for the mid-day meal. Yuri had given them a basket to take with them for anything they might buy.

Along the way were many purple and blue sage bushes in full bloom, filling the morning air with a wonderful fragrance. They also passed a grove of purple asters that had not yet succumbed to the bitter cold temperatures of winter. As the sun rose higher in the sky the cold air became a little less challenging and since there were no clouds in the sky the sun's rays warmed their faces.

"On our way back, I think I'll gather some sage blooms for Yuri, and maybe some aster blooms for Ludi's table," said Tomi as they passed several sage bushes in full bloom that were hanging over into the path.

After about 30 minutes, they came upon a large stone that looked like a perfect place to sit and rest for a few minutes. It was near a fork in the road with a path leading off to the left going towards the Klyzama river and another leading to the right towards town. Soon a young boy, around the age of nine or ten, came walking up the path from the river carrying a basket full of fish, *gustera*[66], by the looks of it.

"Good morning," Alexeev said to the boy. "It looks like you've had a good catch this morning."

The boy was obviously pleased by the compliment and sat next to Alexeev. "Yes, I'm hoping they will bring a good price at the market."

Tomi leaned over to Alexeev and whispered in his ear, "Ask if he'll sell you half of his catch. I think Ludi would like that…let's make sure he gets a generous amount for his efforts." Tomi handed Alexeev several coins.

"I am Lexee, and this is my friend Tomi," said Alexeev as he reached out and shook the boy's hand.

"I am Maksim," said the boy as he set down his catch.

"So how much do you usually get for your fish in the market?" Alexeev asked.

"Mister Volkov at the fish market usually gives me ten kopeks for each fish," he said proudly.

"And how many did you catch this morning?"

The boy smiled wide and said, "Nineteen today, that means he will give me almost two rubles."

---

[66] *gustera*: White Bream (fish)

Tomi whispered again to Alexeev, "You have two rubles. Ask him for six of the largest fish he has, and we'll give him four rubles." He took more coins from his other pocket and discretely handed them to Alexeev.

Alexeev felt a tear coming on at the thought of Tomi's generosity. He bent down and started looking at each fish. "I know this might be an inconvenience for Mister Volkov, but could I buy six of your fish?"

"Well…only if I can get the same price for them," the boy answered.

"Oh certainly, I wouldn't want it any other way. But I also need to ask a favour," he said as he continued to look over the fish. "Do you know Ludmil Markov who lives at the end of the path?"

"Yes, he's the painter," said the boy.

"I will give you four rubles for six of your largest *gustera* if you will deliver them to his servant, Yuri," Alexeev held out the coins.

The boy's eyes opened wide in disbelief. He counted them out, then he smiled and quickly started sorting out the six largest fish. "I will take them to Yuri right away." He had a cloth strip and wrapped it around the six fish.

Alexeev stood up and counted out 20 more kopeks to the boy. "It was nice doing business with you, young man. Now be sure to tell Yuri the fish are already paid for."

The boy flung his arms around Alexeev's waist. "Thank you, sir." Then he hugged Tomi as well. "*Bol'shoye spasibo*[67]," he said as he ran down the path towards Ludi's house. "*Spasibo, spasibo!*[68]"

Alexeev sat back down next to Tomi and held his hand, "That was a good thing you did. That little boy will never forget your kindness." He gave Tomi a kiss on the cheek. "Are you rested enough to continue?" Tomi nodded. So, the two started up again on their walk towards town.

It wasn't long before the path met the main road into town, and then just a few minutes later they saw a few buildings along the roadway and the church just past the house that was used as a town hall. The first building was a *kabak,* so they stopped in to quench their thirsts. The local drink was *Medovuhka*[69]*,* so they both decided to have a mug. The tavern keeper was Igor Ivanov. He was a kindly, very large man with a shiny bald head, rosy cheeks and a half-rim of

[67] *Bol'shoye spasibo*: Thank you very much

[68] *Spasibo, spasibo!*: Thank you, thank you!

[69] *Medovuhka*: A Slavic honey-based alcoholic beverage

white hair on the back of his head that crested from ear to ear. He was not the typical *tselovalnik*[70] who cared for nothing but the profit he could make off his patrons, but was cheerful, friendly, and made it a point to be helpful to visitors and strangers.

"Good morning, gentlemen. I am Igor, your host. What brings you to our quaint little town?" He set the two mugs of *Medovuhka* on the table.

Tomi set a few coins on the table and pulled one of the mugs towards him. "We're visiting Ludmil Markov for a few days."

"Wonderful! It's been nice weather for travelling lately. Just a bit of snow…I hope you have a pleasant stay while you're here. Let me know if there's anything I can do for you." He wiped the end of the table with a rag he had in his pocket and set down a basket of biscuits.

"Thank you," they both said as Igor walked away.

"I saw the *pekarnya* [71] next door, Tomi. Did you want to pick up something else for dinner?"

Tomi took a bite from one of the biscuits. "Well, I don't think I want to get biscuits." The tavern-style biscuits tasted like they had been left out for several days, or perhaps they had been purchased from the bakery in early summer. They were hard, dry and rather tasteless.

Alexeev took a bite of the same biscuit. "I agree…but don't say anything to Igor," he whispered as he leaned in towards Tomi. He was tempted to lean in a little farther to kiss Tomi but wasn't sure how the locals might react. So, they finished their drinks and walked next door, nodding to Igor as they left.

"Umm, the smell of fresh-baked bread on a cold day is one of the most wonderful smells there is," said Tomi as he took a deep whiff of the aroma coming from the bakery.

"*Guten Morgen*[72]*…dobroye utro*," said the baker with an obvious German accent. "I am *Herr*[73] Cohen. How can I help you this morning?"

Tomi immediately noticed a large loaf of *challah*[74] bread. "How much is the *challah* loaf?" he asked.

---

70 *tselovalnik*: Literally, kisser. A tavern keeper, who was allegiant to the tsar.

71 *Pekarnya*: Bake shop, bakery

72 *Guten Morgen* (German): Good morning.

73 *Herr* (German): Mister

74 *challah*: A traditional Jewish braided bread

"50 kopeks. We also have some fresh *rugalach*[75]." *Herr* Cohen handed them each a pastry to try.

"I've never heard of *rugalach*," said Alexeev.

"It's a traditional Jewish pastry to celebrate the eight-day festival of Chanukah," said Tomi. "My mother was Jewish, and this was one of my favourites…almost as good as Sveta's cookies." He took a bite of the pastry. "Umm, mine is filled with apricot."

"And mine is cherry," said Alexeev.

"We'll take the *challah* loaf and ten of each of the *rugalach*."

"*Sehr gut*[76]," said *Herr* Cohen as he put the *challah* loaf and the 20 pastries in Alexeev's basket. Then Alexeev covered them with a cloth that was folded at the bottom of the basket. "20 pastries and a challah loaf…that will be 150 kopeks."

Tomi paid the baker and shook his hand. "*Fröhliches Hanukkah, grüss gott*[77]."

"*Zdravstvuyte*[78]," said Alexeev.

They walked out with their basket full of delectable treasures and decided it was time to walk back. Neither of them was too sure of the time, but they wanted to get back before the afternoon meal. On the way back, Tomi stopped at the sage bushes. Alexeev handed him the knife from his pocket so he could cut a few fresh branches. Tomi selected seven of the best-looking branches and laid them on top of the cloth in the basket. Then Alexeev stepped off the path and cut several stems of the asters and set them on top of the sage.

As they got closer to the house they could smell the aroma of fish baking so they knew it was about time for lunch. When Tomi opened the back door, Yuri promptly thanked him for the beautiful fish and directed them to the dining room. Alexeev took the asters, stood them up in a vase and poured in some water, then he found a cord and tied the sage branches together so they could be hung to dry. He left the *challah* loaf and *rugalach* with Yuri and brought the vase into the dining room and set it on the table.

Ludi had just finished setting the table and was opening a bottle of white wine. "Good afternoon, gentlemen. Did you have a nice walk?"

---

[75] *rugalach*: A Jewish crescent-shaped pastry

[76] *Sehr gut* (German): Very good

[77] *Fröhliches Hanukkah, grüss gott* (German): Happy Hanukkah, good day

[78] *Zdravstvuyte*: Hello or good day

Tomi walked over to Ludi and kissed him on the cheek. "Yes, we did, Ludi. It is such a beautiful day."

"And little Maksim brought the fish you bought from him. That was a wonderful surprise."

"Little Maksim…is he Maksim Kozlov's boy?" asked Tomi.

Ludi's face turned serious. "Yes, yes. But unfortunately, Mister Kozlov passed away last year from influenza. His poor widow is having a tough time making ends meet, that's why the boy sells nearly everything he catches."

"I'm so sorry to hear that, he was always so nice to me. So, what happened to his business? Wasn't he a carpenter?"

"Yes, he was a pretty good one too," said Ludi. "I heard his brother came and took all his tools after the funeral. They never did get along. The family claimed Maksim's wife coerced him into marriage. Now they won't even acknowledge her or little Maksim as part of the family."

Tomi shook his head. "That's a shame. No one deserves to be forgotten and neglected like that, and family should never ostracise one another."

"No more depressing talk," said Ludi.

"Tell Ludi what else you bought in town," urged Alexeev.

"Oh Ludi, have you ever had *challah* bread and *rugalach*?" asked Tomi.

"Ah, you must have gone to *Herr* Cohen's *bäckerei*[79]. I don't think I've tried that…*challah*? But we go there regularly for many of his breads and pastries." Then he whispered to Tomi, "You must have remembered that Yuri doesn't like to bake bread." They both laughed. Then Ludi motioned to Alexeev and Tomi to sit down at the table. "Let me pour you some wine while Yuri finishes preparing the meal." Then they lifted their glasses and Ludi proposed a toast, "*Za lyubov' i schast'ye!*[80]"

Tomi and Alexeev joined in unison, "*Za lyubov' i schast'ye!*" And they all drank together. Yuri brought the baked fish and *challah* loaf to the table, along with sautéed mushrooms with carrots and pickled onions. As they ate the delicious meal, the conversation led to Ludi's artwork and Alexeev expressed his interest in the themes of Ludi's work.

---

[79] *Bäckerei* (German): Bakery, bake shop

[80] *Za lyubov' i schast'ye!*: For love and happiness!

"I must admit, Ludi, I have never seen any paintings quite like yours. I've enjoyed looking at each of them. I have been captivated by their beauty. They are so expressive, so realistic, so..."

"*Chuvstvennyy*[81]?" asked Ludi. "Not many people, especially men, would admit to looking at my paintings and enjoying the experience. In fact, most men pretend like they don't even see them. They walk down my hall like they are wearing horse's blinders. Well, except for the men who are in them, of course. But even some of them later wish I had not painted their portraits."

"Ludi has been painting for many years, and has known many, many men," said Tomi with a wry smile.

"Now, Tomi, you make me sound like an old lecher. But I do appreciate the male form...and Tomi is right, I have had many, many, many men come through my doors over the years."

"So, why have you never painted Tomi?" asked Alexeev.

"He has never let me," he answered matter-of-factly. "I've been begging him for years, haven't I, *moy robkiy drug*[82]." Ludi nudged Tomi on the shoulder.

Tomi shook his head a little sheepishly. "I'm not like those men in your paintings. They are all strong, handsome, beautiful men."

Alexeev shook his finger at Tomi. "Now, I don't want to hear things like that from you. You are the most handsome man I've ever known, *robkiy.*" Alexeev smiled and winked at him.

Ludi looked at Tomi with a serious look on his face. "I want you to know I think the two of you make a wonderful, handsome couple. I think you were made for each other and I think you are both beautiful people."

Alexeev mustered up his courage. "Ludi, would you consider painting a portrait of Tomi and me?"

Tomi was taken by surprise. "Oh, no Alexeev, I wasn't trying to—"

"Wait, wait, Tomi," said Ludi. "Before you object, I want to assure you I did not put him up to this. Hmm, I have just finished a painting and I don't have anything planned."

"But I can't pose naked, Ludi," said Tomi with a hint of terror in his voice.

"Don't be silly, Tomi. Not all my paintings are nudes." Ludi thought for a few moments. "Tomi, would you let me talk to Lexee alone for a few minutes? I want to negotiate."

---

[81] *Chuvstvennyy*: Sensual, erotic

[82] M*oy robkiy drug*: My timid friend

"I don't like not being in on this negotiation, but I guess I'll let the two of you talk it over. But Alexeev, I won't pose nude!" Tomi stood up in a huff and walked towards the kitchen, then turned back around. "I'll bring out the *rugalach* and some tea in a few minutes."

Alexeev smiled and chuckled to himself at Tomi's bashfulness, and at his hint of stubbornness and righteous indignation.

Ludi took Alexeev by the arm. "Let's go into the parlour."

Alexeev talked as they walked down the hallway, "I don't have money to pay for the portrait, but I wanted to know if you would let me work for your pay? I noticed the wall in the front of your yard has collapsed. I could repair it and I could chop wood or make any other repairs you need…anything you need done, I can do."

"Yes, yes, yes, but the work is not important," he answered. "Tomi is a friend and I would have painted his portrait anytime he asked for free." He thought for a few more minutes. "I have been wanting to do a painting of wrestlers. What would you think about posing for a portrait like that…along with a formal portrait of the two of you, of course."

"Oh wait. Tomi would never agree to pose as a wrestler—"

"No, that's not what I meant," Ludi continued. "There is a local man I know. He is about your size and build, but he has different features that would complement your muscular stature. He has told me he would like to be painted as well, but I haven't been able to find a wrestling partner for him."

"So, you would do two portraits?"

"Yes, but I would finish the formal portrait first so you could take it with you. I will do sketches for the wrestling composition. I should be able to finish your portrait and the sketches in about two weeks." Ludi put his hands on Alexeev's shoulders then turned Alexeev's head to the side. "Would you mind taking off your shirt. I'd like to see what I have to work with."

Alexeev looked down the hallway to make sure Tomi was not yet coming, then he closed the parlour door and removed his shirt.

"Hmm, you have quite a bit of hair, but it looks good with your frame." He turned Alexeev around. "Good, not much hair on the back. What about below the waist?" Reluctantly, Alexeev loosened his belt and pulled down his trousers, exposing his cock and balls. "Very nice. I like that you trim your hair. That will help with perspective." He pulled Alexeev's trousers back up. "You can get dressed, I don't want to have to explain this to Tomi." Alexeev quickly put his shirt back on and tucked it into his trousers. "Have you wrestled before?"

"Of course. I used to wrestle with my troops all the time. It was a good way to get their aggression out so they wouldn't fight with the civilians."

"Have you ever wrestled naked?"

Alexeev paused for a moment. "No, but I've seen your paintings and I like what I've seen."

"Good. Now, I'll leave it up to you to tell Tomi what you want him to know. We'll start the formal portrait tomorrow." They shook hands. "One more thing, after I finish the formal portrait, I want you to stop shaving. I want you to have a rough look about you for the wrestling sketches."

"I can do that, and I'd rather keep this a secret from Tomi for now. I'll let him know later."

"The young man's name is Timur. I'll find a way to get Tomi out of the house for a few days while I get the sketches I need for your painting, but we'll finish Tomi's painting first. I know he'll want to take the painting with him, so he'll have to stay at least a week after its completed to let it dry enough to be safe for transporting."

Tomi soon came into the parlour with the tea and pastries, and the three of them discussed the details of the formal portrait. "Ludi and I have come to an agreement about payment for the painting. I am going to repair his wall and chop wood for him for the next two weeks while he paints."

Ludi explained the sittings for the painting would be one hour at a time, three times each day for the first four or five days. After that, he would be secluded most of the remaining days while he finished the portrait. Tomi agreed they could take the time to stay two weeks. He thought it would be a good time for him to catch up on his reading. He had purchased a copy of *The Lay of the Twelve Dreams of Emperor Shakhaishi*[83] while he was in Moscow, and he hadn't yet had the opportunity to read it.

The three finished their pastries and tea. They were all excited about the painting. Tomi also saw this opportunity as a way of solidifying his relationship with Alexeev and he was very proud of him for taking the initiative to arrange for payment. He admired Alexeev and loved him dearly. Later that evening, he

---

[83] *The Lay of the Twelve Dreams of Emperor Shakhaishi*: 14th century Russian literature of unknown source, possibly Tibetan in origin

tried to get him to tell him what he and Ludi had discussed, but Alexeev simply answered, "Ludi and I agreed on a reasonable payment for the painting."

Hmm, there is something he is not telling me! Tomi thought, but decided not to press the issue any further.

Chapter 11
Wrestling Conscience

The next morning, Alexeev got up early again so he could start to prepare for his work on the stone wall. After he built up the fire in the bedroom fireplace, he went out to the stables. He found a pair of gloves to protect his hands and a shovel to help free some of the stones from the ground. Most of the stones looked like they weighed between 20 and 40 kilograms, with about two-thirds of them at 30 kilograms or more. He counted at least 25 of the largest stones, so he figured the job could take three or four mornings if he could devote two hours each day, and if the weather was favourable.

When he examined the part of the wall that was still standing, it appeared most of the smaller stones were used to fill in the centre and interior of the wall, with the larger stones on the outside as support and the flatter stones on the top. His first task would be to sort the stones and identify which ones had flatter sides for the outer sides and top of the wall. After a few hours he had half of the stones arranged by size and shape. Once he saw the sun start to come up over the horizon, he decided to stop for a while and make some tea.

He lit a fire in the oven, filled the water pot and set it on the stovetop. Yuri and Ludi were not yet awake so he went up to see if Tomi was ready to get up. The coals were still glowing in the fireplace and Tomi was just getting out of bed.

"Good morning, Tomi. Did you sleep well?"

Tomi yawned and stretched his arms over his head. "Very well, my love." He stood up and kissed Alexeev on the cheek, then went over to the basin to rinse his mouth. "You got up early. What have you been doing?"

"I've been repairing the wall. You know…the section in front that had collapsed." Alexeev joined Tomi at the basin and washed his hands. "I think it will take about three, maybe four mornings like this, for me to restack the stones.

I think I saw a few more areas of the wall that could use some repair as well. But it's good work and I like to be kept busy."

"I hope Ludi appreciates what you are doing for him. Those stones must be very heavy."

Alexeev got behind Tomi and picked him up. "Well, I think if I can lift you this easily, the stones shouldn't be any problem." He set Tomi back down, took off his shirt and flexed his biceps. "What do you think? Are these strong enough?"

Tomi wrapped his hands around Alexeev's biceps and squeezed as hard as he could. "Arrr, you're plenty strong for me!" He kissed Alexeev's chest and gave him a hug. "I love you…"

"I love you too." Then he kissed the top of Tomi's head. "I put water on the stove for tea. Are you ready to come downstairs?"

"Yes, I'll be down in just a few minutes. I need to put on my shoes."

"Do you want your special tea? I saw Ludi also has a tea with cinnamon. Would you like to try that?"

"That sounds good, I like cinnamon. I'll get some of my own tea later if I need it." He finished putting on his shoes, then went downstairs for breakfast.

For the next four days, Alexeev worked on the wall each morning, then he and Tomi would eat breakfast with Yuri, and after breakfast they would walk to town. Each day they would wait for little Maksim by the sitting rock where the path forked off to the river, and each day Tomi would have Alexeev negotiate for several of whatever he had in his basket at a ridiculously high price. He always had at least a dozen fish, one day he had a rabbit, another day he had six duck eggs and the last day he had four pheasants. Yuri was pleased to get the fish, rabbit and eggs, but had never cooked pheasant, so Tomi had the opportunity to make his braised pheasant and sauerkraut (his mother's recipe).

Ludi got up around noon each day, so the couple would sit for the painting for two or three hours, one hour at a time between one and six o'clock each afternoon. They wanted to be able to display the portrait in Tomi's front parlour, so Ludi let them borrow a few formal outfits for the sitting. Alexeev's costume was a green velvet robe, nearly ankle length, with patterns of gold crescent moons and stars, and a dark green sash around the waist. The robe was open at the top, revealing a darker green silk collared shirt open down to about mid torso. Tomi's costume was a burgundy satin shirt with horizontal pleats across the chest, and a dark red satin pantaloon at mid-calf length. Tomi wore dark brown highly polished boots while Alexeev's boots were grey deerskin.

They would usually break around two o'clock for tea and biscuits, and then again around four to stretch and walk around for a bit before the third sitting. By the end of the fourth day, Ludi was far enough along he no longer needed the boys, except for an occasional brief examination by Ludi to study their eyes, or hair, or skin complexion. Ludi was especially impressed by the colour of Alexeev's eyes and made sure he viewed them in full daylight.

He secluded himself in the parlour most of the afternoons and painted well into the night. Yuri said this was his normal routine whenever he did a painting, and not to be concerned. But Tomi was tempted to knock on the parlour door. But Ludi was very sensitive when it came to his painting habits and was vehemently opposed to anyone viewing his artwork before its completion. Alexeev tried to keep Tomi busy. He brought him along when he went to the woodshed each afternoon to chop wood. He asked him philosophical questions, and Tomi talked on and on about his views, opinions, values and beliefs. He was well-read and knew many of the ancient scholars' and philosophers' views on spiritual and social matters. Alexeev loved to hear Tomi talk about current events, political leaders, religious morays and cultural practices.

Finally, on the fifth day, Ludi woke up early and joined Tomi and Alexeev for breakfast. The painting was progressing nicely and Ludi decided to take a break from painting for a day. He wanted to go into town because today many of the town residents would be meeting to discuss their annual celebration for the New Year's holiday. Each year, they met as a town family to celebrated together, and most of them would celebrate in town at some point during the seven-day festivities. There would be plays, concerts, sing-alongs, children's games, bonfires, dancing and of course, traditional foods of every kind.

Tomi had put together a few children's plays in his own town in previous years, and since he wasn't able to be home for the holidays this year, Ludi thought it might be a good way to keep him busy while the sketches were being finished. Since Alexeev didn't want Tomi to know about the wrestling painting, he convinced Tomi to go with Ludi into town while he stayed behind to work around the house. Yuri decided to ride along with them in the carriage so he could visit his sister on the other side of town while they scoped out the holiday activities.

Ludi also gave Yuri a note to deliver to Timur privately, inviting him over for the day, so Yuri would deliver the message before continuing to visit his sister. Timur was the only son of the baker. He was a little taller than Alexeev, had black hair, broad shoulders and a muscular build like Alexeev's, but Timur was about 15 years younger.

It was a few hours later when Timur showed up. Alexeev met him at the back door and invited him in for a cup of tea so they could talk and get to know each other. Timur was shy at first, but soon warmed up to Alexeev and felt comfortable with him. He shared that he and his father had lived alone since he was a baby. His mother died giving birth to him so he never knew her, and his father never remarried. His father's sister, Aunt Sarra, lived in town with her husband, so until he was five or six, he stayed with her during the day, and his father brought him home at the end of each workday. When he was six, he started school, and at the end of his schooling he began working mornings with his father in the bakery, and as an apprentice with a mason most afternoons. He was always a very active child and teenager. He played all the sports including *lapta*[84], his favourite team sport, and wrestling, his favourite contact sport.

They had a few common interests and Alexeev shared how he used to wrestle with his troops. He also shared how he lost both of his parents when he was very young and raised by his aunt and uncle. The two men felt comfortable talking about the intimate details of their lives, and how their experiences helped to shape who they had become. Alexeev felt like he could talk and listen to Timur all day long and still not exhaust the conversation or get bored with the content. He thought what it might be like with Timur and Tomi together, and he imagined the activities they could engage in as a sexual threesome. These thoughts were new to Alexeev, but the paintings in Ludi's home were challenging his imagination and expanding his desires. But he was afraid to tell Tomi. He loved Tomi, but he was also very attracted to Timur.

While they talked, Alexeev made *buterbrody* and portioned out some leftover rabbit from the day before and vegetables from last night's dinner. He also brought out a bottle of spiced vodka Ludi had given him. Alexeev mentioned his fondness of spiced vodkas to Ludi, and there was a full bottle he had been saving. Ludi had more of a taste for wines, beers and ales than for vodka, so he had made a gift of the bottle to Alexeev. Timur welcomed a drink, since the

---

[84] *lapta*: A traditional Russian bat and ball game

morning air was still a bit chilly. There was a fire in the kitchen stove but the rest of the house was cold. They both had a cup of vodka and drank to each other's good health.

After they finished their meal, they decided it was time to get down to the business at hand. The reason Ludi wanted the two of them to get together was so they could become comfortable with each other without feeling intimidated by each other's bodies, and so they could wrestle in private to get used to wrestling naked. As for Alexeev, he was very comfortable with his body and wouldn't mind walking around the house naked all day long, but only if it was acceptable to Tomi and anyone else who happened to visit.

Ludi had a large room in the attic that he used as a playroom for his sexual escapades. The floor was covered in several layers of thick rugs sewn together to create a padding over the hardwood floors. There was also a fireplace at each end, and the only windows were shoulder-high, so no one could see what was happening inside from the ground. On the walls were pegs with all sorts of interesting toys hanging, ready and available for anyone who wanted to live dangerously. There were chains, whips, leather harnesses, masks, spiked collars, clubs, paddles, ropes and many more toys Alexeev couldn't imagine their purpose or the pleasures they might cause. Once the men got upstairs, they built fires in the two fireplaces and lit the candles on the wall sconces. Soon the room was warm and they both stripped down to their undershorts.

"How about we arm wrestle first, just to get a little warmed up," said Alexeev.

"Sounds good to me."

They both stretched their arms, twisted back and forth at their waists, stretched their knees and legs. As they stretched, they couldn't help checking each other out, flexing a bit and visually making comparisons of the size of the other's biceps, chest, and legs. Then they both laid down on the floor facing each other. Alexeev held up his right hand with his elbow firmly on the floor, then Timur did the same. They clasped hands and Alexeev counted down, "three…two…one…go!"

They both flexed their biceps, forearms, wrists, and shoulders. At first, they seemed to be evenly matched. Their arm size was about the same and so was their overall musculature, but while Timur grimaced and strained, Alexeev remained fairly calm and steadfast. He waited until his opponent had spent the greater part of his strength, then he released the power he was holding back and slowly forced Timur's arm to the floor.

Immediately, Timur raised up his left hand as a second challenge, and without hesitation, Alexeev clasped Timur's left hand. This time Timur counted down, "three…two…one…go!" And with the same grimaces and strain from Timur, and the same calm restraint on Alexeev's part, the result was the same. Although this time, Alexeev did not wait so long. Timur's arm was forced slowly to the floor a second time.

Timur was a strong man though. His muscles were well defined and the veins on his arms and neck were pumped. He wasn't used to losing. He had very little hair on his chest unlike Alexeev, who had a nice covering of hair from the top of his chest to the base of his stomach. They both stood up, Timur's nipples were hard and he flexed his arms, then his chest, then he stretched his arms above his head as a signal to Alexeev he would not accept defeat so easily. Alexeev returned the posturing with arm and chest flexing of his own.

"Ludi left some oil for us to use. He said we could use it to enhance the wrestling. The idea is if your opponent is difficult to grasp the match would take longer." He poured out some of the oil onto his hands and applied it to his chest and arms.

"I've never used anything like that before," Timur sounded a little apprehensive.

"Don't worry, I learned about this when I was down in Armenia and Curdistan. It's just olive oil," assured Alexeev. "They use this when they wrestle down there. It makes the match a little more challenging. Come over here and I'll help you put it on, then you can put some on my back."

Alexeev poured a generous amount into his hands, then Timur rubbed it on his chest, arms and legs.

"Here, let me help you." He began rubbing it around on Timur's back and shoulders. Timur soon followed the example by rubbing some on Alexeev's back. They both removed their shorts and rubbed oil on each other's buttocks and cocks. Both of their bodies glistened with oil. The attic now felt rather warm, partly from the fires but the oil also had a mixture of pepper oil to warm the body (an addition of Ludi's meant to increase pleasure). They were both feeling the heat and starting to sweat. Alexeev set the bottle down then returned to Timur. He raised both hands above his head towards Timur, who raised his hands to interlock them with Alexeev's. Now the match had begun.

At first, they slipped from each other's grasp a few times, then tried to wrap arms around one another's waist, or chest, or legs but the oil made prolonged contact difficult. Each one could slip out of the other's grip without much difficulty. They wrestled for a while, then applied more oil, and occasionally they would throw another log on the fire. The heat felt good and both of them could feel the sexual tension pouring out through the sweat. The match went on for more than two hours without any rest except to apply more oil or to build up the fire.

Then as Alexeev was applying more oil, Timur rushed onto him from behind and tackle him to the floor. He laid on Alexeev's back and wrapped his arms underneath Alexeev's arms and interlocked his hands behind Alexeev's neck. Alexeev struggled, but his face was forced onto the floor and his arms were being pulled back so he couldn't lift himself off the floor. Then he felt Timur's hard cock pressing against his buttocks and making its way near his ass hole. With all the strength in his chest, he pulled his arms forward to break Timur's grip, then he wrapped one of his arms around Timur's neck and flipped him on his back onto the floor. With the other hand, he held Timur's forearm to the ground. Timur's bicep was flexed so he could see the peak bulging but it had nowhere to go. Both of their cocks were hard and throbbing now as they wrestled face to face. Alexeev grabbed Timur's other arm and flattened it to the ground as well. He smiled as their two cocks rubbed against each other, then as if drawn together by instinct, they kissed.

Passionately and violently, their tongues lashed out at each other. Alexeev let go of Timur's arms and grabbed Timur's hair and held his head to the ground. Timur wrapped his arms around Alexeev's back then wrapped his legs around Alexeev's waist and locked his ankles together. In one motion, Alexeev's cock plunged into Timur's hole as if it knew exactly where and how to insert itself. Alexeev pumped in and out, in and out, in and out, in and out, his ball sac slapping against Timur's buttocks each time. Then Alexeev rolled over onto his back and Timur sat on Alexeev's cock and pushed himself up and down with his legs. His cock, still hard and thick, slapped up and down on Alexeev's stomach.

Timur raised his arms and folded his hands behind his head and flexed his biceps and chest. Alexeev reached up and tried to grab Timur's nipples but the oil made them too slippery. Then he reached his hand behind Timur's neck and pulled his face down to his and they kissed. He sucked the sweat and oil off his face, then licked his neck and shoulders, then licked his chest and sucked Timur's nipples, first the right one then the left. Then Timur held Alexeev's arms down and kissed him, licking the sweat from Alexeev's chin, then neck, then shoulder. He kissed and sucked Alexeev's nipples and grabbed his pectorals hard so the nipples protruded more. His tongue flicked at the one on the left and his teeth gently bit the erect nipple.

Alexeev cried out, "*ya sobirayus' vzorvat'sya vnutri tebya*![85]" Then with a few strong thrusts into Timur's hole, his cum was released.

Timur gasped, then reached down to his own cock and started stroking it fiercely. He stood up over Alexeev's face. Alexeev reached up around Timur's waist and sucked his balls. Timur kept stroking his cock with one hand and pinching and twisting his nipple with the other. He convulsed as his muscles tightened and flexed. Then he groaned and lurched forwards as his cum spewed out onto Alexeev's face. The hot, milky liquid dripped and ran down the side of Alexeev's unshaven face as he continued to suck Timur's balls. Then Timur dropped to his knees and wrapped his arms around Alexeev, and they embraced. They kissed intensely as if their mouths were starved for attention. The excitement of the moment was overpowering their common sense and taking control over Alexeev's sense of loyalty and devotion to Tomi.

But suddenly, he stopped. He looked into Timur's deep blue eyes and felt the shame of his actions. He saw Tomi's brown eyes looking back at him. He felt the condemnation of what he had done. Timur saw the pain on Alexeev's face and immediately knew there was guilt behind those green eyes. A burden was building on Alexeev's heart. With tears in his eyes, Alexeev stood up and found a towel. He began wiping off the cum, sweat and oil.

"What have I done? What have I done?" he repeated over and over again.

Timur ran over to him. "It's not your fault…it just happened—"

Alexeev interrupted him, "No, it should not have happened. Ever! I love Tomi. I am in love with him. I wanted to pledge my life to him but now I have betrayed him." He picked up his clothes and ran out of the room and down the stairs.

Timur quickly wiped himself off and got dressed then went downstairs. He had never had a relationship with a man before. He played around with some of the boys from school and there was a customer who came by the bakery every now and then, and they sometimes escaped to the back of the building and sucked

---

[85] *Ya sobirayus' vzorvat'sya vnutri tebya*!: I'm going to explode inside you!

each other's cocks. But Alexeev seemed different. There was a passion and sincerity behind his actions. He wasn't just trying to relieve his carnal needs. It almost seemed Alexeev thought he was making love to Tomi, and Timur was envious of that kind of relationship. He wondered if he would ever find a man like that, someone to love and to make love to. He wondered if the passion and physical ecstasy he felt with Alexeev could ever be duplicated with anyone else. It was an erotic rush and a sexual stimulant to wrestle, dominate, abuse, and conquer or be conquered, but there was also a tenderness exuding from Alexeev. Timur felt it from the moment they met. He cared about how his partner felt, he wanted to make sure the pleasure he felt was reflected onto the one he was with so the pleasure he felt was exceeded by the pleasure he gave in return.

When Timur got downstairs, Alexeev was still getting himself dressed. He was distressed, shaking his head and making vile accusations against himself in self-condemnation.

"Alexeev, it's not your fault and Tomi doesn't need to know. I won't ever tell anyone," he pleaded as he reached out to Alexeev.

"No, you don't understand. I can't lie to him. Our relationship can't start out like this." He fumbled with his shirt, then threw it to the floor. "Please, just get cleaned up and leave."

Timur took Alexeev by the shoulders and shook him. "You're being foolish. Tomi doesn't need to know what happened here. He is just an old fool anyway. I don't know why you are with him—"

"Don't you ever say anything like that about my Tomi!" Alexeev suddenly smacked Timur's arms off him.

Without thinking, Timur drew back and punched Alexeev in the gut, then with the other fist gave him an uppercut to the chin and immediately threw a blow to the eye. Alexeev fell back and nearly lost his balance but returned the blows with a side swipe to Timur's cheek and a blow with the other fist flat onto Timur's nose. Timur immediately buckled and held both hands to his nose. Blood gushed from both nostrils and the result was undoubtedly a broken nose. Alexeev grabbed his shirt from the floor and quickly put it up to Timur's nose to catch the blood.

"I'm sorry, I'm sorry," he said as he rushed him to the kitchen's water basin. "It was an instinctive reaction." As Timur washed the blood from his face, Alexeev removed Timur's blood-spattered shirt and rinsed it in fresh water, then took a clean cloth and started tending to Timur's wounds. "I'll rekindle the fire in the oven and heat some water so you can bathe."

Timur nodded and continued to hold Alexeev's shirt to his nose. It took almost an hour for enough water to get hot enough for bathing, so in the meantime, Alexeev washed out Timur's shirt and gave him a fresh shirt of his own to wear home. Timur's nose stopped bleeding, but after the blood was wiped away, there was a dark red bruise running across his nose from eye to eye, and the nose was very tender to the touch. Alexeev had a cut lip from the uppercut and the side of his face was a little pink, but other than that, he was relatively unscathed.

There was a large bathtub in back of the kitchen, so Alexeev filled the tub with the water as it heated. Once there was enough water for Timur to bathe he got undressed and sat in the tub. Alexeev brought him a washcloth and soap to wash off the oil. Timur was feeling better about the whole experience and he understood why Alexeev needed to be with Tomi, even though he hadn't experienced that kind of love himself. But he hoped one day he would find a special person to be with, someone he could commit his life to.

When Timur finished bathing and while he dried himself off, Alexeev took his turn in the tub and washed off the oil, sweat and blood. He wondered how he would tell Tomi what happened. How could he tell Tomi he was unfaithful and had given his cock to another man? How could he be so foolish? And for just a few minutes of pleasure. He grieved at the possibility he may have ruined his life with Tomi and jeopardised their future together.

Timur finished drying himself and put his shorts and trousers back on, then he put on Alexeev's clean shirt and finished with his stockings and boots. Alexeev got out of the tub dried off, then wrapped the towel around his waist and walked over to Timur.

Alexeev held out his hand. "I am sorry for the way things turned out. Please forgive me for my indiscretion and foolishness."

Timur shook his hand. "I wish the best for you and Tomi. I only hope someday I find someone as good as you to spend the rest of my life with. Tomi is a lucky man." With that, Timur put on his coat and left. Alexeev bowed his head, knowing the next few hours would probably be the hardest he had ever faced before. He went into the parlour and laid down on the settee to rest and think.

Chapter 12

Confrontation and Release

Yuri arrived home around five o'clock in the afternoon. He had walked from town so Ludi and Tomi could stay for the festivities planning mccting, which was taking longer than expected. Alexeev had fallen asleep in the parlour, so Yuri didn't wake him but began to prepare dinner. He brought home a few loaves of black bread from the bakery and picked up a few vegetables from the town market. There was leftover pheasant from the night before, so he decided to use it in a stew, also adding the vegetables he bought along with leftover cabbage. He also brought out some pickled onions and a jar of peach preserves. Before long, the kitchen was warm from the stove, and the smells of dinner soon found their way down the hall to the parlour.

Alexeev was still a bit sore from wrestling but managed to get himself up. He went up to his bedroom to see if there were any noticeable marks on his face and to see if there were any other telltale signs of his encounter with Timur. He didn't want to have to explain the incident to Tomi right away, or to Ludi, for that matter. His long-sleeved shirt would cover the few red marks on his arms and chest, but the cut on his lip would not be easily explained. There was a mark on the side of his neck he could cover by buttoning his collar. But there was also a light red patch on his right cheek, undoubtedly a result of Timur slugging him. Maybe Tomi wouldn't notice, and even if he did notice and ask about it, he could always say it happened when he was chopping wood. *No, I haven't ever lied to Tomi and I'm not going to start now*, he thought. *I'll have to tell him everything or I'll never be able to live with myself.* He unbuttoned his collar and went downstairs to the kitchen.

Yuri was standing at the stove stirring the stew and adding in a few spices. "I saw Timur when I was at the bakery." He paused as if he was waiting for a response, or perhaps a confession. But Alexeev sat down at the table without making any comment. Yuri turned towards him, folded his arms and tilted his head. "He said you're a very good wrestler…" Then he leaned in towards Alexeev to complete his comment, "…and not a bad fuck." Alexeev dropped his head down, not knowing what to say. "Don't worry, I haven't said anything to Tomi or Ludi. I saw them coming out of the bakery though…that was before I went in."

"Don't keep secrets on my account. I didn't stop myself when I should have and I'm not proud of what happened."

"But Timur is altogether another matter. He didn't say anything to me about whether he told Ludi or Tomi, and I don't know if he has the experience or the maturity to be discrete with anyone else." Yuri was worried Timur might brag to his friends about what he did. Then the whole town would know. "Not that these kinds of things haven't gone on in this house before, but Ludi has never been one to advertise his business…his colourful activities…to the town's people."

"I'll talk to Ludi tonight," said Alexeev. "But I don't think Timur will say anything. I think he wants this painting as much as he wanted to wrestle…and as much as he wanted me. And if he does say anything, he risks being ostracised as much as Ludi."

"Tomi and Ludi were going to stay for the rest of the town meeting but they should be back around seven, I think," said Yuri.

"Is there anything I can do before they arrive?"

Yuri thought for a moment. "Oh yes, could you make a trip out to the woodshed and bring in another wheelbarrow of wood, then start a fire in the dining room?"

Alexeev picked up his gloves on the way out. While he brought in the wood, he contemplated how he would tell Ludi what had happened. Timur was only 19, so Alexeev should have exercised more self-control and resisted temptation. But he also didn't want to let Ludi think Timur was completely innocent in this matter. Ultimately though, Alexeev knew it would be Tomi who would bear the greatest weight of this pain, and Ludi would have to live with whatever consequences resulted if Timur revealed where the event took place. This was a small town where gossip could spread very rapidly and Alexeev didn't want to make things any more difficult for Ludi than they already were.

He changed into clean clothes for dinner and dabbed some of Vanya's cologne on his chest and neck. He knew Tomi liked the fragrance, but he liked it too. It reminded him of the flower shop in Moscow where they renewed their friendship. Alexeev still felt quite guilty about adding to Tomi's physical injury a month ago, and now he was faced with yet another event that may end up harming Tomi. But this time, the emotional consequences might be irreparable. He wished he could turn back time to avoid the morning altogether, but what happened could not be undone and Alexeev would have to live with the cost of his indiscretion.

He could smell the black bread Ludi was warming for dinner, so he knew supper would be ready soon. He ran a brush through his hair, took one last look at himself in the mirror, then went downstairs. Ludi and Tomi had just arrived and were already in the dining room setting the table.

Alexeev walked up to Tomi and kissed him on the cheek. "How was the meeting? Did you get everything planned for the holidays?"

Ludi answered before Tomi could open his mouth, "Tomi was a veritable genius with the townspeople. He is going to help the children with a stage production of one of the stories of *Baba Yaga*[86]."

"I thought I would try to do the fairy tale about the *Apples of Youth and of Living Water*[87]," said Tomi. "I remember my mother helped with a production of that story when I was in school…I played one of the princes." All through supper, Tomi and Ludi shared the plans for the town's holiday festivals with Alexeev. Tomi would work with one of the activity organisers over the next several days. He planned to take a few days to write the dialogue, then share his ideas about the stage scenery and costumes. He knew he and Alexeev would leave within a week but he wanted to put in as much effort as he could while they were still around. Alexeev was so proud of Tomi he could barely keep from smiling, and every few minutes he would either kiss Tomi's hand or caress the back of his head.

At the end of the meal, Alexeev went around and gathered the plates, bowls and silverware from the table and took them into the kitchen.

"Now Alexeev, I won't have you doing any more work tonight," said Tomi as he followed him into the kitchen. "You've been working hard all day long and I want you to go into the parlour with Ludi and relax for a while. Let me wash these dishes and then later, I will join you." Tomi could be very persuasive and

---

[86] *Baba Yaga*: A famous Russian fairy tale character, Baba Yaga is a wild witch of the east

[87] *The Apples of Youth and of Living Water*: A traditional Russian fairy tale

insistent when he wanted to be, so Alexeev gave in and went into the parlour with Ludi.

He sat next to Ludi on the settee. "I'm glad we have a little time alone together. I need to talk to you about what happened here today."

"You mean with Timur?" he asked.

"Yes, I'm afraid so," he said solemnly. "I have to confess I was not a very good host today…the fact is Timur and I did more than just wrestle."

Ludi patted him on the back and started to chuckle. "Oh my boy, wrestling is a very sensual sport, especially if you are already attracted to men." He put his arm around Alexeev's shoulder and whispered, "My work involves capturing this male attraction on canvas. That's why I brought the two of you together. I didn't intend for this to upset you though."

"Then you have done this before? Didn't you even consider how this might affect Tomi or the relationship he and I have?" Ludi could hear in Alexeev's voice how upset and irritated he was.

"Tomi knows what I do. He has known me for many years and he has never made any objections to the way I conduct my business. I think some of his views might even surprise you." Ludi stood up and grabbed his pipe and continued, "if I had known this was going to upset you, I would have spoken to you about it before I invited Timur over. But honestly, I thought you knew where this was headed. You seemed so enthusiastic about the paintings. I thought you understood what posing with another man could and would lead to. You are both young and virile, and I think you are both attracted to each other. There is nothing wrong with that. It doesn't have to interfere with your commitment to Tomi. You can still love him while you are attracted to other men, and you can't keep the way you feel bottled up inside you…that isn't healthy."

Alexeev thought for a moment. "Ludi, I don't think I can go on with this painting. It wouldn't be fair to Tomi. And Timur might interpret it as something more that it really is. I don't want him to think this is leading into any kind of intimate relationship, but that's where it's headed if I don't put a stop to it. I won't deny I am attracted to him, but my heart belongs to Tomi. If I continued with this painting, with wrestling Timur, I only see it as heading into disharmony and a painful ending."

"I understand, Lexee. I don't want you or Tomi to feel uncomfortable while you are here. If there is anything I can do to help, just let me know."

"I would still like you to paint me though, but I want this painting to be for Tomi…not for me." Alexeev shook Ludi's hand. "I think I want you to paint me the way you think would be most appealing to Tomi. After all, the painting is for him. It is something I should have done from the very beginning."

"It would make me proud to do such a painting. And don't worry, I will have Yuri explain things to Timur." Ludi smiled and patted Alexeev on the back. "And I'll make sure he won't be coming back here while you and Tomi are around."

"Thank you, my friend. Now I think I will go in and relieve my love from his kitchen duties. I don't like him doing so much work."

Alexeev went into the kitchen and helped Tomi finish washing the dishes, then they dried and stacked them neatly in the cupboards.

Tomi rested his head on Alexeev's shoulder. "Would you mind if we went to bed early? I'm feeling a bit tired and my head is pounding. It really has been a long day."

Alexeev smiled and kissed him on the forehead. "Of course, but let's stop by the parlour and say goodnight to Ludi before we go upstairs." So, they passed by the parlour and said their goodnights.

As soon as Tomi got inside the bedroom, he fell down onto the bed and threw his arms back over his head. "I think I could sleep all day tomorrow if I didn't have to go into town and write that darn play."

"I thought it was something you wanted to do." Alexeev sat on the bed next to him. "You know, you don't have to write it if you don't want to."

"I'm just being selfish. I do want to help out." Tomi reached up and took Alexeev's hand. "I'm just tired and the headache started early this afternoon. I'll feel better in the morning."

"Here, let me help you out of your clothes." Alexeev took off Tomi's shoes and stockings then untied his trousers and unbuttoned his shirt. He kissed Tomi's chest and patted his belly then put his arm beneath Tomi's back. "Sit up so I can get these clothes off you." Tomi sat up reluctantly, and Alexeev undressed him the rest of the way. Then he walked around to the other side of the bed and started taking his clothes off. Tomi put his pillow against the headboard and sat with his legs under the covers.

Alexeev was trying to think of the right words to tell Tomi what happened earlier, but the more he thought about it, the more upset he got. He sat on the bed facing away from Tomi. He stared directly ahead trying to put the words together in his head. He loved Tomi and he needed to be honest with him in every way, even if the results might be painful. But the six years they were apart had not been kind to Tomi. Alexeev could see the physical difference. His hair had receded more and there was more white hair than brown, especially in his beard and moustache. There were dark circles under his eyes and his wrinkles were more pronounced. But probably the biggest difference was his lack of energy. Even with all these physical failings, Alexeev loved him now more than ever before. He knew he needed to be with Tomi and he knew Tomi was the only one who could ever make him happy.

Then a single tear rolled down his cheek. "I need to tell you something, Tomi. I need to tell you what happened today." The words struggled to get past his lips.

Just then, Tomi came up to Alexeev from behind and wrapped his arms around him and caressed Alexeev's chest. "Please don't say anything more, *lyubimyy moy* [88]. I don't need to know what happened." That touch when Tomi caressed his chest was the same touch, the same caress from six years ago when they first met. It was the first time Tomi, or any man, had touched him in that way, and Alexeev had never forgotten that feeling. It was a feeling of energy, tenderness, compassion and love. The feeling flooded Alexeev's mind. Tomi put his hand on the side of Alexeev's face and turned his head towards him. His hand touched the tear, and as he felt the moisture, he put his finger up to his mouth and kissed the precious tear.

"I am not angry, my love. You need to know that you are and always have been my hero and my champion, ever since that winter day six years ago when you called to me from the road in front of my house." He kissed Alexeev's cheek. He kissed the red mark on the side of Alexeev's face, then he touched the cut on his lip. A single droplet of blood marked his finger. He put his finger in his mouth and sucked the blood from his finger then he gently kissed Alexeev's lip. "You rescued me from my broken and bleeding heart, and you opened my heart after it had been shut for so very long. You make me feel like I am worth…" then he stopped. He looked at those bright green eyes so full of tears, so full of sorrow and…shame. "I don't ever want to see those tears again…not from sadness or regret. You have always been honest, kind, loving and faithful to me. And I don't want you to ever think I won't believe what you tell me. I will never doubt you, but you must promise me you will never hold anything back to spare my feelings. You can tell me anything: your joys and successes, but also your regrets and

---

[88] *Lyubimyy moy*: My love, my lover

failures. I will never doubt your love for me. And you should never doubt or question my love for you." There was a determination in Tomi's voice, almost to the point of scolding.

He kissed Alexeev then took both of his hands, "I will always love you. And nothing happened today to change that." Tomi paused for a moment. "Do you know what today is?" Alexeev shook his head, wondering the significance of the date. "It has been exactly six years today since the day we first met."

The tears poured from Alexeev's eyes. It grieved him to know he had betrayed Tomi on the very day marking the anniversary of their first meeting. He had never loved anyone as much as he loved Tomi, but the events of the day showed him how vulnerable he was when he let his guard down. "I love you with all my heart, Tomi." They kissed again and laid down on the bed underneath the covers. Thcy kissed and cuddled, and held each other, both crying and laughing, then falling asleep in each other's arms.

They never discussed the events of that day again, but Alexeev always felt he was to blame for allowing himself to be enticed by another man's beauty. Tomi didn't feel the same though. He knew it was a natural attraction and an innate response, and he continued to show Alexeev respect, admiration and love. He wouldn't let himself be deceived into thinking his physical appearance was enough to maintain their love or their relationship, but he also knew he was having a profound effect on Alexeev. They knew they were meant for each other and were both determined not to let circumstance, events or any person come between them ever again.

They both slept late the next morning. Tomi was exhausted from the activities in town and Alexeev just wanted to be close to his Tomi for as long as he could. He wanted to hold him almost as much as he wanted to be held and comforted. Alexeev was a strong man and very confident and secure in his abilities, but the encounter with Timur had troubled him greatly. If he had controlled his lust, the events would have certainly taken a different turn, he thought. But his love for Tomi was strong and he knew in his heart he would never cheat on him again or cause him emotional or physical pain. In fact, he had sworn an oath several years ago, if he and Tomi ever found themselves together again, he would protect him with his life.

Tomi was sleeping on his side, facing Alexeev who had already gotten up once to rekindle the fire. But that was several hours ago and now the fire was dying down again. Alexeev got up and put another log on the fire. Tomi was in a deep sleep with his gentle snore, like a kitten purring. Alexeev shivered for a moment then he got back into bed and under the covers. He backed himself up against Tomi and reached back and took Tomi's arm and pulled it over him so it laid across his side. It felt good to have someone holding him for a change, even if he was asleep and not aware of what he was doing. Tomi's body was warm under the covers and he fit neatly up against Alexeev's buttocks. He could feel Tomi's cock gently pressing against his butt crack. Alexeev smiled and pulled Tomi's arm a little closer and tighter to his chest. Then Tomi gently and ever so slightly clutched Alexeev's chest. Alexeev could feel Tomi's cock getting a little firmer. Alexeev jutted his hips back in response. Tomi caressed the nipple on that furry chest until he felt it getting hard, then he ran his hand down to the other nipple and caressed it as well.

Tomi whispered, "I want you on top of me, *moy general.*"

Alexeev raised his arm up and over Tomi and turned towards him. "I love you so much, *schast'ye moye*." He positioned his forearms on the bed on either side of Tomi's shoulders with his knees on either side of Tomi's hips, then he leaned down and kissed him. Their tongues united inside their mouths and they both began to breath more heavily. Alexeev's hard nipples brushed against Tomi's chest, and their cocks pressed against each other as if they were dancing. Alexeev's ball sack drooped itself over Tomi's sack and covered it thoroughly. Tomi could feel Alexeev's muscles getting tense and then sensation was exhilarating. Alexeev kissed Tomi's neck then fondled his cold ears. He raised Tomi's arms above his head and kissed his chest and arms then kissed his belly.

As Alexeev went even lower, Tomi arched his back reacting to the sensation of the tongue on his skin. He licked the base of Tomi's cock lightly just above the ball sack. The he licked the ball sack and sucked one of the balls into his mouth. His tongue enveloped the ball and pressed it firmly against the roof of his mouth, then he did the same to the other ball. The sensation was incredible. Tomi felt an ecstasy deep inside his gut. There was a burning and pounding feeling that travelled from his groin up through his gut and deep into his torso. Alexeev took hold of the small, hard cock and started to rub and stroke it, but he continued to lick and suck the balls gently and slowly. Then Alexeev licked his forefinger and middle finger, covering them with saliva. He gentle inserted them into Tomi's anus, just a little way at first. After a few insertions, he slid them in deep and began to massage to top of Tomi's colon from the inside.

Tomi gasped and cried out, "Fuck me deep, *moy khoroshiy*[89]." He could barely contain the excitement, the elation and the thrill of this exquisite, carnal pleasure. He pounded the bed with his fists, then he grabbed the pillow beneath his head and clutched it tightly. His legs were bent at the knees and they started quivering. Alexeev kept up the anal massage and began stroking Tomi's cock harder and faster. He licked and sucked the head of Tomi's cock as he stroked it. Tomi's cock was hard and rigid. Then he took the entire cock into his mouth and reached up to Tomi's chest and began to pinch and pull the nipples. He felt Tomi's body begin to convulse and spasm.

"Alexeev!" he cried out. "Fuck! Fuck! Fuck me!" His cum discharged into Alexeev's mouth. He swallowed, but he kept sucking, massaging, pinching and pulling. For a few moments, Tomi's body stiffened as if it was releasing every last bit of cum into Alexeev's mouth. Then he collapsed in exhaustion. Alexeev swallowed again and continued to kiss Tomi's cock. He pulled his fingers out of Tomi's ass and released his nipples. Then he crawled back on top of Tomi and kissed him on the lips. He wrapped his arms around him and rolled over onto his back, pulling Tomi on top of him.

"You mean everything to me, Tomi. I love you with all my heart." He held Tomi on top of him for several minutes, and Tomi kissed him again and again.

"You are my master…my hero…*moy general.* I love you, Alexeev."

The two of them stayed in bed for a while longer, not wanting the moment to end. But the sun had come up, and soon they could smell the aroma of breakfast from the kitchen. They both knew the lovemaking helped each of them put the events of the previous day behind them. It was time to move on. As they got up and dressed, they would occasionally glance at each other and smile, and as they sat on the bed, ready to put on their shoes, the thought occurred to each of them that the day could be spent in the bedroom. But there were things that needed to be done because commitments had been made. Tomi was still going into town to write the play for the town children and Alexeev was still going to have Ludi paint his portrait. But the picture would be of Alexeev alone and not of him wrestling with Timur.

Over the next few days, Tomi went into town each morning and Alexeev made sure Yuri went with him. He didn't want Tomi driving the carriage by himself. Yuri didn't mind since it gave him the chance to visit with relatives he

---

[89] *Moy khoroshiy*: Literally, 'my good'—referring to complete satisfaction

didn't see often. So Ludi and Alexeev spent several sessions each day on the painting for Tomi. As a bargain for the painting, Alexeev chopped wood each afternoon, stacked it neatly in the woodshed, repaired a few more areas of the stone wall, and allowed Ludi to make sketches of him for future reference as he saw fit. Ludi still wanted to paint a picture of Alexeev wrestling, and with the sketches he could do so without Alexeev having to be present with Timur.

The sittings for the painting and sketches were much more difficult than Alexeev had anticipated. Ludi wanted to capture masculine strength and charisma, so he would have Alexeev flex in different positions for long periods of time. There were poses concentrating on the biceps, the chest, the legs, and back, but also the abdomen, buttocks, forearms, neck and shoulders, and even the feet and hands. He especially wanted intricate sketches of the cock and balls, before, during and after ejaculation. Many of the sketch poses captured combinations of body parts, or the position of the body at different angles. But the painting was the masterpiece. Alexeev chose the pose with a little advice from Ludi, and both were very satisfied with the result. At the end of the fifth day Ludi had completed the painting and had drawn enough sketches to give him a good and sufficient portfolio as reference for future paintings.

Tomi was also finished with his obligations for the town's holiday celebrations. He wrote the play for the children, drew up a design for the different stage sets needed for the play, and even searched out the local talent for the many festivities. The town council was very grateful for all his effort and even offered to pay him to stay through the end of the holiday celebrations, but Tomi already had plans of his own, so he graciously declined. He was anxious to continue their journey home, and there were still a few relatives and friends he wanted to visit on the way.

The morning of their departure came too soon though for both Tomi and Ludi. The distance between them seemed to grow farther with each year but they promised to visit at the next opportunity, if the gods and fates would allow. Ludi had designed a wooden box to contain and protect the two paintings on the long journey home and he had Alexeev build it. The paintings would take a few months to dry completely before they could be framed and displayed, but Tomi had not yet seen the painting of Alexeev.

"Won't you show me the painting now before we leave, so I can at least thank Ludi for his good work?" he asked.

Alexeev shook his head. "So impatient…but I guess you have waited long enough. Go ahead, Ludi, remove the lid so my impatient lover can have a look before he goes into a spasm."

Ludi chuckled and removed the lid. "Now Tomi, I want you to know your boy here has been my most cooperative model. He strutted and flexed every time I asked…and he even stayed still for the painting as well." Ludi chuckled but Alexeev blushed.

Tomi shook his head at Ludi's attempted humour and Alexeev, though he was embarrassed by the comment, took it in stride and helped him steady the box to tilt it forward so Tomi could see the painting.

Tomi gasped, then hugged Alexeev. "Thank you, *moy sladkiy.*" Then he hugged Ludi and kissed him on the cheek. "Thank you, my dear friend. This makes me very happy. As usual, you have done an excellent job. Now we have two beautiful paintings by a true artist."

"You are very welcome, my friend. You have a fine man here." Ludi kissed Tomi on each cheek, then hugged Alexeev and kissed him on the lips, plunging his tongue deep into Alexeev's mouth. It startled Alexeev so much that he almost dropped the box. "Easy there, handsome, I was just taking the last of my payment." Ludi smiled and winked at Tomi. Then Alexeev repacked the paintings and secured them in the back of the carriage with the rest of their belongings. There were tears all around, including Yuri, who brought out two large baskets of food for the journey. It even included a loaf of *challah* bread and 20 or 30 assorted *rugalach*, along with several kinds of dried meats and cheeses, pickled vegetables, hard boiled eggs and a few bottles of vodka.

"Well, we won't go hungry, will we…thank you Yuri," said Alexeev as he shook his hand and loaded the baskets onto the back of the carriage.

"I will send you a case of my blackberry wine as soon as we get home," assured Tomi. Alexeev helped him into the carriage then climbed up next to him where they both sat on the padded seat cushions Sveta had made for them. "Oh Ludi! I almost forgot to give this to you for little Maksim." He tossed Ludi a small sack of coins. "Each day I was in town, I bought a token for the weekly drawing…you know, the one they have to raise funds for the festivities. Well, I won yesterday's drawing. The total win was 25 rubles, 30 kopeks. I want you to give the winnings to Maksim for him and his mum. And—"

Ludi opened the sack. "But there is much more than 25 rubles in this sack," he exclaimed.

“Yes, I’m getting to that,” said Tomi, a little annoyed ay the interruption. “After I wrote the play and designed the stages and costumes, and planned for the music and entertainment, the city council voted to pay me 20 rubles. And since I wasn’t doing any of it for pay, I decided to give my salary to Maksim as well.”

“You never cease to amaze me, my friend,” said Ludi as he cinched up the sack. “I will certainly see he and his mum get this money. And on their behalf, I thank you.”

Tomi leaned down from the carriage and gave Ludi another hug and kiss. They were both in tears. “I am going to miss you, my friend.” Ludi was at a loss for words but clutched the sack of coins and wiped his eyes and smiled at Maksim’s new benefactor. Then Alexeev unfolded a blanket and draped it over Tomi’s legs to make sure he stayed warm. As they rode off, there were still many goodbyes from the carriage. They would always remember their wonderful visit with Ludi, and as a reminder, the beautiful paintings would be hung in Tomi’s front parlour for all his visitors to admire.

The next leg of their journey would take them to Tomi’s Aunt Galina Pavlovna who lived in Nizhny Novgorod. During good weather with no snow, they could make this part of the trip in about four days, but because of the intermittent snow, Alexeev estimated it would take about six. Fortunately, the roads leading there were generally well-travelled as it was a popular trade route to Moscow. The road would also continue to follow the river, so Alexeev was confident he would be able to find food if they ran out, either fish or game, and Tomi had plenty of spices, turnips, tea and powdered cocoa, along with several food items they still had from Vanya, Sveta and Orlov. Yuri made sure Alexeev loaded a few bundles of wood into the back of the carriage, in case they stopped and couldn’t find any by the roadside.

Alexeev was planning on making camp each of the six nights on the road to Aunt Galina’s, and Tomi would diligently prepare their meals with whatever food items they had in the carriage, or whatever fish or game was brought back from the daily hunt. After the first two days on the road, the cold air began to bother Tomi, so he spent most of the rest of the journey to Galina’s in the back of the carriage with a blanket wrapped around him and his fur cap pulled down over his ears. He also had a knitted wool scarf he wrapped around his neck. Alexeev was used to the cold weather so he fared well in the front with the reins, with his long wool coat that was lined with fur. Tomi insisted he wear his fur-lined coat and a scarf to stay warm, and he finally realised it was the same woollen coat he had given to Alexeev when he and his men first stayed with him six years ago. It gave him a special feeling inside to know the coat was still useful. But it also bothered him to see the coat was now showing many signs of wear: the fur had fallen out in several places, there was a tear under one of the sleeves and both sleeves were frayed and the seat looked like it would be worn completely through by the end of this trip.

Alexeev stopped every hour to rest the horses, but also to check on Tomi and make sure he was keeping himself warm. Alexeev later tied a chair on the inside of the carriage near the front opening so Tomi could sit in the enclosure, but still had a view through an opening to the front so they could talk. He secured one of Sveta's cushions to the seat and the other to the back for comfort so Tomi was protected from the cold wind and they could both enjoy each other's conversation.

As they talked and planned their futures together, Alexeev's mind wandered and he dreamed of all the episodes they had yet to experience: the countless nights of passion together in each other's arms, the new friends they would meet along life's journey, the old friends and relatives to visit in renewed fellowship, the anxious moments, the surprises, the myriad of joys and happiness and yes, even the pains and sorrows life oftentimes brings. But his glance was always towards his one true happiness, Tomi, and he couldn't help but smile every time their eyes met as if it was that first encounter six years ago when he had first fallen in love.

Chapter 13

Tea With *Tetushka* Gala

The sun shone bright for the rest of their journey to Aunt Galina's home and the pig farm, so they made good time on this leg of their trip. Each night they stopped by the side of the road, made camp, had a simple meal and then held each other all night long in their compact and cosy bed in the back of the carriage. Tomi rode in the back and rested for two days. He felt better and well-rested on the third day, so he spent a few hours up front next to Alexeev once they got started on the road again after breakfast.

Surprisingly, there was still some *buterbrody*, and Alexeev complemented his meals with pickled vegetables, fire-roasted fish from the river and cider. But Tomi could only stomach a few slices of bread soaked in cider or sometimes a little broth with a few finely cut vegetables. Alexeev also made his special lentil stew the second night from the dried lentils and peas Tomi had brought from Moscow, so they had something hot to put in their stomachs. Tomi managed to get several spoonfuls down after he diluted his portion with warm water, and there was still enough soup to last a few more nights. Alexeev had also bought some cocoa while they were in town visiting Ludi, so he surprised Tomi with a special sweet dessert: wild blackberries topped with powdered cocoa, sprinkled with a little cinnamon and honey. The gallant effort impressed Tomi even though the flavour combination was a little different than what he was used to, but he enjoyed it nonetheless because it was made with love.

Shortly after their lunch break on the sixth day, they arrived in the town of Nizhny Novgorod. Tomi wanted to stop at the town bakery to pick up something special for Aunt Galina. She loved pastries, especially the ones baked at *Pekarnya* Morozov in the centre of town. Tomi stopped there on the way to her house nearly every visit, and this time of year they made a special Italian dessert called *Nociata*[90], and it was a favourite of hers. She always looked forward to sitting down to tea with her company, and especially with Tomi. He reminded her of her younger brother, Dmitry, Tomi's father. Dmitry had died of influenza when Tomi was a child. He and his wife Anya lived in Prague until his passing, then Anya and her sons immigrated to Minsk.

Dmitry was born and raised in Sochi along the banks of the Black Sea. When he was a teenager, his family, including Galina, his younger sister Olga and his younger brothers Toma, Yuliy and Fedya, migrated north to Moscow, but Dmitry had other ideas. He decided to part from the family, so he boarded a ship to cross the Black Sea to *Ahelo-Pirgas*[91] in the Ottoman Empire. From there he made his way into Habsburg, and finally settled in Prague where he met Anya and her family. She and her family were Jews living in the Ashkenazi community. Her father owned and operated a small, yet very successful Deli. They also had four acres of land and raised sheep, cows, goats, grains, vegetables and fruits. Their land supplied goods for the local store, and Anya and her four brothers and three sisters helped run the farm and the Deli. Dmitry got a job as a farmhand for Anya's father, and very soon fell in love with Anya. They were married in the Jewish temple two years after they met.

Tomi was the third of four sons. But soon after his younger brother was born, Dmitry became sick with influenza and so did Tomi's younger brother, Desya. Both Dmitry and Desya died when Tomi was four. Anya saw an immediate need to find a husband to replace the father her sons had lost, so she remarried a gentleman twice her age and outside her community. She was 38 and he was 76 years old. Within a few months after their Christian marriage, her new husband moved the family northeast to Minsk in Belarus and then to *Nyen*. His stepfather died when Tomi was fifteen, and when he turned sixteen, Tomi joined the army as a company clerk.

He had been good at numbers since he was a young boy, and he worked a few years in a local grocery store in *Nyen* as an apprentice inventory clerk starting at age fourteen. He quickly familiarised himself with bookkeeping practices and maintaining records, and what he didn't already know, he was able to learn quickly. At sixteen, he enlisted in the army and for twenty-two years, he

---

[90] *Nociata*: An Italian treat traditionally made in the Sabine area in Lazio, especially during the Christmas season.

[91] *Ahelo-Pirgas*: Burgas, Bulgaria

worked as a clerk and records keeper. When he was 38, he was injured when a building collapsed during a fire and he was caught in the debris.

The injury was not permanent but he was dismissed from any further service. He felt it was time for him to choose a different career path and settle down in the countryside. He also wanted to seek out any fragment of his heritage or ancestry he could find. He had been told by his mother of his grandfather's intentions to move the family north to Moscow, so that was where he decided to start his journey. During his travels across the country, he discovered his birthfather's siblings had settled between Moscow and the Ural Mountains, so he travelled from family to family, getting to know relatives he had never met and building new kinships and friendships along the way. He finally settled in Storozhevsk-Shoynaty and obtained a job with the mayor as the town treasurer. By the time he was 48, only seven years after arriving in Storozhevsk, he had saved enough money to purchase the green and white cottage along the Vychegda River.

Tomi earned enough to hire several farmhands and a few house helpers who would clean the house, launder the clothes and linens, help with the marketing and assist in jarring preserves for sale in the local store. Tomi also sold fresh produce from his gardens, blackberry and raspberry jams and homemade wines and cordials. Within a year of buying the cottage, he stopped working as town treasurer and devoted his time to perfecting his wine and cordial industry and was able to purchase additional acreage on either side of his property. He planted a new field of his own special hybrid of blackberries, producing fruit about twice as large as the common wild berry.

Now it was early afternoon and Aunt Galina's farm was in sight. The smell of the pastries was making Alexeev's stomach rumble, and they were both anxious to settle in, sit down to tea and have a pleasant afternoon with Tomi's aunt.

"There it is, Alexeev!" He grabbed Alexeev's shoulder and pointed up the road. "See the red-trimmed house? Look at the beautiful detail on the flue graces and the ornate gables around the windows. That is the finest home in town. My *Tetushka*'s house has six bedrooms, two parlours, a huge dining room and a very large kitchen, and a fireplace in almost every room," Tomi spoke with a lot of pride in his voice. "You just have to get used to the smell of the pigs."

Along with the six bedrooms, there was a large divided attic. In previous years, when the army would march through town, Galina would donate the space in the upper floor and attic to bed down the troops for as long as they needed (that was where Tomi got the idea of hosting travellers in his own home). Then, when relatives would visit, the attic was used for the children and young people to bunk down. There was also a large second floor above the barn with smooth, waxed hardwood, where the young people from town could have parties and dances. Galina loved to encourage her young relatives and young people from the community to use her home for their pleasure and special events.

"If I could tolerate two dozen soldiers who think bathing is a fate worse than death, I think the smell of pigs will be easy to get used to." He did not want Tomi to think a little thing like that would upset him in the least. In fact, he was already planning to help with the farm chores in any way he could while they were there. Tomi smiled and put his head on Alexeev's shoulder. He was grateful Alexeev was so cooperative and eager to engage himself in his life, such as it was.

Alexeev rode the carriage onto the wayside up to the barn, locked the brake, then hopped out and ran around to the other side to help Tomi down. The week had been a long one, and Tomi suffered occasionally from his rheumatism as well as frequent headaches. His back was very stiff from the morning ride. Alexeev wrapped his arm around him as they walked together up to the side door of the house.

As Tomi opened the door, he called out, "*Tetushka*, *Tetushka* Gala! It is me, Tomi. I have come here to visit you with my friend, Alexeev." The door opened to an inner porch area lined on each wall with various herb plants and potted mint bushes and tea leaves hanging to dry from the ceiling. There was a wonderful combination of smells in the air. The inner porch led to the kitchen door, propped open by a smooth black stone about the size of a small loaf of bread. Aunt Galina was standing by the stove heating a pot of water for her afternoon tea. The boys were just in time.

She looked up and smiled. "*Moy malen'kiy chelovek*[92], Tomi, my Tomi, how good to see you." The white-haired dowager, barely five feet tall if she could stand up straight, held out her gnarled hands to hug the two boys. Tomi was five feet six inches so her head came up just below his chin, but Alexeev at six feet towered over the 96-year-old by more than a foot.

[92] *Moy malen'kiy chelovek*: My little man

Alexeev was a gentle giant though, as he knelt on one knee, kissed her on both cheeks and wrapped his arms around her. "I am so happy to finally meet you, Galina Pavlovna."

"Oh, my dear, call me *Tetushka* Gala," she said as she patted Alexeev's head. "Everyone here is family."

"*Tetushka*, this is my dear friend, Alexeev." Tomi kissed her on both cheeks and gave her a big hug. "He is going to live with me in my cottage in Shoynaty."

"How wonderful, Tomi. But what a long trip!" The look on her face suddenly showed concern. "You must stay here for a while and rest up before you continue your journey…you look so pale!" She put her hand up to his forehead to test his temperature then patted his cheek. "Come and sit at the table. I have hot water for tea almost ready. And bring in your bags, my dear, you know where your room is. I will get the tea ready."

"I will bring in our bags so you can help *Tetushka* with setting out the tea." Alexeev stood up, gave Tomi a kiss on his cheek and went quickly out the door to the carriage. On the way to the carriage he saw the *khozyain*[93] standing in front of the stables, so he asked him to tend to the horses. Then he grabbed their four bags from the carriage along with the box of pastries.

Tomi opened the door for Alexeev and placed the box of pastries on the kitchen table. "We brought your favourite pastries. What plates would you like me to use?"

"Oh, use the Delftware plates from Holland. I always like those when company is here…or family." She smiled and pinched Tomi's cheek then patted it gently. "You are good to me, Tomi. You always remember my favourite pastries. It will be a few minutes before the tea is ready. You go show your young man where the bedroom is."

He led Alexeev through the kitchen and into the living area, then down the hallway to the second bedroom on the right just past the parlour. The dresser and night tables were honey oak, and the design and carvings on them were unmistakably the handiwork of Vanya. The bed had a brass frame with a dark blue silk canopy lined with white lace roses. There was a brass candelabra on the dresser and a pink ceramic vase for flowers, and a honey oak and pink ceramic wash basin next to the dresser.

---

[93] *Kozyain:* Hostler or stableman

"I don't want to keep *Tetushka* waiting. Just put the bags down by the bed and we will come back later to unpack." So, he set down the bags and walked back down the hall to the dining room where *Tetushka* was ready to pour the tea.

"Would either of you like honey in your tea? Alexeev, I have my own bees and the honey here is especially good."

"I would love to try your honey. Yes, please," answered Alexeev. He pulled out *Tetushka*'s chair to help her get seated.

"You are such a gentleman, Alexeev. It is no wonder Tomi is fond of you."

"Oh? And what has Tomi told you about me?" Alexeev asked. He sat down next to her on her left and Tomi sat down to her right.

"When Tomi comes out here, he always tells me about how much he misses you. You made quite an impression on him, but I don't want to talk out of turn. What adventures do the two of you have planned?"

"Our adventures are just beginning. I think we can stay here for about two weeks, if you can tolerate a couple of boys in your home for that long," said Tomi.

"But we want to do some work for you while we are here," Alexeev added. "Tomi can help in the house and I will make myself useful in the woodshed or the pigsties or anywhere else you need a good strong back or strong hands."

"Oh, that sounds wonderful, but I don't want you to wear yourselves out while you are here. I have servants to do the housework and farmhands to tend the pigs and the farm."

"You just tell us what needs to be done and let us worry about the rest," assured Alexeev. "Now let me give you a pastry to go with this wonderful tea." She gave a big smile as Alexeev placed a pastry on one of her special Delftware plates.

"Speaking of tea…" said Tomi, "do you have some of that bath tea? The kind with willow bark and peppermint…and something else…"

"Juniper and lavender, it is my special recipe. Yes, yes, I will get you a bag to use," she said. "Are you still having problems with rheumatism?"

"Yes, I am afraid so. And long trips and cold weather seem to aggravate it and make the pain more intense." Tomi grimaced and placed his hand on his back.

"It has been getting worse over this last week, *Tetushka*," said Alexeev. "Maybe you could give me your tea recipe so I can keep some on hand for him?"

"Of course, my dear. After we finish, Tomi can show you to the boiler so you can get the fire started for the hot water. You are a sweet man, Alexeev." She smiled at him and patted his hand. Tomi was glad the two of them were getting along so well. He wanted Alexeev to be part of his family in every way, and Galina was very special to him.

The three talked until the teapot was empty. Alexeev could see the look of pain on Tomi's face so he wanted to start heating the water for the bath. He told Tomi to go into the bedroom and rest until the bath was ready. "I will help you to the bedroom if you can't walk on your own."

"I am afraid you may need to, Alexeev, I don't think I can stand up." The look on Tomi's face turned from pain to desperation.

Alexeev jumped up and gently scooped Tomi into his arms. "I will be right back, *Tetushka.* Would you fetch one of the tea bags for me?"

"Of course, my dear, you get Tomi settled in the bedroom. Get him into bed for now."

Alexeev carried Tomi to the bedroom and laid him on the bed, then gently removed his clothes. Tomi was exhausted. The pain wore him out and he could barely move without aggravating the rheumatism. Once Alexeev got him undressed, he draped a quilt over him and tucked it around him. "Now try to rest here while I prepare your bath. Is there anything I can get you?"

"You are a good man. You are so good to me, my love. I will be fine now." Then Tomi shut his eyes and tried to fall asleep. Alexeev started a fire in the bedroom fireplace before he left.

The boiler was in a room next to the kitchen and there was a large ceramic bathtub in the same room on top of a raised slatted floor. The floor underneath the slats was tile, and there were several drainage canals crisscrossing the floor leading to a small opening on the outer wall where the water could drain out into the gardens. There were also rows of earthen basins filled with porous lava rocks. Underneath the basins were firepits. The firepits would heat the rocks, then hot water could be poured over the rocks to create steam. There were also three wooden benches, long and wide enough for a man to comfortably lie down on each one or several men could sit side by side.

Alexeev built the fires under the boiler and in the firepits. He checked the water in the boiler and saw it was full. Soon the room warmed up, so Alexeev stripped off his shirt and boots. Within a half an hour, the water was hot enough for a bath so he opened the valve and filled the tub. Then he filled several pails with water so he could later pour the water over the hot stones. Now he was ready for the teabag and Tomi.

Tetushka had left the teabag on the dining room table. It was about the size of a ten-pound bag of sugar. He lifted the teabag up to his nose and took a sniff. There was a soothing smell of mint and lavender. He dropped it in the steaming bath water then went to get Tomi. Although his eyes were closed, Tomi still looked tense and in pain.

Alexeev brushed his hand over Tomi's forehead. "The bath is ready for you now, my dear." He lifted Tomi up, together with the quilt, and carried him to the boiler room. He set him down on one of the benches and removed the quilt. Then he tested the water to make sure it was not too hot, then he picked up Tomi again and gently lowered him into the bathtub. As Tomi settle in, Alexeev poured the pails of water over the hot rocks and soon the entire room was full of steam.

"Come join me, my love," said Tomi. So Alexeev removed his trousers and shorts and sat down in the tub next to Tomi. The tub was large enough for the two of them to sit side by side with their legs outstretched. The water was very soothing and soon the tea's medicinal qualities were easing the pain. Tomi leaned back onto Alexeev's chest, and Alexeev wrapped his arms around him, clasping Tomi's hands in front of him. He slid their bodies down under the water so only their heads were exposed. The air in the room was now very warm, nearly as warm as the water in the tub but comfortable nonetheless.

They sat in the tub until the fires died out and the water began to cool. Tomi was nearly asleep and still weak from the pain. Alexeev gently rose from the water and gathered Tomi once again in his arms and set him down on one of the benches. There were towels at one end of the bench, so he dried off Tomi then dried off himself. He put his trousers back on and wrapped the quilt around Tomi to cover him, then he carried him back to the bedroom. He laid his naked body in the bed, removed the quilt and covered him with the sheets and bedcovers. The poor fellow was already asleep before his head hit the pillow.

Just then, the clock on the bedroom dresser chimed six o'clock. Alexeev tucked the blankets around Tomi to prevent him from getting a chill and he put a few more logs in the fireplace. The blaze soon warmed the room. Alexeev went over to the bed and brushed Tomi's forehead. He did not have a fever but he was fast asleep. Alexeev left the bed canopy open so the warmth from the fireplace could reach Tomi and he left the bedroom door open slightly so he could occasionally check back on him without disturbing his sleep.

Alexeev found Galina in the front parlour in her rocking chair knitting something blue and white. She looked sombre, as if the act of knitting took her into a therapeutic trance of some kind. Her left eyebrow would twitch up and down in rhythm with the knitting needles and the motion of her hands and she pursed her lips as if from determination. Alexeev stood in the archway of the parlour and leaned against the column with his arms folded in front of him. He was still in his trousers, shirtless and barefoot. He was worried about Tomi, but watching Galina knit seemed to put him somewhat at ease. He already felt like *Tetushka* had taken him in as her own nephew, and it felt good to think of her as his own auntie. A single tear slowly rolled down his right cheek and he started to tremble. Just as the tear reached his lower jaw, Galina looked up at him and saw his sorrow.

"You are worried about Tomi, my dear?" Alexeev nodded as he wiped the tear from his face. "You are a good boy, Alexeev. I saw the way you cared for Tomi, the way you carried him so gently to the bedroom. His papa would have liked you." She set her knitting down in the basket next to her and stretched her arm towards him. "Come, sit with me for a while."

"Let me build up your fire first." He noticed there was only a meagre fire the fireplace. She only had the strength to place small logs in the fireplace. Alexeev picked up a few larger logs with ease and placed them on top of the dying embers. Soon, they caught fire and started making the parlour a little cosier. He sat down of the floor next to the rocker, pulled his knees up to his chest and drooped his head and wept. "*Tetushka*, I am so worried about him. I have never seen him like this before…it frightens me." Galina patted his head and stroked his hair. "We have been apart for six years…we weren't even together for one week before…and now we are together again…but I don't know how to help him." He gasped, trying to hold back the tears. "*Tetushka*, what should I do, how should I help him?"

"Does he make you happy?" she asked. Alexeev nodded. "Then love him, my dear, just love him." She leaned down and kissed the top of his head. "He just needs to rest, Alexeev. He is not as young as you are, and sometimes the injuries he had when he was younger come back and cause pain in his bones. That is the trouble with wars and fighting, the damage always seems to come back to continue the suffering." She paused for a moment then squeezed Alexeev's shoulder. "Come to the kitchen with me, my boy, you must be hungry.

I will fix you something to eat, then we can come back here and talk some more while you eat." Alexeev stood up and helped Galina up from her rocking chair.

"Let me go get dressed. I will just be a moment." He wiped the tears from his face and walked down the hall as Galina made her way to the kitchen.

He opened the bedroom door and walked in quietly, then leaned over the bed to see how Tomi was doing. The glow from the fire gave just enough light to see that Tomi's eyes were still shut. He was sleeping peacefully. Alexeev sat on the edge of the bed and pulled out a shirt from one of the bags on the floor. He dug around in the bag until he found a pair of stockings, then he finished getting dressed. He leaned back on the bed and kissed his forehead. "*Khoroshego otdykha moye schast'ye*[94]." Then he got up carefully and adjusted the covers.

Galina was busy at the stove heating water in a kettle for tea and heating a small pot of soup. She had already placed fresh rye bread, butter, and a jar of honey on the table, and had arranged two Delftware plates and two matching cups. She also had a plate of cheeses and sliced sausages and another plate of pickled onions, cucumbers, and carrots. The soup was simmering as Alexeev entered the kitchen, and from the wonderful aroma he knew it was cabbage *Borscht*, one of his favourites.

"That smells wonderful, *Tetushka*, and I am so hungry. May I help you with that?" He took the potholders, picked up the soup pot from the stove and placed it on an iron trivet on the table. Galina poured the hot water into the teapot and had Alexeev transfer it to the table as well. There was a large tray at one end of the table, so Alexeev began placing the plates of food onto the tray. He poured them each a cup of tea. "Honey?" he asked.

She nodded and smiled. Alexeev dipped the spoon into the honey and spun the spoon with his fingers until the dripping honey string released itself from the honey pot. Then he held the spoon over her teacup and they both watched the amber sweetness drop into the hot tea. He again spun the spoon a few times to release the tiny string, then replaced the spoon into the honey pot and repeated the action for his own cup of tea. They both watched as if the process was the most fascinating and intricate procedure they had ever seen.

Then they both picked up their own spoons and stirred their tea to mix in the honey. He placed both of the delicate cups with the sweetened tea on the tray with the rest of their supper, then he took the tray into the parlour and set it on

---

[94] *Khoroshego otdykha moye schast'ye*: Rest well, my dear (literally, my happiness)

the table between the rocker and settee. Then he went back to the kitchen and escorted Galina to the parlour. She held onto Alexeev's arm to steady herself as she walked. She had a cane she would often use when she was by herself, but on many occasions, she would leave it in one room or another and forget where she had left it.

Alexeev helped her to the rocking chair, then he pulled up a chair next to her and handed her the cup of tea. They both took a sip of the wondrous potion and smiled. The steam warmed their cheeks as they drank the tea and it felt almost as good as the tea tasted.

Alexeev picked up Galina's soup bowl and ladled the hot *borscht* for her, then served himself. He passed her the bread plate, then the butter, and finally the cheese and sausage plate and pickled vegetables. He served himself last and commented how wonderful everything looked. After he buttered his bread, he tasted his first spoonful of soup and took a bite of bread. "Ummm, this is so good, *Tetushka*. I think this is the best *borscht* I've ever tasted."

"Thank you, my dear. This recipe was my mother's, handed down from her grandmother. It has been in our family for many generations. But my grandmother didn't use beets. She used something else, I think hogweed…or maybe it was mushrooms. I am sure Tomi has the recipe though. He likes his *borscht* cold."

She was very proud of her simple cooking and especially because most of what she made was a product of her own gardens and farm. She had her indoor spice garden and another larger indoor garden behind the barn so she could grow some of her vegetables in a few of the winter months, an acre devoted to grains and corn, an acre devoted to turnips, beets, leeks and onions, and other root and bulb vegetables, and yet another acre of various fruit and nut trees including a few varieties of apples, pears, peaches, apricots and cherries, walnuts and pecans.

Her servants put up preserves every year and made enough to sell the greater portion of her efforts with enough left over to store in her root cellar for her own winter supply. Her profits helped her hire local young people in town to plant, harvest, and tend the fields, as well as take care of her livestock. Of course, at this point in her life, she no longer did any of the work, but offered her advice every now and then to her workers. Even though they were her employees, most of them considered her as close as their own mother or grandmother. She paid all of her workers more than they could get at the other local farms with the added benefits of free boarding if they didn't have a place of their own.

But her pig farm was the real money-maker. She had herds of between 600 and 800 pigs of various breeds (not including piglets): Czech White, Black Slavonian, Red Iberian, Belarus Spotted Pied and German Landrace. She raised and sold piglets to neighbouring farms looking to start their own herds and sold mature adults to butchers from local and neighbouring villages. And her prices were always very competitive. For more than 50 years, she had had the same few pig handlers, and now their sons cared for her herds. They were all loyal workers who were experts in their field. Brothers Kolya and Semyon (their father was a suitor of Galina's two oldest daughters) now in their mid-40s, and Stefan who was a local lad she originally hired to slop the pigs 20 years ago when he was a teenager, and Vladimir who was the manager and overseer, man-in-charge and head *Svinopas*[95] of the business.

Vladimir was 59 years old and still going strong. He had been secretly in love with Galina ever since he was first hired. Vladimir was only 14 at the time and she was much older than he, even then, but he had only had eyes for her. She was the sophisticated, very brilliant, older woman whom he adored. He never crossed her or questioned any orders, but immediately obeyed and followed her instructions with precision detail. He never gave up hope someday she would accede to his advances. He pined for her and never married, but Galina never considered an intimate relationship with him. She was satisfied to remain a widow and independent of anyone hindering or changing her way of life. She appreciated his company though and had many long talks with him, but rejected any intimate references or advances. And now, since she was advanced in years, both were satisfied with their relationship as it was. She always thought of him as the son she never had.

Alexeev had nearly finished eating but had not spoken much. Galina sensed he was still overwhelmed with worry about Tomi, but she knew dwelling on something he had no control over would eat at him until it consumed him completely. "Alexeev, would you do me a favour?" she asked. "My *svinopas*, Vladimir, has gone to market in one of the neighbouring villages with a dozen of my pigs, and he took Kolya and Semyon with him this time. They are selling the pigs in the town where the brothers grew up. They are staying to visit with their mother and sisters during the holidays. Vlad will return here before the new year, but that is still several weeks away. I am afraid Stefan will be overworked,

[95] *Svinopas*: Swineherd, a person who tends pigs

and he has never been left in charge before. Tomi said you were a lieutenant in the army, so I know you have much more experience overseeing duties and organising a day's work. Would you mind giving him a hand and taking charge while you are here until Vlad returns?"

Alexeev was a little relieved he would have something to keep his mind off Tomi's recovery, and he knew Galina would be around the house to look after him. "Of course, I will," he said as he placed his large calloused hand on hers. Galina's hands were so small and delicate in comparison to his. "I will get up early in the morning and meet with him to see what needs to get done. We will manage, don't you worry."

"Vladimir has a register in his office in the barn. It lays out all the daily duties and the agendas and rotations of certain obligations." Then she smiled and said, "He and I wrote it years ago when I first hired him to run things for me."

Although Alexeev had never raised or cared for pigs, he was confident he could handle this task. He always knew he could manage any circumstance if he put his mind to it and had the proper resources. He helped Orlov tend the animals in his barn in Moscow, but Orlov only had a few pigs for a short time. Alexeev had learned to milk the cows and toss their hay, feed the chickens, slaughter, pluck, and clean them for cooking, and milk and tend the goats. He also learned the art of making butter and cheeses, and knew how to candle eggs to determine fertilisation. The idea of learning how to care for pigs never crossed his mind before, but he welcomed the challenge of learning something new.

When they finished their dinner, Alexeev ladled a bowl of soup for Tomi (since the soup was now cold), buttered a piece of bread and poured him a hot cup of willow bark tea with honey. Galina had a special jar of willow bark tea that was good for soothing aches and pains. She showed him where she had a smaller lap tray so Tomi could eat in bed without having to get up and come into the kitchen. "Give Tomi a kiss for me and tell him I will say prayers for his health." Alexeev thanked her and kissed her goodnight, then took the tray of food into the bedroom for Tomi. He noticed Galina's tray was the same design as the one he had used when they were at Vanya's.

He backed himself into the bedroom and placed the tray on the dresser, then lit the candles on the candelabra and moved it to the nightstand on Tomi's side of the bed. Then he slowly opened the canopy all the way and tied it back against the bedpost. He placed his hand gently on Tomi's shoulder and whispered,

"Tomi, how did you sleep? Are you feeling better? I brought you something to eat."

Tomi slowly opened his eyes and smiled when he saw his sweetheart sitting next to him. "You make me feel much better, my love. I am feeling better, but still tired."

"Do you think you could eat something?" he said. "*Tetushka* made some delicious *borscht* and rye bread, and I also brought you a cup of hot tea with honey." As Tomi raised himself up on one elbow, Alexeev placed his hands under Tomi's arms to help him sit up.

"It smells so good and I am a little hungry." Alexeev took the pillow from the other side of the bed and tucked it behind Tomi's back for support. Then he got up and retrieved the tray from the dresser. He brought it to the bed, unfolded the tray legs and set it gently over Tomi's lap, then took a cloth napkin and laid it on Tomi's bare chest.

"You have some cold soup and hot tea while I build the fire back up," he said, as he handed him a spoon. Then he kissed him on the forehead. "You are going to be all right." Tomi smiled and nodded. He tossed a few large logs into the fire, then poked them with the fire prod until they started to blaze. He took off his shirt and trousers and slipped into bed next to Tomi. He put his strong arm around Tomi and snuggled up next to him. "I will always be right here by your side to take care of you, but you must promise me one thing."

Tomi turned his head towards Alexeev. "And what is that, my dear?"

"You must promise me that you will never leave me alone." A tear rolled down Alexeev's cheek and he almost choked on the words.

Tomi rested his head on Alexeev's shoulder. "I promise, my love, I promise."

The two sat side by side while Tomi ate the bread and soup and drank the tea. Alexeev watched him intently, stroked his back and shoulders and told Tomi all about how he was going to take charge of the pig farm to assist Stefan. Tomi smiled and listened and thought to himself how wonderful it was to be with a man who cared so much about his well-being. He was amazed Alexeev was so willing to care for him. Tomi had known many young men who were only concerned with themselves. Once they discovered Tomi's maladies and afflictions, they quickly disappeared. Whenever he would meet a new man, he always held out hope he would be the one to sweep him off his feet and fill his deep sense of loneliness and despair. Then six years ago, when he met Alexeev, he had the same high hopes and dreams. But six years is a long time to wait.

Hope starts to fade and dreams become vivid reminders of one's failures and unaccomplished goals. But now those hopes and dreams seemed to be making their way back into Tomi's reality. At least Alexeev had not decided to leave yet, and Tomi held out hope the two of them would remain together.

When Tomi had finished eating, he leaned back onto the pillow, stretched his arms and legs and yawned. He was still exhausted from the pain and needed to sleep through the night. Alexeev gathered the dishes and tray and took them back into the kitchen. Galina had already gone to bed, so Alexeev quickly washed and rinsed the few dishes and dried them with the tea towel, then set them on the counter. There was still some willow bark tea left in the teapot so he poured another cup for Tomi and added a spoonful of honey, then he brought it back into the bedroom for Tomi.

"Here, have some more of the tea. It will help you sleep a little better." Tomi drank the tea slowly and then Alexeev got back in bed and laid down next to him. He wrapped himself around Tomi's body, cuddling him gently. Within a few minutes Tomi was fast asleep. For a while, Alexeev listened to the soft sound of Tomi's breathing. It was a welcomed sound and Tomi's face was no longer tense with pain. It looked like the tea had done the trick and eased the pain. Alexeev was looking forward to the next few weeks, not only because he wanted to learn more about pigs but also because he knew the respite from riding in the cold would be good for Tomi's recovery. Now they had the remainder of their lives together to look forward to.

Chapter 14
Behind the Woodshed

Over the next few days, Tomi gained some of his strength back, and he took daily tea baths to reduce the pain from his rheumatism. He even began to help with the housework, although Alexeev insisted he refrain from any kind of lifting or other strenuous activities. Meanwhile, Alexeev was getting acquainted with raising and tending the pigs, but he had daily rows with Stefan about efficiency and use of his time. Having been in the military for such a long time, he was very familiar with how to get things done quickly with the least amount of manpower. He prided himself on knowing intuitively how to manage activities, and he tended to take charge of every situation and even barked out orders without thinking. Tomi understood this about him and admired him for his ability to apply practical ingenuity, even if the situation was completely unfamiliar to him. It was one of the reasons Tomi was attracted to him. Alexeev was never mean-spirited or unkind but could be straightforward and direct, which was sometimes interpreted as arrogance. Stefan, on the other hand, was not used to taking orders from strangers. He had been doing things the same way for nearly 20 years and was unwilling to change his style or method for anyone, even a former lieutenant in the army.

Alexeev woke up early one morning, stoked the fire in the bedroom then built fires in the dining room and oven. He filled the water in the kettle for tea and set it on the stove. Then he lit a lantern and went down to the cellar and picked out a few jars of jams, peach preserves and a few apples and sausages for breakfast. When he got back upstairs to the kitchen, Galina was preparing the biscuit dough. "Oh, thank you, my dear. I was hoping you would be up early," she said. "It gets more and more difficult to manage those stairs."

"I am happy to do it, *Tetushka.* Tomi does not usually let me help out with meals…he enjoys cooking and baking for me. He says I cook like I am still in the army…too much meat and spices and not enough fruits and vegetables." Alexeev smiled and placed the food on the kitchen counter. "Would you like me to do anything else for you?"

"No, dear, you go about your business. I know you have many things to do," she said. "I will ring the bell on the back porch when the biscuits and sausages are ready."

Alexeev paused before he headed outside. He leaned down and kissed Galina on the cheek. "I hope I am not speaking out of turn, but I think of you as my own *Tetushka,*" he said, "and I think you should let your servants prepare your meals for you. You should be taking it easy—"

She interrupted him, "I may be old, but I can still manage the simple things. Cooking every now and then gives me pleasure and especially when I can cook for my nephew and his new beau." She patted his cheek. "Don't worry about me. I know my limitations." He gave her a hug then went out to start his work for the day.

Two days each week during the winter months, logs needed to be chopped for the fireplaces, oven and boiler, and this week a little more was needed for Tomi's baths. Today was one of the days to chop wood. Alexeev put on a pair of gloves and made his way to the woodshed where Stefan was already preparing to chop wood. He had already removed his shirt in anticipation of the sweaty activity. Alexeev removed his as well and hung it on a nearby tree limb. Both men were roughly the same age and similar build. Both were taller than average and very muscular. Alexeev's forearms were hairy, but his back was bare and smooth except for a small amount of hair in the small of his back just above and continuing beneath his trouser line. His skin had a slight olive tone giving him the appearance of being well tanned and healthy.

Stefan had black hair with hints of grey in his temples and chin. He had a short patchy beard and moustache that made him look a little older than he was. There was a small patch of hair between his pectorals filling the cleavage, and a few dark hairs around his areolas. His armpits had a small amount of short black hairs, as did his wrists and forearms, but the rest of his body was hairless and smooth. He had dark brown eyes topped by thin black eyebrows. Stefan's chin had a deep cleft that was nearly covered by the white hairs in his beard, and his cheeks were always rosy and stood out because of his pale white skin.

Each of the men grabbed an axe and began to chop wood from the large pile of logs. They continued chopping steadily, almost as if in competition with each other. The sweat was dripping down their chests, backs, and arms. Both had tied a scarf around their foreheads to help keep the salty sweat from stinging their eyes. After about an hour, they heard Galina ring the bell. Breakfast was ready. They both went over to the water bucket and dipped a rag into the cold water and wiped the sweat from their faces, chests and armpits. They dried themselves off, put their shirts back on and walked to the house for breakfast. Galina had set the table and laid out the food for the boys. As Alexeev and Stefan entered the kitchen, Tomi came in from the hall.

Alexeev smiled and gave Tomi a kiss and a hug. "Good morning, *schast'ye moye*, did you sleep well?"

"Very well, *moy sladkiy*," he replied.

Stefan looked on with disdain as he perceived the relationship between Alexeev and Tomi was more than friendship. From the backyard, he would occasionally catch a glimpse into Tomi's bedroom and see them kissing or hugging, and he had noticed Alexeev doting on Tomi incessantly. Stefan suspected their relationship was indecent and perverse, yet he had never witnessed this kind of relationship between two men before. Nevertheless, it stirred up an anger in him and contempt for the couple. "The pigs are better company than this wretch," he said. As he passed by, he elbowed Tomi's back, then spat on Tomi's plate and walked back outside. As he slammed the door behind him, he yelled, "I won't share a table with a *mamen'kin synok*[96]."

Galina picked up Tomi's plate immediately and replaced it with a clean one. She shook her head. "I don't know what's gotten into that boy."

Tomi reached out and took Alexeev's hand. "Why would he say those things? He's known me for years. I've always been kind to him."

"I won't let him disrespect you like that, Tomi. I will teach him some manners." Alexeev's muscles were tense with anger but Tomi held him back.

"Now just sit here with me and calm down. We don't know what's going through his mind," said Tomi. "Maybe he has never been loved before. He doesn't know what it's all about."

"Obviously, there's not much of anything good going through that little mind of his," said Alexeev as he clenched his fists.

"We are probably the first men he's seen who care for each other like we do. When he finds his own true love, maybe he will understand." Alexeev wasn't

---

[96] *Mamen'kin synok*: Sissy boy

satisfied with Tomi's response and felt Tomi was giving in to being bullied. But he sat next to Tomi and put his arm around him as if to shield him from any further humiliation.

The three of them sat together at the table, and though Galina and Tomi both ate their meal, Alexeev barely touched the food on his plate. He was fuming and his anger towards Stefan grew with every breath he took. None of them said anything about Stefan until they had finished.

"You should take a plate of food out to Stefan and talk to him, Alexeev," Galina said as she handed him a plate of food. "Just be patient with him, my dear, and give him a chance to apologise."

Alexeev said nothing, but took the plate and walked out the door. Stefan had gone back to the woodshed to resume chopping. Physical activity could sometimes take his mind off his troubles and worries. He chopped quite a large stack of wood by the time Alexeev returned to him.

"Galina has prepared a plate for you," he said as he held out the plate to him.

"I have no hunger," he replied in between chops.

"You have been working for two hours. You should eat something," insisted Alexeev.

"I do not need you to tell me what I should do or how long I should work," he said still swinging his axe.

Then Alexeev put the plate of food down on a stump and grabbed Stefan's arm, forcing him to stop his work. "Then you are going to go back inside the house and apologise to Tomi."

Stefan threw his axe to the ground and turned towards Alexeev. The anger on his face was obvious, his muscles were flexed and his fists were clenched. He drew back his arms ready to throw a punch but held himself back for the moment. "Take your hand off me, you pervert. You are just as bad as he is. Neither one of you deserves the swill we give to the pigs."

Alexeev had heard enough of Stefan's insults and posturing. He ripped his shirt off in one stroke, then clenched his own fists. "No one says that to me without getting a beating." The two locked arms and wrestled each other to the ground. Stefan punched Alexeev's side repeatedly, but Alexeev soon got the upper hand and thrust his elbow into the side of Stefan's neck. He grabbed Stefan from behind, wrapping his arms under Stefan's armpits and locked his hands together behind Stefan's neck. He forced him to his knees then rammed his knee onto Stefan's calves, pinning him down. Finally, Alexeev let go and flipped

Stefan onto his back, and with one arm brought his fist down on Stefan's chest once, then twice, then a third time. He flipped Stefan over again and held his face to the ground with his forearm and twisted Stefan's right arm behind him so he could not move. Then he plunged his knee into Stefan's side but lost his balance with the motion.

Stefan took advantage of the situation and grabbed Alexeev's ankle, forcing him to his back, then he sat on his stomach and began punching Alexeev's face wildly: right, then left, repeatedly. He reached out and took Alexeev's hands and held them down to the ground, raised himself up from Alexeev and then came down with with his knee onto Alexeev's gut. He came down a second time, this time on Alexeev's groin. But suddenly, he saw Alexeev's chest and arms flex. Alexeev lifted his arms off the ground with the full weight of Stefan still on top of him. Then he reached his legs up behind Stefan and grabbed him around the sides with his feet and pulled Stefan off him, plunging him to the ground onto his back.

The two jumped to their feet and continued to fight and throw punches at each other. But soon Alexeev's experience and superior strength gave him the advantage. He got behind Stefan and placed one arm around Stefan's neck and locked the other behind Stefan's head then secured his grip, tighter and tighter. Stefan flailed his arms in desperation to no avail. He couldn't breathe, and the blood flow to his head was being cut off by Alexeev's mighty forearms and biceps. Soon, Stefan began to go limp, and within a few seconds he passed out. Alexeev learned how to stop the flow of blood to an opponent's head long enough to make him lose consciousness. He only used this method a few times as a defence, but he had mastered the technique. Alexeev lowered Stefan's limp body to the ground and released his grip, making sure his victim was breathing again. The skirmish was exhausting, but it was now over, at least for the time being. Alexeev had a cut lip and eyebrow, sore ribs, and a bruise on his chest, but Stefan wasn't quite so fortunate. He had a cut forehead, bruised eye and cheek, bloody nose, and bruises on his legs, arms, chest, side and neck. He would also have a nasty headache when he regained consciousness.

Alexeev left him on the ground to recover by himself, then he grabbed his shirt and walked back to the house. He tried to figure out what he would say to Tomi and Galina. This was hardly the kind of behaviour expected of a respectable former army lieutenant. What would Tomi think of him, thrashing one of his aunt's workers? And what would *Tetushka* think of him now? He had just bonded with her and was getting to know her, and now he had ruined everything. As he walked up to the house, the door opened. It was Tomi. He ran to Alexeev and threw his arms around him.

"What happened, Alexeev, are you all right?" He took out his handkerchief and began wiping the blood from his lip and eyebrow.

"I'll be all right, Tomi. Don't fuss over me."

"But what happened?"

"Stefan wasn't hungry," he said, hoping Tomi would not press him to explain further.

"Let me get you inside and clean you up. Did Stefan do this to you?"

"Yes, but he is in worse shape than I am. He will recover on his own. He's out by the woodshed." Tomi followed him inside but grabbed a wash rag and turned to go back out.

"*Tetushka*, will you tend to Alexeev? I am going to see how Stefan is doing." He ran to the woodshed and found Stefan still on the ground, but he was starting to sit up and recover, although he did look a bit disoriented. Tomi quickly plunged the rag into the water bucket and began wiping Stefan's face. "Are you all right, Stefan?" he asked. "What happened?"

Stefan batted Tomi's hand away from his face. "Don't touch me, *pedik*[97]," he yelled. "I don't want your help. You are a curse to this house." Then he bolted to his feet and slapped Tomi in the face with the back of his hand. Tomi lost his balance but was still standing. Then Stefan lunged forwards and began hitting Tomi repeatedly. "Let's see how your new boyfriend likes your face after I get done with it."

Stefan hit Tomi with closed fists several times in the face and within a few blows, Tomi was down on the ground. He didn't fight back; he couldn't fight back. He knew he had no chance of overpowering Stefan and he wasn't fast enough to escape. His only hope was that Stefan would take his anger out on him quickly and stop before he killed him. Stefan was now on top of him with Tomi wedged between his knees. Within a few more blows, Tomi collapsed and passed out. Then finally, the beating stopped and Stefan stood to his feet. He kicked Tomi in the side in one last attempt to inflict some final damage. His fists were red with Tomi's blood and his chest was blood-spattered as well. He still felt

[97] *Pedik* (Kyrgyk): Fag, queer

disoriented and held the side of his head with one hand. He ran down the path leading to the road, stumbling now and again as he ran.

Galina had wiped the blood from Alexeev's face and held a dry cloth to Alexeev's brow to stop the bleeding. "You boys should know better than to fight like this," she said. "Don't you know nothing good ever comes from violence? And what will Tomi be able to do after you and Stefan have fought like this?"

Suddenly, Alexeev was worried for Tomi's safety. He had a bad feeling something was desperately wrong. "*Tetushka*, I must go to Tomi!" He quickly got up and ran out the door. He ran all the way to the woodshed. With each stride he felt more uneasy something horrible had just happened. "Tomi! Tomi!" he called out. But by the time he arrived, Stefan was no longer in sight and Tomi was unconscious and motionless on the ground, covered in his own blood. "Tomi, Tomi, what has he done to you. Oh, my dear Tomi, I am so sorry." As he cried out, the tears streamed down his face. He scooped Tomi into his arms and carried his flaccid, bloody body into the house. He laid Tomi on the kitchen table and gently dabbed his face with a wet rag to remove the blood and clean the wounds. Galina brought over a pan of fresh water and clean rags and took the bloodied rags from Alexeev to soak them in the basin.

After a short while, Tomi was breathing more easily. He opened his swollen eyes and gazed up at Alexeev, "Don't take it out on Stefan," he said as he gasped for breath. "He didn't know what he was doing. He wasn't in his right mind." He reached up with one hand and held on to Alexeev's forearm. "It won't do any of us any good, my dear. Violence from violence is never the answer."

A single tear rolled down Alexeev's cheek. "But I love you, Tomi. It pains me to see you get hurt because of me."

"You must let it go…for me."

Over the next few days, Tomi continued his recovery. The wounds gradually healed, the swelling went down and the bruises began to fade. Galina made sure they both ate well and the two boys regained their strength. Alexeev convinced her to let her housekeeper do the cooking. Stefan did not return while Alexeev and Tomi were there, so Alexeev took over all his chores to ensure all the farm work and duties of maintaining the pigs were taken care of in the meantime. It was hard work, but the farm seemed to run more smoothly without Stefan. Alexeev made sure he kept his thoughts to himself and did not talk negatively to Galina about him. Before long, the incident behind the woodshed seemed like a nightmare from the past and any ill feelings towards Stefan were locked in a vault inside Alexeev's mind, never to be opened again, for Tomi's sake.

Galina was happy to have the boys stay for an extended time, especially during this holiday season, but she was sorry their long stay was a result of injury. Tomi assured her they had intended to stay through the Christmas and New Year's celebrations to begin with, and said he was glad they would now be staying a few weeks more. She enjoyed sitting in the parlour with the boys; recounting stories of her childhood and especially sharing stories of Tomi's father Dmitry. She told stories about when they were children, and the years after the family was separated when Dmitry migrated to Prague. Tomi's mother never told him much about his birth father, mainly because she wanted Tomi to accept and respect her new husband as his true father. He had rescued her and her children from living in the streets, and even though their marriage was not always perfect, she was thoroughly devoted to him and grateful for all he had done for them. Listening to all her stories helped Alexeev feel more a part of their family. Galina had a treasure trove of wisdom to pass on and an immeasurable quantity of family history that might never have been communicated to Tomi if they had not been inclined to stay the extra weeks.

It was three weeks before New Year's, and Galina had many assorted decorations for the house she had collected over the years. Some of them were handmade gifts, given to her by visiting relatives or neighbours or city officials. But many were treasures handed down from her mother and grandmother, a few of which contained centuries of history and memories hidden within them. Galina's mind was still clear enough to tell the stories behind each memento as she removed them one by one from her cedar chest and curio cabinet, although sometimes her memory seemed to loop the same events repeatedly. But she was happy and she was not in any pain, so for the most part, Galina's life was good.

She had a miniature hand-carved, hand-painted village set. Her niece, Kapeka, started it for her many years ago. Each year she and her husband, Daniil, would bring her a new addition or two to the village so it would grow each year. Each year she would clear the table in the front parlour and set out the village pieces with care to make them look like a miniature rural hillside. Fedya, her youngest brother, had given her a set of miniature carved wooden animals: dogs, cats, deer, horses, cows, sheep and of course, a variety of pigs that were all hand-painted. She placed these throughout the display. She also had dozens of brass and silver candlesticks to adorn the fireplace mantels, shelves, and tables throughout the house. She had multiple sets of hand-painted wooden icons and each set was designated for a specific room in the house. There were also many glass and silver balls and metal bells and stars she collected for decorating the New Year's branches.

The boys helped Galina sort through all the treasures and place them diligently wherever she told them. They treated each item as an adventure, listening intently to each story then singing traditional New Year's and Christmastime hymns, chants and carols. Galina taught them a few songs they had never heard before. She learned some of them when she was a child: songs taught to her by her mother and grandmother. She even remembered a few pagan chants in her great-grandmother's language, Adyghe, native to the Shapsug tribe when they lived in Sochi.

The boys had a great time over the next week as they transformed the house into a glorious holiday setting and magical wonderland. The final touch was bringing in hay from the barn and spreading it over the dining room floor, and ironing the large, white, silken tablecloth for the dining table. The silk tablecloth had been purchased in Cathay by Galina's father (Tomi's grandfather) when she was a child. It was pure white, with an embroidered border of dragons, cherry trees, and maidens holding fans. Even though the scenes were not Christmas nativities Galina treasured the silken cloth and displayed it proudly every New Year's and through the end of the Christmas celebration.

The boys also helped Galina make the large Christmas candle from the beeswax she saved for the special holiday event. Of course, most of the wax she harvested was used for everyday candles, but she took special care to make sure her servants saved a large amount of the purest, whitest wax for this special time of year. This was the largest candle she would make every year. It had three thick, braided wicks, stood about one metre high, and was about 10 centimetres in diameter. For the final touch, she took rose petals and boiled them, then reduced the liquid so all the water was boiled out, leaving a fragrant oil. Then she added the oil to the beeswax. The result was a candle with a distinct rose fragrance when lit. It was one of the envies of her neighbours and Galina was careful not to share her secrets with anyone outside of the family. So, this year she passed on the secrets and the tradition to Tomi and Alexeev.

Finally, the home looked festive, had an aroma of pine and roses and was filled with the holiday spirit just in time for the holiday celebrations. Tomi had been planning a special dinner for the three of them as a pre-celebration festivity, and Alexeev was waiting for this day because he had a special surprise planned for Tomi. Before they had left Moscow, Alexeev had concluded his business Mister Dvorkin. He had asked the jeweller to remake his mother's brooch into two identical silver bands, each with one of the two emeralds. He had hidden them away in his bag, so his gift had remained a secret.

Meanwhile, Tomi was planning a surprise of his own and intended to reveal it to Alexeev before the special dinner as well. While he was recovering and confined to his bed, he thought a lot about how he truly felt about his relationship with Alexeev. He never knew anyone who could read his thoughts and feelings like Alexeev could. He loved him with all his heart and soul and wanted to always be by his side. He borrowed some paper, a pen and inkwell from Galina, and over the last few weeks he wrote a vow to Alexeev. Tomi's mother had taught him a few aspects of the Jewish faith she was raised in. One of them was the *Ketubah*[98], which is a marriage union vow. She had read hers to Tomi; the vows made to her by Tomi's birth father for their engagement. Tomi had kept the idea in his heart, in hopes one day he could write a *Ketubah* for the one he loved. He had found his one true love in Alexeev.

While Tomi and the housekeeper were busy preparing the meal, Alexeev was busy tending the animals and then stoking the fireplaces. Galina had many sets of clothes she kept on hand for her workers or for relatives who visited. So, she found festive clothes for both of the boys to wear for dinner to make them feel a little more jovial. She knew Tomi never bothered to bring fancy clothes with him when he visited, and she doubted Alexeev had anything fancier than what he was already wearing. While the housekeeper finished preparing the dinner, Galina sent Tomi to his room to change. Then she rang the bell for Alexeev, so he could come in and bathe. She had laid out Tomi's clothes in his bedroom, and Alexeev's set was in the bathing room. Unfortunately, Alexeev had forgotten to restoke the fire in the boiler after Tomi's morning bath, so his bath would be a cold one. But the cold water was refreshing after a rigorous day on the farm and in the barn. He found some lavender oil Galina had set out for him, so he rubbed it on his chest and underarms.

They finished getting ready about the same time, and both made their way to the dining room. The table was set with Galina's favourite Delftware and sterling silver utensils, and she had placed her special crystal goblets rimmed with gold

---

[98] *Ketubah* (Hebrew): Written thing. A traditional Jewish prenuptial agreement, part of the marriage ritual

at each place setting. The boys transferred the food from the kitchen to the dining room table. And lastly, Galina asked Alexeev to go to the cellar and bring up a bottle of her *Mors*[99] wine, made from her own foxberries. There was a special eight-tiered candelabra on the table, white silken napkins with silver napkin rings shaped like maple leaves. On top of Tomi's plate were two little velvet boxes, one white and one blue, and on top of Alexeev's plate was a scroll tied with a lavender silk ribbon. Next to Galina's plate was a tall thin crystal vase with a single, long-stemmed red rose with a sprig of pine.

When Alexeev returned with the wine, they were all ready to be seated for the meal. Tomi dismissed the housekeeper for the evening then he pulled out Galina's chair and helped her get seated. Alexeev set the wine bottle on the table and pulled out Tomi's chair for him. Alexeev picked up the white velvet box from Tomi's plate and then knelt down between Tomi and Galina.

He took Tomi's hand, and as he began to speak, he felt like he was almost choking on the words and his hands began to shake. "Tomi, you are my true love, my destiny and my true source of happiness. I think of you every second of the day. I miss you when we are apart, and I love you with all my heart. You are my *odin yedinstvennyy*[100] love, and I am your only, beloved Alexeev. Will you accept this ring as a token of my love, my devotion and my promise to protect you and stay by your side for as long as we both live?" Alexeev opened the box and removed the shining silver ring. The green emerald was sparkling in the candlelight. As Alexeev placed the ring on Tomi's ring finger on his right hand, he gazed into his eyes and saw tears rolling down his face.

"Oh yes, yes, my love." Tomi flung his arms around Alexeev's neck and kissed him. Galina was glowing and smiling from ear to ear. She was full of joy to witness such an expression of love. Alexeev handed him the blue velvet box and opened it. Tomi smiled, then took Alexeev's right hand and slipped the second ring on Alexeev's finger. Then Tomi picked up the scroll from Alexeev's plate and untied the ribbon. "Now I have something for you, my love." He opened the scroll and read it to his Alexeev:

You are my best friend, my hope, my future, my strength, and my soul mate. As we embark on life's journey together, I promise to love, cherish, encourage, and inspire you. Our hearts will fuse together, creating a unique bond with

---

[99] *Mors*: A sweet, non-fermented juice made from foxberries

[100] *Odin yedinstvennyy*: One and only

friendship and compassion at its core. Through this union, I vow to value and support you, always striving to show sensitivity to your needs.

In your eyes, I see my love, and in your heart, I see my dreams, and in this promise, I see a union that is true and steadfast, uniquely devoted to compassion, kindness, and sincerity. We shall nurture one another emotionally, spiritually, and intellectually, always mindful of our respective qualities and strengths. May we continue to grow together, maintaining the courage and determination to pursue our desired paths. I promise to celebrate life's joys with grace and overcome life's adversities with tenacity. Through all time and space, there has been no love like ours, and our story will unfold with beauty, grace, and meaning. May we maintain the intimacy that fosters trust, honesty, and communication.

I pledge to cherish and sustain you, meeting life's trials with quiet strength and courage, and meeting life's blessings with wonder, joy, and laughter. As life partners, we shall build a home that emanates love, peace, tolerance, and charity. We will grow as individuals, and delight in an elegant freedom born from mutual respect. Through each other's eyes, we will see the world anew: that we may be better together. And through all time and space, there will be no happiness like ours.

When he finished reading, he looked into Alexeev's eyes. They both had tears rolling down their cheeks. Alexeev placed his hands on either side of Tomi's face, rubbed the tears away with his thumbs, and leaned in and kissed him. Then they both embraced and wept together.

Galina was crying too, but finally she picked up the bottle of wine and handed it to Alexeev. "Pour us some wine, my dear, I have a blessing for the two of you." After he filled their goblets, Galina raised hers up and said, "*Pozdravlayu*[101], my boys. May the gods and fates bless your lives forever. Now let's eat in celebration of your new life together! *Chtoby vse horoshee iz starogo goda pereshlo v novy*[102]."

---

[101] *Pozdravlayu*: Congratulations

[102] *Chtoby vse horoshee iz starogo goda pereshlo v novy*: To carry the best from the old year to the new, or all the good things of the old year are transferred to a new

Moye Schast'ye[103]

Part 2

Do Smerti[104]

[103] *Moye Schast'ye*: My happiness, my joy

[104] *Do Smerti*: Until death

Chapter 15

A Joyous Beginning

Tomi and the housekeeper spent the better part of thc afternoon preparing food for the special dinner following Galina's instructions and guidance. The menu included baked pig, *vinegret salad*[105], *farshirovannyy sladkiy perets*[106], dark rye bread and butter, berry jams, pickled vegetables, mushrooms stewed in cream, honey-almond cookies, *sbiten*[107], black tea, *blini cake*[108] and of course, *Mors* wine.

Rings were exchanged, vows were given and Galina blessed the new couple as they drank wine to seal their new relationship. Tomi, Alexeev and Galina ate, shared stories, laughed and cried over dinner. Galina was so happy that she could witness the beginning of Tomi's new-found relationship with Alexeev. Tomi felt stronger than he had over the last few weeks and his aches and pains from rheumatism were almost completely gone, as had the bruises from his unfortunate encounter behind the woodshed. He was grateful Alexeev was by his side to see him through his illness and tend to his injuries, and Alexeev had never been happier now that Tomi was in his life again. He was no longer lonely, no longer had to make decisions on his own, and no longer placed his own welfare above everything else in his life. This, he thought, is true happiness.

When they finished dinner, Galina felt the need to let the two boys have some time by themselves. "I think I will go lie down for a while. Tomi, take Alexeev for a walk out in the garden. There is a beautiful moon tonight and there are no

---

[105] *vinegret salad*: A Russian salad made with diced cooked vegetables (beetroots, potatoes, carrots), chopped onions as well as sauerkraut and/or brined pickles

[106] *farshirovannyy sladkiy perets*: Stuffed sweet bell peppers

[107] *sbiten*: Hot drink made from spices and herbs with honey or sugar

[108] *blini cake*: Stacked *blini* with custard or cream filling separating each layer. Topped with custard cream sauce and fresh fruit.

clouds in the sky…a lovely night for a walk." Galina got up from the table and wrapped her shawl around her shoulders. "When you come back in, we can have some hot *sbiten* and *blini* cake in the parlour."

"I'll light the fire in your bedroom before we take our walk." Alexeev put his arm around Galina and helped her down the hall to her bedroom. Meanwhile, Tomi cleared the table and put the leftover food away.

As they walked down the hall, Galina said, "I am so glad you and Tomi were able to find each other again after all these years. You know, Tomi has been alone for a long time and he hasn't always been very happy. Sometimes the pain and loneliness can be very depressing."

Alexeev opened the door to the bedroom and helped Galina into her bed. He removed her shoes and shawl and set them on the wooden chest at the end of the bed then he covered her with a soft, multi-coloured, knitted blanket. "Did you knit this, *Tetushka*?"

"No, my dear, this blanket was knitted by my younger sister, Olga, the year before she died. She and Tomi's father were only a year apart. It broke her heart when Dmitry left the family." While Galina continued with her story, Alexeev busied himself with building the fire in the fireplace. "I think she was secretly in love with him even though he was her brother. Sometimes brothers and sisters can have relationships that can't be easily understood. She never married, and later when we found out that Dmitry had died, she withdrew even more. After our parents died she stayed with me until she passed away about eight years ago."

"That must have been hard on you, losing your husband, then your brother and parents and finally your younger sister."

"When you get to be my age, most of the friends you once knew are gone. Life is not always easy. *Chemú byt', togó ne minovát'*[109]." Galina closed her eyes while Alexeev finished making the fire.

"I will let you know when Tomi and I come back in. Then we can have the cake and *sbiten* to celebrate." The fire was now going strong, and Galina could feel the warmth filling the room. "Rest well, *Tetushka*," he whispered as he patted her head and gave her a kiss on the cheek.

After Tomi put the food away, he gathered together their coats, scarves and hats from their bedroom and brought them out into the parlour. He also came across a few old pipes he left during previous visits. He had started smoking a

---

[109] *Chemú byt', togó ne minovát':* What must be, must be (literal)—which have not been avoided

pipe when he entered the army as a teenager, and smoked a pipe somewhat regularly ever since, especially during the winter and holidays. It seemed to take him to a romantic place in his mind and a place where his imagination could take over his thoughts. It was peaceful and soothing and would often have a calming effect if he was upset or nervous. He took the two pipes and stuck them in his coat pocket, then went back into the kitchen and found a fresh bag of tobacco. Galina always made sure she had fresh tobacco on hand for visitors and relatives, and especially for Tomi.

"Are you ready for our garden walk?"

"Yes, I have our coats and scarves in the parlour. I don't want to get a chill."

"That reminds me, I want to start the fire in the parlour to take the chill off the house," said Alexeev. "I'll be right back. It won't take but a moment." He returned in a few minutes and the two went outside hand in hand.

It was a beautiful evening; the moon and stars were mirrored in the frozen river below, and the snow on the ground was glistening white and seemed to sparkle from the sky above. They could see the spray of stars thickly strewn haphazardly across the sky as if they were thrown by a farmer sowing seeds in the field. The pine trees were covered with water droplets, and occasionally a branch would catch the wind and a spray of unexpected sprinkles would mist down on passers-by. The sculptured bushes in Galina's garden were bare, but their shapes could still be identified: deer, squirrels, giraffes, elephants, turtles and fish, and some were also shaped into spheres, cubes, and pyramids. The garden was a wonderland even in the dead void of winter. Alexeev could hardly imagine how it would look in the spring and summertime when the leaves were green and the flowers were in full bloom. It must be a spectacular sight he thought. He wished he and Tomi could stay and see the magnificent blooms in their full glory together. *Perhaps next year*, he thought.

In the centre of the garden was a circle of four stone benches and a large stone firepit. Behind one of the benches was a brightly painted shed filled with wood for burning in the pit. Alexeev opened the door to the shed, took an armful of twigs and placed them in the pit. Then he retrieved several large logs and placed them strategically on top of the twigs. Tomi had found the flints and attempted to light the wood to no avail. "Let me do that for you," said Alexeev. "You stick to mastering your skills in the kitchen." He smiled wryly at him and took the flints. Within minutes, the fire was roaring and warming their bodies and souls. The stream of smoke swirled overhead and the occasional sparks rose upwards and disappeared into the hazy cloud.

Tomi took the pipes from his pocket and handed one of them to Alexeev. "Would you like to smoke?" he asked.

"Sure. I don't smoke too often but I like the smell of the tobacco."

"That pipe was one my father left me. It was a wedding gift from his father-in-law, my grandfather." The pipe was made of cherry wood, carved with Hebrew lettering underneath the rim and it had brass bands below the lettering and between the mouthpiece and base of the pipe. The highly polished red and black grains in the wood were especially beautiful in the light of the fire and starlight.

"What do the symbols around the rim mean? I don't recognise the lettering."

"The words are in Hebrew, it says, 'Love, trust, and forgiveness.' It is a statement of the foundations of marriage."

"It is very beautiful." Alexeev held it up so it reflected the light of the fire.

"Here. Take some tobacco." Alexeev took a pinch and stuffed it into his pipe with his thumb then handed the pouch back to Tomi.

"It has a sweet smell."

"Yes, it has essence of cherry in the tobacco," he said as he stuffed some into his own pipe. "The pipe I am using is a clay pipe I bought here in Nizhny Novgorod several years ago." Tomi's pipe was a blue glaze and had the face of an old man with a beard. He pulled a burning twig from the fire and handed it to Alexeev to light his pipe. They sat on the bench in the moonlight, smoking their pipes in front of the fire, warming themselves and feeling very romantic. "I would love to have a garden like this someday."

As they finished smoking their pipes, Alexeev wrapped his arm around Tomi and rubbed his shoulder to keep him warm. "That feels good," said Tomi as he rested his head on Alexeev's chest. Tomi enjoyed feeling Alexeev's strong chest muscles on the back of his head. They were massive and hard and made Tomi feel protected and safe. And he loved placing his ear on Alexeev's bare chest to listen to his heartbeat.

"It feels good to have you in my arms, my love," Alexeev whispered as if he didn't want the bushes and trees to hear the passion in his voice. He took Tomi's hand and held it up so he could see the ring on his finger. "It looks good on you, *schast'ye moye.*" He smiled and kissed Tomi's hand.

"I have never felt so loved, Alexeev. You make me feel complete like I have never felt before," Tomi's voice sounded a little broken, like he was having trouble finding the right words. "You make me feel more alive than I have felt in years. You brighten my days." Then his voice changed, and it sounded surer and more confident, "I want to be able to brighten your day also, to make you feel warm inside and brighten your path and fill your face with happiness. I want to fulfil your every need and desire, to protect you from harm, to shield you from unhappiness and shelter you from the storms that life can bring. I want you to run to me if you are afraid, and I want you to rest in my arms if you are tired. I want to caress your brow and kiss your lips to arouse you." He paused for a moment, then continued, "You already do all that for me, *moy general*[110]. I feel protected by you and I feel safe in your arms."

Alexeev squeezed Tomi a little tighter. "Now that is what I like to hear, *schast'ye moye*." He turned Tomi towards him and kissed him. His tongue felt so comfortable inside Tomi's mouth. His lips opened wide and his tongue licked Tomi's chin, neck and then his earlobe. As he sucked his face and neck, he reached his hand into Tomi's shirt and found his hard nipple. Tomi inhaled deeply in anticipation of the passion to come. "I love to get you excited, my dear." Alexeev lowered Tomi backwards onto the bench and covered Tomi's body with his own. They were breathing heavily and their exhaled breaths looked like smoke trails from two chimneys in the cold air.

Alexeev unbuttoned Tomi's shirt and sucked one of his nipples as Tomi ran his fingers through Alexeev's hair. Then he wrapped his legs around Alexeev's waist and grabbed his hair, pulling Alexeev's head closer onto his bare chest. Alexeev stood up with Tomi still clinging to him. His hands had found their way underneath Tomi's shirt and were caressing his back. He spun around on the cobbled walkway and danced his way around the firepit. Tomi hummed a familiar melody in Alexeev's ear and one of his hands ran through Alexeev's hair while the other steadied itself around Alexeev's strong, thick shoulder and neck muscles. They danced for a while in the moonlight, enjoying their moment alone together.

In the distance, they could hear the howling of a lone wolf and an owl hooting somewhere in the trees. But the cold air was making Tomi shiver. So, Alexeev gradually stopped dancing and set Tomi back down onto the stone bench. He

---

[110] *moy general*: My leader, my master

started buttoning Tomi's shirt. "We should go back in before you get winter fever. You have been through a lot lately and I don't want you getting ill with the rest of our trip ahead of us."

"You're right, my love, and *Tetushka* will be expecting us inside for cake any time now." Tomi sat up and pulled his coat back around him to button it. "Do you see my scarf anywhere?"

"Here it is. You were sitting on it," Alexeev took it from the bench and wrapped it around Tomi's neck. Then he smiled and kissed him on the forehead. "I love you, Tomi."

"I love you too, Alexeev." They embraced and hugged each other for another brief moment. The fire was almost out, but Alexeev took a stick and pushed the logs apart so their flames would die down a little faster. Then they walked arm in arm back to the house.

Galina was still in bed, so Alexeev went to wake her while Tomi brought the cake to the table and put the pot of *sbiten* over the fire to get it hot. It smelled good and spicy, and reminded him of the pleasant holidays he used to spend in Minsk and *Nyen* when he was a child. He found some candied orange peel in the pantry and added some to the hot brew. Then he poured the *sbiten* into a porcelain pot and brought it out to the table.

Alexeev slowly opened the bedroom door. "*Tetushka*, are you ready to get up and have some dessert with us?" he said quietly. He walked over to her bed and gently touched her shoulder. "*Tetushka*, it's time to get up and have some *blini cake*. It's Tomi's special recipe."

She slowly sat up and manoeuvred her legs over the side of the bed. "Would you hand me my shawl and shoes, dear?"

Alexeev picked up the shawl and placed it over her shoulders and helped her with her shoes. Then he took hold of her hands and gently raised her to her feet. "Did you have a pleasant rest?"

"Yes, it was good to sleep for a while," she said. Then she raised her head up a little to smell the air. "Oh, doesn't that smell wonderful. I love the smell of hot *sbiten.*"

They were soon in the dining room. Tomi was just getting ready to cut and serve the cake. Alexeev helped Galina to her chair then poured the *sbiten.* The steam from the three cups swirled above the table like hypnotic trails: wispy and mystifying. Tomi served each of them a slice of cake, then he poured custard sauce over each piece and spooned raspberry jam on top of each slice.

Alexeev stood up and raised his cup, then Tomi and Galina raised theirs also. "To the New Year. May it bring happiness, hope and fulfilment."

"To the New Year," said Tomi and Galina.

Then Alexeev sat down next to Tomi and put his arm around him and kissed him. Just then the clock in the parlour struck twelve o'clock. They continued eating the delicious cake and drank the hot *sbiten* while they talked about Tomi and Alexeev's plans for their future together. Galina was glad she could give the boys a good start. She was coming to the end of her life's story, but their story was just beginning. Galina had been much more than an Aunt to Tomi over the years. She was more often his advisor, his confidante, and his friend. He would speak to her about his relationships with men, his disappointments and tragedies, and his loneliness and despair. Even though he could only visit once a year, they created a bond between them, greater than any friendship either of them had with those they saw daily. Tomi would send her regular messages by courier, along with his new wines, cordials, or special gifts he managed to purchase. And Galina, in turn, would send back samples of honey, pork sausage varieties and an occasional porcelain figurine she would come across. He had a treasure of thirty figurines he displayed on his writing desk in the parlour, each one a treasured gift from his beloved *Tetushka*.

Their celebration was complete and each of them had special memories to take with them. They shared the memory of Tomi and Alexeev's new union, and with that, Galina was contemplating what more she could do to give the boys a good beginning. She remembered when she was first married to her husband Nikolai, what a struggle they went through those first years. How she hoped and prayed so many times the gods would smile on the two of them and the fates would be kind, but after only fourteen years of marriage, Nikolai was taken from her, and she was left to raise her children on her own. With only a small herd of pigs, she continued her husband's business and made it a success. But because she poured every bit of her soul and spirit into the business and her family, she was never able to give any of her soul or spirit to another lover.

Each of her children left, one by one, and over the years the business thrived. Nikolai built their home before he died and gave her the foundations of a business she was able to manage after he was gone. Much of Tomi's business savvy was a result of Galina's influence in his life. She encouraged him to start up his own business while he was still a city treasurer, and even sent her business manager to Shoynaty for a year to help him get the company established. She funded his first investment in wine and farm equipment and made a gift of several cows and horses.

And now Galina was ready to invest once again in Tomi's future, this time with Alexeev by his side. She wanted to make sure the boys got a good start together. Tomi had talked about how he thought Alexeev needed to be kept busy in some kind of business activity, but they hadn't decided what that might be. She knew the boys would be staying for only a few more weeks so she needed to make her decision quickly.

It was a long day and a very long evening. Tomi and Alexeev escorted Galina to her bedroom and helped her get ready for bed. After she got into bed, Alexeev kissed her on the forehead, then Tomi leaned over and gave her a hug. "Thank you for welcoming him into your home, and thank you for celebrating with us," he whispered. Then he kissed her on the cheek.

Galina patted Tomi's cheek and reached out and held Alexeev's hand, then she held Tomi's hand as well. "I am happy for the two of you. I was glad to take part in your happiness tonight. I will always remember this special evening." She squeezed both their hands then put both her arms under the covers while Alexeev tucked the covers in around her.

The boys extinguished the lamplight and walked together, arm-in-arm down the hall to their room. For a few minutes, they recounted the memories of the evening. They held each other's hands and admired the rings. Then Alexeev took the scroll from his coat pocket, kissed it and set it on the nightstand next to the bed. After they got undressed, they pulled back the covers and slipped into the bed and Alexeev held Tomi close to him. They talked for a while longer, but finally they both fell asleep, smiling and bringing the good memories of the day into their own private dreamlands.

Chapter 16

Christmas Preparations

Over the next few days, Tomi and Alexeev continued to talk about their future together. It would not be easy and Alexeev would have to find work. Tomi had not worked as town treasurer for a few years, but made enough profit from his farm produce, and especially from the sale of his blackberry wine and cordials, to make his life more than comfortable and prosperous. He could regularly afford trips like this to spend time away from his business and rely on his workers and servants to take care of things. He could also afford to provide charity to many different individuals during the year, and still manage to give gifts to friends and relatives when the opportunity arose. But they both knew it would be good for Alexeev to keep busy and active in the community.

There were few opportunities for work in town though, so Tomi wanted Alexeev to consider managing a lodge for travellers. He knew Alexeev's cousin Orlov had taught him a great deal about the business of his boarding house, and a lodge on the banks of the Vychegda River could be profitable, especially since it was a prime fishing and hunting location for travellers. Tomi had some money he had set aside, waiting for a good opportunity to invest in.

The idea sounded appealing to Alexeev, but he insisted the lodge should be within walking distance of the cottage, so he could manage it each day without having to travel far. There were several advantages to opening a lodge. The farm could supply most of the produce for the guests' meals and selling Tomi's wines and cordials in the lodge could be an added benefit and attraction and mutually beneficial for Tomi's business as well. They could even arrange tours of the winery or provide guided nature walks or horse rides for travellers who want to see the countryside.

They had fun talking about the possibilities and variations on lodge designs, menus, furniture styles and landscaping ideas. Once they agreed on the project,

Tomi would write to Vanya to propose commissioning him to build the lodge's furniture. They even discussed ways to entertain their guests. Tomi knew how to play the gusli and Alexeev played the zuma and both knew most of the traditional songs. Some of Tomi's farmhands also played different instruments: tambourines, flutes and pipes, and the bandura, and every autumn they would form a small ensemble and play music at the town's harvest festival. There were so many possibilities. Galina even joined in their enthusiasm and gave them samples of her various bath teas along with the recipes.

When Alexeev was a teenager, he helped Orlov build several extensions to their house, so he tasked himself as the chief builder and architect of the lodge. He would search out local young men in the village to assist him, and he was confident the outcome would be an amazing and beautiful structure and the envy of the towns throughout the valley. He got some advice from Galina; whose husband designed and built the fabulous home she now lived in. Then he sketched out a few designs, and he and Tomi talked about how many rooms they should include, how large the kitchen should be, how many parlours, the size of the dining room and bathing rooms for the sauna areas, like the one in Galina's home but on a larger scale with separate sections for men and women. They also talked about adding on a Great Hall with a high ceiling for dancing, large meetings, and parties, and make it available to the rest of the town for local functions.

Galina collected seeds and bulbs from her garden over the years, so she gave them an ample supply to start a large garden area for the lodge. Some of her collection included very rare plants: miniature roses of every hue, lilies, peonies, wild columbine, several varieties of mint, chamomile and varieties of camellia. She also decided to give them her Delftware collection. It included service for 20, five large serving bowls, three platters, four pitchers, five salt cellars and many other miscellaneous bowls and serving dishes. And she gave them her collection of crystal ware that included goblets, glasses, carafes, vases and pitchers. At first, Tomi refused to accept such an expensive gift, but Galina explained how this was probably one of the last times they would see her, and she had other sets of china she would leave to other relatives, along with furniture, ornaments, pictures, books, clocks and much more than she would ever possibly miss. So, Tomi and Alexeev accepted the gifts graciously. And of course, none of the items could be packed up until after the Christmas celebration. Galina had invited relatives and many of her neighbours to the house for the upcoming festivities, as she had every year since her husband's passing.

She recruited the boys to plan the celebration this year, including the twelve course Christmas Eve dinner and all the meals that would follow, along with arranging all the entertainment and group activities. This, of course, included music and dancing. It was a tall order, but they felt sure they could make all the necessary arrangements. But Alexeev ensured Tomi would take it easy and rest every afternoon for at least an hour. Tomi started pulling out recipes from Galina's collection for the *Rozhdestvo Khristovo* [111] festivities and Alexeev went into town to arrange for musicians and to pick up necessary supplies, decorations and food. Galina invited around 70 people to the celebration, which also included clergy from the local parish and a few of the city officials. Most of the guests would come in carnival or festive costumes and those who did not would be provided fancy dress to change into. Galina's home was not far from the church, so after the twelve-course meal ending Lent, all the guests would sing songs and walk in procession to the church for the Christmas Eve service.

After the service, the guests would procession back to the house, singing all the way and stopping at neighbours' homes along the way, bidding them well wishes and leaving gifts of cakes, cookies, gingerbreads or other sweet breads. Then the guests partake of the elaborate Christmas meals prepared over the next three days of celebration. There were a thousand things the boys needed to do to prepare and only a few more days to get most of the things done. The first thing they needed to know was exactly how many guests had responded back to Galina. Who planned to attend and how many were expecting to stay for any of the four nights? Galina's housekeeper made a list of everyone who planned to attend. The first group of relatives would arrive four days before Christmas, and the second group would arrive by the end of the day before Christmas Eve.

There were 17 relatives who were visiting:

From Yoshkar-Ola: Tomi's niece Klara (age 54), her husband Nikolai (age 56) and their twin sons Alik and Anton (age 23).

Also from Yoshkar-Ola: Klara's oldest daughter Ania (age 31), her husband Mikhail (age 34), their son Mikhail (age 12) and daughters Faina (age 9) and Nina (age 6).

[111] *Rozhdestvo Khristovo*: Nativity

From Moscow: Tomi's niece Tasha (age 41) and her husband Alexandre (age 43), and her two daughters Galya (Galina)—*Tetushka's* namesake (age 17)—and Nadya (age 15).

Also from Moscow: Tomi's grandnephew Toma Daniilovich (age 37) and his wife Darya (age 43), their son Vadim (age 18) and daughter Akilina (age 15).

Tomi was planning to use most of the women folk to help prepare the meals, and especially the baked goods to give to neighbours during the procession after the midnight service. Galina wanted to have at least 30 baskets of baked goods available for the procession. Tomi's recruits included Klara, Tasha and Darya, and his three grandnieces, Galya, Nadya and Akilina. They would need to start baking almost as soon as they arrived so all the items could be made on time. Galina had many neighbours between her home and the church and she never missed an opportunity to give them a Christmas basket of baked goods.

Alexeev was counting on the younger men and boys to help him with the farm chores, chopping wood, arranging tables and chairs, setting up the beds and cots and any other physical activity he could find to keep them busy and out of mischief. The boys and men were Klara's husband, Nikolai, and his two sons, Alik and Anton; Ania's husband, Mikhail; and finally, Toma Daniilovich and his son, Vadim. Ania was put in charge of watching and taking care of the three youngest children: Mikhail, Faina and Nina. They would be enlisted to set and clear tables, wash and cut vegetables, fold napkins and even do some light housework. All able bodies were expected to contribute in some way.

Twenty-three neighbours replied they would attend on Christmas Day after the Christmas Eve service, and four of the clergy from the church planned on joining the Christmas Eve dinner and procession to the church: Father Matvei, Father Petya, young Father Yuli and Father Andrei. And the mayor and the city treasurer along with their wives were expected to join as well. By Tomi's reckoning, there would be about 40 people coming to the house sometime during the holiday week. Most of the relatives would arrive before Christmas Eve so, for Christmas Eve dinner, which included Tomi, Alexeev and Galina and eight of the workers, the count was 28 for the first night.

Alexeev needed to decide who would sleep in which bedroom and who would get the attic. Of course, the married couples were given priority for the bedrooms on the main floor since they had the most comfortable beds and are easiest to access. Cousin Klara and her husband Nikolai had the front bedroom on the west side of the first floor, cousin Ania and her husband Mikhail had the bedroom next to it and cousin Toma and his wife Darya were in the third bedroom on the west side. Aunt Galina's bedroom was the front bedroom on the east side of the hall. Tomi and Alexeev were in the second bedroom on the east side, but they gave up their room for cousin Tasha and her husband Alexandre.

On the second floor, there was a large bedroom above the parlours, so the five girls were assigned that room: Faina, Nina, Galya, Nadya and Akilina. The final sleeping place was the attic, which was above the sauna and bedrooms. The younger boys (Tomi's grandnephews)—Alik, Anton, Mikhail and Vadim—could share the front part of the attic, which was divided, then Tomi and Alexeev had the back portion.

After diligently working to get the house ready, purchasing supplies, preparing the bedrooms and attic, along with keeping up with all the other duties of the farm, Tomi and Alexeev were exhausted. The night before the first relatives were to arrive, they finally got to bed just before midnight. Tomi fell back onto the bed and flung his arms back above his head. "Well, Alexeev, we finally finished. All that's left is to prepare the meals. I am so tired..." He yawned.

"You shouldn't work so hard, my sweet. You will have your hands full once the family starts arriving tomorrow." Alexeev kept talking as he started to undress. "I am afraid I will need to be out in the barn most of the day tomorrow. I have five gallons of milk in the cellar, but I wanted to get at least another two, and you'll probably need more cream."

"How much butter do we have?" Tomi asked.

"Oh, we have plenty of butter and cheese. Twenty pounds of butter, eight five-pound rounds of hard cheese, and ten pounds of *tvorog*[112]." Alexeev walked over to the fireplace and threw a few logs in, then lit the fire. "We also have about five gallons of cream. Does that sound like enough?"

"I think that will be fine. How much meat do we have in the larder?"

"Five pigs, ten chickens, two lambs, a goat, four geese, a buck and about a hundred eggs. We can feed a fucking army. Anyway, we have another five or six hundred pigs in the sty if we get desperate...don't tell Galina I said that." Alexeev stood in front of the fireplace, completely naked, and stretched his hands out towards the fire.

---

[112] *tvorog*: A traditional Russian cheese, similar to farmer's or cottage cheese

Tomi started laughing. "You've never seen my family eat before. They eat like a herd of elephants!" Then he looked up at Alexeev. "*Moy golyy general*[113], you are so beautiful. Ludi didn't do you justice in that painting. Oh, it is a beautiful painting, but you are beyond beauty that can be captured with oil paints on canvas." Alexeev bowed his head down and started to blush. "Come over here and help me get undressed."

Alexeev flexed and posed playfully as he made his way over to the bed. "I will use my superior strength to remove your boots and my powerful grip to undo your shirt buttons. Like *Ilya Muromets*[114]!"

The silhouette of his body in front of the fireplace looked ominous. Tomi could see the definition of Alexeev's muscles as the glow from the blaze glistened on his masculine bulges and curves. Even though he was tired from the last few days' activities, Tomi was aroused. "You're silly… Do you know how much I love you, my dear?"

"Show me, my love." Alexeev removed Tomi's boots, then slowly removed his pants and stockings, and finally unbuttoned his shirt with his teeth. After each button, he licked the part of Tomi's chest that was revealed.

Tomi was reclining on the bed, leaning back on his elbows with his legs dangling over the bed towards the floor. He tilted his head back. "That feels so good." Alexeev opened the shirt all the way and saw Tomi's nipples, firm and pert with the expectation and anticipation of satisfaction. He reached his tongue out to the nipple on the right and circled the hard erection, then flicked it with his tongue. Then he leaned over to the left nipple and repeated the foreplay. Tomi moaned in response. Alexeev kissed his shoulders and neck, then rubbed his chin against Tomi's chin. He plunged his tongue forcefully into Tomi's mouth as if with a ravenous appetite. He put his arms around Tomi's back and gently lowered his body all the way to the bed. His cock rubbed against Tomi's cock. Then Alexeev put his knees up onto the bed on either side of Tomi and he pulled him all the way onto the bed. They continued to kiss. Tomi reached around and put his arms around Alexeev's neck. He felt the brawny muscles of Alexeev's back and grabbed his powerful sides, feeling the sturdy ribcage that framed the magnificent torso.

Then Tomi tapped Alexeev's back. For a moment, they stopped kissing, "What is it, my dear? Am I going too fast? Did I hurt you?"

---

[113] *Moy golyy general*: My naked general.

[114] *Ilya Muromets*: A folk hero of ancient Kievan Rus', a knight errant.

"No, my love, but I am so tired. Could you just hold me tonight?" He started to cry. He wanted to please his handsome, virile lover but he was exhausted from all the work they had done. "I want to do it but I am so weak tonight."

"Oh, don't feel bad, Tomi," he said as he kissed his brow. "I should have known better." Alexeev brushed his hand over Tomi's forehead. "We'll just get under the covers and I'll hold you close to me."

"Thank you, my sweet."

Alexeev got up and helped Tomi sit up, then he pulled back the covers and let Tomi put his legs under the covers. "Will you be warm enough?"

"Oh yes, you have made a nice fire for me, *lyubimyy moy*[115]."

Alexeev went around to the other side of the bed and cradled himself against Tomi. He gently put his arm over Tomi's chest and kissed him on his cheek. "Sleep well, *schast'ye moye*."

"I love you, Alexeev."

"I love you too, Tomi."

As they held each other that night, they realised not every night needed to end in passionate lovemaking. They could be content in each other's arms, knowing they were in love. They could give each other physical pleasure without having to exert much energy, just by holding hands, or wrapping an arm around a shoulder, or leaning onto the other's chest, or just looking lovingly into each other's eyes. Their relationship would not be built on how many times they could ejaculate, or how deeply one could throat the other's cock, or how effectively one could penetrate the other's ass. But it would be built on their love for one another, and their consideration of each other's needs, even if those needs sometimes required the omission of physical exertion or quieting a physical passion for a time.

Soon, Alexeev heard Tomi's quiet purring and knew his one true love was content. He pulled the covers up and gently tucked them under Tomi's chin then kissed him on his cheek. He smiled and closed his eyes and soon he was fast asleep with his arm still resting on Tomi's chest.

It was three days before Christmas Eve, and Alexeev woke up early, as usual. He prepared to busy himself with his routine chores on the farm. He put another log on the fire in the bedroom fireplace and then got dressed but made sure he did not wake Tomi in the process. Then he went to Galina's room and built her

---

[115] *lyubimyy moy:* My love, my lover

fire as well. The clock struck five. He hurried to the kitchen and cut a slice of *chyorniy khleb*[116] and cheese, started the fire in the oven, then filled a pot with water for tea.

As he waited for the water to boil, he looked out the window. The sky was clear, and he could see the stars. It should be a good day to get things done. He noticed the jar of raspberry jam on the counter was almost empty and knowing how much Tomi enjoyed jam on his bread every morning, he decided to go down to the cellar and bring up another jar. He looked around to see if there was anything else he needed to bring up. *Let's see, we are almost out of turnips and eggs. Hmm, looks like I need another onion and maybe a few carrots…and a few sausage links for me and a cup of cream.* He grabbed a basket.

He found everything he needed in the cellar and came back up and set the basket of food on the counter. The water in the kettle was still heating so he started to prepare the vegetables for frying. He diced the turnips and carrots then sliced and diced the onions. Then he pulled one of the iron skillets from the cupboard, twirled it playfully in the air, then set it on the stove and spooned a few globs of butter into it. As the butter melted, he slid the cut vegetables from the cutting board into the skillet and spooned a small amount of salt from the salt cellar over the frying vegetables, then took a pinch of white pepper and sprinkled it in as well.

While the vegetables cooked, he pulled a large bowl from the cupboard and cracked six eggs into it. Then he added some cream, a little salt, a pinch of pepper and began to whisk the mixture together. He pulled out another skillet from the cupboard and set it on the stove and spooned some butter into it, then he stirred the vegetables again. Once the butter had melted, he slowly poured the egg mixture into the skillet. He could hear the eggs bubbling as their liquid settled on top of the hot butter, then he placed a lid on top to cover it. Once the vegetables started to brown, he added several sausages into the mixture. Then he lifted the lid from the egg skillet and poured a little water from the kettle into the skillet around the sides, then replaced the lid as the water began to steam.

As the breakfast continued to cook, he got down some plates and cups from the cupboard, and placed them around the kitchen table, then got out some utensils and set them next to each plate. He heard the water in the pot starting to boil so he placed the ceramic tea kettle on the table and wrapped the tea cloth

---

[116] *Chyorniy khleb*: Russian rye bread or black bread

around it. As he poured the hot water into the tea kettle, the back door swung open and a tall, white-haired man walked in.

"Good morning, good morning!" he said. "I am Vladimir, Galina's *svinopas*." He held out his hand in a friendly gesture.

Alexeev grabbed his hand and gave him a strong, firm handshake. "Good morning, I am Alexeev, a friend of Galina's nephew, Tomi."

"Ah, yes. Galina told me Tomi would be visiting but I thought he would be gone by now. I am glad to meet you though."

"It's good meeting you as well." They both smiled and nodded. Alexeev took down another cup and offered it to Vladimir. "Can I pour you a cup?"

"*Da, pozhaluysta*[117]. Will you and Tomi be staying through the holidays?"

"Yes, we will. And I am glad you are back. Tomi and I have much more work to do before Galina's relatives arrive." He poured the tea and handed it to Vladimir along with the jar of honey and a plate of bread and cheeses. "Would you like to join us for breakfast?" Then he cut another slice of bread and cheese for himself, and they both sat down at the table.

"Thank you, the bread and cheese will be fine." Then he leaned in towards Alexeev and whispered, "I've already had one breakfast." Then he chuckled. "But that's why we returned a little early. I didn't want Stefan to have to work alone over the holiday week…Galina always invites a crowd for Christmas. By the way, where is Stefan? I didn't see him in the workers' quarters."

"I am afraid he and I had a few disagreements. We haven't seen him for a few weeks now." Alexeev stood up and checked the eggs and vegetables, gave each a quick stir, then covered them again.

Vladimir laughed. "Stefan always was a bit of a hothead; he's got quite a temper. But you look like you can hold your own… Ah, don't worry, he will be back once he's had time to cool off. It is not the first time he has let his temper get the best of him."

"Well, I am sorry I fought with him anyway."

"What's done is done." Vladimir was obviously not upset in the least, which made Alexeev feel a little more at ease. "My crew and I arrived late last night. Kolya and Semyon are already starting the morning chores so we will take care of the farm work. You can help Tomi and Galina with whatever they need to get done in here."

---

[117] *Da, pozhaluysta*: Yes, please

"Thank you, I appreciate that. Although I was glad to learn about tending the pigs. It is a lot of work. Once the relatives arrive, I will send the boys out to the woodshed to cut more wood for the fireplaces along with any other chores you want them to do. I also wanted to get a few more gallons of milk this morning."

"Very good, we need to keep those little devils busy so they don't get underfoot inside the house. I will have Semyon help you with the milk though. Kolya and I will take care of the rest. And just send the little devils out to me once they get here. There is plenty to do around the farm, as you well know." Vladimir took the last swallow of his tea and stood up to leave. "Come on out for the milk any time you are ready." He reached out and shook Alexeev's hand again then turned and walked out the back door.

Alexeev took the last bite of his bread and cheese and set the skillets on the warming shelf, then went down the hall to his bedroom where Tomi was still sleeping. He put his hand gently on Tomi's shoulder and whispered, "Tomi, Tomi. Is my little *sonya*[118] ready to wake up?"

He rolled over towards Alexeev, yawned and stretched out his arms. "Is it time to get up already?"

"Yes, breakfast is almost ready and the tea is already made. Oh, and I wanted to let you know, Vladimir is back this morning. After I get the milk, I can help you out in the kitchen or whatever else you need me to do in the house."

"Oh, that's wonderful," he said as he yawned again and sat up on his elbows. "I'll get dressed and come right out. Mmm, I smell eggs and turnips…but I wanted to make *syrniki*[119] for you this morning." He sounded a little disappointed.

"You've got to get up earlier than this if you want to make breakfast for me!" Alexeev kissed him on the forehead. "Now, I've got to hurry back to the kitchen to make sure our breakfast doesn't burn." He looked back as he opened the door, "I think I heard *Tetushka* getting up when I passed her room. Would you mind checking in on her and help her to the kitchen?"

"I will." He waved his hand at Alexeev to motion him away, "You go ahead and finish getting breakfast ready. We'll be there in a few minutes."

Tomi pulled on his trousers and a warm shirt then stepped into his slippers. He could feel a slight headache coming on, but hoped it would pass. He walked

---

[118] *Sonya*: Sleepyhead (literally, dormouse)

[119] *Syrniki*: Fried cheese cakes

down the hall and knocked on Galina's door and slowly opened it. "Good morning, *Tetushka*. Are you awake?"

"Yes, Tomi. Come on in." He opened the door and saw she had already lit a candle on her nightstand, and she was dressed and sitting on the edge of her bed. "Could you help me with my shoes? They get harder and harder to put on each morning."

He knelt in front of her, put on her stockings, then slipped her shoes onto her tiny feet. "Let me get your shawl so you don't catch a chill." He struggled a little to get up, but managed to steady himself by hanging on to the bedpost. He wrapped the shawl around her shoulders then helped her to her feet. "Alexeev has made us breakfast this morning. Eggs and turnips, I think. And he said Vlad is back. Now Alexeev can help us with anything we need him to do."

They walked slowly down the hall and into the kitchen. Alexeev had everything ready. The eggs were in a serving bowl, and the vegetables and sausages were on a platter. There was also black bread, raspberry jam, and of course, hot tea and honey. After the three of them ate breakfast, they talked about the plans for the day. Most of the relatives were expected to arrive sometime today if the letters were accurate. The weather had been favourable the last few weeks, so there shouldn't have been any delays due to snow, and most of them made it a point to be on time or early.

Mikhail and his son were coming down from Yoshkar-Ola on their own, while his wife Ania and their two daughters would ride with Klara and her family. They were meeting in Cheboksary a week earlier and were planning to meet up with Mikhail later to continue in caravan. So, by late afternoon or evening the first nine guests would grace Galina's home.

The menus were all planned, and Alexeev made sure he had all the food Tomi needed in the cellar and larder. Galina added her advice and shared several recipes that were family favourites, including a few pie recipes she hadn't used since before she was married. They were recipes her mother gave her: ones she remembered from childhood that might be particularly memorable for Klara, and she also wanted to pass these recipes on to her kin.

But Tomi still showed signs of exhaustion and the dull headache from early morning had morphed into a pounding and throbbing behind his eyes. His hands trembled as he ate, his eyes were bloodshot and he seemed to have difficulty concentrating. Alexeev worried about him and decided to help with the meals so Tomi would be able to rest during the day before the family arrived. After all, he knew his way around a kitchen and could follow recipes. And he thought, once the family started to arrive, he could enlist some of the wives to help with the meals, just as Tomi had already intended.

Tomi had already done all the work to plan the meals, even figuring the ingredients and amounts necessary for all the preparation. Plus, he worked out a schedule for the children to assist in setting the tables, clearing, and washing the dishes, cutting vegetables, kneading bread, churning butter and other various tasks to keep them busy. Tomi didn't like loose ends and always needed a plan to follow. Likewise, Alexeev had a list of chores for the boys for barnyard activities, feeding the livestock, milking the cows and goats and chopping wood for the fire. Vladimir made a list of the chores and duties that needed to be covered, so it was simply a matter of assigning the tasks.

"Tomi, I want you to go rest for a while, and you too, Galina. I will finish the chores for this morning and then I'll go down to the cellar and bring up all the food we'll need for lunch and dinner." Alexeev felt Tomi's forehead to make sure there was no fever. "I don't want you getting sick. I don't think you've been sleeping very soundly the last few nights. You've had too much on your mind."

"But you can't do all of this by yourself," he said.

Alexeev leaned over and whispered into Tomi's ear, "You must have forgotten, I am the powerful *Ilya Muromets*." Then he flexed his arm and smiled.

Tomi put both hands around Alexeev's large, rock-hard bicep and smiled. "Yes, I did forget for a moment. What would I do without you, my love?"

"Even if you don't get to sleep, I want you to at least rest for a while. *Tetushka*, I want you to go rest also, or maybe go and knit for a while. This is going to be a long week and I don't want you to wear yourself out either." He got up and went to Galina and helped her to her feet and started escorting her to her room. "I'll let you both know when lunch is ready." Tomi waited in the kitchen for Alexeev to return then he got up and leaned on Alexeev as they walked down the hall to their bedroom. "After lunch, I'll change the linens on our bed and move our things to the second floor. I already have our bed prepared for us upstairs along with all the other beds and cots, and I have clean sheets for the bed in our room."

"But that's so much work." But he knew he could hardly stand, let alone prepare a large meal. "I love you so much, *moy general*."

"Yes, yes, yes. I love you too. But let's get you back in bed so I can get busy."

After they walked to the bedroom they sat on the edge of the bed for a moment, then Alexeev knelt in front of him and took off his slippers, unfastened his trousers and unbuttoned his shirt. “Can you stand up, my dear? Just lean on me so you don’t fall.” Tomi stood up slowly and put his hand on Alexeev’s shoulder. Then Alexeev pulled down his pants as he stepped out of them. He stood up slowly and wrapped his arm around Tomi’s waist to steady him then pulled off his shirt and lowered him back onto the bed. He put his feet under the quilt and pulled it up around his neck. “Now you sleep as long as you want. I’ll get the chores done and get you in a few hours.” He softly kissed Tomi’s forehead, smiled, then kissed Tomi on the lips. He pulled the canopy shut over the bed to keep the light out, then closed the bedroom door behind him.

Alexeev stopped just outside the bedroom and leaned up against the wall outside the bedroom door. His cock was hard. He missed their physical interaction. The simple act of kissing or caressing, or even Tomi’s hand on his shoulder aroused him. He wanted to stay and thrust his cock into Tomi’s mouth or ass. He wanted to stretch out on top of him and feel their two cocks converge and intertwine between their hot bodies. He wanted to suck Tomi’s beautiful hard nipples and he wanted Tomi to massage and pound his chest as he had before.

Alexeev untucked and unbuttoned his shirt and reached his hand in and gave his left nipple a rough twist and pull. Then he reached down into his trousers and felt his swollen cock. He closed his eyes and imagined making love to Tomi, and he stroked his cock a few times. After only a few minutes of his fantasy, he took a deep breath and released his cock, then rebuttoned his shirt and tucked it back into his trousers. He looked back towards the bedroom door then walked down the hall and into the kitchen where he started to clean up the breakfast dishes.

He decided *buterbrody* and soup would be the best option for a simple lunch. He brought up some salted pork from the cellar along with a few carrots, pickled beets and onions and a jug of apple cider. They had eaten the last few slices of black bread for breakfast so Alexeev proceeded to make a few loaves. He found the recipe, mixed all the ingredients together, then began the kneading process. His cousin Orlov would never let him make the bread at the boarding house. Alexeev remembered when he was in his teens, Orlov would give him the chore of making bread and butter for the family, but every time he tried, the bread would turn out rock hard. After several failures, Alexeev was assigned butter churning instead. Every other day, he would churn butter, working his shoulders, biceps and forearms in the process. He was also the oldest boy in the family, so he also chopped wood, forked hay and dug postholes for the fences. It was all hard work, but he appreciated the discipline it taught him when he entered the army.

He set the kneaded dough in a few pans, covered them with a cloth and placed them near the stove for warmth. Now he had time to move his and Tomi's belongings from the bedroom to the attic. As he walked down the hall he quietly opened Galina's bedroom door just enough so he could glance at her resting in her bed. She looked peaceful and comfortable. The fire in her fireplace was still blazing, so he carefully shut the door.

Then he opened Tomi's bedroom door and quietly packed their clothes and belongings into their trunk, then set the trunk out into the hallway. He went back into the bedroom and proceeded to wipe down the dresser with a dry cloth. Then he noticed the bottle of cologne Vanya had given him. He removed the cork and put the bottle up to his nose. He smiled as he took a deep breath. Then he replaced the cork and put the bottle in the case on the nightstand with their other toiletries. He pulled back the bed canopy slightly and saw Tomi was still sleeping. He gently touched Tomi's cheek then brushed his hand over his hair and bent in to kiss his forehead. Tomi moved slightly but didn't wake up.

Alexeev went back into the hallway and picked up the trunk and carried it up to the attic. Their part of the attic was in the back behind a dividing wall, so they would have a little privacy, although he wasn't sure how quiet the boys would be. He had placed crates in between the beds and cots, so the fellows would have places to store their bags and belongings. The back portion of the attic had a full-sized bed for Tomi's sake, so at least they would get some good rest at night. Alexeev wanted to make sure Tomi had a comfortable place to sleep or escape to, so he chose one of the most comfortable beds. He even moved a small dresser up to the attic for Tomi and placed one of Galina's best candelabras on the dresser.

For the final touch he borrowed one of Galina's crystal vases and filled it with cypress branches and a few sprigs of blooming witch hazel. Just as he finished placing their clothes in the dresser he heard a carriage pull in alongside the house. *Could it be Klara and Nikolai so early?* He rushed down the stairs to the side door and opened it.

In the front seat of the carriage were a young man and boy. *It must be Mikhail and his son, Mikhail Mikhaylovich.* He walked up to the carriage and guided

Mikhail to the carriage house. Alexeev stopped the carriage just outside the carriage house so they could get out a little easier. He helped them get down from the carriage then introduced himself.

"Good morning, I am Alexeev Kondurov, a friend of your Uncle Tomas." He shook Mikhail's hand and bowed his head slightly.

"So very nice to meet you, I am Mikhail Petrovich," he said. Then he placed his hands on Alexeev's shoulders. "You are a fine-looking man. Have you been taking care of our Great Aunt Galina Pavlovna and Uncle Tomi?"

"Yes sir. And now that you are here, I can tend to your needs as well," Alexeev stood at attention as he answered. He wanted Mikhail to be assured he had the utmost respect for him and his family.

"No need to be so formal," Mikhail said as he smiled. "You and I are probably around the same age." Then he leaned in and kissed Alexeev on both cheeks. "This is my son Mikhail, and there are two stowaways in the back…they would be Alik and Anton."

"Let's get you and the boys something to eat, then we can come back out and tend to the horses later." Alexeev offered his hand to the boy as he stepped down from the carriage. "So, you are Mikhail. What a strong grip you have," said Alexeev as they gripped hands to get down. "Are you looking forward to the celebrations?" The boy just nodded in response.

"He is a little shy at first, but after he gets to know you, he'll be under your feet every minute." Mikhail patted his son on the back then stretched his arms out to his side. "The last few miles were a little bumpy."

Alexeev called into the back of the carriage, "Boys, are you coming out? Do you want to join us?"

Two identical heads popped out of the carriage curtain and spoke in unison with rather low, husky voices, "Who are you calling 'boys'?"

"Oh, I beg your pardon." Alexeev bowed. "I should have said 'gentlemen'."

Mikhail leaned into Alexeev and whispered, "Be on your guard with these two. They can be terrors when you least expect it."

"Well, let's get everyone settled in. Mister Petrovich, I have you and your wife in the third bedroom on the left once you pass the parlours. Are your wife and daughters coming separately?"

"Yes, they decided to come with Aunt Klara and Uncle Nikolai. But they should be arriving soon. They weren't far behind us. And please, call me Mikhail."

Then Alexeev bent down to the lad. "And you, young man, will be sleeping in the attic with me and your Uncle Tomi. Captains Alik and Anton will be sharing the attic with us along with your cousin Vadim when he arrives." Alik and Anton hopped out of the carriage and they each shook Alexeev's hand.

"Anton, could you and Alik bring in the bags?" asked Mikhail.

"I'm Alik, but we'll bring them in anyway," he said, then he rolled his eyes and shook his head in a very disapproving manner.

Alexeev knew there was some rebellion going on and started making mental preparation and plans on how best he could handle these two. Perhaps he should treat them like he used to treat his troops. That was his first thought. But maybe they just need a positive influence in their lives. Someone they can look up to and follow instead of feeling like they have to compete for attention.

Alexeev picked up one of the smaller bags and held it out to Mikhail's son. "Mikhail, do you think you can carry this bag in for us?"

He smiled and nodded his head. "You can call me Miki." He looked like he was looking forward to the adventure of staying in the attic. He had only been to his Aunt Galina's once before and that was seven years ago when he was five. He and his father and sister Faina had come to stay while his mother was in her last few months of pregnancy with his youngest sister, Nina. They had arrived in late February and stayed until September. Nina was born in May, but Ania had some bleeding during her last four months of pregnancy. Her mother stayed with her, but the family thought it would be best if the children were not present during the birth or while Ania recovered. There was a possibility Ania would not survive the stresses of labour, so it was decided Mikhail and the two children would visit their *Tetushka* for the summer.

When he was here before, the attic was full of old furniture, beds, cots, paintings, statues and many things a little boy could explore. It was like a jungle of old furniture. He remembered *Tetushka's* farm well though and was especially looking forward to seeing the pigs and playing with the piglets. "Is Uncle Vlad going to be here also?" Miki asked with a look of excitement on his face.

"Oh yes, Uncle Vlad is here," answered Alexeev, then he bent down and whispered to Miki, "And I think he will need help with his piglets, too!" Miki smiled and giggled. "Mikhail, I want to let Aunt Galina know that you've arrived. There is hot water on the stove for tea."

"Of course, of course. We know our way around." He patted Alexeev on the shoulder and helped direct the group into the house while Alexeev walked ahead of them into the house and down the hall to Galina's room.

Alexeev knocked on her door. "*Tetushka*, may I come in?" He slowly opened the door and walked over to her bed. "Mikhail and Miki are here with Anton and Alik."

Galina sat up slowly in bed, "Oh, they are here early."

"Would you like to rest a while longer?"

"No, no, I should get up and welcome them." Galina had a look of anticipation on her face that merged into a broad smile.

"Here, let me help you with your shoes." He knelt in front of her and placed her shoes gently on her feet. He helped her to her feet then opened the bedroom door for her. "I'm going to see if Tomi is ready to get up. I think they will want some tea after they get settled. Would you like to get out the tea? The water is already on the stove…hmmm, I may need to light the stove again but I'll be there in a few minutes."

Galina walked slowly out to the kitchen and Alexeev went into Tomi's bedroom. "Tomi, Tomi, my love…your nephew and grandnephews are here early. Would you like to get up now?"

Tomi rolled over towards Alexeev and suddenly realised what was said. He quickly threw the covers back and sat on the edge of the bed. "They're here already? Oh, my goodness, I wasn't counting on them arriving until after lunch."

"Now, Tomi, calm down. Everything is going to be fine. The bread dough has had plenty of time to rise, so I just need to bake it." He sat down next to Tomi and put his arm around him. "*Tetushka* is getting the tea ready. So, we just need to slice some cheese and put some vegetables together in a pot for some soup."

"Thank you, *moy general*. What would I do without you?" He kissed Alexeev then finished getting dressed. "I'll be out in just a few minutes, then I'll start chopping the vegetables for the soup."

"And I'll go fire up the oven and put the bread in to bake." Alexeev cradled his hand under Tomi's cheek. "Did you get enough sleep, *schast'ye moye*? I don't want you to wear yourself out over the holidays."

"I'll be fine, don't worry so much about me." His head felt a little better, but there was still dull ache behind his right eye.

"And who else should I be worrying about?" he said as he looked Tomi straight in the eyes. "You, my dear, are the only one I worry about." He kissed him on the forehead, then on the lips. "Mmm, I can hardly wait for tonight!" Then he jumped up, took Tomi by both hands and pulled him up to his feet. "Everything will be fine. I'll either be in the kitchen or out helping Mikhail unload the carriage." He kissed Tomi again and then went out to the kitchen.

Galina was in the kitchen getting the tea from the cupboard when Alexeev came in. "It looks like the bread is ready for baking," she said.

"Well, I'm glad to see it rose this time. Usually, my bread turns out hard as a rock. Let me heat up the stove and oven so we can get the water hot for the tea." He loaded several logs until there was a nice blaze. Then he filled the water pot and moved it onto the stovetop and opened the oven and placed the pans of bread inside to bake. "*Tetushka*, I'm going out to help Mikhail unload the carriage. Tomi should be here in a few minutes. Would you let him know to check the bread so it doesn't burn?"

"Oh, yes, yes. Don't you worry about it. We will take care of everything in here, my dear."

Alexeev walked quickly out the back door and jogged out towards the carriage. Just then, Kolya and Semyon came out of the barn carrying two five-gallon containers of milk. They stopped directly in front of Alexeev and stood at attention.

"*Gospodin*[120], I am Kolya. Vladimir said you wanted more milk. Shall we take this down to the cellar?"

"Yes, please do. I am so sorry I didn't make it in to help with the milking." Alexeev bowed in gratitude. "Thank you so much for helping out, and please call me Alexeev."

"Nice to meet you, Alexeev. It was our pleasure." He reached out with his free hand and shook Alexeev's hand. "This is Semyon." Alexeev promptly shook Semyon's hand as well. "Be sure to let us know if you need anything else." They bowed and tipped their hats, then walked inside the house with the milk jugs.

Alexeev continued to the carriage where Mikhail and his son were unloading the trunks. He grabbed one trunk and set it on his shoulder and grabbed a second trunk and carried it under his arm. Miki had a smaller trunk in his arms and was waiting for instructions. Mikhail was still pulling trunks off the carriage. Alexeev called up to him, "Mikhail, whose trunks are these?"

"The two larger ones are Ania's, and Miki has his own."

---

[120] *Gospodin*: Lord, master, gentleman, mister, sir, monsieur

"We'll take these in then, and I'll send the boys…I mean, the men out for the rest. Follow me Miki, I'll show you where you'll be staying."

"Yes, Uncle Alexeev," said Miki. Alexeev paused for a second, then smiled. It made him feel good to be called Uncle by one of Tomi's grandnephews.

The two of them walked into the house and down the hall to Mikhail's room. Alexeev set one of the trunks down and opened the door. He set the two trunks down on the floor in front of the bed, then he and Miki walked out and closed the door. "Miki, let's go up to the attic and get you settled, then we'll get some water for your papa's room. You can help me fill the pitchers for each of the rooms." They walked into the dining hall, then up the stairs to the attic.

The windows upstairs were open to let in the fresh air and the breeze was blowing the curtains that hung in front of the windows. Alexeev had also hung a few curtains throughout the attic to divide the space where the boys would be sleeping to give them a little added privacy. The waving curtains looked a little eerie to Miki, and his eyes opened wide as if some mysterious monster might be lurking in the shadows behind the curtains.

"Follow me Miki, your fortress is here in the back," Alexeev sensed Miki's uneasiness but he was used to interacting with children. He took Miki's hand as they passed through a few folds in the curtains, then through an opening into a good-sized area sectioned off with a bed and a crate. "Here are your quarters my lad. Your Uncle Tomi and I will be sleeping just behind this door over here. So, if you need anything in the night, we are nearby." He showed Miki the door leading to the room where he and Tomi would be sleeping. Alexeev opened the door partway so Miki could see in. He knelt next to him. "If you need anything, you just knock on this door and I'll come right out for you." Miki set his trunk down by his cot, then they found their way back through the maze of curtains and back down the stairs to the dining hall. "Now, let's get that water for the rooms."

As they went into the kitchen, Alexeev could hear the water boiling in the pot on the stove, so he got down the ceramic teapot and set it on the table, then wrapped the tea cloth around it. Galina spooned some tea leaves into the teapot and Alexeev poured the hot water over the leaves. "I'll let Mikhail know the tea is ready. We're going to take some fresh water to the rooms, then we'll be right back."

"Thank you, my dear. There are several pitchers on the counter in the pantry you can use for the water."

Alexeev filled the pitchers with water. He gave one to Miki while he carried two in one hand and one in the other hand, then he and Miki went around to each room and placed a fresh pitcher of water by each basin. They passed Mikhail in the hall. "Aunt Galina has the tea ready for you in the kitchen and she's anxious to see you."

"I'm helping Uncle Alexeev, Papa," Miki called out.

Alexeev smiled. "I'd like you to call me Uncle Lexee. Another fine man called me that before and I like the sound of it." The two of them continued down the hall with the other three pitchers. Miki had set his in the first room, so now his job was to open doors and make sure the towels were straight. When they finished setting the last pitcher, Uncle Lexee grabbed Miki by the waist and raised him up over his head and set him on his shoulders. Then he ran up and down the hall a few times, ducking and spinning around, jumping up and down. They both laughed and giggled. Finally, they made it to the kitchen. Alexeev lifted him off his shoulders and set him on the floor just in front of the kitchen door. He whispered into Miki's ear, "Now, we don't need to tell *Tetushka* that we were racing in her halls. It will be our secret." Miki smiled and nodded, then he hugged Alexeev around his neck.

"It will be our secret, Uncle Lexee." Miki opened the kitchen door and ran in.

Tomi was just coming down the hall, so Alexeev waited for him at the kitchen door. "My love, I have a new name. Miki calls me Uncle Lexee."

"I like that, it suits you. Lexee it is then." Tomi reached up and kissed him on the cheek. Alexeev smiled, then kissed Tomi on the lips.

Anton and Alik had been upstairs in the attic putting their things in the make-shift dresser, but they came down just in time to see Alexeev kiss their uncle. They looked at each other and smiled deviously, as if they had a cunning or shrewd idea planned out. They waited for Tomi and Alexeev to go into the kitchen, then they whispered to each other. Tomi and Alexeev hadn't seen them, and they lingered back for a moment before they went into the kitchen.

"Oh, Miki, how you have grown," said Galina. "You are nearly as tall as I am. How old are you now, my dear?"

Miki blushed, then gave Galina a hug and kiss. "I turned twelve in October, *Tetushka*."

"My, my…time goes by so quickly. Soon you will be a young man." Galina patted his cheek. "Hop up to the table and your uncle will pour you some milk."

One of the twins came through the door. "Oh, Alik, it is so good to see you too. And where is your brother?"

"I'm right here, *Tetushka*," said Anton, stepping out from behind his brother.

"I don't understand how you can tell them apart so easily," said Tomi.

"I've been able to tell them apart since they were born. It's the shape of their heads, I think." Galina put her hands on the side of each of their faces, then gave them each a kiss.

"That's right, I remember Klara telling me you helped her deliver them when they were born. You've helped deliver several of your grandchildren and great-grandchildren, haven't you?"

"Yes, many, many joys…and a few tears," she said as a tear rolled down her cheek. She remembered her granddaughter, Faina Andreyevna, who died while giving birth to her second daughter. She was Roza's only child. But Faina's daughter, Gavrilla, grew up to have a son, Andrei, who turned 23 this year. Both mother and child died. And then her granddaughter, Klara's firstborn daughter, Rada Nikolayevna, who died in her sleep only a few days after birth. Rada would have been the same age as Alexeev if she had lived. But Galina always marvelled at the twins. They were the only twins she had ever delivered. And there were other grandchildren and great-grandchildren she had delivered. Each with their own special memory for Galina.

Though her body was frail and weakening more as the years passed, her mind was still sharp. She could still remember events of her childhood, of her marriage and also of her later years when she would take time from her work and daily duties to visit and care for relatives who were pregnant, or ill, or fading into death. She couldn't always remember the events or conversations of five minutes ago, or who visited two weeks ago, or the plans she made for upcoming events, but she had a staff of good, caring workers who took care of her business and looked after her as if she was their own grandmother.

Chapter 17
Holiday Plans and Pains

Later that afternoon, Klara and Nikolai arrived with Ania and her two daughters Faina and Nina, just before sundown. Then Toma Daniilovich and Darya arrived with their son Vadim and daughter Akina. Vadim also brought his friend Leonid; whose parents were both ill with diphtheria and were not expected to recover. Toma already committed to Leonid's parents he would make sure Leonid had a place to stay until he could find work, and they would welcome him into their family like their own child. Vadim and Leonid had known each other since early childhood. Since Leonid's family had moved to Moscow from Chatanga in the northern region before Leonid was born, he had no contact with any other family members. Alexeev quickly brought in an extra cot from storage and set it up in the attic, and Tomi laid out clean linens and blankets. Toma also told Uncle Tomi how Alexandre and Tasha were delayed but they should be arriving before noon on Christmas Eve.

Tomi asked Mikhail to bring up a ham from the larder for dinner, along with other necessities, like pickled vegetables, fruit preserves, milk and honey. He had the housekeeper prepare most of the meal. But he insisted on supervising what went into each dish. He also had to check how things were stirred and cooked and needed to approve when they were deemed to be ready for the presentation. He enlisted Faina and Nina to cut vegetables, and Akina and Miki were given the honour setting the table. Klara made several more loaves of bread.

"You can never have too much bread around in this family!" she would say. She brought a large bag of fennel seed for her special holiday fennel loaves, which was not Tomi's favourite, but she insisted on making it anyway. Tomi still had a few loaves of black bread left over that Alexeev made earlier that morning, so he would have black bread he could enjoy, and Klara promised to make several different kinds of bread as well over the next few days.

Tomi rested as much as he could and let the younger generation take charge of the tasks more difficult or labour-intensive, but by the time dinner was ready, his head was pounding. He had sharp pains behind his eyes and the vision in his left eye was blurred and slightly darkened. But he didn't want to give anyone cause for alarm and especially didn't want Alexeev to worry, so he kept quiet. These headaches usually went away within an hour or so, and the vision generally cleared up shortly after that.

Dinner was finally ready and the entire family sat down around the grand dining room table in the great hall. Twenty-five in all, which also included Vladimir, Semyon and Kolya; Helga and Klava, the housekeepers; Helga's three sons Klaus, Johann and Hendrick. Galina always made sure her hired hands were included in festive and holiday celebrations, especially those who could not visit their own families very often. But she also gave them time off to visit their relatives as often as she could. She had learned that a good employer not only looks out for the profitability of the business but also for the welfare and happiness of its employees. The workers never had any problems with Galina, and the business never suffered as a result of her generosity. In fact, it thrived.

The feast was fabulous and everyone had their fill. There was enough variety of foods everyone was happy, and no one left the table without a full belly, except Tomi. His headache did not subside this time as it had in the past. The pain behind his eyes also made him nauseous and dizzy, so he only had a few bites of food and a few sips of wine.

While everyone talked back and forth about their journeys, family business, new and old romances, children's school grades, church gossip, recipes, births, deaths, marriages, new dresses, old styles, weather, politics and religion, Tomi found it difficult to focus on any of the conversations. His mind was overcome by the pain and he began feeling unsteady. He reached over and grabbed Alexeev's hand and squeezed it hard. Alexeev looked at Tomi and immediately knew something was wrong. Tomi's face was pale and his eyes were red and filled with tears.

"Tomi, what's wrong?" he asked.

"Take me to my bed, I'm not feeling well." He was nearly choking on his words.

Alexeev helped him up from the table and led him over to the staircase. Then he picked him up in his arms and carried him up to the attic and laid him down in the bed he had prepared for the two of them. Alik had been observing, so he rushed and followed them.

"What's wrong with uncle? Is he sick?"

"I don't know, Alik. He fainted when we got to the stairs. He said he was feeling sick, but I think it's…he probably just needs to rest, you know, he's been so busy planning this whole gathering." He hesitated to say any more. "Would you go down and ask Mikhail to come up?" Galina had told Alexeev earlier that Mikhail had studied for several years to become a doctor at the University of Bologna in Italy, but gave it up when his wife had their first child, Miki. He and his wife were in Bologna for six years while he studied there, but when she became pregnant, they moved back to Yoshkar-Ola so Ania could be with her mother for the birth. After Miki was born, they never returned to Bologna, so he worked on his father-in-law's dairy farm instead.

But he put some of his training to good use: birthing calves, tending the livestock medical needs and occasionally treating other animals in the neighbourhood. He had learned a lot about medicine but never got his certificate to practice. Alexeev knew it was too late in the evening to get the doctor, so he thought Mikhail could at least look Tomi over and make a preliminary assessment of his condition.

Alik dashed down the stairs and brought Mikhail up to see Tomi.

Mikhail motioned for Alik to stay where he was and not come into the bedroom as he looked Tomi over. He felt his skin for temperature, looked under his eyelids for any discolouration, opened his mouth to see the colour and texture of his tongue, then unbuttoned Tomi's shirt and listened to his heart and lungs. "He has a fever and his eyes are very bloodshot, but I don't see any other signs indicating what might be the cause." He shook his head, frustrated that he was unable to see any other signs. "Did he say anything to you before he fainted?"

"When we were at the table, he said he wasn't feeling well and he wanted to lie down. He only had a few bites of food. Then just before we got to the stairs, he put both hands up to his temples as if he was in pain and then he fainted." Alexeev remembered what happened during their visit with Vanya, so he recalled those events to Mikhail as well. He explained how Tomi fell from a stool and injured his side, and that he was having headaches regularly, and when the doctor had come to see him, he had talked to Tomi privately.

Mikhail didn't want to alarm Alexeev since he didn't have all the information and there truly wasn't anything they could do until the doctor arrived, except try to make Tomi comfortable and try to get the fever down. "I think we will just have to wait, either for Tomi to wake up to tell us more, or until the doctor can examine him. This is beyond my training." He went to the water basin and soaked a cloth in the water then wrung it out. "We need to get his fever down tonight, so I need you to keep applying a wet cloth to his face, forehead and chest. I'll stay and check on him throughout the night to see how he's progressing and then, in the morning, I'll have someone get the doctor."

Alexeev thanked him and shook his hand then sat down next to Tomi and dabbed his face and forehead with the damp cloth.

Mikhail opened the bedroom door but kept back when he saw Alik. "It's very important no one else comes up here in Tomi's room until after the doctor sees him and determines what's wrong. You haven't touched him, have you, Alik?"

He thought for a moment. "No, I haven't. I was going to help Uncle Lexee but he managed without me."

"Good, then you can go back downstairs. Both Alexeev and I must stay up here alone with Tomi until the doctor arrives." Mikhail looked around the room. "We have enough firewood for the night. I need you to ask *Tetushka* where the doctor lives, then go fetch him as soon as you can tomorrow morning. Also, ask my Ania to come up so I can give her instructions."

Alik ran downstairs and carried out Mikhail's orders, then informed all the relatives of what had happened. There were many gasps and wringing of hands and a lot of speculations about what was going on. Ania suspected the worst but went upstairs as requested. She knew if her husband told Alik not to enter the room, he suspected a quarantine might be necessary, and if that was the case, anyone who was exposed to the illness could be in danger of contracting the disease. Quarantined illnesses were often fatal. Ania saw many such diseases in her short lifetime, mainly because Mikhail was studying these particular diseases. He was already exposed to many of them, so he was more than likely immune, but many in the household could become ill since Tomi had encountered everyone after their arrival. Only Alik was permitted to leave the house and only on the condition he go straight to the doctor's house and promise not to interact with anyone either on the way or on his return. Mikhail knew the dangers of epidemics, and didn't want to be the cause of a city-wide disease that could possibly take the lives of many. He explained everything to Ania and asked her to try to calm the relatives. There was enough food in the house to last for several weeks, and hopefully, the dangers of spreading the illness would be gone well before the food or firewood ran out.

Early the next morning, Alik walked down the road to the doctor's house and brought him back to Galina's house. No one had yet awakened except for Ania, so the doctor was able to see Tomi without interruption. Alexeev and Mikhail took turns in the night watching Tomi and managed to get his fever down. He had not had any convulsions and he was awake when the doctor arrived.

"Tomas Pedorov, you gave everyone quite a scare yesterday. How are you feeling now?" the doctor asked as he felt his forehead.

"My headache is gone and I don't seem to feel dizzy anymore," he said. "But I feel weak."

The doctor thought for a few minutes and looked at Tomi. "You had a similar incident when you were here a few years ago, didn't you?"

"He's had this before?" asked Alexeev.

"I'm afraid so. But it's not a disease," he reassured them. "Tomas, I think they need to know." He looked at him and rested his hand on his shoulder. "Will you let me tell them?" Tomi nodded reluctantly. "The truth is we aren't completely sure what is wrong. He gets headaches that eventually cause his vision to blur, and sometimes the headaches are severe enough they cause nausea or even unconsciousness. How long has it been now? About ten years or so?"

"Yes, I think I had my first severe headache and fainting spell about twelve years ago, and my doctor in Storozhevsk diagnosed it about two years later," said Tomi. He looked at Alexeev and held his hand. Tomi was ashamed he had not said anything to Alexeev before this, but he hoped the symptoms would go away on their own. "I'm sorry for not telling you."

"The truth is we don't know why Tomi has these headaches. It could be due to indigestion, changes in the weather, too much iron in the blood or a whole host of other things. One of my colleagues suggested an imbalance of humours that would require bleeding. We tried that, much to Tomi's objection. Another said there could be spiritual aspects of this illness that may be taking place, but he refuses to see a priest. Personally, I think there might be something pressing on the back of his eyes from the inside." The doctor reached into his bag and held out a bag of powders. "I know your doctor has prescribed a tea for you to drink and I want you to keep drinking it as often as you have these headaches. But this is a new powder I've been giving a few of my patients who also have headaches similar to yours. It's called cinchona. I'm not saying it will work for you, but I think it might be worth it for you to try it. You can mix it in with a hot water bath, but you can also drink it like the hot tea like you currently have. Send Alik to me tomorrow if the bath powders work and I'll give him more."

Alexeev shook the doctor's hand and accompanied him to the stairs, then went back to Tomi. "How are you feeling, *schast'ye moye*?" he asked. "Do you feel like getting dressed and coming downstairs, or would you rather sleep for a while longer?"

"I feel like all I've been doing lately is sleeping," he said as he sat up. "I'd like to come down for breakfast. I don't want the family to keep worrying about me." He held on to Alexeev's hand. "Oh, Lexee, I don't want them to bleed me again, don't let them…please don't let them bleed me." He was nearly in tears.

"No one is going to bleed you, my dear. But will you allow me to worry for a while longer?" He kissed Tomi on the forehead. Tomi rested his head against Alexeev's chest. He was glad he didn't have to keep any secrets from him anymore. Alexeev stood up and got out a fresh pair of trousers and shirt from their trunk. "Can you get dressed on your own? I want to go down and get breakfast started for you."

"Yes, I think I can manage."

Alexeev washed his face and changed his shirt. "And I think I'll get the bath started for you after breakfast." Then he kissed Tomi and went downstairs. Mikhail had gone to his room to rest for a while since he had been up most of the night. The children were still in bed but Anton was already awake and getting some of the early morning chores taken care of. He was building the fire in the dining hall and had already started the fire in the oven and stove. Alexeev caught him before he finished the fire. "Anton, could you also start the fire under the boiler when you get a chance? I want Tomi to get a bath after breakfast."

"Of course, Uncle Lexee. I'll get it started once I'm done here," he said.

Then Alexeev went back into the kitchen. Klara was starting to prepare the morning meal. She had a mixture of *blini* batter and chopped vegetables and a few loaves of bread. She asked Alexeev to go down to the cellar and get some sausages for breakfast, another jar of honey, a few jars of fruit compote, ten more eggs and a jug of milk. He carried out her orders like a true soldier: precisely and immediately. When he returned with the bounty, he laid everything out on the counter, then filled a pot with water and set it on the stove for tea. "Tomi should be down for breakfast shortly."

"How is our Tomi doing this morning? I saw the doctor leave a while ago."

"He's doing much better. The doctor said it's something he's had for a while and there's no danger of anyone else getting sick." Alexeev got a few cups down from the cupboard along with the tea pot.

Klara came over to him and put her arm around his waist. "You were very worried about him, weren't you?"

"Yes, but now that I know he's going to be all right, I am very relieved." He scooped some tea into the teapot. "I just wish I could help him more than I do."

"Believe me, my dear, you are helping him more than you know just by being here with him." She sat down at the table and started to arrange the sausages on a baking tray. "You're different than the other men he's been with." She spoke cautiously and hesitated, but then continued, "Did anyone ever tell you what Tomi's life had been like before he met you?"

Alexeev shook his head. "No, and I didn't want to pry. I always thought he would tell me what he wants me to know."

"Well, that's a polite way of thinking but you might be waiting a few decades. Tomi is not one who shares his life easily, even with those he loves." Alexeev sat down next to her. "You need to know he has had many, many disappointments in his life. It all started when he left the army. He lost his first lover in battle. Then he made his way across the country. Uncle always says he was looking for his family…and I guess that's what he wanted everyone to believe. I think he's been looking for that special person though…someone he could fall in love with again. We all saw the tortures he would put himself through. He would take in a young man who happened to come his way…or one with a nice smile who happened to wink at him or give him the slightest amount of attention, and the men got younger and younger. At first, they would appear to be very loving and attentive. Tomi would take them into his home, buy them new clothes, get them jobs and pamper them in every way. Most of them started with nothing, many were drifters, or had spent all their money on drink or gambling. Some of them were kicked out of their homes either by their parents…or their wives.

"But Tomi always managed to find them…the worst of the lot. He was like a moth and they were the flames. I remember one of them, I think his name was Dani. He was 15 or 16 years younger than Tomi…this was just before Tomi turned 43. Dani was a strong, handsome young man, and at first it looked like he adored Tomi. He added a room onto the barn for Tomi to use as a studio where he could paint. I'll bet he never told you he was a fine artist many years ago.

"Then Dani remodelled Tomi's wine cellar…or at least he started to. He was very handy around the house and good with tools…and in return, Tomi would give him anything he wanted, anything he asked for. Tomi bought him all new clothes, a new carriage lined in fine brass with velvet cushions and satin fringes, he even bought him a building in downtown Storozhevsk because Dani said he wanted to start his own business. But the projects he started around the house never seemed to get finished because he kept telling Tomi he had to spend more time planning his new business.

"Well, the months went by and no business was ever opened in that building. Instead, Tomi found out later that he was using the building to entertain both men and women. And then he found out Dani had sold the building…or lost it gambling…we never found out for sure. It broke Tomi's heart but he kept right on supporting that man. Three years into their relationship, Dani started getting restless and wild. He beat Tomi several times. He went into fits of anger and would tear up the furniture, break the good dishes and then he ruined much of Tomi's artwork. We found out later from the neighbours that Tomi had frequent unexplained bruises on his face, arms, and neck.

"Nikolai and I went to visit Uncle one summer and found the whole house in shambles and he had a bruised eye and swollen nose. He said he was getting ready to redecorate the house and was going to throw away all his junk. He also said he had fallen down the stairs, but we knew better. He was terrified of Dani but didn't want anyone to know. You've seen my husband, he's no small man…but Dani was bigger and stronger, about your size. But Nikolai told Tomi he would go to town and get one of the magistrates to come back with him to forcibly remove Dani. And that's exactly what we did.

"We took Tomi with us so he wouldn't be alone. We came back with the magistrate who had drawn up a written notice of immediate eviction and we also brought the constable to carry out the duty. Dani never came home that day…he must have heard what was going on. And he never was heard from after that. I think that was Tomi's last romance before you. And it was probably the most devastating. Tomi has been alone ever since then."

Alexeev didn't know what to say. What could he say? He was more than 20 years younger than Tomi, he was strong and handsome, but he was in love. He could never take advantage of Tomi. He didn't want anything Tomi had, and he didn't want his money. All he wanted was to protect Tomi, to share his life with him…all their joys and sorrows alike. He wanted to be with Tomi to comfort him and also to encourage him to try new things. He wanted to explore the world with him. He wanted to grow old with Tomi and if the gods and fates willed it, to die by his side or carry him to his grave and lay him to rest.

It saddened Alexeev to know there were those in the world who had such little regard for their fellow man, especially those who would take advantage of one so loving and giving as Tomi. He looked down at his ring and thought about the commitments and vows the two of them exchanged just a few nights before. Alexeev was now determined more than ever to stay by Tomi's side and protect him from anything and anyone who might harm him.

As the smells of breakfast cooking meandered through the halls, reaching each bedroom and sleeping area, the family soon came to the dining hall for breakfast, Tomi included. The very spot where, the night before, Tomi was feeling so poorly, this morning he was filled with joy and relief. Each family member came to Tomi one at a time and kissed him, wishing him well. Even little Nina brought him a sprig of pine and a pinecone she found on the ground when they arrived the day before.

Tomi smiled and thanked her, then he kissed her little hands as she handed him her treasures. He found a vase and filled it with water then placed the sprig of pine in it and set it in front of his place at the table. He invited Nina to sit next to him so she could enjoy the beautiful pine during breakfast. As everyone else sat down around the table Klara and Alexeev brought in the platters with the food while Faina and Miki brought in two large teapots and went around the table and filled everyone's cup with tea. Ania followed them with a pitcher of milk and filled the children's cups and also offered milk to anyone who wanted it in their tea. Honey seemed to be the chosen favourite though, especially since it was harvested right here at Galina's ranch.

Many conversations from the night before continued as if they had never been interrupted by the previous night's trials, and several new conversations were sparked as the relatives got reacquainted with those whom they hadn't seen for a while. Soon the last of the relatives would be arriving from Moscow: Tasha and Alexandre and their two daughters were expected sometime after noon. Alexeev gave Tomi a cup of tea with a few pinches of the new powder from the doctor and it seemed to keep the headaches away, but Tomi added plenty of honey to disguise the bitter taste. Miki sat next to Alexeev during breakfast. He adored his new uncle and wanted to be close to him as much as possible. While they were eating, Miki noticed the ring on Alexeev's finger. He liked the sparkle from the green emerald. Then when Tomi passed the tray of bread to Alexeev, Miki noticed that Uncle Tomi was wearing the very same ring.

"Uncle Lexee, why do you and Uncle Tomi have the same ring?" he asked.

Alexeev didn't want to say anything to upset or confuse the lad, especially since they were starting to form a strong bond between them. He glanced over at Mikhail, who smiled and nodded in approval. "Your uncle and I are very close friends, just like your mum and papa. We wear these rings as a symbol of how much we care for each other."

At first, Miki looked a little bewildered. But he thought for a moment, then put his hand on Alexeev's hand. "Do you love my uncle?" he whispered.

Alexeev wrapped his arm around Miki and gave him a hug. "Yes I do, very much."

Mikhail smiled and reached across the table and took his son's hand. "When you fall in love someday, you can give a ring to the one you love too."

Then Tomi leaned over and kissed Alexeev on the lips. "Is it all right with you that your uncles love each other?"

Miki smiled and nodded. "I love Uncle Lexee too." Then he kissed Lexee on the cheek. Alexeev was so touched by Miki's kiss that he could barely hold back the tears. He had never seen such innocence, such purity and such honesty. He smiled and squeezed him a little tighter.

"Would you like to take a walk down to the river after breakfast, Miki?" he asked. Miki's eyes suddenly got brighter and he nodded enthusiastically. "Tomi, come with us. It will do you good to get out and get some fresh air. And it's such a beautiful day."

Klara overheard the conversation. "We can manage things around here, Uncle. Maybe you and the boys can do some fishing while you're down by the river."

"Well, all right, as long as I'm not needed around here. It sounds like fun," he said. Then he stood up. "Uncle Lexee and I are taking a hike down to the river if anyone is interested in coming with us."

Alik and Anton quickly chimed in they wanted to go and so did Mikhail. Klara whispered to Nikolai and gave him a few nudges, and Darya convinced Toma it would be good for him as well. "It will be good for Vadim…and Leonid can take his mind off his troubles for a little while." It would be all the boys and menfolk hiking to the river, and the women and girls would stay behind and socialise with each other and with Aunt Galina. Usually, Tomi would choose to stay behind with the women so he could catch up on all the gossip and exchange a few recipes, but this time he decided he would rather be with Alexeev.

"Oh, Uncle Lexee," said Anton, "the water in the boiler should be hot by now."

"Good, thank you, Anton." He leaned towards Tomi. "I think you should take a bath with the doctor's herbs before we go."

Mikhail overheard. "That will give us just enough time to get things cleaned up in here."

So, they went into the bathing room and Tomi took his bath with the doctor's new medicine. The soothing medicine was a very relaxing remedy, especially in the hot water, and Alexeev made sure he massaged Tomi's neck and shoulders to release any tension. Then they dried off and proceeded to get ready for their hike.

The hike to the river wasn't very far, only about a half an hour's walk, but the air was still cold, so everyone would need to bundle up. The twins quickly bounded up the stairs to get their coats. Miki looked at his father, as if to get approval to pick out his clothes on his own.

Mikhail rose from the table and motioned to his son. "We'd better go find something for you to wear." Miki looked a little disappointed that his papa had to go with him to get dressed.

Alexeev sensed Miki's embarrassment. "Mikhail, I have to go upstairs for my coat. Would you like me to go with Miki? I'll make sure he finds something warm to wear." He patted Mikhail on the shoulder and nodded.

"That would be splendid," he said. "Miki, go ahead and go up with Uncle Lexee. I'll meet you all back down here."

"Let's go, Miki!" Alexeev swooped down and grabbed Miki and swung him on top of his shoulders, then he turned around. "Tomi, I'll bring down your overcoat and scarf. Is there anything else I can bring for you?"

"Oh, yes. Could you bring my knitted cap and gloves also, please?"

Alexeev winked and blew a kiss through the air, then he and Miki trotted up the stairs like a horse and rider. When they got to the attic, Anton and Alik were changing into their woollen trousers and overcoats. Alexeev couldn't help but notice that the twins were very well-built. Their chests and arms were very muscular and their abdomens were rippled. They had strong, thick thighs and calves that looked like melon halves. Neither of them had much hair, except a small amount of blond hair on their stomachs, just above and below their navels and some hair on their thighs. Alik caught him staring and winked at him. Alexeev quickly turned his head and blushed.

"Let's find something for you to wear," he said to Miki as he sat him down on the floor. The two of them looked through his clothes, then Miki picked out a thick shirt to wear with the trousers he already had on. "That's a good warm shirt to wear. Do you have a long coat?"

"Yes Uncle, here it is. And here's my cap and scarf." Miki showed them to Alexeev. Miki pulled the shirt on over his head, then put on the cap and scarf.

"That's fine. You will match your Uncle Tomi. He has a cap and scarf just like yours. Now let's see if you can find something for me to wear." They went into the back room of the attic where Tomi and Alexeev were staying. He pointed to the dresser. "My drawers are the ones on the left. See if you can find a nice warm shirt for me to wear." Alexeev took off the thin shirt he had on, then took off his house shoes.

"Here is a nice blue one, Uncle Lexee." He held it up to show him.

"Oh, that's a nice choice." Alexeev put on the shirt, then sat on the bed and put on his hiking boots. "Do you have a pair of boots for hiking in the forest?"

"Yes, I'll go put them on," he said as he scampered into the other room to find them. Alexeev smiled then picked up Tomi's coat, cap and scarf. He thought for a moment about Anton and Alik. He rubbed his hard nipple through his shirt and felt his cock starting to get hard. "Don't forget your coat, Miki," he called out. He shook out his trousers and pulled on his crotch to make a little more room and to adjust the trousers so that any enlargement wasn't as noticeable, then he went out and joined Miki and the two of them started down the stairs. Alexeev called back to the twins, "Don't be too long, we want to go as soon as we can so we can be back before lunchtime." The twins followed just moments later.

Nikolai, Toma and Mikhail were all dressed and ready for the hike, and Tomi and Klara had packed a few snacks in a basket: cheese, rolls, some dried fruit and sausages. "Growing boys need a little sustenance between meals," she proclaimed.

Lexee handed Alik the basket of food then he asked Anton to get another basket and put in a few bottles of wine and a several of towels. "You never know when someone might want to take a swim," he whispered. Anton smiled and quickly rushed to gather some towels. Tomi put on his overcoat, and soon the ten of them were ready for their morning adventure.

"This isn't going to be too much for you, is it?" Alexeev asked as he helped Tomi on with his coat.

"Of course not. Besides, you were the one who said the fresh air would do me good." Then he looked up at Alexeev and winked. "And you've never been to the river, so you might get lost without me."

Tomi and Miki both pulled out a pair of gloves from their coat pockets and put them on as they walked outside. "The two of you really do look alike! Just like two of my men on patrol!" said Alexeev as he observed the two from behind. They both smiled and reached back to him, one on each side, to take hold of his hands. The three of them walked together holding hands much of the way: Miki on the left, Tomi on the right and Alexeev in the middle. Nikolai, Toma and Mikhail followed close behind and Anton, Alik, Vadim and Leonid followed at the end. Most of the way, the path was flat and clear, but as they got closer to the river there were a few places that were not as easy to manoeuvre through.

Alexeev called back to the four stragglers, "Boys, come up front while we go over these rocks. Watch how Tomi and I go over the rocks with Miki. I want you to help Mikhail, Toma and Nikolai as they go over, then help each other." Although Alexeev didn't doubt any of them could make it on their own, he wanted to make sure the boys were paying attention. Tomi had pointed the way, but Alexeev knew from experience that one wrong move or careless step could result in a twisted ankle or worse.

Alexeev went first, then turned around and took Tomi's hand and steadied him over the rocks. Then he went back and took Miki's hand. "Now just hold on to my hand. I won't let you slip or fall." The three of them were safely at the top of the rock. "All right Anton. You go first, then help Nikolai." Anton stepped up without any difficulty, then turned around and took Nikolai's hand and guided him to the top and then came back for Toma. Alik followed close behind and turned around and assisted Mikhail. Then Alik helped both Vadim and Leonid traverse the rocks. "Good job, men!" said Alexeev as he patted each of the boys on their backs.

Soon they could all hear the rushing of the river. It was only a few hundred feet away, just over the next hill. There was a crisp scent in the air and they were all anticipating the cold refreshing water. The sun was shining bright and even though the air was cool, their faces were warmed by the sun's rays. The twins had taken off their scarves and tied them around their waists and had unbuttoned their shirts. Vadim and Leonid had taken off their coats and tied the sleeves around their waists. Alexeev had tied his coat around his waist as well and had unbuttoned his shirt too.

As they reached the top of the hill they looked down and saw the beautiful river, not yet frozen by the harsh winter, but there were icy patches on the edge of the water. There were several levels where water had pooled together as it gradually cascaded down to a larger pond. The sight was breath-taking. Tomi, Mikhail, Toma, and Nikolai had all been to this part of the river frequently in years past. Galina had told them it was called the Ponds of the Seven Maidens because of the seven ponds that were formed here. Miki had been here once before also, but it was several years ago and he didn't remember much about it. Anton, Alik and Vadim had also been to the ponds as children with their fathers.

In fact, they had hiked for a 30 mile stretch along the river a few years ago with a few more cousins during the summer. Alexeev had never been to seven ponds but found it to be a very inviting place, welcoming, and very peaceful. The group soon found a flat rock suitable for the ten of them to sit and enjoy the scenery. Alexeev had taken off his coat, so Tomi made quick use of it by folding it over and setting it beneath his head so he could lean back and relax for a while after the long walk.

They had brought a clay jar and several wooden cups, so Mikhail went down to the river and filled the jar, then came back up to the group and offered water to anyone who was thirsty. Alexeev and Miki scouted out the riverbank and soon Miki was back up on Uncle Lexee's shoulders. From that height, he could reach pinecones that had not yet fallen. Nikolai and Toma had settled next to Tomi and were sharing Alexeev's coat-turned-pillow and were simply enjoying the view and the company. Anton and Alik were getting ready to take a winter's plunge into the freezing river, and soon Vadim and Leonid decided to join in. They had already removed their shirts and shoes and were getting ready to remove their trousers.

"Uncle Lexee!" they called. "Are you ready to go for a swim?" The invitation sounded a little more like a challenge, and Alexeev was not about to be shown up by the likes of these young bucks.

"Of course," he called back. Then he and Miki walked back up the bank to the flat rock. Miki started to take of his coat but Alexeev stopped him. "Hold on there, this is not something you want to do. The water is very cold and it is not good for someone as young as you." He rustled the top of Miki's head. "After my swim, maybe we can take a walk upstream and see if there are any good places to fish. Then maybe we can come back tomorrow morning with a few fishing lines and get some fish for tomorrow's lunch. Does that sound good?" Miki was satisfied with the answer. When he thought about jumping into freezing water, he had second thoughts and was a little relieved he wouldn't have to jump in after all. "Tomi, do you want to join us?" he asked.

He hesitated for a moment. "Well, I don't think I want to go in all the way, but maybe I'll go down and get my feet and ankles wet."

Alexeev smiled and started stripping off his clothes. The boys were waiting until the last minute to remover their trousers. They could already feel the effects of the cold. Their muscles were getting tense, their cheeks were rosy and their nipples were getting hard. They started to punch each other to stay warm. "All right boys, are you ready to go in?"

All five of them quickly took off their trousers and ran screaming all the way to the river. Nearly in unison, they all jumped into the deep pond at the far end of Seven Maidens. As soon as their heads came up out of the water, they continued to scream shouts of victory, then they splashed each other and wrestled vigorously in the water to burn energy to keep from being overtaken by the cold. Nikolai, Toma and Miki watching from the rock laughed at the sight, and pointed as one after the other would dunk or splash the other, while Tomi and Mikhail made their way down to the riverbank a little more slowly. Then Alik and Anton, Vadim and Leonid all ganged up on Alexeev and held his arms out, then pushed him under the water backwards. But suddenly, Alexeev rose up out of the water with all four of them in tow, two on each arm, then he threw them all in at the same time. The boys were amazed at his strength and were certainly taken by surprise. It had only been a few minutes, but the five of them knew they needed to get out of the cold, frigid water and dry off. They all ran back to the rock where Nikolai quickly handed each of them a towel.

Miki's eyes opened wide when he saw the five men running naked back to the rock. He had seen his papa naked before when they would bathe together, but he had never seen men so muscular before. It was a strange feeling. He saw how beautiful and attractive they each were, especially his Uncle Lexee. He felt a peculiar urge in the pit of his stomach. It was a little like the feeling he would get when he stood on a balcony high above the street. Or the time his papa set up a rope from a tall tree branch and fastened a wooden board at the end of the rope. He sat on the board, then he swung him on the rope until he was far above the ground. The feeling was exhilarating, and exciting, and strange.

As he watched the men dry themselves off, he watched how they caressed and patted their muscles and how they held their cocks and stretched them out to dry them and how they lifted their balls to pat their sacks and buttocks dry. He watched them run the towel over their thighs and how they would tense up then release. It was a fascinating thing to watch. He saw them dry their armpits. Anton, Alik, Vadim and Leonid barely had any hair under their arms, but Alexeev had a thicker patch of light brown hair under his. As he dried his pits, the hairs gently fluttered in the breeze. Then he watched as Alexeev dried his thick chest and shoulders.

The muscles seemed harder and more defined than they were before he got into the cold water, and the veins on his arms were full of blood. There were even blue veins on his neck, shoulders and chest that were visible. It was beautiful. Miki couldn't take his eyes off Uncle Lexee. Then he dried off the hair on his head and shook his head rapidly afterwards to settle the hair since he didn't have a comb or brush. Some of the spray from his hair fell on Miki's face. Uncle Lexee glanced around for his trousers.

Miki jumped up and grabbed the trousers and handed them to him. He was so close, he could see the veins in Alexeev's thick cock. He wanted to touch it, he wanted to hold it in his hand, he wanted to know what it felt like. Suddenly, he stumbled a little, just enough that Lexee instinctively reached out his arm and kept him from falling. He scooped him up in his arm and lifted him up to his shoulder. He said something to him, but Miki was thinking about Lexee's muscles and about his large thick cock. He put one hand on his strong shoulder, and the other on his chest. He was overwhelmed with excitement. His small cock was up against Lexee's bicep and it felt wonderful. For a moment he wondered how it would feel if his cock got pressed between the forearm and bicep and how the squeezing pressure might feel. As he rested his hand on Alexeev's chest, he felt his hard nipple. Instinctively, he gave it a gentle squeeze. Alexeev looked at him and smiled, then set him back down on the ground.

Suddenly, there was another new feeling. This time it was an uncomfortable feeling in his trousers. It had started when his cock was pressed against Uncle Lexee's bicep. His penis was getting harder and stiff. It was pressing against his trousers now and making that area feel very tight. As he thought about what was happening he started to feel very conscious about his physical change, and even though he didn't know why it was happening, he felt embarrassed. He sat down on the rock to hide what was happening in his trousers but he couldn't stop looking at the men. He wanted to touch Uncle Lexee's muscles again, but he also felt like he wanted to hit him. Not to harm him but as some kind of playful competition. He wanted to prove he was also a man, that he was strong and could hurt him if he really wanted to. But he didn't want to hurt him, he wanted to be close to him, he wanted to touch him and to be touched by him. That's what he liked about Uncle Lexee. He was always playing with him, getting rough with him. He liked to feel Uncle's muscles press against him. Uncle Lexee would also let Miki use his muscles to try to overpower him as well. Even though Miki knew it was just play, it felt like more than just play.

He started to think about Uncle Tomi and how he and Uncle Lexee would sleep together at night. He saw the two of them kissing, holding hands, caressing each other and gazing into each other's eyes. He wondered how Uncle Lexee and Uncle Tomi would play when they were in bed together.

Then the feelings started to make sense. He was beginning to realise he liked Uncle Lexee in a similar way Uncle Tomi must like him. He imagined the two of them play-fighting in bed and rubbing each other's muscles. He also knew he wanted to rub his cock, but he wasn't sure why. He felt a sensation in his nipples but didn't understand that either. He would have to explore these mysteries when he was alone in his bedroom, where he could have some privacy.

Now, Alexeev was an excellent soldier and knew everything there was to know about how men reacted to each other and how they played together in jest and in lust, but he was naïve and inexperienced when it came to interpreting children and understanding how they react to different circumstances, especially when it came to feelings and emotions of the heart. He didn't realise that Miki was becoming physically attracted to him, but simply thought Miki was reacting like any other boy with an older male relative.

Alexeev was only six years older than Orlov's oldest boy, but Orlov had several grandsons Alexeev would play with often while they were growing up. They would run, swim, play games and wrestle, but he never picked up on any physical or emotional attractions, possibly because there weren't any. He was always cautious with the little girls though. He was keenly aware that they, as they got older, would sometimes start to see him as more than an uncle. So, he would often distance himself from them as they started to mature. But he never imagined the feelings he had as a child and as a maturing young boy, could be directed towards him by another boy, especially one of his own nephews.

So, when he felt Miki's cock pressing against his bicep and when Miki reached down and pulled his nipple, Alexeev was taken by surprise. He had grown very fond of Miki in these few short days and he was starting to feel very protective of him, especially when he would observe Anton and Alik tease him for being shorter, or slower, or weaker, or any number of other things. The twins were in their twenties and should know better than to pick on someone so young and impressionable. But he didn't feel it was his place to correct them or scold them, so he would just remove Miki from the situation and spend more time with him. This new revelation caught him off guard. He didn't know what to do or how to react. He didn't want to ignore Miki, but at the same time he didn't want to pretend nothing was happening. He decided he would discuss the matter with Tomi tonight and get his advice.

After he and the twins dried themselves off and got dressed, they all had some of the snacks Klara had packed for them, with a cup or two of wine. They enjoyed the rest of the morning together, talked and played a few games, then decided it was time to go back and join the women once again. Alexeev still had a few chores to get done before lunchtime: wood needed to be brought in for the stove, oven, and fireplaces. And Tomi kept thinking about the menu and what needed to be prepared. Nikolai and Toma wanted to go to town to pick up some more tobacco and Mikhail just wanted to spend more time with his wife.

Chapter 18
Good News

All the boys arrived back at Galina's home just in time for lunch. The women prepared meat pasties, a platter of pickled vegetables, several platters of cheeses, fruit preserves and a cream-based mushroom soup. Of course, there was always tea, milk, wine and vodka, and several kinds of desserts the women were trying out before the Christmas celebration, and the baking would continue through tomorrow. A few of the desserts included almond *kulich*[121], fruit cake, honey-almond cookies, *pryaniki*[122], *rugalach*[123], *romovaya baba*[124], cranberry-orange cookies (Sveta's recipe), tea cakes and molasses snowballs (Tomi's recipe). Galina had more than twenty neighbours she wanted to give sweet treats to, not including the clergy and city officials who planned to attend. And certainly, there would have to be desserts made for the family as well.

Tomi tried to stay away from the kitchen as much as possible for the rest of their visit—at Alexeev's request—and only baked when it came to preparing Sveta's special recipes and his own molasses snowball cookies. He left Klara and Ania in charge of overseeing the rest of the food preparation, including the meals. After lunch, Alexeev gathered the boys and took them out to the barn so Vladimir could assign them chores for the afternoon. While the women continued to bake, Alexeev and Tomi escaped up to their attic room for some time alone.

Tomi laid down on the bed as soon as he got into the room. "That was a long walk. I'm glad we're back."

---

[121] *Kulich*: A traditional Russian and Ukrainian Easter cake

[122] *Pryaniki*: A Russian spice cookie or honey bread

[123] *Rugalach*: A Jewish crescent-shaped pastry

[124] *Romovaya baba*: Yeast cake saturated in syrup made with rum

Alexeev shut the door then came over to the bed by Tomi. "Let me take off your boots." As he set the boots next to the nightstand, he thought about what he wanted to ask Tomi about Miki. He didn't want to embarrass either Tomi or Miki and he wasn't sure how the family might react if they found out what happened at the river.

"You look pensive, *moy general*. Is something wrong?" he asked.

Alexeev sat down on the bed next to Tomi. "I need some advice and I'm not exactly sure how to ask. I don't want to upset you."

Tomi placed his hand on Alexeev's knee. "I know you love me, Lexee, and you know I love you too. I don't think there is anything you could say to change that."

Alexeev looked into Tomi's eyes. "I think Miki may have feelings for me. I mean, he doesn't just think of me as his uncle…no, that's not exactly what I mean…hmmm, this is not easy to explain."

Tomi thought for a moment. Deep down, Tomi could see the signs of Miki's affection towards Alexeev but he didn't see anything wrong with it. Tomi had been fond of several adult male figures when he was growing up but nothing ever came of the misplaced affections. He gradually learned that most men focus their attention and their affections on women. After many years he started to pick up on signs that certain men were either attracted to him or desired something more than friendship, but he was always cautious.

There were many men who would want to inflict physical harm on him if they knew he wanted more than basic male friendship. And Tomi always knew, even from a young age, he couldn't fight back. Not only was he physically weaker than most men, but his conscience wouldn't permit him to strike or harm anyone or anything. In recent years, he had even begun to question the need to eat the flesh of animals because it meant ending the life of an innocent creature. So, unlike Alexeev, Tomi was incapable of defending himself if it meant inflicting physical pain or striking an aggressor.

"Do you think he is attracted to you?" Tomi asked. "Because that is an easy thing to understand. Miki is a young boy who has not been exposed to very many social situations. You are a very attractive and very masculine man, and you are paying a lot of attention to him. You are kind, intelligent, attentive, talented and fun to be with. You don't treat him like a child but you treat him like a person, like someone you want to be with." Tomi paused for a moment. He looked into Alexeev's eyes. "It is no surprise if he is falling in love with you…those are all the qualities I fell in love with too." He brushed Alexeev's cheek. "Tell me more about what happened."

"When we were at the river, I picked him up, and I think…no, I know his cock was hard. And I sensed he was embarrassed when he thought I knew. I didn't say anything to him about it…I didn't really know what to say. And while I was holding him, he reached down and touched…then squeezed my nipple."

Tomi could tell this was difficult and embarrassing for Alexeev to recall, but he also knew it might be good for him to express these feelings too. He needed to know what Alexeev felt so he could understand what advice to give him. "How did that make you feel inside? The touching, I mean."

"It was awkward, especially coming from someone so young," his voice trembled a little. "Tomi, it wasn't anything I wanted, you know that, don't you?"

"I know you wouldn't have done anything to him and I know you wouldn't have harmed him." Tomi kept looking into Alexeev's eyes. "But that's not what I asked."

"You want to know how it made me feel." Alexeev knew he needed to be completely honest with Tomi. He needed to trust Tomi would understand even if it was something painful to hear. "I feel excited when I'm with little Miki. It's not the same way I feel excited about you, it's something different. I get excited by his youth and enthusiasm, by his eagerness and willingness to learn from me. It wasn't anything sexual or even arousing…not until he touched my nipple. My first reaction was it was wrong and I needed to remove myself from the situation."

"That's when you set him back down on the ground," Tomi interjected.

"Yes, and as soon as I sat him down, I realised I needed to get dressed as soon as possible."

"Why did you think you needed to get dressed so quickly," asked Tomi. He sensed there may be something more.

Alexeev hesitated but decided to tell everything he could recall. "Because I felt myself getting hard. I knew if I didn't put my trousers on right away someone might see…you might see my cock was getting hard."

"It was a natural reaction," said Tomi without hesitation. "I know how sensitive your nipples are and I know it doesn't take much to get you aroused. And I also know we haven't been intimate nearly as often as you would prefer." Tomi was trying desperately to try to make Alexeev feel better about the situation without making him feel guilty about things he didn't have control over. "But when you realised what was happening, you got dressed."

"Tomi, I don't want to feel like this about anyone except you. And especially about someone as young as Miki."

"I don't doubt that, Alexeev. I think you are a man of honour and I know you love me. I don't want you to worry about the feelings you might have had. You stopped before anything happened. And I don't want you to be overly concerned about Miki's feelings either. You are a good influence on him and I think it would do him more harm than good if you suddenly stopped paying attention to him. He needs men like you in his life. He needs to see there are masculine men like you. And he needs to understand those men can be very good, and decent, and kind, and honourable." Tomi held Alexeev's hand. "Just be his Uncle Lexee."

Alexeev kissed Tomi's hand and felt a tear forming. "How did you get to be so wise, *schast'ye moye*?" The two of them laid back down on the bed and held each other.

After a few hours, Alexeev heard the sound of a carriage coming up the driveway. He looked out the window to see who had arrived. A large carriage had pulled in alongside the house, so he surmised more family was arriving from Moscow. He walked back over to the bed and patted Tomi's shoulder. "Tomi, Tomi, I think Tasha is here from Moscow. Are you ready to get up?" Tomi rolled over and groaned out a few words that didn't make much sense. "I think you need to get up, *schast'ye*…or maybe I will have to tickle you." Alexeev put his hands by Tomi's side, just below his armpits, then began to tickle him vigorously. "Now you will have to succumb to the master. My forceful ways will make you do as I command."

Tomi squealed, and wriggled, and twisted from side to side, all the time laughing and pleading for his conqueror to stop. "All right! All right! Just let me go! Let me go! Please, please stop!"

Finally, Alexeev stopped tickling and wrapped his arms completely around him and kissed him. Then he brushed his hand over Tomi's forehead, "I love you, *schast'ye moye.*" They both got out of bed and put their shoes on, then went downstairs to greet the new arrivals.

It was indeed Tomi's niece Tasha, her husband Alexandre and their teenage daughters Galya and Nadya. Mikhail, Toma and Nikolai were already greeting their kin and helping them down from the carriage. Anton and Alik, Vadim and

Leonid also came from the barn and started unloading the trunks and bags, then they led the carriage into the barn and got the horses settled into the stables.

Tomi introduced everyone to Alexeev, who promised to try to remember their names. They all exchanged kisses and hugs, then they all went inside where Galina was resting and waiting in the parlour. They filed by their *Tetushka*, gave her a kiss and wished her well for Christmas. Once all the pleasantries were finished, the family all adjourned to the great hall and dining area where Klara and Ania had set out afternoon refreshments. Everyone was busy getting themselves plates of food and cups of tea or spiced vodka.

Tasha made it through the crowd to Tomi. She had a huge smile on her face and she looked like she could hardly contain herself.

"What is it?" Tomi asked. "You look like you're going to explode!"

She grabbed his arms. "I have some news from Vanya and Sveta." She said almost singing the words. Then she smiled and started laughing. "They are going to have another baby!" Everyone in the room started cheering and talking back and forth among themselves. Glasses were raised to the baby's health and everyone exchanged hugs once again. "They didn't want to say anything until they were absolutely sure. If you had just stayed another day…she saw the doctor the day after you left."

"So, my dear Vanya and Sveta are going to have a fourth child." He reached out to Alexeev and hugged him, then he started to cry.

"Now what are you crying about? This is a happy occasion." He kissed Tomi on the top of his head.

"I'm afraid I won't see them again until long after the baby is born."

Alexeev held him closer and patted his back. "We'll have to plan a special trip back after the baby is born. Don't worry, Great Uncle *Medved'*[125] will make his appearance before you know it."

That afternoon, the women baked the cakes and cookies for the Christmas Eve procession through the neighbourhood after the midnight service at the church. The children decorated the food baskets with paper flowers, pinecones, ribbons, and colourful dried leaves. Vadim and Leonid walked into town with Anton and Alik, and Mikhail, Toma and Alexandre decided to go with them. Tomi discussed the menus for Christmas Eve dinner and the Christmas meals with his nieces, Karla and Darya, who promptly elected themselves as head

---

[125] *Medved'*: Bear

cooks (which annoyed Tomi greatly), and Alexeev and Miki sat in the parlour with their *Tetushka* and listened attentively as she told stories of her childhood Christmases. Later they were joined by Faina and Nina, Galya and Nadya, and Akilina.

Once all the children were present, Galina decided it was time to tell her favourite Christmastime story. It was about the birth of her youngest brother, Fedya. "My mother's name was Nina. She was short like me, and she had long black hair. It came down all the way to the floor when she let it down, but most of the time she kept it braided and wound around her head like a crown. Quite often, she would braid in coloured ribbons: either red, or green, or yellow, or pink. She loved to adorn her hair with colour. My papa's name was Pavel. He was tall, and handsome, and strong, much like Alexeev."

Uncle Lexee sat up straight and puffed out his chest. "He had blond hair he kept cut very short, but he also had a beard that was long and white and it wobbled up and down whenever he ate or talked. He would let me grab hold of it every once in a while, and I would pull it down so his mouth would open. Then he would cross his eyes and make a noise like a braying donkey."

Alexeev crossed his eyes made a sound like a donkey, "EeeAwww, eeeAwww," and all the children laughed.

"Mama was expecting a baby, and by December, her tummy was very big and she was tired all the time. She could barely walk from her bed to the kitchen. She already had five of us children and Papa had to work at the flour mill every day, so she was left alone to take care of us. I did my best to help with the household chores, but I was only twelve years old…just about your age, Miki." She reached out and patted Miki on the head.

Miki smiled, and the girls giggled. "Things got harder and harder for her to do and her tummy kept getting bigger and bigger. Papa would leave for work very early in the morning, so he wasn't there to help her, and none of us children were strong enough to get her out of bed. I would make breakfast…usually porridge and sometimes sausages…and then I would fix *buterbrody* and *tvorog* later in the day, but not all the chores were getting done. We ran out of wood a few times and I had to walk to the next farm to ask the neighbour boy if he could come over and chop wood for us."

Just then, Nadya and Galya remembered this part of the story. Nadya said excitedly, "Was that Nikolai?"

Tetushka smiled. "Yes, that was your Great-great-uncle Niki." She reached out and patted Nadya's cheek. "He was a very handsome young man when I first met him…of course, I was far too young to get married, but I already had my eyes set on him.

"Niki would come over almost every day to chop wood or shovel the snow from the lane in front of the house. He would check in on mama and make sure she was doing fine. He would even help us wash the clothes. And I remember a week before Christmas, he brought a buck he had shot and killed so we could have meat on the table. I knew a few recipes for breads, cookies and cakes, so I baked him a loaf of black bread and thirty little tea cakes. Working at the mill, Papa always had plenty of flour, so we often traded with the neighbours for vegetables, or chickens, or eggs. And we had two cows, so we always had plenty of milk and butter also.

"But it was now a few days before Christmas…" She paused and looked at Galya and Nina. "You see how busy all the women have been today…just think if the children had to do all of this! Mama said we shouldn't worry about baking baskets for the neighbours and she said we wouldn't be able to go to church Christmas Eve. We were so disappointed. When Papa got home late in the afternoon on Christmas Eve, he brought Niki with him. We all had a cup of fruit porridge and Papa found some berries to sprinkle in our bowls, and I made several *pierogi* pies that had cabbage, turnps and carrots. After we ate, he let Niki take us all in the carriage to the church so we wouldn't have to miss the service. I got to sit in the front seat with Niki. He put his arm and coat around me to keep me warm.

"We got to the church just in time for vespers. The service was wonderful, telling how the holy child was born so long ago and how the star in the sky shown overhead. It was magical. Then, I remember riding home and we sang songs all the way back. It was well after midnight by the time we got home, so we were all very tired. But as soon as we opened the door, Papa greeted us. He was holding our new baby brother. Fedya had been born just after midnight on Christmas Day. That was the most wonderful Christmas I ever had."

Tomi leaned into Alexeev and whispered, "And this is the most wonderful Christmas I've ever had. To be with you, here at *Tetushka's* house, and to hear that Vanya and Sveta will have another child."

It was a beautiful evening. After dinner, Alexeev and Tomi took a walk in the moonlight. The half-moon was high in the sky, and there were only a few clouds, so the starry sky was a spectacular sight. They walked up to the top of the hill, just in back of Galina's estate and sat on a rock in the middle of a clearing. From the top of the hill they could see most of the valley below and the town that spread from one side of the river to the other. On the other side of the river, beyond the town, they could see the rolling hills with patches of snow and trees among the farms. There was a peacefulness in the air, a calm in the slight breeze that came up from the valley below.

"I don't want to spend much more time here, Alexeev. I love Galina and my family, but I think we need to get on with our life together, by ourselves."

Alexeev sat up and stared into the sky. "It will probably take another five or six weeks to get to Storozhevsk." He was worried about riding that far in the cold with Tomi not in the best of health. "Are you sure you can travel right now?"

"Tasha's brother-in-law, Pavel, lives in Murygino. That's about halfway home."

"That could take three or four weeks if the weather holds out. Longer if the weather gets bad."

"We could also stay in Kiknur with my friend, Gevorg. I haven't seen him for many years, but I send him a case of wine every other year and he sends me a clock in return. He always says I am welcome anytime." Tomi took hold of Alexeev's hand.

"He doesn't paint, does he?" He smiled, then winked at Tomi.

"No, he's a clockmaker. I have known him and his wife for about fifteen years now." Tomi sensed the uneasiness in Alexeev's voice. "I was going through Kiknur one year on my way to Moscow, and my carriage broke a wheel in front of his house. He came out to help me and let me stay in his guest room while the wheel was being repaired by one of his neighbours, and we have been friends ever since."

"Well, he sounds like a good man." Alexeev patted Tomi's knee. "It's settled then. We will leave the third day after Christmas and plan to stop in Kiknur…and visit Gevorg."

Chapter 19
Gevorg of Kiknur

The Christmas festivities went over very well, just as Tomi had planned and hoped it would, and Alexeev stood by him constantly to make sure he didn't overdo it. The women baked forty-two baskets of pastries, cakes and cookies for Galina's neighbours and friends, the men donated one elk, three geese and four sturgeon to the church for the poor, and Galina donated twenty of her largest pigs and ten logs of cheese. The clergy and the city officials joined Galina and the family for the traditional Christmas meal after the procession home, and all their guests made merry until nearly sunup Christmas morning. After the Christmas meal, Alexeev escorted Tomi to their attic bedroom so they could get some well-deserved rest.

Over the next few days, the family visited and played games, baked, ate and had a good time together. Some committed to coming back next year, and some regretted they wouldn't be able to come back for a few years. Travel was not easy, especially during this time of year. The weather was not always this favourable and often, the roads were impassable during the winter season. But this year, it looked like the weather would continue to be drier and warmer than usual, at least for another few weeks. Galina had her servants pack up the Delftware and crystal sets so Tomi and Alexeev could take them back with them. They made sure they were carefully packed away in crates with plenty of straw and sawdust to prevent breakage.

Finally, on the morning of the fifth day after Christmas, the boys were ready to leave. It was two days later than Alexeev had planned, but they were ready to get underway. They said their goodbyes and exchanged hugs and kisses. The carriage was loaded with baskets of food: *buterbrody*, dried elk meat, pork sausages, cheese, pickled vegetables, fruit preserves and a few cases of wine and vodkas. Alexeev was also able to ride into town the day before and restock their supply of spices, cocoa and tobacco, and Galina gave them a box of candles and a case of honey.

For the first week and a half, the days were clear but cold and the nights were clear and breezy. Alexeev built fires under their canopy each night, and continued to keep the fires burning until morning. But he was getting more and more concerned about the weather. This was an unusually late holdout for the snow season. Generally, the snow season would start in October and not stop until May. The fourteenth night of camping on the side of the road was a particularly clear night, almost a full moon in the sky. Alexeev could see the long stripe of stars draping their way across the night sky. He even saw a shooting star. It was so beautiful it almost made him weep. In fact, it was probably the most beautiful event he had ever witnessed in the sky. It lasted for several seconds, and glowed with hues of pink and orange and left a grey trail that could be seen for several minutes.

Alexeev had been taking this leg of the trip rather slowly and resting the horses longer than usual because of the cold, but also to give Tomi a chance to recover from the holidays. The next afternoon, they passed through a small town called Uren which was only a day and a half away from Kiknur, so this would be their last night on the road for a while. As Alexeev set up their camp and canopy and started their campfires, he noticed the clouds were thicker than they had been the last few nights. He hoped the snow would at least be delayed another two days so they could make it to Gevorg's safely and without snow.

Tomi took out a pot from the back of the carriage and started to heat some water over the fire, then he poured some of the water into the tea kettle. He added a few cut up carrots to the pot along with some of the elk meat, some pickled cabbage and a few spices. Then he placed one of their last loaves of black bread on a rock near the fire to warm it up. Alexeev went into the woods to gather more firewood for the night. While the food was heating, Tomi stepped up into the back of the carriage to get the folding chairs and a few blankets for the evening. As he was inside, he heard a noise in the camp. Maybe Alexeev had decided not to gather wood or maybe he had forgotten his gloves.

Tomi opened up the back of the carriage and saw a huge brown bear rummaging through the basket of food he had left by the fire. Fortunately, the horses were partitioned by the canopy and they had not yet sensed the danger. Tomi slowly pulled down the carriage door and latched it closed. He started shaking and didn't know what he should do. If he tried to make noise to scare it away, it might startle the horses. He decided to just wait it out and hoped it wouldn't disturb the horses and woultn't figure out he was inside the carriage.

He continued to hear the noise for close to an hour and every once in a while, he would hear scratching along the outside of the carriage. Then he would hear the beast knock over something in the camp or he would hear it's breath up against the wall of the carriage, sniffing. He started to cry but tried to remain quiet. The inside of the carriage was getting cold because they had not yet set the flap opened to allow the heat to enter. Then he thought he heard the bear lumber off into the forrest, but he was still too scared to open the carriage door. He could only see through a tiny slit between two of the carriage boards that gave him a limited view of the campsite.

Finally, when he decided he had waited long enough and thought he had mustered up enough courage to open the carriage door, he heard the bear return. It sounded like it was throwing things inside the camp. Then he saw the latch on the carriage door jiggle up and down. He was terrified. There was no way he could defend himself from such a beast. It would easily overpower him and tear him to shreds. He suddenly started crying again and then he picked up a skillet from the floor next to him. He held it firmly in his hand but he was shaking uncontrollably. He had never struck another living creature in his life and he wasn't sure he could now, even to defend and save himself. He was sure this would be the end of his life, and Alexeev would come back to the camp to find him half eaten by the bear.

The latch jiggled up and down again and he could feel his heart pounding faster and harder. It was nearly bursting through his chest. Again, the latch went up and down and the carriage door rumbled as if the bear was trying to tear it off its hinges. "Tomi, are you asleep? Why did you latch the door?" It was Alexeev's voice. Tomi leapt forward to the carriage door, unlatched the lock and swung the door open. He jumped into Alexeev's arms still crying and shaking.

"Oh Alexeev, thank the gods you are here," he heaved and cried.

"Oh my goodness, my dear, are you all right? What happened?" He sat down on the ground with Tomi still shaking and clinging to him. He rubbed Tomi's back and tried to comfort him.

Tomi was still crying and shaking and looking back and forth into the woods. "It was a huge bear! It came into camp while you were gone…I was trapped inside the carriage."

“I’m here now, my love, I’ll protect you.” Alexeev continued to hold him but the threat of the bear returning was a little disconcerting. He glanced around to see if he could determine if it was still nearby. “Well, it looks like he’s gone and at least he didn’t scare the horses off…I don’t think he’ll be back tonight.” He continued to hold Tomi and rub his back. “Maybe you should go inside for a while and rest while I finish fixing dinner.” He opened up the flap so the warm air from the fire would heat the inside of the carriage then he helped Tomi into the carriage. “I’ll clean up out here while you rest.”

Tomi stepped up into the carriage, laid down and almost immediately fell asleep. Alexeev set up several torches around the camp and made sure the horses were safe and secure for the night. Then he picked up the fragments of the basket that had been torn apart by the bear. The stew Tomi had been making had burned, so he got more food from the carriage and cooked another stew. He heated more water in the kettle and poured some in a cup with some tea leaves, then he poured another cup for Tomi and sprinkled in some powders from the doctor. Alexeev had discovered these powders also had a calming effect and might help Tomi get a better night’s sleep as well.

He hopped up into the carriage and gently placed his hand on Tomi’s shoulder. “Tomi, Tomi, dinner is ready. Do you feel like eating something?”

Tomi rolled over towards Alexeev. “Yes, I think I’m all right now. I was so scared, Alexeev. I didn’t know what to do.”

“It’s all right now. You don’t need to worry about it anymore.” He helped Tomi down from the carriage. “You did the right thing. You locked yourself in the carriage and just waited until the bear left.” They both sat in front of the fire. Alexeev handed Tomi a bowl. “Here, have some stew. And I’ve made you a cup of tea.”

After the two of them finished dinner, Alexeev had Tomi go back into the carriage and get to sleep. Meanwhile, he cleaned up and gathered all the food together and brought it back into the carriage. He went around the camp and made sure all the torches were still burning and put more wood on the campfire. He didn’t join Tomi but kept watch in the camp. Every hour or so, he would walk through the campsite, relight any torches that had gone out and keep the campfire burning. The bear didn’t return that night but Alexeev was anxious to leave as soon as there was light. He knew Kiknur was no more than a day’s ride and he wanted to make sure Tomi was safe and secure in a sturdy building for at least a few nights before they set out again. Fortunately, there was only a light dusting of snow in the night, so the road was still clear.

He woke up Tomi early the next morning so they could get an early start. The clouds overhead seemed to predict an upcoming storm, but to their good fortune, the snow held back yet another day. They arrived in Kiknur at two o'clock in the afternoon, and Tomi convinced Alexeev to stop at the town bakery before they got to Gevorg's home. The temperature was falling fast so they would need to decide what to buy quickly before it started to snow.

Once inside the bakery, Tomi immediately knew what he wanted to purchase. He saw fresh *Vatrushka*[126], one of his favourite sweet breads, and fresh *nareznoy baton*[127], the best bread for *buterbrody.* He purchased twenty of the *Vatrushka* and four loaves of the *baton.* Now they were set to make an appearance at Gevorg's. Tomi firmly believed that no one, not even a good friend or relative, should ever show up empty handed, especially when they were hoping to spend a few nights.

Of course, Alexeev's ideas were much the same: he insisted he work to help minimise the burden of his stay. He was good at many things, especially if it involved physical labour. He could figure out how to do just about anything he put his mind to. They were quite a pair, each having their own ways of expressing gratitude and each appreciating what the other had to offer.

Gevorg's home was on the far east side of town, almost the last house before the woodland swallowed up the countryside. It was a modest home with three bedrooms, a living room and kitchen. Gevorg lived there with his wife, Alma, and two sons: Slava, who had just turned twleve, and Volya, who was fourteen. Gevorg's grandparents had migrated north to Russia from Mesopotamia after the Ottoman-Safavid War of the 1620s and 30s. He met his wife Alma in Kiknur when they were both in their teens. Tomi was passing through Kiknur a month before Gevorg's wedding when his carriage broke down. Gevorg was kind enough to take him in while his carriage was being repaired, and Tomi returned the kindness by staying for the wedding, taking charge of the menu and preparing all the food for more than a hundred guests. Even though the miles often kept them apart, their friendship never waned.

Tomi wrote to Gevorg often and he poured out is heart more than a few times in his letters. And Gevorg would write back with words of comfort and advice.

---

[126] *Vatrushka*: Sweet rolls with a creamy cheese filling

[127] *Nareznoy baton*: A popular Russian wheat bread

They both had troubles and successes of their own over the years, and they always made sure to take each other into their confidences. Tomi always worried about how Gevorg would make ends meet, and Gevorg was always concerned about Tomi's isolation and lonliness.

"Now Alexeev, I want you to know that Gevorg makes a modest living and doesn't have a lot to spend. But he has always been insistent on extending to me every kindness he can think of. He is overly generous, sometimes beyond his means, so I want to make sure we don't make him feel he has to spend money on us."

"You know I value a person for who they are and not for what they can do for me or what they can buy. I'm surprised you would think it necessary to remind me of that." He held Tomi a little closer. "You are a very kind person and from what you have told me, Gevorg is very much like you."

Tomi patted Alexeev's chest. "You have the biggest heart I have ever known. I know you and Gevorg will become fast friends."

They pulled up to Gevorg's home and Alexeev led the carriage around to the side of the house, then he helped Tomi down.

"He's not expecting me. I hope we won't be an inconvenience," he said as he stepped down.

They walked up to the front door and Gevorg came out just as they stepped up onto the porch. "Tomi?" he said with excitement. "What a wonderful surprise this is!" He hugged and kissed him, then looked at Alexeev. "And who is this fine-looking young man?"

"Gevorg Voskerchyan, this is my good friend, Alexeev Kondorov." The two exchanged hugs and kisses then Gevorg rushed them inside out of the cold.

"Here, let me introduce you to my family. We have some additions for you to meet," he said as he guided them into the living room. "Tomi, you've already met my wife, Alma." She nodded and shook their hands. "And these are my two boys, Slava and Volya." They both shook hands.

"What handsome boys you have, Yegor," said Tomi. "I'm sorry I haven't visited in so long, I didn't realise your boys would be so tall and handsome, just like their father."

"They grow like weeds and eat like pigs. So, now you are here." Gevorg smiled and led them to the setee.

Alexeev remained standing. "I should go tend to the horses before it starts snowing."

Gevorg forced him onto the settee. "Nonsense, you're my guest. Volya, you and your brother take the horses to the stable and get them fed and covered for the night…Tomi, you are staying for a few nights?"

"We don't want to be an imposition—" said Tomi.

"You have never been an imposition, you have always been a pleasure and delight." Gevorg took Tomi by the shoulders and looked him straight in the eyes. "I am so happy to see you." He gave Tomi another hug. "It's all settled then, you will stay for a few nights so we can get all caught up and it will give me a chance to get to know your friend, Alexeev."

"I should at least bring in our bag for the night…and the package?" Alexeev said to Tomi as he got up again.

"Yes, yes, of course…" said Gevorg. "I will have Alma heat up the tea while you bring in your things." Alma quickly got up and excused herself to the kitchen and Alexeev followed the boys out the back door to the carriage.

"Your father is a very kind man," said Alexeev as he hurried to keep up. Volya nodded and smiled.

Now that they were alone, Gevorg seized the opportunity to get some answers out of Tomi. "So Tomi, tell me about Alexeev. Remind me how the two of you met?"

"We met six years ago. Alexeev is…was a lieutenent in the army," he said.

"I thought you had left the army before you met me. You didn't go back, did you?"

"No. He was leading his troops through the wilderness and just happened to pass by my home." Gevorg shook his head in amazement. "He came up to my door and asked if they could spend the night—"

"That was a little bold of him, wasn't it," he nudged Tomi, making sure he knew he was teasing him. "But knowing you, that was what you had in mind all along…aye?"

Tomi continued, "But they only stayed for one week and then we didn't see each other for six years."

"You must have been going crazy, not being able to see him." Gevorg's interruptions were beginning to annoy Tomi.

"I was miserable! Finally, I was out visiting my nephew, Vanya—"

Gevorg interrupted again, "Isn't he the carpenter…the one who lives in Moscow."

"Yes…now let me finish!" Tomi was getting frustrated, not being able to finish two sentences. Gevorg just smiled and chuckled to himself. "So, we met a second time by chance in a flower shop. And after that, we decided we were meant to be together. We are on our way back to Storozhevsk and I thought I had better stop in and see my good friend, Yegor."

Gevorg smiled, then gave Tomi another quick hug. "I am glad you did. I was beginning to wonder if I would ever see you again. But it has been good to hear from you by messenger…and get a case of wine every now and then." He nudged Tomi playfully.

Meanwhile, Alexeev followed the boys out to the stables. "Not so fast, boys. I haven't had to run that fast since we were chasing after the Turks!"

"Were you really in the army?" asked Slava. "Did you ever meet the Tsar?"

Alexeev ruffled Slava's hair and bent down to him. "Yes I was, and yes I did. Our Tsar is exceptionally tall and very handsome." He grabbed their bag and the package of baked goods. "Maybe later I can tell you a few stories of our adventures together." The two boys smiled, then hurried to the business of tending to the horses. "As soon as you're done, we brought some *Vatrushka*. I don't want you to miss out."

Volya smiled. "We will only be a few minutes."

Alexeev came in with the bag and the package. "Did I miss anything important?"

"Tomi was just getting me caught up on how the two of you met." He reached out and grabbed Alexeev's forearm. "You are a lucky man to have found Tomi," he whispered. "And I daresay that Tomi is fortunate to have found you."

Tomi stood up and took the package from Alexeev, "I'm going to join Alma in the kitchen so the two of you can get better acquainted." He gave Alexeev a kiss on the cheek and disappeared into the kitchen.

Gevorg sat down next to Alexeev and put his arm on his shoulder. "Tomi is a good man. Sometimes a little too good. He gives his heart away without considering it may cause him heartache in the long run." He didn't have any reason to think Alexeev was taking advantage of Tomi, but he knew quite often Tomi made hasty decisions about the men he was with, and his decisions often proved to be unwise. "You are a strong, handsome and healthy younger man, who has decided to live with a man I care about very much. It is true, Tomi and I don't see each other very often. In fact, I think he has only been here to visit twice since our first meeting—"

"—but you are not convinced I am the right man for Tomi," Alexeev interupted. "I can't explain all the reasons I love him. He makes me happy. I want to be a better person when I am around him…and even when I am not. He makes me laugh and cry. I find pleasure in him, even when we are doing nothing, and I don't know who I would be or how I would be different if he were not around…if we had never met. I love the way he talks and I love the way he makes me think about the world around me.

"I feel like he was with me…with my soul…when I was growing up. He was that part of me that wouldn't give up, he was that voice that kept telling me to try harder, or try again. But I don't want you to think he is just someone who encourages me or someone who prods me into doing the right thing. He is the most important piece of my puzzle. Without him my life has no form, my story has no plot, and my future is futile. I want only to make him happy, to try to fulfill his dreams…and in return, maybe I can find the purpose within me that makes me want to be his mate."

As soon as Alexeev finished, Gevorg threw his arms around him. "Thank you, my brother, thank you for loving my Tomi."

Alma and Tomi couldn't have timed it any better. They walked in with the tea and warm *Vatrushka* just as Gevorg and Alexeev were embracing.

"I trust this is a hug of friendship and you are not trying to strangle the best part of my life," said Tomi.

Gevorg wiped his eyes and laughed. "He is a good man, Tomi, a very good man."

Alexeev stood up and stretched. "I've been sitting in that carriage all day. I think I'll walk out to the barn and let the boys know the tea and pastries are waiting for them."

Gevorg, Alma and Tomi sat and drank tea and shared the *Vatrushka* and got caught up on some of the events they had missed in each other's lives. Alexeev brought the boys in so they could have some of the pastries while they were still warm. Then he told them a few stories of the Tsar's accomplishments and victories. Not only was he a victorious leader in battle, but he was also a very modern thinker. Alexeev boasted how the Tsar was bringing Russia into the western world: introducing new forms of government and new ways of thinking about Russia in the bigger scheme of things. He was even introducing an education reform that would ensure all boys would learn how to read, write, and understand basic arithmatic before they entered adulthood. Alma was already seeing some of the education reform in their local school. Gevorg had not always heard favourable stories coming from either Moscow or *Sankt Piter-Burkh* when it came to the Tsar, but he was fascinated all the same.

As the afternoon went on, Alexeev asked about any chores needing to be done around the house. Gevorg was reluctant to discuss such things with a guest, but Alexeev was very persuasive and persistent. Although they had plenty of firewood to last at least another month, Gevorg had been trying to get the boys to fell a large pine tree in the back of the property that had been struck by lightening during a summer storm last year. There was a danger it might fall and damage the barn. The boys always had some kind of excuse, either school or other commitments that couldn't wait, and with Gevorg going into town everyday to work in his shop, the tree-felling looked like a hopeless cause.

So, Alexeev offered to help the boys get the job done over the next few days. He convinced the boys to help out by telling them it would give him a chance to tell them more stories about the Tsar. Tomi was proud of Alexeev's cunning way of getting the boys to do something they should have volunteered to do to begin with. Alexeev told Tomi it was a tactic he often used on his men when there were undesireable jobs that needed to get done. He had a way of talking and a certain charisma about him that made people want to do his bidding. Sometimes Tomi had the feeling Alexeev was using the same technique on him to get him to change his mind about certain things. But it was always just a suspicion.

Alexeev didn't waste any time. He got up at five o'clock the next four days. Actually, there were ten or fifteen clocks that announced the hour at the same time. They chimed throughout the house all night long. Since Gevorg was a clockmaker, many of his clocks were on display at home, and he also had dozens at his shop in town. Although Alexeev wasn't usually bothered by the chime of a clock, even one that chimed every quarter hour, he was not used to so many clocks all chiming together. It took him nearly half the first night trying to put the noise out of his head. He finally fell asleep around three o'clock. But he got used to the noise a little more each night.

Gevorg had brought a straw mattress into the living room from the boys' bedroom. It was small, but they managed to make the most of it. The boys too were having to share a mattress, which did not go over very well until Papa reminded them that Tomi and Alexeev were guests and if they continued to complain, they would find themselves sleeping on the cold ground in the barn. Originally, Gevorg wanted the boys to give up their room, but Tomi would have no part of that idea. He and Alexeev both insisted the living room floor would be more than sufficient for their needs. It had a fireplace, plenty of wood and it was situated on the side of the house opposite the kitchen so they would not be in anyone's way in the morning. They humbly accepted the mattress and thanked the boys for their enormous sacrifice. All was well after Alma brought out another tray of warm *vatrushka*.

The first thing Alexeev did after he got up each morning was to build the fire in the fireplace. Although he and Tomi managed to keep each other warm during the night, he knew Tomi would soon feel the cold once he realised the warm body next to him was gone. There was a pot hanging in the fireplace so Alexeev filled it with water, then got himself dressed. By that time, the water was hot, so he poured himself a cup of tea to ward off the cold of the morning. He had told the boys he would wake them early so they could work on the tree each morning for a few hours. That way the boys would still have time for their regular chores and schooling. When he opened the door to their room each morning, the two boys had their arms wrapped around each other in much the same way he and Tomi would sleep all night.

For two hours, the three of them chopped and chopped until the tree finally gave way and fell to the earth in a tremendous crash and thud. Alexeev decided that was enough for the first day and told the boys to go inside and wash their hands and faces, put on some clean clothes and get ready for breakfast. He saw there were flickering lights in the kitchen and supposed Alma was already awake and making breakfast. He gathered the axes and took them back to the barn just in case it started to snow, then he went inside to get himself washed up.

Alma was indeed awake and starting to fix breakfast, but to Alexeev's surprise, so was Tomi. The two of them were making breakfast together. Alma had some bread that was starting to get hard, so she was soaking it in an egg and milk mixture. Once the bread had soaked up the excess egg, she fried the slices on a buttered griddle. Then she topped them off with a dollop of tvorog, or fruit compot. It was a good way to make use of old bread so it wasn't wasted. Tomi was busy heating up sausages and he also had a pot of water on the stove for tea. The smells were wonderful.

Alexeev passed by and went to the water basin to wash up. When he noticed what Alma was preparing, he couldn't resist. "Oh, Tomi, can I bring in a jar of *Tetushka*'s honey? I think it might go well with this."

"That's a wonderful idea. Please bring in a few jars, I know we have plenty to spare." Alexeev dashed out to the carriage and retrieved three jars and brought them back in to Alma.

The boys were already cleaned up and getting the table set for breakfast. A few minutes later, in walked Gevorg. He had been out in the barn milking the cow and gathering a few eggs, so he was just about ready for breakfast. Alma and Tomi brought in the food and tea, and the whole family sat down to breakfast. Gevorg thanked Alexeev for helping the boys fell the tree, he thanked Tomi for helping Alma prepare breakfast and for the gift of the honey and he thanked the boys for eagerly helping Alexeev. Then he kissed Alma and thanked her for being his wife and always taking care of him. Everyone started their day with this positive assertion and it put smiles on all their faces and good thoughts in their minds.

Over the next three days Alexeev and the boys sawed the branches from the tree trunk, and then to cut the trunk into manageable sections. Just before noon on the last day, there were a few snow flurries, so Gevorg brought his horse and cart around to the back where the logs were. He and Alexeev loaded the largest logs onto the cart, and the boys gathered the smaller branches and loaded them as well. Then they unloaded the cart into the woodshed. Gevorg would be able to manage cutting the remainder between him and his two boys, and he was grateful to Alexeev for taking charge of the tougher portion of the task.

As soon as they finished, the snow started coming down more heavily and soon the yard was covered in a few inches of fluffy white snow. It was a beautiful sight but one that came untimely for Tomi and Alexeev. They hoped the snow would stop and give them a few more weeks of clear weather so they could safely make it home. But in the meantime, they took advantage of the weather, such as it was. Alexeev played in the snow with the boys.

Soon, several of the neighbouring boys joined in the fun and the yard became a battleground for the pint-sized troops. They made snowballs and pretended they were soldiers fighting a fierce battle with an imaginary enemy. Everytime someone would walk by the house, they chanced being pummelled by hoards of flying snowballs and shouts of victory and triumph. The passersby were in relatively good humour and didn't seem to mind, and ocassionally bent down to form a white weapon of their own to return fire.

Tomi watched from the living room window and laughed as the friendly war progressed. Then he laughed even harder when the boys ambushed Alexeev, and

Gevorg joined in and made a surprise attack on the lieutenant. He crept up behind Alexeev and held him tight while the boys fired their stockpile of snowballs one after the other, relentlessly at their victim. But Alexeev wasn't about to be beaten so easily. He overpowered his captor and forced Gevorg's face into a snowbank. They all had much fun, and none were anymore than soaked to the skin when the game had finished.

The four soldiers eventually came into the house to warm themselves by the fire. Alma was busy with the housework, so Alexeev, Gevorg and the boys stripped off their water-drenched clothes and stood by the fire to get warm and dry. Tomi hurried to find towels for the four rapscallions, then rounded up some dry clothes for them to change into. He was glad Alexeev had a chance to have some fun, especially with Gevorg and his children.

As the day ended, Tomi was glad for the snowfall, even if it meant a probable delay in getting home. After a late supper and a long fellowship in front of the fireplace with their hosts, he and Alexeev again brought out their mattress and made up their bed by the living room fireplace. He rested his head on Alexeev's bare chest, listening to him breathe and counting his heartbeats.

When he was sure everyone else had turned in for the night, he turned himself over on top of Alexeev and kissed him. He smelled the faint scent of lavendar oil on Alexeev's chest mixed with a musky scent of masculinity. He buried his head between the thick chest muscles and licked and sucked the sweat from his skin. Alexeev had been holding back ever since they got into bed because he didn't want to wear out Tomi, but the wolf was now aroused and could not be put back in his cage. He rubbed Tomi's back and massaged his neck and shoulders.

Then Tomi reached out to Alexeev's arms and guided them all the way back onto the mattress above his head, exposing Alexeev's bare chest and armpits. He started licking one of Alexeev's armpits. It was a sensation Alexeev had never felt before, except perhaps in a dream. There was a slight tickling sensation, but also a poignant sense of overwhelming emotion deep within his chest that felt like it was welling up inside him, waiting to burst forth.

Tomi reached down under the sheets. Alexeev was naked and his cock was rock-hard and thick. Tomi reached over to the side of the mattress where he had set a bottle of oil. He poured out a small amount on his hand then reached back and spread it over the hard cock. He raised himself directly over the cock, then slowly lowered himself onto the cock while guiding it between his buttocks.

Alexeev reached out to steady Tomi as he went up and down, up and down, up and down.

In just a few minutes, Tomi had no more strength in his legs to raise himself, so he leaned forward onto Alexeev's chest. As he paused for a few moments on top, he stared deep into Alexeev's bright green eyes. Then he felt Alexeev carefully turning him over onto the mattress. He felt his lover's strong calloused hand cupped behind his neck as it drew him down to a passionate kiss. The kisses were long, and tender, and deep, and the boys were reminded of how much they loved each other. They didn't simply love the physical pleasure the other one gave, nor was it the feeling of closeness and how it makes one feel protected or needed. No, their bond went beyond the physical.

They could look into the other's eyes and see the joy, or laughter, or distress, or fear, or sadness, or whatever emotion happened to be making it's mark on the other's heart at the moment. Alexeev wanted to make love to Tomi but he also wanted to fulfill whatever it was Tomi needed at this particular moment.

He reached down to Tomi's legs and drew them up and rested them on his shoulders. He slid the cock back over Tomi's asshole and slowly wedged it back in. Tomi took a deep breath and gripped his legs at the bend in his knees. He pulled them as close to his chest as he could, then waited. He saw the look of anticipation on Alexeev's face. "Do it!" he said. "Pound my ass and get your cock deep inside me."

Then Alexeev began to thrust his cock in and out, in and out, in and out. Tomi's body was relaxed, but the pleasure inside him was welling up like a wave. Then as he looked into Alexeev's eyes, he saw something curious, like a shadow from the fire…no, it was another pair of hands caressing Alexeev's shoulders. They were masculine, strong hands massaging his lover's shoulders. One of them reached down and expored the massive pectorals and the other touched the side of his face and guided it to the side.

Gevorg's face came into view as he kissed Alexeev. The two of them sucked each other's faces while Alexeev continued to pump himself inside Tomi. Alexeev didn't seem to mind the third person and as Tomi realised what was happening, he was overtaken by an overwhelming sense of calm and release and happiness. Gevorg made his way around to Tomi. He looked him in the eyes and smiled then he slid his tongue deep into Tomi's mouth.

Tomi had always been attracted to Gevorg, but they never talked about their feelings for each other because when they met, Gevorg was already engaged.

And he never talked to Alexeev about bringing anyone else into the relationship because he didn't want to make Alexeev feel uncomfortable. But bringing Gevorg into the relationship could never be permanent either because of Alma and the two boys. Even though it was turning into a very pleasurable experience for all three, they each knew this could only last for the night.

Gevorg spread his legs above Tomi's face and lowered his dark, hard, uncut cock into Tomi's mouth. Then he reached up and pulled Alexeev's face towards his and kissed him. They entwined their arms around each other. They could feel each other's strong, muscular bodies. Gevorg was a tall man like Alexeev. He had a thick bush of hair around his long cock, and dark, thick, curly hair on his pectorals, stomach, back and legs that covered his olive complexion. His biceps and triceps were thin but well-defined, angular and strong, and he had a lean and muscular body. His eyes were dark brown, almost black, and they were capped by long black eyelashes that were unusually curved upwards and thick eyebrows that nearly met in the middle above his nose. The hair on his face was shaved, but the dark, thick stubble gave him a wild appearance. And he had short, black, curly hair on his head that always seemed a bit dishevelled. Overall, he was a good-looking man and a stunning example of dark, sensual, male beauty.

Alexeev thrust himself deep inside Tomi, but Tomi's energy was spent. He pulled himself away and laid back and watched his two wolves in their quest for dominance. Then he pulled out his pipe and tobacco bag. Gevorg was used to taking charge in his marriage bed, but this was a different arena. Alexeev turned him over and clung to his back until he submitted. Gevorg lifted his buttocks high in the air and lowered his head to the ground in submission. Alexeev slapped Gevorg's round, firm, muscular buttocks as a play for dominance. He spread open the buttocks and ran his oiled finger around the tight hole, then gently inserted his massive, thick cock into the virgin ass. Gevorg let out a controlled cry of pain, then clenched his fists and pushed himself up onto all fours, then lowered himself down again.

Tomi crawled over and whispered to him. "Relax and take deep breaths," he advised. "It hurts more when you are tensing up." He stuck the pipe in Gevorg's mouth for a quick puff of relief. Then Gevorg grabbed Tomi by the back of the head and forced a passionate kiss on him. It felt as if he had been waiting all these years to taste Tomi. There was no resistance. Tomi plunged his tongue down Gevorg's throat, then released him and smiled. Gevorg's eyes were watery and his gaze was like an animal in heat.

Alexeev slowly removed his cock almost all the way, then slowly reinserted it, this time holding and squeezing Gevorg's hips and buttocks as he kept them spread wide. Gevorg took a deep breath. He and Alexeev were both perspiring and their bodies glistened in the firelight. Tomi wiped the sweat from Gevorg's brow then leaned up and kissed Alexeev while he carressed his face and ran his fingers through his hair. Then he got up behind Alexeev and reached around to his bare chest. Alexeev brought his arms up and clasped his hands behind his head and began to flex. Tomi gripped the tightening pectorals then began fondling the hard nipples.

Gevorg's hole was beginning to relax and he was experiencing the pleasures of penetration. He reached back with both hands and spread his buttocks wider. Barely able to speak, he cried in a low murmur, "*Glubzhe! Glubzhe!*[128]" It sounded more like a growl than human words.

Alexeev leaned into his pumping motion for greater impact, then he rammed his cock in as deep as it would go. He pulled it all the way out, then jutted it back in with precision force and accuracy. He repeated this several times, and each time Gevorg would gasp and clench the mattress. Tomi pumped Alexeev's nipples to enhance his lover's pleasure and Alexeev cried out to Tomi, "*Ushchipnut' ikh!*[129] Aaarrrgghh! Aaarrggh! *Yeshcho'! Yeshcho'!*[130]"

He was pumping Gevorg violently now. "Pull them harder, Tomi! Uurrgghh!, Aarrrgghh! *O Bozhe! Divnyy!*[131]" Gevorg let out another cry and Alexeev released his shot of cum deep inside Gevorg. Tomi massaged Alexeev's pectorals, shoulders and biceps, and licked the sweat from his body. Alexeev reached down and massaged Gevorg's back then slowly pulled his cock out. He turned Gevorg over so he was face up.

As Alexeev kissed Gevorg, Tomi sucked Gevorg's cock and balls. His muscles tensed and the sweat rolled off his chest and down his side. He thrusted his pelvis upward into Tomi's mouth and pounded his fists down against the mattress, then wrapped his veinous arms around Alexeev's neck and looked him in the eyes like a leopard ready to devour his prey. Alexeev could see the sexual tension building in Gevorg's eyes and he could see the reflection of the fire in Gevorg's pupils. He reached his arms around to Gevorg's back and squeezed his

---

[128] *Glubzhe! Glubzhe!*: Deeper! Deeper!

[129] *Ushchipnut' ikh!*: Pinch them!

[130] *Yeshcho'! Yeshcho'!*: More! More!

[131] *O Bozhe! Divnyy!*: Oh my God! Marvellous!

muscles. Gevorg huffed and panted and continued to pump his cock into Tomi's mouth. Then suddenly, Gevorg became tense all over, his muscles tightened and flexed, and in one final gasp his cum exploded into Tomi's mouth and onto his face. He writhed for a moment as if he was in great pain, then relaxed his entire body.

Tomi and Alexeev laid down on either side of Gevorg and kissed his face. There was mutual ecstasy between the three of them. They were nestled in each other's arms for a while, each one resting and relaxing from the strenuous encounter. Gevorg looked like the weight of the world had been lifted from his shoulders. Any tension or apprehension there may have been previously was now washed away. Gevorg turned to Alexeev and kissed him, then he turned to Tomi and kissed him. He stood up and put on his robe and walked back to his bedroom. Tomi and Alexeev smiled at each other, kissed, then fell asleep in each other's arms.

Chapter 20

Surprise

It was a beautiful Sunday morning. The sun was shining and the skies were clear. Alma was getting breakfast ready, and the young boys were already in the barn milking the cow, gathering eggs, and feeding the animals. Gevorg and Alexeev took stock of the carriage and made sure it was in prime condition to continue, and they ensured the horses were healthy, well-fed and rested. The clouds from the previous day had disappeared and the birds were in the trees singing. Even the snow was beginning to melt. Tomi woke up just as Alma finished preparing breakfast, so he set the table and poured the hot water into the teapot, then called the men and boys in for breakfast.

As they all ate, they discussed the best plan of action for Tomi and Alexeev for the rest of their trip. Tomi had a niece, Alena, who lived in *Khlynov*[132], which was about a third of the way from Kiknur to Storozhevsk. It was a ten-day ride, depending on the weather, so they decided to leave as soon after breakfast as possible. While Alexeev and Gevorg loaded the carriage, Tomi and Alma prepared food for the road. Tomi left several bottles of *Mors* wine from Galina, several jars of honey and three bottles of his own blackberry wine. Alma helped Tomi prepare a dozen *buterbrody* with cheeses and dried meats, a few jars of pickled vegetables and a few jars of fruit compote. They also planned to spend one night in Kotel'nich, which was about a week away. There they could restock their supplies and bed down in the inn, if necessary.

Just as they were all packed and ready to go, Gevorg came out with one last crate. “Wait, wait, don't leave without this. It's a gift for the two of you as you start your new life together.” Alexeev opened the crate. It was a beautiful eight-day, chiming wall clock. It was dark walnut wood with oak inlays, and the

[132] *Khlynov*: former name of Kirov, Kirov Oblast.

interior was lined with cedar. It had a bevelled glass door in front that gave a view of the silver-plated face and pendulum and two brass weights. At the clock's crest above the face, was a carving of two bucks with intertwined antlers. Alexeev was stunned at its beauty and Tomi was overwhelmed with gratitude.

Tomi gave Gevorg a big hug and whispered, "I never can visit you without you giving me an expensive gift." He had a tear in his eye but he was smiling with joy.

"I have missed you all these years. Let me give you this to celebrate my new friend, Alexeev," he whispered back. He kissed Tomi on the cheek then gave Alexeev a hug and kiss. "Take care of this man," he said to Alexeev, "I love him dearly."

"You can be sure I will," replied Alexeev as he hugged him back and kissed his cheek.

They exchanged hugs and kisses with the boys and Alma, then Alexeev helped Tomi up into the carriage and placed the crate carefully in the back and tied it in place to secure it for the ride. Alexeev put on his old tattered gloves that had holes worn in the thumbs and palms where the reigns rested, but "they were a good and comfortable fit", he would say as an excuse not to get another pair. Tomi smiled to himself and they got underway.

The roads were good and mostly snow-free due to the unusually warmer and moderately dry winter. It was difficult to tell there had been a snowball fight the day before. They hoped the weather would remain clear for the rest of their journey so they could make good time through the wilderness to Storozhevsk.

In just a matter of minutes they passed the last house in Kiknur. It was the last house they would see for many miles as they were entering a densly forested area that was largely unpopulated. Once they entered the forest, Tomi became very troubled and appeared to be quite disturbed.

"Is something wrong, Tomi?" asked Alexeev.

Tomi looked all around the front seat on the carriage then looked in back of the seat. "I think I have forgotten it. I don't see it anywhere." His frustration grew worse.

"What are you looking for, my love?"

"I think you should stop. I need to check the back," he insisted.

Alexeev stopped the carriage. "I'll look in the back for you, but what am I looking for?"

"It's a big package. It's tied with a red ribbon," he said almost in tears. "Oh, do hurry, my love."

Alexeev jumped out of the carriage and went into the back. "I don't see anything back here other than our trunks, the baskets of food and the crate from Gevorg. There are the blankets, our pillows, a few bottles of blackberry wine…what am I looking for? What could be so important?"

"Nevermind, my love. I guess it wasn't important after all," Tomi called back to him.

This change of attitude towards something that had seemed extremely important a few minutes ago was very upsetting to Alexeev. Tomi wasn't one to get disturbed or troubled very easily and now he was fine even though the package could not be found anywhere. He looked around one last time then walked back around to the side of the carriage and hopped up to the seat. There on the seat was a large package tied with a red ribbon. There was a white envelope tucked under the ribbon, and on the envelope was written '*For My Love*' in Tomi's handwriting.

"I'm sorry, it was here under the seat all along," he said as he smiled and handed the package to Alexeev.

"What's this for?" he asked. "And why are you playing games with me?" He smiled and held the package up and shook it a little.

"Open it and find out."

Alexeev opened the card and read:

Moyemu lyubimomu, Alexeev, v yego tridtsat' shestoy den' rozhdeniya.
Ty sdelal menya schastliveye, chem kogda-libo.
S dnem rozhdeniya, moy general!
Pri vsey moyey lyubvi,
Tomi
To my sweetheart, Alexeev, on his thirty-sixth birthday.
You have made me happier than I have ever been.
Happy Birthday, my master!
With all my love,
Tomi

"How did you know it was my birthday? I've never told you, and you've never asked," he said, rather puzzled.

Then they both said in unison, “Orlov!”

Alexeev opened the package. On top was a new pair of leather riding gloves and underneath was a beautiful, deep-blue, silk-lined, full-length woollen coat, just right for cold-weather riding. There was also a matching hat and scarf.

“You are too much, *schast'ye moye*,” he said. Then he hugged Tomi and kissed him. He promptly took off the old gloves and put on the new ones. They were a perfect fit. Then he took off his old tattered coat and put on the new one. It fit perfectly! And because it was silk-lined, it was very comfortable and slick to the touch. “This is the best birthday I've ever had. Usually, Orlov just bakes a cake in my honour, but this is very special. Thank you!”

Then Tomi reached under the seat again and pulled out another smaller package. “Here, this is also for you, from Yegor and Alma.”

Alexeev looked a little puzzled but opened up the box. It was a small *blini* cake covered in raspberries and cream sauce. “Awww, it's just enough for two!” He hugged Tomi and gave him a big kiss.

They sat by the road for a few minutes and enjoyed the birthday cake, and Alexeev couldn't stop admiring the fine workmanship of the coat and gloves. Tomi had even embroidered the initials *AK* on the coat in white silk thread over the heart. It was nice to have someone who cared enough to find out the hidden details of his life, even though he didn't feel he deserved such attention. Alexeev smiled the whole time he was eating the cake and savoured every bite.

The next several days went smoothly. They stopped on the side of the road each night like they had so many times before. Even though the nights seemed to be getting colder, there was still no more snow since they left Kiknur. Alexeev had plenty of hay and oats for the horses and he and Tomi spread out their food over several days. Alexeev would ocassionally catch a few fish in the river, so they had plenty to eat. Tomi ran out of his medicinal tea, though. He guessed he left one of the tins at Galina's house when they were there.

But Alexeev made sure he was getting plenty of rest. He kept him out of the cold air as much as possible and set up the chair as he had before, so they could sit and talk while Alexeev took the reigns, so Tomi sat inside the cabin protected from the elements.

They made it to Kotel'nich the afternoon of the eighth day after they had left Kiknur and decided to stay in the inn for the night. There was a nice stable, so the horses would have good care, shelter and plenty of food. Alexeev also made sure he purchased enough hay and oats for the next leg of their journey. It was early in the afternoon, so Tomi walked over to the deli next to the inn while Alexeev was settling the horses in the stable. He ordered several *buterbrody* with cheese, a few *pierogi* and also purchased a few general food items. He also noticed the deli had a large variety of hard candies, so he stocked up on a variety of the sweet treats. He never could resist candy that was well made.

He took a few of the items with him for dinner for the evening meal, but made arrangements to pick up the rest in the morning before they left. The deli owner remembered Tomi from some of his previous trips, so he was very accomodating and Tomi always made sure he tipped him well.

They were able to get a good night's sleep. Even though the floor in Tomi's carriage was padded, it was not the most comfortable sleeping arrangement. The cabin was narrow, the mattress was thin and the air that came in through the opening was warm and frigid, alternately. In addition, the crates of dishes, the paintings and the clock had to be secured underneath the carriage floor, so Alexeev put the padding on top of the crates and trunks. Their bed was still flat enough, but they now were sleeping only a few feet from the ceiling, so they had to be careful getting up in the morning. A night in the inn was a welcome change. Alexeev was able to keep a fire going most of the night, and the bed was much more comfortable than the cabin. They both got up early and their food items from the deli were ready and waiting with the innkeeper. The next stop was Khlynov, less than a week away. They would stay there with Alena for a night or two.

Tomi had visited Alena on his way to Moscow, and told her he would stop by on his way back, so she was expecting him. She was the oldest daughter of Tomi's older brother Ludmil, who had passed away sixteen years ago. Although she never married, she had a close friend with whom she lived since her father died. Together they took in boarders to earn most of their money and both were seamstresses as well. Alena was one of Tomi's favourite neices because she always listened attentively to all his stories about his relationships, and she always gave him good, sound advice. In past years, when he was unable to go to Moscow, he always made sure he went to Alena's to spend the holidays with her.

On the second day after leaving Kotel'nich, Tomi developed a severe headache just after waking. Alexeev thought he also had a fever. He had some cinnamon, ginger, and cloves he mixed with peppermint leaves in a hot tea then he added some honey to sweeten the brew. He also learned from Orlov that cayenne pepper mixed with oil could be used as a rub. Its stimulating effects sometimes helped to reduce headache pain. Rather than continuing on, Alexeev decided to stay for the day where they had camped overnight. He thought it was possible Tomi's headaches could be the result of travelling so much. Tomi lost his appetite, which was often the case with these episodes. But he did manage to drink several cups of the tea throughout the day. Alexeev gave him cayenne pepper paste massages throughout the day in between naps. By late afternoon and early evening, the headaches were nearly gone and he was feeling somewhat back to normal except for a slight blurring in his left eye. He went to sleep early that night and by morning they were ready to continue the trip.

Two nights later, they arrived in Khlynov. Alena and her friend, Katia, greeted them at the door and welcomed them in. Katia was an attractive woman in her early forties, a few years older than Alena. She had long black hair with streaks of grey, and she usually kept it up in a bun on the back of her head. She was taller than Tomi by a few inches, but not as tall as Alexeev and she had wide hips and thick, strong arms. Alena was a lovely woman of thirty-eight years, only just taller than Tomi. She was thin and wiry and she had dark brown hair she usually wore loose on her shoulders, or tied in a ponytail to one side. Alena had a younger sister, Anzhela, who had left home two years before her father died, and the family had not heard from her ever since. Alena suspected she had run off with a boyfriend to get married.

They lived in a beautiful house with eight bedrooms, a parlour, a dining room and a large kitchen. They rented out four of the bedrooms on a full-time basis and two of them were usually available for travellers who needed a place to stay for a small fee. They had a reputation for very reasonable rates and the local businesses were happy to direct customers their way. On the side of the house, were the stables that boarded up to ten horses along with their two cows. They also had a chicken coup beyond the stables and a storage building just beyond the hen house.

They employed two other women to help with the farm duties, and Katia had a sixteen-year-old son Ivan, who tended to the horses. The inside of the house was beautiful with rich burgandy paint offset by cream coloured boarders, sturdy oak furniture, and paintings of every kind of flower imaginable. Both Alena and Katia had dabled in art throughout their years together, but realised as the years went on they had less and less time to pursue their painting talents.

Alena had a room ready for Tomi so Katia showed Alexeev to their room so he could get their bags out of the way. Alena wanted to know all about Galina's holiday party and all the latest gossip. She was especially thrilled to hear about Vanya and Sveta's announcement of their expected new arrival. It was hard to believe Faina, their oldest, was already twelve, and Feodora, their youngest, would be eight in just a few months. Alena and Katia took a trip to Moscow three years ago and had such fun with the three girls. They even made them matching outfits for the harvest festival while they were visiting and were able to stay to attend the party themselves. While Alexeev unloaded the carriage, Tomi filled in Alena about his new relationship with Alexeev. He didn't want any awkward questions Alexeev might not know how he should answer. But Alena was thrilled Tomi and Alexeev were in love and they had decided to live together as a couple.

"You know, Katia and I are in the same kind of relationship," she whispered.

"Well, I've known for some time now," he replied. "I remember when the two of you first started living together, there were a few eyebrows raised…let's see, it's been almost twenty years now, hasn't it?"

"Nineteen years in March," she replied.

"Katia moved in here with you and your father a few years before he died…rest his soul. I remember Galina came here for a four- or five-month visit." He thought for a moment. "And I was able to come for about two weeks… Oh, we had a nice time…a very nice time."

Soon Katia and Alexeev rejoined the group in the parlour and Alena excused herself to get the tea and some refreshments. Katia gave Alexeev the short tour of the house and Ivan was already taking the carriage around back for the night and was tending to the horses.

"My Ivan's a good boy," she told Alexeev. "Don't you worry about those horses," she said. "Ivan's the best there is, and he knows everything there is to know about horses."

"It's good you're giving him a chance to get some experience before he has to go out on his own," said Alexeev. "Not all young boys have the opportunity to get that kind of hands-on experience." As he walked around the parlour, he admired the paintings one by one. He spent several minutes studying each painting and absorbing their exceptional beauty. This, of course, was one of Alexeev's favourite things to do: to admire artwork and lose himself in the images.

"I see you like our paintings," said Katia. "Some of them were painted by Alena and some were painted by me."

"Now you'll never get him out of this room, unless of course, you have more paintings in another room," said Tomi.

Alexeev was quite surprised the two women were such wonderful artists. He had not known any female artists before. "You and Alena are remarkable artists!" He walked up to a brilliant painting of a rose garden with arbours and roses of every hue and shade. It reminded him of some of the gardens in Moscow when they were in full bloom in the springtime. "The roses are so vivid and realistic," he said. Then he looked closer to examine some of the detail, "You've even painted bees and butterflies on the flowers!"

"That one is called Mosaic Garden," said Katia. "It is one of Alena's favourites."

He glanced down at the signature and saw a large *K* followed by a few nondescript letters scribbled in the lower left corner. "You are a very talented artist."

She smiled and patted him on the shoulder. "Thank you, thank you. That's always nice to hear."

Alena brought in the tea along with some cookies and candied fruit. "Well, here we are…" She set the tray on the table. "Please, everyone help yourself."

They each took a cup of tea and a plate of cookies and fruit and had a wonderful evening of conversation and getting acquainted. Ivan joined them once he finished caring for the horses and he sat himself down next to Alexeev. They were talking about Alexeev's adventures in the army while they were out by the stables, so now Alexeev had a chance to finish a few of the tales. Tomi was busy getting Alena's recipe for her fruit cake and the method Katia used for her candied fruit, and he was giving them his recipe for molasses snowball cookies. But the night soon caught up to Tomi, and the tea was helping him relax. He was ready to get to bed. Alexeev had just gotten to the end of one of his adventures, so he was ready for bed as well.

The boys went up to their room on the second floor right across from Ivan's room, and the women stayed up a while to put the food away and wash the dishes before going to bed in their own room on the first floor.

"I'm glad we stopped here, Alexeev. Alena and Katia are the nearest relatives I have, and I wanted to make sure they knew about you."

"They seem like wonderful people. I especially like their paintings. Did you know both of them paint?" Alexeev quickly got undressed then built a fire in the fireplace.

"I don't think we have time to sit for another painting, my love," he said as he tugged on Alexeev's chin. "Help me get my boots off."

He knelt down and unlaced Tomi's boots, then removed them along with the stockings. "*Schast'ye moye*, you know I would never think of asking anything like that. I simply think they paint beautiful pictures." Then he started laughing. "I think Katia thought I was going to ask her if I could buy that painting though…she was getting ready to bargain with me!"

Tomi put on his long-sleeved nightshirt then got into bed underneath the covers. Alexeev folded up the clothes then washed his hands and face in the basin. "Come to bed, love, I'm getting cold here by myself." Alexeev got underneath the covers and held Tomi. "I think we should stay tomorrow night as well. I don't want Alena to think we are just here for convenience alone…besides, I like my niece."

"Yes, I think that would be a good idea. I like getting to know your family." Alexeev was rarely disagreeable, in fact, he didn't usually offer his own opinion unless he was asked. Tomi knew Alexeev had a very good sense of judgment though, and wanted him to start taking charge. Tomi always felt more comfortable obeying rather than giving orders, even though he sometimes had a stubborn streak. But he wanted Alexeev to decide for himself to take charge of things. Just how he would accomplish this was still a mystery though. For now, Tomi would have to be satisfied with Alexeev the way he was. He loved him too much to try to force him to change, especially if it would alter the character Tomi had fallen in love with.

Alexeev hugged Tomi a little tighter then kissed his neck. "Goodnight, *schast'ye moye*."

Chapter 21
The Mosaic Garden

Morning didn't come soon enough for Alexeev. He awoke around five o'clock, restless and ready to start his day. He decided to let Tomi sleep in and thought a brisk walk around the neighbourhood could be just the thing he needed to brighten up his morning. He got dressed and went outside. It was a beautiful morning. The stars twinkled through the backs of the trees and danced above the mountains in the distance. He heard the call of wolves in the hills and finches singing in the nearby trees already starting their morning choruses. There was lamplight coming from the barn so he knew the cows were already being milked and fed and soon the chickens would be disturbed from their slumber for egg-gathering as well. Off he went, down the stone walkway on the side of the property.

Alena was another early riser. She was in the kitchen making several loaves of bread and figuring out what to make for breakfast. She knew her Uncle Tomi loved her recipe for *olad'i* [133]. The recipe was handed down from Tomi's great grandmother on his mother's side (Alena's great-great-grandmother, Nita)—Nita always added a little nutmeg to the batter—so she decided to make them this morning. She would serve the cakes with sour cream and fruit compote and would also scramble some eggs. She and Katia didn't often eat a big breakfast, usually porridge with fruit or jam. Katia also loved coffee though, so that drink was always available, especially on cold mornings.

She had had her first introduction to coffee while she was in *Sankt Piter-Burkh* five years earlier and had fallen in love with the flavour and its versatility. She especially liked the fact that she could add cocoa, cream, vanilla or sugar to

133 *Olad'i*: Similar to traditional American pancakes, but usually smaller in size and thicker

her concoction to give it an added flavour kick and variety. Alena thought coffee was a little more of a dessert drink and something one shouldn't indulge in very often. Nevertheless, she made a fresh pot of coffee along with her usual pot of chamomile tea. She thought the coffee and cocoa mixture might be appealing to Tomi since she knew he liked a cup of hot cocoa every now and then.

Soon, Ivan came in from the barn. He had finished his chores and tended the horses, so he came in to wash up before breakfast. He brought in the milk jug and nine fresh eggs. They had thirty laying hens, and since the cold weather had settled in, the hens were tapering off their usual bounty of egg-laying. But nine was still a decent gathering for this time of year. Three of the boarders soon joined Ivan in the dining room, and finally, the last couple came down and sat at the table. There were already hot tea kettles in the centre of the tables along with the serving bowls of eggs. Then Alena brought out a platter of *olad'i.* The boarders were pleasantly surprised and wondered what the special occasion was. Just as they were asking, Tomi walked into the dining room and Alena introduced her uncle to the boarders. Alena invited him to sit down next to her, then she served him the eggs and cakes.

"Do you want tea this morning, or would you like to try Katia's coffee?" she asked.

"Coffee? I don't believe I've ever had that...yes, I'd like to try some." He looked around the table. "Where is Alexeev? Have you seen him this morning?"

"I think I heard him go outside early this morning," said Alena

Ivan added, "I saw him walking towards town about two hours ago."

"He likes to explore," said Tomi. "But he'll be back once his stomach tells him he's hungry."

"Uncle Tomi, did you know your Alexeev was admiring some of our paintings?"

"Yes, he was talking about them last night," he said. "He is very impressed with your artwork. He was especially fond of Katia's painting. I think he said you call it Mosaic Garden."

"He has very good taste. That is one of Katia's best pieces. Did you know it is the painting of our rose gardens in the back?"

"Oh, he would love to see them in the spring when the flowers are in full bloom," said Tomi. "I think we will have to plan a trip here one of these years during the warmer months."

Just as Tomi poured his second cup of coffee, Alexeev walked in through the front door. "I'm sorry I'm late. Good morning!" He walked over to Tomi and kissed him on the cheek. "It was such a beautiful morning I decided to go for a walk and then got caught up in the beauty of the countryside."

Alexeev sat down next to Tomi, and Alena loaded up a plate with *olad'i* and eggs while Tomi poured him a cup of coffee. After his second helping of cakes and eggs and his third cup of coffee, he decided that was probably enough.

"Now what can I do to make myself useful while we are here?" he asked. "I can chop wood or mend fences. I can do any kind of farm work or house repairs. But I don't want to just sit around and do nothing."

After quite a bit of discussion, Katia finally agreed to let Alexeev help Ivan repair the roof on the barn. During the last rain they noticed the roof was leaking. Since the weather had been good the last few days, and since Alexeev was here, Katia agreed to let Ivan go up to the roof with him. She was sometimes a little overprotective of her son, as most mothers are. Alexeev promised to look after the lad and keep him out of harm's way. Of course, Ivan protested the need to have anyone else watch over him, but he was glad for Alexeev's help all the same.

Tomi decided he could be a better help inside the house since he dreaded being out in the cold, plus he was terrified of heights. After the breakfast dishes were washed and dried, he immediately took to the mop and pail and cleaned the kitchen and dining room floors. While he and Alena worked on housecleaning, it gave them some time to gossip and get caught up on family events and happenings.

Meanwhile, Alexeev and Ivan prepared to get busy with the roof repairs. Ivan took Alexeev out to the barn and showed him where the leaks were coming from. There were several wooden slats that were damaged, probably in the last storm or from wind, so those would have to be replaced. Ivan brought out the ladder, and they got up on top of the roof to remove one of the slats for measurements. Alexeev counted ten slats needing to be replaced. There was plenty of wood in the barn, so the two of them got busy measuring and cutting the new slats.

By lunchtime, they had all the slats cut and ready to be nailed onto the roof. So, the boys took a break for lunch. Tomi and Alena made a pot of mushroom and squash stew and there was a fresh loaf of black bread. Tomi went out to their carriage and brought in a few jars of Aunt Galina's honey so they could have honey on their bread and in their tea. Tomi felt a headache coming on so he made some tea with cinnamon, ginger and cloves. It smelled so good, both Alena and Katia were eager to try it also.

After lunch, the boys were ready to return to the barn to finish repairing the roof. Alexeev let Ivan climb the ladder first. Once he was safe on the roof, Alexeev followed with five of the slats. He handed them to Ivan, and had him place them beside him until the rest were brought up. He returned to the ground, grabbed the rest of the slats and climbed back up the ladder. Ivan carefully took the remaining slats and set them beside him with the others. Alexeev had two hammers and more than enough nails to get the job done. First, they removed all the damaged slats and threw them down onto the ground. Then Alexeev climbed to the location where the first slat needed to be placed, and had Ivan hand him the first slat. He wanted to make sure the fit was correct before he let Ivan continue next to him.

The fit seemed to be perfect. Ivan took the second slat and put it in place. One by one, they placed the slats then nailed them in. The job was soon finished so they prepared to climb down the ladder. Alexeev wanted Ivan to go down first. As Ivan approached the ladder, Alexeev gathered the two hammers and a few random nails from the roof. Unfortunately, he didn't see one of the nails and stepped right on it. His foot slipped out from under him and he went tumbling down towards the ladder and Ivan. He desperately reached out to try to grab onto anything but there was nothing to hold onto.

Just as he tumbled towards the end of the roof, Ivan reached out and grabbed Alexeev's arm and held on tight. Ivan was still sitting on the edge of the roof and had not yet stepped onto the ladder, but as Alexeev's momentum carried him over the edge of the roof, his body hit the ladder and it fell to the ground. Ivan was now flat on his stomach on the roof with one arm dangling over the edge, holding onto Alexeev.

"You need to let me go, Ivan, otherwise we will both fall," Alexeev called out. "You aren't strong enough to pull me back up and I cut my other hand as I slid down…I can't grab onto the roof to help myself back up."

"But I can't let you go," Ivan was obviously in pain trying to hold on with all his strength, but he was losing his grip. He yelled out, "Mama! Mama! Help us. Alena! Tomi! Help us!" It was no use. He couldn't hold on any longer. Sobbing from his impossible situation, his strength finally gave way and Alexeev fell to the ground.

Ivan heard the thud of Alexeev's body as it hit the ground below. He couldn't bear to look, but he had to. He leaned over the edge of the roof and saw Alexeev's body stretched out on the ground, face up and unmoving. His right arm was tucked under his body and Ivan could see the other hand, red with blood, and it looked like there might be blood coming from his mouth as well.

Ivan raced over to the other side of the roof facing the house. He yelled out for Katia, Alena and Tomi. Katia came out running, then Alena and Tomi came running out behind her. "He's on the ground around back!" Ivan cried out and pointed to the far side of the barn. "He fell from the roof…I couldn't hold him. I couldn't hold him." He sobbed and sobbed with regret.

Alena and Tomi quickly ran around the barn and tended to Alexeev while Katia stood the ladder back up against the barn so Ivan could come down.

Alena ripped open Alexeev's shirt and put her ear to his chest, "I can hear his heartbeat but he's not breathing." She remembered when Ivan was born he also had a hard time breathing right away, and the midwife slapped him hard until he started breathing. Alena slapped Alexeev's face several times, then listened to his chest again. It startled Tomi and it pained him to see his lover getting slapped in the face, but he trusted that Alena knew what she was doing. Then she slapped him several more times. Finally, Alexeev gasped and started breathing again.

Tomi hugged Alena. "Oh, thank you, thank you, Alena!"

As they tried to raise Alexeev up, he grabbed his right arm that had been pinned behind him. "I think it's broken, Tomi," he said as he winced in pain.

"Are you hurt anywhere else?" he asked. "What about your head?"

"I think I bit my lip, but I don't think anything else is broken. I cut my hand on the way down trying to grab on." He was having a difficult time sitting straight and he gasped for breath.

Alena examined his arm and looked over his cuts and scrapes. "The arm is not broken, but it looks like it's dislocated from the shoulder." She carefully brought it around and rested it on Alexeev's stomach.

Once Ivan got down, he and Tomi and Katia lifted Alexeev and carried him into the house. Alena steadied his arm so it wouldn't fall. They set him down on one of the parlour sofas.

"We don't have a doctor anywhere near here, Tomi," said Alena. "But if it's dislocated, I know how to reset it. Then we can put it in a sling so it can heal."

She looked around for a moment. "Katia, find a long piece of cloth we can use as a sling."

Alexeev had seen broken bones and dislocations set before, so he knew what to expect. It would be extremely painful but at least it could heal properly afterwards. He also saw men who were not able to get their broken bones or dislocations set properly. The arms or legs never were the same again, because the bones mended improperly, and sometimes infection or gangrene would cause complications, or even make it necessary to amputate the limbs. He told Alena to do what she needed to do to reset the arm.

Katia got out a bottle of vodka and had Alexeev start drinking to help numb the pain, or at least reduce it a bit. Alena made Tomi leave the room. She knew he was an emotional wreck and wouldn't be of any use until after she had done her job.

"Ivan, I need to you to hold Alexeev around the chest very tightly," she instructed. "You can't let him move." Katia held Alexeev's other hand so he wouldn't try to struggle. "Alexeev, you know this is going to hurt…" With a sharp tug and jerk, and without warning, she reset the arm. It was quick as a wink, but extremely painful. Alexeev gasped but didn't cry out.

Alena quickly placed the cloth around his arm and tied it around Alexeev's neck. "I think we should also get a cloth to tie the arm around your waist so you aren't tempted to raise your arm."

Alexeev looked down at his arm and sighed. "Well, at least the job is done."

"Yes, you will need to wear this for about three weeks while it heals," said Alena.

Alexeev put the bottle to his mouth and poured the vodka in. "No, that's not what I meant…the roof is fixed," he said, as he reached out and tried to pat Ivan on the leg but missed. The vodka was affecting his mind and coordination.

"You men are all fools," said Katia, spitting out the words. "You could have both been killed!"

Ivan put his arm around his mother. "But we weren't killed, Mama. And Alexeev is going to be fine." Then he sat down next to Alexeev. "Why did you make me let you go, Alexeev?"

Alexeev put his hand on Ivan's knee. "Life is very precious, Ivan." His words came out slurred and were starting to become incoherent, but he took another swallow of the vodka. "I knew you couldn't pull me up…but I also knew if you didn't let go…we could have both fallen together…down. It would have been worse if one of us…were to land on the top…and I wasn't willing to take the chance…you could have been hurt or killed, even."

Katia started crying, then she hugged Alexeev. "Thank you, thank you! I'm sorry I yelled at you. I owe you so much."

"Everything is fine now," he said. "Your son is safe…my arm will too…and Tomi…where is *moye...schast'ye…*" The alcohol was clouding his mind. "Tomi!" he called, as his eyes wandered back and forth.

Alena secured the arm around his waist then bandaged the other hand while Tomi came back into the room. "And drink lots of milk and eat plenty of meat. You need to keep up your strength so it will heal properly."

"I'm right here, my love, I'm right here." He stroked Alexeev's sweaty brow then kissed the bandaged arm. Alexeev took a final drink from the bottle then laid his head on Tomi's shoulder.

"I think the two of you should rest in here for a while. Now Tomi, make sure he doesn't move that arm. It needs to stay still for the next three weeks…and take him to your doctor as soon as you get him home." Then she brought a blanket and draped it over the two boys while Ivan lifted Alexeev's legs onto the couch. He was already asleep and he had his good arm wrapped around Tomi. Alena pulled the door shut and she and the others left them to rest for the afternoon.

Even though Alexeev would recover quickly because he was already in peak physical condition, it would still be a few days before he would get used to not favouring his right arm. He was an active person, and confining or restraining his abilities in any way was very frustrating and most inconvenient.

Tomi did his best to encourage him and help him in any way he could, but Alexeev didn't take assistance well. He wanted to do things for himself and he wanted them done his way. Tomi was beginning to think they would need to stay with Alena and Katia until Alexeev's arm was completely healed, but he always thought in the extremes, which often prevented him from seeing reality very clearly.

The second day after the accident, Alexeev was very restless and wanted to go for a walk. Tomi insisted on accompanying him, so they set out to go together. It was after breakfast and there was plenty of daylight. Alexeev had taken this same path a few days before, the morning before the accident. Tomi carefully helped him put on his new coat, and insisted he wear his hat and gloves as well.

"I don't want you getting a fever on top of your injury." He patted the top of Alexeev's head after he put his hat on, then tugged it from side to side to straighten it.

Alexeev was reluctant, but compliant with the request while he let Tomi help him on with his coat and gloves. He insisted Tomi bundle up as well. "And you, my dear, should try to stay as warm as possible so you don't sneeze on me and cause me any more grief!" he replied, but as soon as the words left his mouth, he realised how ungrateful they sounded. "Forgive me, Tomi. I know I haven't been the most cooperative patient lately."

Tomi patted his cheek and kissed him. "It has already been forgiven and forgotten."

They took a nice long walk, and made plans to leave as soon as they got back to the house. Alexeev felt sure he could manage driving the carriage as long as the weather held out. He was a little apprehensive about delaying their trip any longer and was afraid the weather could quickly turn worse. Tomi was eager to get back on the road as well, although he wasn't looking forward to spending nights out in the cold again. Once they returned to the house, they started getting their things packed and ready to go. They went to their room and Alexeev got the last of his things together in his bag.

Tomi's things were all packed but he still wanted to get some food ready to take with them on the trip. He was still thinking about how Alena revived Alexeev and how he might not have lived if she hadn't been there to help him regain consciousness.

"I want to give Alena and Katia the set of Delftware *Tetushka* gave us. I have my own set of china. I don't need another set just gathering dust on my shelves." He paused for a moment. "Besides, if she hadn't been there for you, you might not be here for me."

Alexeev turned to Tomi and hugged him. "I am always so proud of you, *schast'ye moye*."

Tomi and Alena prepared a basket of *buterbrody* along with Alena's *houska*[134] and other pastries, and Katia made sure they took a bag of coffee beans so he could make a few pots of coffee along the way as a special treat. She also gave him a small tin of cocoa powder since Alexeev had used the last of their supply several days before they arrived.

---

[134] *houska* (Czech): Bohemian sweet bread

Ivan made sure the horses were well fed and he inspected their shoes to make sure they were well-shod and in good condition for the road ahead. He also loaded several bags of oats, grain and hay. He had made a new friend in Alexeev, and they formed a special bond over the last few days. Alexeev encouraged him to find his place in the community and in the world at large, and to not be afraid to try different things. Since Storozhevsk would be a more reasonable trip than Moscow, Alexeev assured him whenever the opportunity arose he would make it a point to visit.

Katia was so grateful of how Alexeev protected Ivan from injury and how he continued to spend time with him, she wanted to reward him in some way. She talked it over with Alena and they agreed that they would give Alexeev the painting he so admired: The Mosaic Garden. Ivan helped them pack it so it could be transported. When they presented it to Alexeev, he was so moved he cried. He hugged Katia and Alena then hugged and kissed Ivan. Tomi's heart was full of pride for his lover, and he knew they had gained a new place Alexeev could call home. Then the boys gave Alena and Katia the crates full of Galina's precious china.

Alena opened up the first crate. "You know, Tomi, this is the set of china I always admired whenever Papa would take us to visit *Tetushka.* We will treasure it always." Then Tomi and Alexeev stepped up into the carriage and rode off while Ivan and the ladies waved goodbye.

Chapter 22
Welcome Home

The winter remained unusually warm and even though he welcomed the advantage they had in travel time, Alexeev was still concerned the weather could change rapidly and snowstorms could come without any forewarning. The afternoon they left Alena's was the toughest for Alexeev since he had to adapt to riding the reins with only one hand. Tomi sat next to him and tried to encourage him from time to time, but the only remedy would be Alexeev's strong willpower and determination.

The real challenge would come that first evening when they would have to make camp. With only one good arm, he would need to rely heavily on Tomi to help him set up the overhead tarp, tie the horses and feed them, build the fires and then maintain the fires all night. They would have to work together to find and chop wood and possibly to hunt or fish after a few days once the provisions run out. Alexeev still felt a dull ache in his shoulder and he knew if he tried to push the healing process too hard, it could result in further injury.

He pulled the carriage over to the roadside a few times that afternoon to rest the horses and also to rest his good arm. But Tomi took the reins in the late afternoon so Alexeev could take a longer break. He found a nice meadow just before sundown where they could make camp for the night. Tomi parked the carriage next to a small grove of trees for shelter. There was a small stream running next to the grove, so Tomi took advantage of the fresh water and refilled their jug, then watered the horses and tied and covered them up for the night. A few downed trees in the grove supplied them with plenty of firewood, and Tomi managed to gather enough small branches and trigs to start a few firepits around the camp, and he found a few large logs nearby that would be perfect to keep the fires going. He led one of the horses to the logs, tied the logs together, then tied the other end of the ropes to the horses and led them back to the camp, dragging the logs behind them.

Alexeev was impressed with Tomi's ingenuity and resolve, and helped him guide the logs into the firepits. Then Alexeev took hold of one end of the overhead tarp and Tomi took the other end. They pulled it out and managed to insert the poles for support. Tomi heated some water in a pot for tea and brought out pieces of dried meat, cheese, and several of the *buterbrody* for dinner, and Alexeev added tea leaves, cinnamon, cloves and ginger to the pot. Soon their dinner was ready, so they relaxed by the fire and feasted on their simple yet tasty morsels.

After dinner, Tomi walked around the camp and made sure the fires were still lit and the horses were bedded down and secure for the night. Then he helped Alexeev finish putting away the rest of the food. They sat a while longer by the fire, and Tomi opened the hatch to the inner cabin so the warm air from the fire could start heating up their sleeping area.

"I'm sorry I haven't been more useful," said Alexeev.

"You've taken care of me plenty of times," said Tomi, "now it's my turn to take care of you."

He helped Alexeev unbutton his shirt, then he carefully slipped it over his head, untied his trousers and took them off. Alexeev got into the cabin and got himself settled in; he was exhausted. He never realised how much he depended on using both hands and arms. With only one good arm, he felt like he was working twice as hard with everything he did while only getting half accomplished. Tomi got undressed, then put on his long bedshirt and joined Alexeev in the cabin. Alexeev was already resting comfortably, so Tomi reclined next to him, next to his good arm. He put his arm over Alexeev's chest and rested his head on his shoulder. Before long, the two of them were sound asleep.

Tomi got up a few times in the night to keep the fires lit and to check on the horses, and Alexeev woke up each time, wishing he was the one making the rounds. He knew this was not something Tomi was used to, but he also knew the experience was probably good for Tomi, to make him feel more useful.

Over the next several days, they managed to form a routine and got used to playing their new roles. Alexeev gained a little more strength, but was still cautious not to use the injured arm, and Tomi seemed to be fitting in well to his role as caregiver. Tomi even surprised Alexeev when he brought back five fish he caught at the river one morning before Alexeev woke up. But Alexeev did his part and cooked the fish after Tomi cleaned them. They had fish for breakfast and lunch and dried and salted the leftovers so they could have the rest the next day. Tomi also had a jar of fruit compote, so they had *houska* warmed over the fire, topped with butter and berry compote as a treat for a few meals.

After a few more days, Tomi started to see the familiar sights and landscapes of the valleys just to the southwest of his own valley and township. Then they went over a hill, and *Ust-Sysolsk*[135] was just in sight. Only a few hills and bends separated *Ust-Sysolsk* and Storozhevsk, but home was still about two days away. Even the smells of the countryside were familiar. There was a decent inn in the town and a store to buy some much-needed supplies, even though they were so close to home.

They pulled into the roadway by the inn just before sundown, and guided the carriage to the stables where Alexeev stayed to get them settled in for the night. Meanwhile, Tomi checked in with the innkeeper. He had known the innkeeper for several years, so they had a good conversation and he gave Tomi the best room in the inn for the night. There was a local *kabak*[136] next door serving food as well as drinks, so Tomi decided they should eat there since they were running low on their food supplies. Their room was not far from the stables, so Tomi met Alexeev at the stables and helped carry their bags back to the room.

"We can get something to eat next door at the *kabak*," said Tomi.

"That sounds good, I am so hungry," Alexeev's stomach growled as he spoke. "I wonder what they're serving tonight?"

"Whatever it is, you can be sure it will taste good," said Tomi. "I've never been disappointed here."

They put on their coats and made their way to the *kabak.* It wasn't crowded, but this was not a very large town. As they walked into the *kabak,* Alexeev could smell the cabbage *pirozhki*[137]. They were also serving *blini* with berry filling, and they had both *sbiten* and tea. Tomi's headaches were coming back, so he thought the spices in the *sbiten* might help. He also had *blini.* Alexeev had *pirozhki*, *blini* and tea, and asked if they also had any pickled vegetables, cheeses or meats. They brought him a large tray of a variety of meats, vegetables and hot pastries so he was happy and well fed. After the meal, the host brought out a

---

[135] *Ust-Sysolsk:* former name of Syktyvkar.

[136] *kabak*: A public ale house, bar or tavern

[137] *pirozhki*: Fried buns stuffed with a variety of fillings

sampling of toffees for them to try. They both raved about how good they were, so they bought a few pieces to take with them.

It had been a long week and Tomi was eager to get to bed early so they could leave before sunrise in the morning. He had been away far too long and was feeling homesick. He constantly thought about how his business was doing while he was away. Although he trusted his servants completely to manage the businesses on their own, he always felt a little more reassured when he gave it his personal touch.

Tomi imagined how Alexeev would feel after several months of being away from the only life he had every known in Moscow and the army. Although he travelled much while on duty, he always came back to Moscow, and to Orlov, the only family he ever knew. Tomi wondered if living so far away from Orlov, Vanya and Galina was a good thing, or if, perhaps, they should consider a move closer to Moscow. It was too much to think about before bedtime and far too many things were going through his mind. He decided to have a few glasses of wine before they returned to the inn, and Alexeev decided to have a glass of spiced vodka. They drank to their health and happiness, then went back to their room at the inn.

Neither of them woke up early. In fact, it was well past breakfast before either of them considered getting out of bed. They cuddled and kissed, happy to be in each other's arms and thankful to have a morning when they didn't have to get up and leave, or get up and start a task or job, or get up and make breakfast for the group. They took their time and made love in the morning.

Alexeev wrapped his strong, good arm around Tomi and gave him a kiss. Then Tomi rolled Alexeev onto his back and started caressing and kissing him. He sucked on his chin and neck then he massaged his neck, shoulders and biceps. He knew Alexeev's arms were tired and tense from riding. He took extra precautions not to disturb the injured arm and shoulder, but he kissed its forearm, fingers and wrist carefully. Then he took hold of Alexeev's chest with both hands and clenched his pectorals. Alexeev inhaled deeply and arched his back. Tomi licked one of the nipples then wrapped his lips around it and sucked. He tugged on the other nipple with his thumb and forefinger.

He felt Alexeev's cock getting harder and thicker underneath him. Tomi slid his chin between the pectoral muscles and down towards the belly then licked and bit his abdomen gently. He followed the trail of hair down to the groin and licked the base of the cock. It sprang up as if it were called to attention. Tomi ran his fingers up and down the thick, erect muscle, then put his lips around the end of the cock. His tongue licked all around it, up and down, and encircled its head. Then he plunged the cock down his throat. He felt Alexeev's hand on the back of his head, pulling it deeper onto the cock, deeper down the throat: the massive muscle expanded inside his mouth, nearly choking him. He gagged and struggled for breath, and saliva poured from the side of his mouth, but he continued to suck. He took hold of the balls and pulled them gently.

Alexeev spread his legs and rested one of them on Tomi's shoulder. Alexeev's shoulders were firmly on the bed but his hard, clenched buttocks were resting against Tomi's chest. Tomi let the balls fall to either side of the large stiff cock then he reached out and started pumping the nipples again while he continued to suck the cock. Alexeev was going wild. His good arm clutched the pillow as he arched his back again and gasped. Tomi anticipated the orgasm and forced the entire cock deep inside his throat. He felt the explosion of cum inside his mouth. He swallowed and continued to suck the cock and pump the nipples. Alexeev continued to flail his arm on the bed and gasped with eager anticipation. His muscles tensed and spasmed, then he released the rest of his cum down Tomi's throat. Tomi swallowed again then licked the cock of all remaining cum.

He concentrated on the balls, sucking on one and then the other. He stroked the cock with one hand while he worked over one of the nipples with the other. Alexeev tensed his muscles, flexed his chest, and pounded the bed with his fist. He grabbed his other nipple and started pulling and pinching it hard. Tomi continued sucking the balls and stroking the cock. He watched his Adonis-like lover flex and thrash like a wounded animal caught in a trap. It was exotic and intoxicating. He glowed with god-like masculinity.

As the last few droplets of cum shot up from the head of his cock, his whole body became erect and rigid in one final moment of elation. Then he collapsed as if all the energy had suddenly been robbed from his body. His skin glistened with sweat, and his chest heaved deep breaths of exhaustion. Tomi saw the smile of satisfaction on Alexeev's face and he knew he had pleased his lover.

They didn't leave *Ust-Sysolsk* until a little before noon, but neither of them was disappointed at the delay. Their horses were fed and rested, so they loaded their bags into the carriage and set off. Tomi made one last stop at the local deli and purchased a few loaves of bread, some cheeses and dried meats for their lunch, two dozen apples and a few bunches of carrots for the horses. The innkeeper put a few bags of oats in the carriage for the horses, but Tomi also liked to give them a treat whenever he could, and they loved apples and carrots. They were especially deserving of rewards, since this had been a very long ride with many nights out in the cold. But they would be home before the next evening.

The countryside was beautiful but bare. The winter had stolen all the leaves from the trees except for the pines, which stood like solitary green giants among the many bare oak and birch trees. But the green grasses could still be seen for miles on end since the winter hadn't yet covered these fields with its white blanket. The river on the south side of the city was starting to freeze, so everyone knew the approach of winter was eminent. Even the birch trees along the banks of the river with their snow-white bark looked like they had been abandoned and left to starve out in the cold. But this was how life existed in the wilderness: cold, stark and naked.

After their first roadside break after lunch the next day, Alexeev gave Tomi the reins. He took out his tobacco pouch and pipe and they shared a smoke while they rode the rest of the way home. The frigid air made it difficult to distinguish between exhaled smoke and one's normal breath, yet the sweet smell of the tobacco seemed to take part of the chill away. Alexeev reached into his pocket and pulled out his handkerchief and unwrapped a few pieces of toffee he had saved from the evening at the *kabak.* He held one up in front of Tomi and placed it in his mouth, then he ate the second one. They both smiled at the indulgence and relished the sweet, smooth richness of the flavourful candy while it lasted.

Alexeev put his good arm around Tomi while his other arm rested from a sling in front of him. Tomi looked at Alexeev's hand and could see the shiny, silver ring and a single green stone displayed proudly on his finger. Alexeev was turning it with his thumb. He gazed at the same ring on his own hand and marvelled at how natural it looked against his skin. He never imagined anyone would care about him the way Alexeev did. He never thought he would be starting a new life with a man who wanted nothing more than to be by his side, and he had never dreamed he would be so in love with a man that he could set aside his own desires, hopes and dreams, and replace them with the needs and wants of someone else.

The sun was setting behind them. They could see the pink and orange hues filling the sky around them. It almost seemed magical as the sun set behind them, they were starting a new life together just ahead of them. Only a few more bends in the road separated them from Tomi's cottage. Alexeev could feel the anticipation of his lover. He could see the difference in the way Tomi was sitting and the way he was breathing and by the look on his face.

"Are you all right, *schast'ye moye*?" he asked. He hugged him a little tighter. "You seem a little tense."

Tomi started crying. "I love you so much, Alexeev. I don't know what I would do if you ever left me." He started shaking and trembling.

Alexeev took the reins and pulled the carriage over to the side of the road. He hugged Tomi, then looked him straight in the eyes. "I am never going to leave you…I love you." He kissed him, then put his hand under Tomi's chin. "You are my whole life now. This is what I want."

Still crying, Tomi wrapped his arms around Alexeev, "I love you, *moy muzh*[138]."

Alexeev wiped the tears from Tomi's eyes then picked up the reins again. "Now let's get home before we freeze to death."

He pulled the carriage around the side of the house and they both started laughing. The reality of making it home had changed any tension and apprehension into happiness and exuberant expectation. Pavel was in the kitchen when he heard the carriage pull up. He ran out to greet them.

"Welcome back, Master Pedorov, welcome back," he said as he helped guide the horses. "It's been a long time. We were starting to get worried." Then he took a long look at Alexeev. "I remember you. Aren't you the lieutenant? Yes…Lieutenant Alexeev. You came to visit several years ago with your troops?"

"You have a very good memory," said Alexeev as he reached out his left hand.

Pavel shook his hand and helped him down. "Looks like you've been in an accident."

"We'll tell you all about it later," said Tomi. "Can you ask Kirill or Anton to tend to the horses? And have them bring in our things from the back of the carriage."

"Yes, sir," Pavel replied. "Then I'll get the water ready for your tea. Will the Lieutenant be staying for dinner?"

Tomi didn't like so much formality, but every time he was away, Pavel treated him like royalty when he returned. He stepped down from the carriage

---

[138] *moy muzh*: My husband

and hugged Pavel. "First of all, please call me Tomi. And second, Alexeev will be staying here with me…permanently."

Pavel was overjoyed by the news. He had always hoped Tomi would find someone who could fill his great void of loneliness. He gave him a big hug then kissed his cheek. "Congratulations, Mast—I mean…Tomi."

"And tell the boys to be careful when they unload our things. There are some very valuable crates in the back. I don't want them damaged," he said. Then thinking for a moment, he added, "Galina's crystal goblets and pitchers are in one of the crates so be sure they are very careful."

Pavel quickly ran to the outbuilding and gave instruction to the boys, then ran back into the house and started making the tea. Tomi and Alexeev walked arm in arm down the cobbled walkway and into the house.

Tomi took a deep breath. "Ahhh… It's good to be home again." The house was full of familiar and welcome scents.

There was a fire in the oven but the only other fire in the house was in the parlour. The servants weren't used to spending much time in the house while Tomi was away on trips, except for the occasional use of his larger oven. Tomi shivered and quickly went to the parlour to put another log on the fire and get some lamps lit.

Alexeev followed close behind. "Let me help with that," he said as he took a large log with his good hand and tossed it in the fireplace. Then he arranged the twigs and kindling around the log. "I'm afraid you will have to help me with the prongs, I don't seem to be able to manage them with only one hand."

Tomi took the prongs from the mantle and manoeuvred the wood around. "Well, I'm glad I can be useful for something."

Alexeev pulled Tomi up to him with his good arm and kissed him. "I can think of many ways you can be useful, and not one of them involves prongs."

Pavel brought in a tray and set it on the table next to the couch. He had a plate of molasses snowball cookies. He had just made a batch using Tomi's recipe. "The water for the tea is almost ready. Here is something to hold you over until I fix some dinner. We're having mushroom soup with black bread for dinner unless you would like something more."

"That sounds wonderful," said Tomi. "Then after dinner, I think we will want to bathe."

"I'll get the water heated for the bathtub," he said. Then he set a few saucers on the table and went back into the kitchen to prepare their dinner. Tomi followed Pavel into the kitchen to fix the tea.

It seemed to Alexeev this was almost like their first dinner together. There were many things that were familiar: the dining room table where he tried desperately to hide the fact that his cock was hard all through dinner, the hardwood floors where they tumbled around after dinner and made passionate love, the fireplace he kept lit each evening and again each morning and the beautiful red-rimmed china with hand-painted pine cones and song birds. But there were also many things unfamiliar: the knitted blanket draped over the settee, the potted spice garden just inside the kitchen, even the bannister on the stairs seemed strange or different somehow, even though he had gone up and down the stairs many times that week six years ago. Then he felt something rub up against his leg. He looked down and it was a black and white cat. There were never any animals inside the house when he was here before.

Alexeev bent down and petted the cat. "And who might you be, my little *koshenya*[139]." He sat down on the settee then picked him up and held him on his lap, stroking its back with his good hand. Then another black and white cat with almost identical markings came around the corner and put its front paws up onto Alexeev's knee. "And here we have another little one." The second cat quickly leapt up onto his lap for attention. He diligently petted each one alternatively so neither one felt neglected. Both started purring and stretched themselves up to his chin and face and began rubbing their scent onto his neck, chest, shoulders and face.

Tomi came back into the parlour carrying the tray with the tea and honey. "I thought I had… Oh, my goodness, you have found my treasures…or they have found you." He sat the tea down on the table next to the settee. "Misha, Mitya, don't smother him…let him have his tea." Tomi picked up Misha. "Yes, yes, I know you have missed all my affection over the last several months." He stroked Misha's head several times, then kissed his nose. "Now you go into the kitchen. Pavel has your dinner ready in there." Then he picked up Mitya and stroked him several times as well, then gave him a kiss and set him back down on the floor. "Go on, follow your brother." They both scampered into the kitchen as if they knew exactly what their master was saying.

---

[139] *koshenya* (Ukrainian): Kitten

"They are very obedient," said Alexeev. "I don't remember them here last time."

"It was about a week after you left, and the two simply appeared on my front porch," he said. "I've always had a soft spot in my heart for cats, and these two were just kittens. Either their mother abandoned them or maybe she was killed by wolves. That happens sometimes out here. I keep them inside almost all the time."

Alexeev put his arm around Tomi. "I'm happy to share my lover with such beautiful companions."

"I know they miss me terribly when I'm gone, especially when it's for such a long time, but they have each other, and Pavel takes good care of them when I'm not here." Tomi was relieved Alexeev took so well to his cats, and the cats seemed to like him as well. Misha and Mitya had kept him company over the last six years, and he didn't know what he would do if they weren't around.

When they finished their tea, Pavel had dinner ready for them in the dining room. The evening was going by so quickly. After dinner, they went into the bathing room where Pavel had already filled the tub with hot water and set out several towels, washcloths and Tomi's favourite scented soaps and lotions. Tomi helped Alexeev undress, carefully removed the sling then steadied him as he sat in the tub. Alexeev immediately sunk himself down to cover the shoulder.

"Oh, that feels so good," he said. "Are you coming in to join me?" There was plenty of room for two in the tub.

"I will, but first let's get you cleaned up," he said. "Sit up a little so I can wash your back and chest, then I'll wash your hair."

He carefully washed Alexeev with the scented soap, making sure he was gentle when it came to washing the injured arm and shoulder. There was still a little redness around the shoulder and a noticeable bruise on his triceps. He removed the bandage on his other hand. "The cut seems to be almost completely healed." There was just a two-inch red line across his palm where the gash had been. "Does it still hurt?"

"No, I don't feel it at all anymore. I think we can leave this bandage off now."

Tomi kept rubbing the washcloth over Alexeev's chest, arms, shoulders and neck. "You're still going to see the doctor."

"Yes sir, *moy general*!" Alexeev said as he snapped his left hand up to his forehead to salute his superior officer. In doing so, water and soap suds splashed Tomi in the face.

"My eyes! My eyes!" he screamed. Tomi quickly put his hands to his eyes as if he was in great pain.

"Oh my god! Tomi, I am so sorry!" Alexeev nearly jumped out of the tub. "…It was just a joke…I didn't mean to…"

Tomi lowered his hands and revealed his smile. "You didn't mean to…what?"

"Why you little…" Alexeev wrapped his good arm around Tomi's back and pulled him in the tub, clothes and all. Tomi screamed in protest all the way but it was no use. He went in as easily as if he had jumped in himself. Even though Alexeev had one lame arm, he could still overpower Tomi without any difficulty whatsoever.

After the initial shock of being overcome and soaked to the skin, Tomi laughed, then Alexeev laughed and then they kissed. Tomi took off his clothes and resumed bathing. Soon all was well, and they finished bathing. Tomi got out of the tub first, dried himself off and wrapped the towel around his waist. Then he helped Alexeev get out of the tub and helped him dry off. He carefully put the sling back around Alexeev's arm and tied the towel around his waist as well.

"We can leave the clothes here for now," he said. "I'll have Kirill wash them tomorrow along with the rest of our clothes."

By the time they finished bathing, it was already eleven o'clock. Kirill and Anton had already unloading the carriage and taken care of the horses. They put the food in the cellar for cold storage, especially the honey from Galina, and took Alexeev's bag and Tomi's trunk up to the bedroom. All the crates were placed carefully in the parlour where Tomi said he would attend to them in the morning. But he and Alexeev were exhausted and ready to get a good night's sleep, and the hot bath helped both of them relax. On this night though, Alexeev wouldn't be carrying Tomi up the stairs to bed. Instead, Tomi put his arm around Alexeev and helped him up the stairs.

"Do you remember carrying me up the stairs six years ago?" Tomi asked.

"I will never forget it, *schast'ye moye.* Never."

Chapter 23

The Blizzard and Unwelcome News

A good night's sleep was what they both needed. Alexeev heard the clock in the downstairs parlour strike nine o'clock but it was still dark outside. He had overworked his right arm even though he had consciously tried to take care of it. It still had a dull ache, and his left arm was sore due to him overcompensating. In the morning, even though he felt very rested, his good arm was still a little tired. He got up and drew the curtain back. There were dark clouds overhead moving in from the west. The winter storm was finally arriving. He got dressed and built up a small fire in the bedroom fireplace, then went downstairs to see if Pavel was up yet.

Tomi heard Alexeev get up, but he rolled over and tried to get a little more sleep. He had gone to bed with a bad headache. But Pavel had a tin of the doctor's tea in the kitchen, so he had made a fresh pot for Tomi before they had gone up to bed. He was feeling much better this morning. Just a few minutes later, he decided he'd better get out of bed and face the new day. He slipped on his robe and slippers and went downstairs.

Pavel had been up for a few hours with the rest of the staff. Due to the approaching storm, he sent Foka and Ivan home since they lived locally. He knew from the looks of the clouds the storm could get severe and he didn't want them to be separated from their families. The rest of the staff continued to prepare the animals for the impending storm. They had plenty of supplies, plenty of food for the animals and plenty of food for the rest of the servants who didn't have any other home to go to. Kirill decided not to try to go home since his family lived nearly a day away. He usually went home about every ten days, spending a few days with family, then returning for another ten days. Pavel and Anton lived full time on the estate but there was still plenty of room for everyone and enough room in the servants' quarters and in the main house for additional guests.

Alexeev built a fire in the parlour then offered to help in the barn with the animals but Pavel said they would manage fine on their own. "Stay inside and have breakfast with Master Pedorov. We will be done soon. Breakfast is all prepared." He showed Alexeev the plates of food, then he went back out to the barn and outbuilding to finish with the animals.

Tomi came into the kitchen and caught Alexeev trying to manage two plates of food along with the pot of tea. "Now what are you trying to do, break all my good dishes?" He took the plates from him and took them out to the dining room. Then he returned and set the teapot and cups on a tray and brought the tray to the table as well. "I can manage things from here. You go sit at the table." He pushed Alexeev out the kitchen door and into the dining room. "I'll join you in just a moment."

Alexeev lumbered out and took his place at the head of the table. He remembered Tomi had insisted he sit there when he was here six years ago. It made him feel good and special that Tomi would consider him worthy to be at the head of the table in his home. The silverware was in a stack at the end of the table, so Alexeev sorted it out and placed a setting at each of the two places. Then he poured the tea and put a spoonful of honey in each of their teacups. He was about to call out to Tomi to see if he could help with anything, when he heard someone knocking loudly at the front door. It sounded like someone was desperate to get in so Alexeev rushed to the front door to see what was wrong.

Tomi came in from the kitchen and placed a vase of fresh Daphne with a sprig of pine in the middle of the table. He retrieved a few dinner plates from the cabinet and arranged them neatly between the silverware that Alexeev had set. Then he got out two of his best embroidered napkins, folded them, and placed one on each plate. He looked around for a moment, not knowing where Alexeev had run off to, then he went back into the kitchen. He filled one of his porcelain pitchers with blackberry wine and brought it back to the table, then he got out two glass goblets from the cabinet. *I can hardly wait to unpack Galina's crystal*, he thought. When he turned around, there was Alexeev standing in the parlour doorway. He had a blank stare and his face was white like a sheet.

"Alexeev, come and sit down for breakfast. I have everything ready," said Tomi. Then he realised Alexeev was upset. "What's wrong? Was there someone at the door?"

Alexeev handed Tomi the scroll he had been clutching. "It was a messenger from Nizhny Novgorod," Alexeev said as the tears started pouring down his face. "Galina has died." Tomi dropped the scroll and the two goblets, shattering them on the floor. His knees started to buckle and he started to collapse. Alexeev caught him with his good arm. "I'm so sorry, Tomi."

"How did it happen…when?" he asked. "We were just there…she seemed fine… How could this have happened so quickly?"

Alexeev set Tomi in a chair and picked up the scroll. "The message said the parish priest came to visit her the the second Sunday after the new year. She passed out while they were talking and then she died that night… Tomi, they have already buried her." He knelt down at Tomi's feet and clung to Tomi's legs. He couldn't stop crying.

Tomi was shocked, but he did not cry. He loved his *Tetushka* dearly, more than any of his other relatives, but the sorrow in his heart couldn't be quenched by tears. Maybe it was the shock of the event, or the sudden news, or perhaps it was Alexeev's tears preventing Tomi from crying. "I didn't realise how attached you had gotten to my *Tetushka.* I think you loved her as much as I did." Tomi put his arms around Alexeev and comforted him.

"There were two scrolls, Tomi," he said as he separated the second one from the first. "It is from your *Tetushka.*"

Tomi took the scroll. It looked like she had written it to him many months before. Maybe she had intended to give it to him while they were visiting, but had forgotten. Perhaps she was holding on to it, just as many people hold on to life, even though they know the end is near. But this message was definitely to Tomi. He was her favourite nephew and he knew it. The scroll was sealed with red wax and the emblem of the three-barred cross was imbedded in the wax, indicating it had been sealed by the priest. Tomi's hand was shaking as he held the scroll. He and Alexeev got up and walked out into the parlour and sat down with their arms around each other, then Tomi broke the wax seal and read the message out loud:

6 August 1711
My dearest Tomi,

Today you went back to your home in Shoynaty. I could not stop crying because I feared for your loneliness. I think you should go and try to find this lieutenant you spoke of. I could hear in your voice how much you loved him. We all go through great tragedies in our lives, but we must learn to either overcome them or somehow turn them around and change the circumstances.

When my Nikolai died sixty years ago, I prayed the gods would take me also so I could again be with him, but the gods had other things in mind for me. I think one of the reasons I am still alive is for you, Tomi. You have been with so many men who have broken your heart, yet you have never been with any who have given their heart and their love to you. That is your tragedy. If you believe Alexeev loved you, you must go to him no matter where he might be. You must be like Ruth from Jewish history, who said, 'Wherever you go, I will go there, and where you will live, there I will live; your people will be my people.' She followed the one whom she loved, just as you must seek and follow the one whom you love. Don't be afraid of what others may think. Love is the most important thing in this world. Without love, there is no hope.

Your father would be proud of you if he had lived to see you grown into the man you are today. He loved you very much and I loved him too. He was taken from this world far too soon. But his wife, your mother, Anya, raised you well. Even though I never knew her, I can see from the way you live your life how she taught you to care for others less fortunate and to be responsible for your actions. She taught you to give in your abundance and not to hoard your money or belongings, because everything of this world is just temporary.

I am ninety-one this year, and I do not know how much longer I may live, but I want to tell you how much I love you. When I die, I want you to make sure my business is given to Vladimir. He has served me well and has given his life and his blood to the business. He has his own house on the property, so anything inside my home may be divided between the relatives as you see fit. If you, or any one of my relatives, wish to buy my house, they must deal with Vladimir and purchase it from him. I am giving him full ownership of all my land, including the buildings, livestock and farm. He already knows this and I have also given a copy of my will to the city clerk to hold until my death.

I will leave you now with these final thoughts. Whatever you choose to do in life, do it with your whole heart and do it without compromise. Love others first and your own happiness will follow. And do not look for those things that you want as much as you seek for those things that you need.

I love you always and want only the best for you.

Your Tetushka Galina

Tomi rolled up the scroll and tied the ribbon around it. As they sat holding each other, the clouds moved in overhead and they could see the sky getting darker outside, it almost looked like the dead of night. They saw flashes of lightening and heard several peals of thunder. Then through the parlour window, they could see the winds pick up and the snow started coming down very heavily. Within minutes, they whole yard was covered in a blanket of pure white snow. For hours, the wind howled through the trees as the snow continued to fall. By noon, more than two feet of snow had fallen.

Alexeev kept himself busy, keeping the fires burning to warm the house, and Tomi invited the servants in from their quarters in the back to join them for tea and fresh baked bread. Pavel, Kirill and Anton would stay through the storm. And Pavel had just hired two new recruits as wine-making apprentices, Viktor and Roman, who were set up in the servants' quarters as well. Anton's best friend, Gugal, was visiting from *Ust-Sysolsk* and was caught off guard by the sudden storm, so he was staying also. Tomi always ensured he had plenty for any visitors who may happen by, and Pavel carried on that quality of charity to make sure everyone felt welcome.

Other than Tomi and Alexeev, Pavel was the only one of the servants who had known or met Galina. He had accompanied Tomi to Galina's home in the summer after Alexeev returned to Moscow six years ago. Tomi suffered from severe depression for several months and his doctor recommended he leave home for a while and visit relatives to get his mind off his obsessions. He stayed with Tomi the whole time until they returned home in August.

Pavel was ordinarily a very cheery young man. He had a constant smile on his face that accentuated his deep dimples. His eyes were very dark brown, which gave him a warm, trustworthy appearance. He had short, dark brown hair and a little tuft of hair on his chin that matched the meagre efforts of a moustache on his upper lip. He was tall and thin, but in good shape, and he walked with a little hint of a bounce in his step. But news of Galina's death wiped the smile clean from his face. For the first time since childhood, his appearance was melancholy and his sadness was quickly spreading to the other boys in the group.

Tomi knew Galina would be very disappointed if she knew people were saddened by her passing. She always wanted to celebrate life rather than mourn over anyone's death. Although she knew full well everyone feels a certain emptiness or loss when someone passes from this life, she also knew any life, and especially one lived with honesty, caring and determination should be celebrated and remembered with joy and laughter. Tomi's first task though was to see to his lover. He could not convince the others to be cheery and joyful if his own partner continued to weep.

The snow kept coming down all morning and afternoon. By two o'clock, all roads were impassable and the paths to the outbuildings and barns disappeared except for the tops of the posts lining the cobbled walkway. Tomi decided the men needed to be kept busy, especially Alexeev and Pavel who were taking the news of Galina's death very hard. He asked Alexeev to organise the men to clear the path between the house and the outbuildings and barn so they would be able to tend to the animals.

Tomi kept tools and shovels in the barn, but also in the mud porch just off the kitchen. so Alexeev grouped the men in pairs to shovel the snow. Meanwhile, Tomi and Pavel began preparing breads, pastries, and hot beverages for the entire group. There was a storage shed just to the left of the mud porch, so once the path was cleared, the men could start bringing wood from the woodshed nearer to the house. No one knew how long the snowstorm would last, so they had to prepare for the worst.

The shovelling kept up until late afternoon when they finally reached the first outbuilding. The barn was connected to the outbuilding on the far side and the woodshed was between the outbuilding and the barn. The servants' quarters were also connected to the outbuilding, but unfortunately the roof had collapsed under the weight of the snow and a fallen tree branch, and it couldn't be repaired until after the storm. Once the paths were cleared enough, Kirill and Anton began removing the belongings and furniture from the servants' quarters and transferring them to the outbuilding. Meanwhile, Alexeev had Viktor, Roman, and Gugal transport the wood up to the house, and then tend to the animals. Tomi kept the men fed all afternoon with Pavel's help. They made tea, hot cocoa, *sbiten*, and even a pot of coffee.

Around five o'clock, Pavel saw a couple of men out by the road, struggling to get by. He and Tomi immediately ran out to invite them inside until the storm passed. Their names were Libor and Milan. They explained they had been travelling from the north and were headed to *Ust-Sysolsk* when the thunderstorm came upon them suddenly in the morning. Their horses threw them and bolted when the lightning started several hours ago and they had been on foot ever since.

The horses took off with all their belongings still strapped to their backs, so they were left with only the clothes on their backs. The snow was so deep they were losing track of the road and they hadn't yet come across any buildings or houses. They would have missed Tomi's house as well, but Pavel happened to be looking out the front window as they were passing by. Libor said the house looked like a mountain of snow, and the trees around it disguised the fact that it was actually a building.

Tomi welcomed them into his home and let them know they could stay as long as they needed. They spent a few hours warming themselves by the fire and drying off and Pavel made sure they had plenty of hot tea and food and a clean, dry change of clothes. Tomi learned they were originally from the Bohemian province in the Habsburg Monarchy, just outside of Prague. They had taken their sister, Svetlana, to Ust'-Kulom for her wedding and were headed back to their homeland. Now they weren't sure they would be able to continue since they had lost their horses with all their belongings. Tomi assured the travellers they would reach their homeland, and he would help them either in recovering their horses or with replacing them. For now, Libor and Milan would join the group with the common goal of surviving the blizzard, and perhaps making new friendships along the way.

Tomi and Pavel had prepared a feast for the boys for dinner. There was *pirozhki* stuffed with cabbage, onion and pork, *borscht* (Galina's recipe), *chyorniy khleb* (Sveta's recipe), cheeses, pickled carrots and onions, honey and jams, and plenty of vodka, blackberry wine and tea. As the boys sat at Tomi's table, feasted on the banquet of food, exchanged stories and laughed together over the good things in life, they forgot for a few hours about the storm and about the death of Tomi's dear *Tetushka* Gala.

The snow didn't let up all day. It would come down in waves of thick white sheets then pound down as large chunks of hail. The posts along the walkway to the outbuilding only lined one side of the path, but Tomi had several dozen posts in the shed next to the house and he also had many yards of tarp. Alexeev decided they should line the other side of the path with the extra posts then stretch the tarps over the path between the posts so they wouldn't have to keep shovelling the snow to keep the pathway clear. The tarps could cover the path and create a sort of tunnel between the buildings if the snow kept coming down as it was. By the end of the day the snow was already more than four feet deep. With everyone's help they managed to get the pathway covered before sundown.

Alexeev and Milan made sure the tarp overhead was also supported by boards running across the top of the path between the poles so the snow wouldn't collapse the tarps.

Tomi had plenty of linens, blankets and quilts for his guests. There were three bedrooms upstairs and two bedrooms downstairs with double beds to accommodate two in each room. Tomi also had extra clothes for Libor and Milan who were happy to accept the charity; in fact, he had extra clothes for everyone who needed them.

After supper, the men sat around in the parlour, smoked their pipes, got to know each other a little better and then played games until about midnight. Most of the men were familiar with *Draughts*[140] and it was one of Alexeev's favourite games, but Tomi only had one board and the game was only designed for two players. So Alexeev suggested *Gnav*[141], which he had learned while he was serving with the Tsar in *Sankt Piter-Burkh* several years ago. Milan and Libor knew how to play *Karnöffel*[142], an old game from the Habsburg area, that could be played with teams of players. So, Milan decided to teach anyone who wanted to learn.

Libor wanted to teach Viktor how to make *Pfeffernüsse*[143], a popular holiday spice cookie from his homeland made with pepper, since he would be the head chef until Foka returned after the storm. Viktor had a few recipes of his own he wanted to share. So, there were two games going in the parlour, *Gnav* and *Karnöffel*, and two chefs in the kitchen preparing a late evening snack for the group. Tomi decided to sit out of the games for a while so he could make some hot *Krupnik*[144] to go with the snacks. He had felt a headache coming on since early afternoon, and thought the spiced drink might help the pain go away. If not, it would at least make it easier for him to fall asleep.

The evening finally came to an end. Everyone went off to their assigned bedrooms to get a good night's rest. Tomi and Alexeev, of course, slept in their room upstairs. Anton and Gugal took one of the downstairs rooms, since they would be getting up early to feed the animals, and Viktor and Libor decided to

---

[140] *Draughts*: Traditional Russian board game similar to parcheesi

[141] *Gnav*: A traditional card game

[142] *Karnöffel*: A traditional card game

[143] *Pfeffernüsse*: A traditional holiday spice cookie, originating in Germany, Denmark and the Netherlands

[144] *Krupnik* (Polish): Hot honey-spiced vodka drink

take the other downstairs room so they could be close to the kitchen in the morning. They decided to work together preparing the meals for the duration of the storm so they could continue to exchange recipes.

Pavel and Kirill slept in the room next to Tomi upstairs, and the last bedroom upstairs was left for Roman and Milan. They had teamed up playing *Karnöffel,* and discovered they had many things in common, including a cunning eye for strategy in card games. Other than the routines of tending to the animals and keeping the fires going, there wouldn't be much to do until after the storm, so most of the men could sleep in as long as they wanted. But breakfast and hot tea would be ready whenever anyone decided to get up.

When Tomi and Alexeev got to their room, Alexeev placed a few logs in the fireplace and Tomi helped him get it lit. Then they both got undressed and got into bed. They were both very tired from all the day's activities and they were content to hold each other until they fell asleep. But it took Tomi a few hours before he got to sleep because the headache lingered well into the night.

Chapter 24
The End of Winter

The blizzard lasted nearly three weeks and dumped almost ten feet of snow on the residents of Shoynaty. By the end of the three weeks, the boys had gotten to know each other quite well. Gugal was feeling right at home and had taken on chores with the animals, Viktor had learned more than a dozen new recipes from Libor, and they were both getting used to each other's styles of cooking. Roman was learning all about the laundry from Kirill and how to maintain the bathing room, but he was also paying close attention to Pavel and had a desire to learn how the wine was prepared. There was quite an art involved, and Roman wanted to learn everything he could; Milan was talking daily with Alexeev about his plans to build a lodge on the far side of Tomi's property.

Alexeev never did keep his appointment with the doctor due to the sudden snowstorm, but his shoulder mended quite well. He started removing it from the sling about a week into the storm for a few hours at a time, stretching the arm, testing its mobility, then later exercising it to rebuild the muscles and keep the joint mobile. A few days before the storm ended, he removed the sling completely, much to Tomi's objection.

"You should wait until the doctor has a chance to look at it," he said. "You could hurt yourself if you're not careful."

Alexeev simply tugged at Tomi's chin. "I think I know what I'm doing…don't worry, I'll take it easy." Then he changed the subject and started talking to Tomi about his plans for the lodge. He showed Tomi the layout of the building incorporating many of the ideas they had talked about on the trip. The layout included seven one-room cabins built in a semi-circle around an inner garden, and opposite the cabins would be the great hall and dining area. The inner garden would be planted with many of the seeds their dear *Tetushka* had given them before she passed away.

Tomi couldn't help but wonder if she somehow knew it would be the last time she would see them, perhaps a foresight or intuition. He didn't regret giving Galina's china set to Alena though, and he still had the set of crystal. He was sure Galina would have made the same decision under the same circumstances, and his *Tetushka* trusted him to do the right thing with her belongings. He sent a message to Vladimir letting him know he would not be able to visit again until late summer at the earliest, so Galina's belongings would have to wait to be distributed to the relatives until then. She had always been an excellent example to him, always considering others above herself, always giving freely to those who were in need, even if it meant she would go without. He admired her and wanted to carry on her legacy in any way he was able and whenever the opportunity arose. Tomi asked Alexeev to make one addition to the garden area. "In the centre of the garden, could we build a circle of four stone benches and a large stone firepit, like the one in *Tetushka's* garden?"

The request nearly brought a tear to Alexeev's eye because that was in his mind as well, but he had omitted it because he thought the similarity might be too much for Tomi to handle. "Of course, we can, *schast'ye moye*."

Both Milan and Libor decided to stay on and help Alexeev with building the new lodge. Even though Libor was an excellent chef, both he and his brother were also experienced carpenters. In their homeland, they had built many homes and barns but never anything so grand as a lodge, so they were eager for the challenge, and they knew their experience would be much appreciated.

Gugal expressed an interest in staying on as well. He was a strong young man who needed a job. He also mentioned to Alexeev he had an older brother who might be interested as well. Gugal had just turned twenty-one and his brother, Nikita, was twenty-five. It looked like Alexeev would have four strong men to help him build the lodge over the summer, as long as Tomi could purchase the supplies. But Alexeev made sure Tomi understood once the lodge was opened for business and started making money, all the profits would be credited as payment for his debt until all that was borrowed was paid back in full.

As winter ended, the days grew warmer. Ivan and Viktor tended the blackberries, Roman and Demyan, a new recruit, managed the farm, Anton and Kirill took care of the animals and general clean-up, Foka prepared the food for the workers and made ready any food items to be marketed and Pavel managed everything. Tomi's headaches were occurring more frequently and becoming more painful, so he decided he could no longer manage the blackberry business.

He had taught Ivan everything he needed to know, so it was up to Ivan to pass on the secrets to Viktor of making a good wine and smooth cordials. Tomi hadn't mentioned the severity of his headaches to Alexeev since before they arrived home in February. He merely said he wanted to give the boys a chance to prove themselves in the business, but Alexeev suspected there was more going on. Their activities in the bedroom had tapered off considerably and many times when they were in the heat of passion, Tomi would suddenly become tired or would seem distracted. He would also isolate himself in the parlour for hours at a time and close all the doors and curtains, and when Alexeev would ask what he was doing, he would simply say he was reading and had lost track of time.

Pavel was usually the man who knew all the happenings in the house, outside the house, in the backyard, on the farm, in the barn, in the attic, in the cellar…yes, Pavel knew everything that was going on. But he was also completely devoted to Tomi. He was only thirteen years old when he and Tomi had first met. Pavel's parents had abandoned him because they believed he was cursed. He was born on the thirteenth day of January in 1690 (13 times 13 times 10), and at the thirteenth hour of the day, under a full moon. And the fact that his twin brother died in childbirth upset the midwife so much she fled the house and never returned. Pavel was born with pitch black hair, while his brother's hair was snow white. The local priest declared that there had been a spiritual war in his mother's womb and the devil had stolen the soul of the child that lived. Coincidentally, on the day of his birth, his father and three of his siblings developed nosebleeds that could not be explained by the local doctor.

There were several other coincidences that plagued young Pavel. Black cats seemed to show up every year on his birthday. At age two, he developed a sinus blockage that caused him to whistle through his nose. This first occurred at night, and the entire household was in an uproar because his father wanted to immediately put him outside to remove the bad omen from the house, but his mother insisted he stay in his crib. Fortunately, the whistling subsided after a few hours after he was given hot mint tea to soothe his breathing.

Then, when he was about five, his parents found him talking at the threshold of the front door. They immediately ran to retrieve him, believing any conversation or exchange at the threshold was a curse, but found he had been talking to no one, or at least no one they could see. There were other signs he might be possessed, like the strands of hair on the top left of his head that turned white when he was six. The priest said it was his twin brother trying to come back from the dead. Additionally, he had a birthmark on the back of his neck that looked like an eye, which the priest declared was a sign of the evil one spying on those he lived with. Then, of course, he also favoured his left hand, which proved he was, at the very least, abnormal.

Tomi knew Pavel's parents, but only in passing. They lived near the centre of town, so Tomi would occasionally see them at town celebrations or in town at the market. He knew them by name but he was not acquainted with their struggles or with any of the rumours surrounding young Pavel. Tomi would often bring his fruits or vegetables to market and sometimes he would sell his baked goods as well. Occasionally, he would see young Pavel and his older brothers and sisters wandering from booth to booth, eyeing the candies, cookies and pastries, and sometimes spending a kopek or two on something sweet to share. But Pavel always seemed to be in the background. Tomi would sometimes hand him a cookie, or a few berries, or a piece of hard candy. That was usually the extent of their interaction until Pavel's thirteenth birthday.

On that morning, Pavel's mother went into his bedroom to wake him and to wish him a good birthday. When she opened his door, there were three black birds perched at the end of his bed and a black cat sitting on the window ledge just outside his closed window, looking in. She screamed, and the birds came flying towards her. As she ran through the house the whole family was awakened by her screams. They all came running, but the birds disappeared as if by magic. None of the other family members saw the birds, and Pavel was asleep until he heard his mother's scream and saw her running out of his room. Later that day, they rode him into town and gave him a few kopecks to spend for his birthday, but they never came back for him. When he finally walked home, which was a four hour walk from the centre of town, the house was completely empty. His neighbours didn't want to have anything to do with him and even threw rocks at him to keep him off their land.

Tomi happened to go into town a few weeks later and saw little Pavel wandering the street. He had a bloodied forehead, several bruises and his clothes were tattered. The poor boy had tear streaks down the front of his dirty face and he obviously hadn't eaten or bathed in quite a while. Tomi took him home, fed him, tended to his wounds, washed him up and gave him some new clothes. It was a few days before Tomi could get the whole story of what happened from the boy, how he was abandoned and how all these circumstances culminated on that tragic day. But Tomi was a generous, well-meaning individual, and though he does not always take to children immediately, and sometimes wishes they were all born with the knowledge and maturity of young adults, he would never tolerate the abuse or neglect of even a single child.

From that point on, he treated the boy as his own son even though Pavel often referred to Tomi as 'sir' or 'master' and eventually as 'Master Pedorov'. It was that habit of innocent politeness Tomi both treasured and detested. He so much wanted Pavel to think of him as a dear friend, or even as a father figure, and Pavel did love Tomi very much, but felt a deep need to show him his unfailing respect rather than the tender feelings of his heart.

Now, Alexeev didn't know the entire story of how Pavel came to live with Tomi but he heard parts of the story over the last several months, especially on their long trip home from Moscow. Yes, if anyone knew what was going on with Tomi, it was Pavel. After all, Pavel had been with Tomi for thirteen years now and they were as close as father and son, perhaps even closer. But Alexeev didn't have an opportunity to speak with Pavel all day because there was much to do now that the weather was warming up. They always seemed to be missing each other, except when Tomi was around. So, for now, Alexeev would have to save his questions until a more opportune time.

Today, the sun was shining and the skies were clear for as far as the eye could see. There had not been any snow for nearly four weeks, and the temperature was unusually warm for March. The seeds were already planted in the new lodge garden and over the next few weeks Alexeev and Roman went into town to pick up many more plants for landscaping. Most of the snow had already melted and the rivers were no longer frozen over. It was a good sign that construction could begin almost as soon as supplies could be obtained.

Alexeev would have his hands full. He needed to start preparing the area on the property where the lodge would eventually be built, which meant he needed to survey the area first. He and Milan took the better part of their Sunday surveying the land, making sure the property was well-suited for the lodge, and discussing any alterations from the original design.

The next day while Libor, Gugal and Nikita continued to clear more shrubs from the acreage, Alexeev and Milan rode into town to see if the lumber mill had reopened and how long it would take to get an order fulfilled. They already calculated what they needed: including the types of wood, sizes and measurements. Milan was excited about getting back to work, since he was unaccustomed to remaining idle for very long. Alexeev listened carefully to all

Milan's advice and recommendations, and incorporated several of his ideas into the lodge's plans and designs. Fortunately, the lumber mill was open and ready to take orders.

Tomi had sent a note with Alexeev guaranteeing payment, and since he was one of their regular customers, they gave Alexeev an expected fulfilment date of one week for the first delivery and one month for the balance. Tomi's note promised full payment upon verification of delivery…and he sweetened the deal with a case of blackberry wine and cordials. Alexeev handed over the case of libations but wasn't quite ready to place the order yet. The owner, Lev Sokolov, gladly accepted the wine and sent back a dozen jars of candied orange peel for Tomi. He assured Alexeev that once he was ready to place his order, it would be fulfilled promptly and with precision, accuracy and care.

The initial order would be enough to keep Alexeev busy at least until the final delivery was received. He could store all the supplies including the lumber, in Tomi's outbuilding. Alexeev was grateful everything was working out so well and it looked like he would have enough workers to complete the job in a reasonable amount of time. Milan speculated the job would take about three months to complete the cabins, and another two to three months to complete the main lodge, which would include the kitchen, dining hall, parlour, bathing rooms, a dance floor and stables. Early in the morning, Tomi asked Ivan to start seeding the gardens as soon as the layout of the grounds was complete, but he was not aware Alexeev had already made other arrangements and Ivan knew Alexeev didn't want Tomi to know anything about the progress on lodge's garden.

When Alexeev arrived home in the afternoon after visiting the lumbermill, he found Tomi upstairs in their bedroom fast asleep. He carefully and quietly sat down on the bed next to him and brushed his forehead. His skin was hot to the touch.

"Tomi, how are you feeling?" he said quietly. Tomi was still sound asleep. Alexeev put his hand on Tomi's shoulder and gently nudged him, "Tomi, Tomi, are you feeling all right?"

Tomi squinted then pulled the blanket over his head. "I don't feel well," he said with a faint voice. "Can you just let me sleep for a while?"

"Yes, you just stay in bed and sleep as long as you want." He quietly got up and went downstairs.

Pavel met him on the stairway and took his arm to lead him into the parlour. "Alexeev, I am very worried about Master Pedorov," he whispered. "He hasn't eaten all day and when I checked in on him after lunch, he looked flushed." Pavel looked like he was ready to burst into tears. "Then I asked him if I could go fetch the doctor for him and he yelled at me…he told me to mind my own business and to leave him alone." Pavel could barely get the next words out, "Then he told me, *ubiraysya k chertu!*[145]"

Alexeev put his arm around him. "I thought something was wrong, but I couldn't make sense of it."

"I don't know what to do," Pavel said through the tears. "He's never spoken to me like that before."

Alexeev sat him down on the settee. "Now listen to me. I need the doctor to come and see him. I know what Tomi said, but I'm telling you, we need to get the doctor." Pavel nodded his head in agreement. "Tell me where the doctor lives and I'll get him before dinner." Pavel gave Alexeev the directions and he left immediately.

Doctor Boris Vasilyev came back with him immediately. On the way, the doctor explained what Tomi had been going through for the last fifteen years or more.

"When he first came to Shoynaty, he came to see me about his headaches," said the doctor. "At first, it was just an occasional headache, usually mild. But the unusual thing was they could last for days. My first diagnosis was the headaches were somehow a result of stress. I recommended he slow down a bit, take trips to reduce tension, even take hot baths to relax the muscles. I started giving him some tea that has been relatively successful in reducing headaches…and the tea was working, at least occasionally. But the headaches always came back. Over the years, the headaches have gotten worse and more frequent. I've been making his tea more concentrated than I usually do for my other patients.

"Then several years ago he started experiencing dizziness and blurred vision that accompanied the headaches…most unusual. Five years ago, he lost all control of the right side of his body. We call this *apoplexy*. It is a condition we have only recently started to understand. The condition is usually caused by

[145]*ubiraysya k chertu!*: Get the hell out!

bleeding inside the brain and it is usually fatal. But in Tomi's case, he recovered within a few months."

"Is there no cure for this, apoplexy?" asked Alexeev. "Isn't there anything you can do?"

"Unfortunately, we don't know enough about what causes it so we don't know how to cure it," he answered. "Many doctors believe that blood-letting could help alleviate the problem, but Tomi refused further treatments after about the fourth or fifth session. He needs to continue to drink the tea though. I suspect he may have had other episodes he either didn't know about or refused to tell me. Tomi is very stubborn, and I know he would rather not take my advice, and he would rather not drink my tea either, but it helps his headaches." The doctor paused for a moment, then continued, "How close are you to Tomi?"

Alexeev hesitated to answer.

"Do you love him? Yes, I know about Tomi. I can't say that I approve, but I know what he is like in his private life." Alexeev still didn't comment. "You need to be prepared for the worst. Doctor Leskov in Nizhny Novgorod sent me a message and said he believes Mister Pedorov may have some kind of growth pressing from behind his eyes inside his head. If that is true, there is only one final outcome."

Alexeev felt a lump in his throat and his stomach felt like he had been kicked by a mule. But he knew he needed to be strong. He knew he needed to be there for Tomi. His love for Tomi grew stronger and deeper on that ride home with the doctor.

The doctor examined Tomi, much to Tomi's protest, but didn't prescribe anything more than the tea he was already drinking and possibly more frequent hot baths. Alexeev promised to make sure he took the hot baths and drank the tea regularly with every meal and even between meals. Tomi knew he should have seen the doctor before, but he was tired of never getting any answers. He was so tired. There didn't seem to be any remedy for his illness, if it truly was an illness. His doctors didn't ever have any specific answers, so maybe this is just the way life is for some people. But if this was the way life was going to be, Tomi didn't want it to last much longer. Oh, he loved Alexeev and he wasn't considering taking his own life, but the weariness and the pain was getting to be too much of a burden, a greater burden than he could bear.

Over the next several weeks, Tomi's headaches continued to be a daily recurrence, and Alexeev urged him to continue to drink the tea. He also made sure Tomi took regular hot baths, and then gave him massages every evening before bedtime with oils mixed with lavender, chamomile and ginger. They seemed to have a soothing effect on him and helped him sleep. About mid-April, Tomi received word that Sveta had given birth to a son, Stanislav, on April 1st. He was so happy, he forgot about his headaches for the rest of the day. He had Foka prepare a special dinner that evening in honour of the new grand-nephew, Stanislav Ivanovich, baby Slava.

After dinner, Tomi asked Alexeev if they could skip the bath and massage, "Let's just go up to bed a little early tonight."

Alexeev wasn't too sure it was wise to break such a beneficial habit, especially when they seemed to be giving Tomi such sound and uninterrupted sleep, but he complied with Tomi's request. "Just this once, *schast'ye moye,* then it's back to our routine tomorrow."

Tomi climbed the stairs slowly, but insisted he climb them by himself. He knew Alexeev was spending far too much time caring for him and wasn't devoting nearly enough time to building the lodge. As he opened the door to the bedroom, he felt the cool air from the unheated room. It made him shiver. Alexeev went in and quickly started a fire.

"You should have at least given me a chance to make a fire ahead of time," he said to Tomi. "I don't like the idea of you getting a chill."

Tomi sat on the bed and started taking off his clothes. His nightshirt was underneath his pillow so he pulled it out and put it on over his head. It was long enough to cover his knees but he rolled it up around his waist. He also had a nightcap with ear flaps that came down to cover his ears at night but he wasn't ready to put it on yet. Alexeev was finishing making the fire and Tomi could already feel some of the heat from the fireplace. "Could you come over here, my love?"

Alexeev stood up right away, thinking something was wrong and he knelt in front of Tomi. "What is it? What did you need?" he asked.

Tomi reached out his hands and took hold of Alexeev's large, strong, calloused hands. He looked deep into Alexeev's bright green eyes. "I love you."

Alexeev wrapped his arms around Tomi and gave him a big hug. "I love you too, Tomi."

"I want you to make love to me tonight…I miss feeling you on top of me…feeling you inside me," he said. Then Tomi started unbuttoning Alexeev's shirt. He pulled it up over his head then he leaned in and kissed him. "You know

I have never stopped loving you," he said. There were a few tears forming in his eyes. "I know I haven't been able to satisfy you as often as you wanted but you know it's not because I don't want to."

"I know that, Tomi." Alexeev stood up and finished taking off his clothes. He suddenly realised the sacrifice Tomi was about to make. His headaches were consistent every day now and offering to make love could not be an easy choice to make. "I don't want to give you any more pain though—"

"You don't understand, my love. I need you to make love to me tonight." Tomi laid back against the pillow. "Today was one of the happiest days of my life, hearing that I have a new grand-nephew. And you are the best thing that has ever happened to me. I want to feel the joy of being with you…I want to see the joy on your face, the way you used to look when we would make love. I want you to know how much I love you…*schast'ye moye*."

That was the first time Tomi had ever used that phrase before, and it would be many years before Alexeev understood what was happening in Tomi's mind that night. It was like a door had opened, a candle had been lit, a dam of cool rushing water had been released. Tomi's whole life had been a quest for a happiness that was based on things he owned or could buy. He made a lot of money and spent it lavishly, both on himself and others, but it was in the spending where he sought his happiness.

When Alexeev had entered his life six years ago, everything had changed. He saw something in him remarkable and precious. Alexeev found his happiness not in things, but in experiences. He taught Tomi that true happiness could never be bought, it had to be lived and experienced. Tomi wanted one last time to give Alexeev the opportunity to experience the happiness he had so richly given.

The only light in the room was from the flames in the fireplace. Tomi could see Alexeev's strong, masculine silhouette standing next to the bed. He could see the muscles glisten and all he could hear was Alexeev's breathing. Alexeev set one knee on the edge of the bed, then brought the other knee across to the other side of Tomi. His large naked body looming over Tomi like an imposing marble tower. Then he bent at the waist and cupped the side of Tomi's face with his hands and kissed his lips. Tomi could taste the familiar sweet savour of Alexeev's tongue. He could feel the rough hands on his face and it made him feel protected and safe.

Alexeev put his arms under Tomi's shoulders and relaxed his body on top of him. The embrace was warm and strong. Tomi could feel Alexeev's cock and balls dangling above him as they gently settled on top of his pelvis, and the chest and torso muscles pressing against him. He kissed Alexeev's neck and chin as he reached his arms around Alexeev's back. Alexeev pushed himself up from the bed with Tomi still holding on. Tomi reached up with one hand and grabbed his hair then wrapped his lips around Alexeev's mouth. As their bodies intertwined Tomi could feel Alexeev's cock getting hard. This was what he wanted, this was what he had yearned for, this was the love he needed to give and also receive, but it was a painful sacrifice.

Alexeev was starved for this physical attention. He had been holding back for Tomi's sake, but now he felt his release was imminent. His muscles were taut and pumped. He could hear his heart pounding in his ears and he could feel the blood coursing through his veins. The rough stubble on his face was scraping against Tomi's cheek and he heard a slight gasp, but it was one of ecstasy not pain. Tomi bit Alexeev's chin in return showing him that it was all right to be playful. Alexeev reached over to the nightstand for the bottle of oil. He turned out a small amount on his hand then spread it over the hard, thick cock. He guided the cock in while Tomi was still clinging to his hair and kissing him. As the cock slipped in, Tomi rocked his hips forward and back, then he leaned back with one arm on the bed for support and rode the cock up and down.

Alexeev pumped vigorously, pounding himself up into Tomi's buttocks. Then he laid Tomi back onto the bed and kissed him and pulled his cock out. He grabbed Tomi's cock and stroked it until it became hard, then he leaned down and licked the tip and sucked the clear, sticky liquid from its head. His mouth began to water as he took the whole cock into his mouth. He plunged his lips all the way to Tomi's pelvis, taking the cock deep inside his throat. Tomi moaned and pulled at his nipples. He rocked his hips up and back again as Alexeev sucked. Then he held Alexeev's head down onto his cock amidst his black and silver hairs. As he felt his cum release into Alexeev's mouth he heard him gag, but that didn't stop him from sucking. He licked the side of the cock, then the head, and then the balls. He reached up and twisted Tomi's nipples and continued to suck until the cock was no longer hard.

But Tomi wasn't finished yet. He raised his legs up and held them in the air to spread them as wide as possible. "Fuck me deep, my love!" Alexeev smiled and wiped his mouth with one hand, then the look changed to determination and domination. He leaned in and thrust his cock into Tomi. He grabbed Tomi's ankles and pressed his weight against Tomi's legs. Tomi tilted his head back and moaned, "Deeper! Fuck me hard!"

Then as Alexeev leaned in, Tomi reached up with one hand and grabbed Alexeev's face. "Don't hold back!" he yelled. His face showed an anger Alexeev had not seen before. Then he slapped Alexeev's face hard and punched him in the chest. "You always hold back! Fuck! I want it all this time!" Although Tomi meant this to anger Alexeev into releasing his tension, Alexeev couldn't have been happier to comply. He played the domineering master and made the angriest face he could, then he wrapped his massive arms around Tomi's legs and locked his hands together. Alexeev's forearms were the same size as Tomi's ankles and calves, and his biceps and triceps were nearly as large as Tomi's thighs. As he pounded his cock into Tomi's ass, their bodies slapped together.

Every fourth or fifth pounding Alexeev would force himself deeper into Tomi, and Tomi would reach back and flail his arms. Then Alexeev turned Tomi over onto his stomach and lunged his cock deep inside him. "Aaarrrgggh! *Moy general*!" cried Tomi. Alexeev kept pounding. He took hold of Tomi's wrists and spread out his arms as far as they would go. His cock was still hard as he forced it in and out of Tomi's ass. An explosion of cum flooded inside Tomi. "Aaarrrgggh! *Dostatochno!*[146]" Tomi let out a cry with a deep exhale.

Alexeev sensed this was Tomi's limit so he pulled his cock out and continued to stroke it above Tomi. He stroked it vigorously with one hand while he squeezed his nipple with the other. His hips propelled themselves back and forth as if they were still engaged in going deeper into Tomi. His chest was solid and rock-hard as he played with the nipple and fondled his muscles. Tomi glanced back and saw this stunning creature glistening in the firelight. He imagined Alexeev was a gladiator standing over his conquered victim, releasing his cum on his back as a final act of dominion and power and humiliation. But the more he looked at his lover, the more he saw his innocence, his purity and his virtue. The last few drops of cum spilled out onto Tomi's back as Alexeev tightened his muscles for the final release. Alexeev let out a deep sigh of satisfaction, then he laid down next to Tomi and draped his arm across Tomi's back.

"I love you, *schast'ye moye*," he said as he kissed Tomi's cheek.

---

[146] *Dostatochno!*: Enough!

Chapter 25
The Darkness of Spring

Alexeev woke up early the next morning feeling refreshed and full of energy. Their romance had been rekindled last night, and everything looked new, and bright, and exciting. He lit the fire in the fireplace and got dressed quickly and quietly so Tomi could sleep a while longer. He gently kissed his lover on the forehead then he prepared to go downstairs to start his day. As he opened the door, Misha and Mitya scampered in and quickly hopped up onto the bed.

"Now don't bother your master. Let him sleep in this morning," he whispered as he picked them up and set them back onto the floor. "Come follow me into the kitchen and I'll get you some breakfast." They looked up at him, meowed and hopped back up on the bed. "Now, don't argue with me. I don't want you bothering Tomi." He picked them up again as they meowed and meowed.

Then Misha bit Alexeev's thumb and Mitya hissed at him. He dropped them both and they promptly hopped back up onto the bed. "I'm not telling you again," he said as he scooped them both up off the bed and quickly set them outside the bedroom door. As Alexeev closed the door, the two cats stared incessantly at the doorknob. "It's no use. I won't let you back in until after your master wakes up, so you might as well follow me downstairs." He started walking down the stairs and the two boys followed him down the stairs and into the kitchen meowing all the way.

Pavel was already in the kitchen heating the water for the tea. "Good morning, lieutenant. I see the boys have talked you into feeding them a second time."

Alexeev bent down to the two felines. "So you thought you could coax me into giving you extra treats? Is that what you were doing?" He petted each one and stroked their backs. They both raised their tails in the air, then rubbed against

Alexeev's legs, meowing and purring. "Well, I guess everyone is entitled to get into mischief every once in a while. Let me see what I can find."

Pavel held out a bag of dried fish pieces. "This is their favourite."

Alexeev pulled out a few pieces and held one in each hand about waist high. "Come on boys, stand up for me and you can have your reward."

Their bright yellow-green eyes focussed on the fish pieces. They both stood up on their hind legs and reached up with their front paws to retrieve the savoury morsels.

"Good boys!" he said, praising the two performers. "They have been well-trained," he said to Pavel.

"Yes, Tomi knows just how to get them to do anything he wants. They are like his own children and they see him as their loving father." Pavel poured the hot water into the teapot. "By the way, how is Tomi this morning."

"He's still sleeping," said Alexeev. "Hmmm…well-trained in some things, but they are rather disobedient when it comes to staying off the bed."

Pavel wasn't quite sure how to react. "How do you mean?"

"Oh, nothing, I guess," he said. "I'm sure they just wanted to be next to him on the bed."

"Wait, do you mean they got up onto the bed?" asked Pavel, obviously a little surprised.

"Yes, but I'm sure it was nothing," he said. "I just had to set them back on the floor…but they kept jumping back up."

"Alexeev, something must be wrong," Pavel's voice was full of angst. "They were trained never to hop up onto the bed…I've only seen them get on the bed when Tomi was very sick." Pavel immediately ran out of the kitchen and up the stairs. Alexeev followed him, as did Misha and Mitya.

Alexeev felt like his heart was going to burst out of his chest. He called out, "Tomi, Tomi!"

Pavel got to the bedroom door first and slowly opened it. Then quickly went over to the bed. "Master, are you all right?" He bent over him and brushed his forehead. His skin felt damp and cold. "Oh, Alexeev, I think he's—"

"Nonsense," Alexeev interrupted. "You can see he is breathing. He is just in a deep sleep." Alexeev went over to the other side of the bed and set his hand on Tomi's shoulder and gently shook him. "Tomi, it's time to wake up." Tomi opened his eyes just a bit and mumbled. Neither Alexeev nor Pavel could make out what he was saying. "I didn't understand you, Tomi. Are you ready to get up?" Again, Tomi just mumbled.

"I think I had better get the doctor," said Pavel.

"I'll stay with him until you get back." He looked into Tomi's eyes and saw confusion. He didn't understand what was happening and neither did Alexeev. Tomi could hear Alexeev's voice but his vision was blurred and he had a difficult time focusing on the words. He was scared, more scared than he had ever been before. More scared than he was when the bear invaded their camp, and more scared than he was when he saw Alexeev lying motionless on the ground after he had fallen from the roof. He wasn't in any pain though, but his right arm and leg felt strange. Like they were only connected to his body but not really part of it, as if their functioning capability had been interrupted or disconnected. His mind was trying to tell his arm and hand to reach up to Alexeev's face, but the arm and hand remained unmoved on the bed. He could feel the skin and the muscles, but his mind had lost the ability to dictate their performance. He started to panic and then he started to cry.

Alexeev saw the tears forming. "Oh, *schast'ye moye*, it's going to be all right. Pavel has gone to fetch the doctor. You are going to be fine." He laid down next to Tomi and put one arm under Tomi's neck and the other over his chest. "I'm here to take care of you, my love." Misha and Mitya had jumped up onto the bed as soon as Pavel had left the room. Mitya was crouched down next to Tomi's shoulder, purring into his ear, and Misha's head was resting on Tomi's forearm. How would these two little ones survive without their papa? They loved him dearly. Their eyes had barely opened when they were found on his front doorsteps, so he could have been the first person they ever saw, and most definitely the first caring person. Like Pavel, they were outcasts when Tomi took them in. Pavel had grown to love these two felines like his own brothers and they reciprocated the affection, but they were absolutely devoted to Tomi.

After a few hours, Pavel came back with the doctor. He examined Tomi and concluded he had another episode of apoplexy, probably sometime in the night.

"He recovered from this once before, and even that was unusual. I just don't know if he will be able to recover from this one. He should stay in bed and get as much rest as possible. Keep his mealtimes very regular though and you will need to mash his food before you give it to him. He will need to be spoon fed, and take care when you give him water. He may tend to choke because he doesn't have much control over his muscles. You will need to help him do everything:

bathing, feeding, dressing, urinating and defecating. He won't be able to do anything on his own."

"But he recovered last time," said Pavel. "Doesn't that mean there is a good chance he will recover again."

"It doesn't make any difference what happened in the past. These episodes are rarely the same and usually get progressively worse." He shook his head. "It's a pity anyone has to go through something like this."

"Is there anything you can give him?" asked Alexeev. "Should I still give him the tea?"

"Keep him from exerting himself, keep his diet simple, keep him clean…and yes, continue giving him the tea. I'll send over a stronger, more potent tea to help him sleep." The doctor looked Tomi over one last time then packed up his bag and left.

Tomi was almost completely non-reactive the entire time the doctor was there. He glanced at him a few times, inhaled when he was asked to do so and would occasionally move his mouth as if he had something he wanted to say. But he remained silent for the rest of the day. Alexeev stayed by his side all day long, hoping Tomi would speak, and Misha and Mitya stayed next to him on the bed as well. They would occasionally stand and stretch, then rub up against him, but then they would take their place by his side again and watch over their master.

Alexeev left only a few times to prepare Tomi's food, or to get clean linens for the bed. In the afternoon he brought up a bucket of hot water so he could wash Tomi off and then change his night shirt for him. He already made up his mind that no matter what happened, he would take care of Tomi for the rest of his life. He would never leave him and never forsake him.

Over the next several weeks, Alexeev got into a routine of caring for Tomi. Every morning, he got dressed and had breakfast before Tomi woke up. Then he prepared Tomi's breakfast, took it up to him and woke him. After breakfast, he helped Tomi use the chamber pot, then cleaned him up and got him dressed. He carried Tomi downstairs to the parlour where they sat for a few hours. Alexeev read to him from the books in his library. If the day was warm enough, Alexeev carried Tomi out to the porch and wrapped a blanket around him so he could enjoy the fresh air for a few hours. After lunch, Tomi took a nap in the parlour on the settee while Alexeev went out to supervise his workers for a few hours.

Mid-afternoon, Alexeev came back to wake Tomi and help him get mobile for a while. He developed a series of stretching exercises he thought might help

Tomi gain some of his ability and mobility back. After the exercises, Alexeev set him back on the settee while he prepared dinner. He carried Tomi to the dining room table and sat next to him and helped him eat.

Although Tomi's right side was paralysed, he had complete use of his left side, so Tomi was got used to eating with his left hand. Of course, there was an occasional spill that needed to be cleaned up, but more often than not, Alexeev took the blame for the unfortunate accident. It always put a half-smile on Tomi's face, even though he knew what was going on. He still couldn't form words though, so communication was rather difficult.

Alexeev didn't tell Tomi he had sent a message to Vanya the day after his episode, but he hadn't heard back yet and it had been three weeks already. He knew Vanya would be heartbroken if he wasn't told about his uncle, but he also knew he probably had his hands full with a newborn in the house. Tomi's birthday was in just a few days and Alexeev hoped Vanya would be able to at least send a message. Unfortunately, sending word across the wilderness was an uncertainty at best.

Alexeev made plans with Pavel and the rest of the servants to give Tomi a surprise party on his birthday though. Pavel sent word to the mayor as well, so several folks whom Tomi had worked with before would be attending. Foka had all of Tomi's favourite recipes ready to prepare and Alexeev had a few recipes Orlov had given him that he wanted Foka to try. One of them was the ten-layer *Medovik*[147] cake Orlov had made when they celebrated Alexeev's retirement. Other menu items included *halupki*[148], mushroom and leek soup, *pelmeni*[149], *vinegret salad,* Galina's cabbage *borscht*, *black bread*, *challah bread* and *houska*, *medovuhka*[150], *krupnik*, vodka and of course, blackberry wine.

While Foka concentrated on preparing the food, Alexeev asked Libor and Milan to decorate the hall in the outbuilding with ribbons and candles. He planned on using Tomi's best china: the set rimmed in scarlet red, with hand-painted pinecones and winter song birds. He was also planning on using the crystal set Galina had given them, along with Tomi's sterling silver place settings, and the embroidered red napkins with hand-stitched snowflakes around the edges. It was going to be a memorable birthday indeed.

---

[147] *Medovik*: Multi-layered Russian honey cake

[148] *halupki*: Stuffed cabbage

[149] *pelmeni*: Russian dumplings

[150] *medovuhka*: A Slavic honey-based alcoholic beverage

The day before Tomi's birthday Foka had the menu all lined up and all the ingredients were on hand and ready to be put to use. He made a few things ahead of time: *Medovik* is always better a few days after baking, and the *Krupnik* just needed to be heated and mixed with a sufficient amount of vodka to keep everyone cheerful.

Today, he would also make the breads and a few of the other desserts and pastries. Tomi knew something was going on but he didn't seem to be aware of the date. Foka used the servants' kitchen in the outbuilding for nearly everything but he decided to make the honey cake in Tomi's large oven since he had ten layers to bake. Tomi caught a whiff of the cake wafers, and for a moment it looked like he knew what the smell was, but he never gave more of an indication other than an occasional glance in the direction of the kitchen.

While Tomi was taking his afternoon nap, Pavel heard a carriage ride up alongside the house. He glanced out the kitchen window. "Well, bless this house after all, if it isn't Vanya!" He ran outside to greet him, waving his hand and smiling from ear to ear. He was nearly in tears by the time he got to the carriage. "Oh Vanya, I knew you'd come, I just knew you would have to come and see your dear *Dyadya Medved'*[151]!"

Vanya parked the carriage and hopped down. "Pavel, my good friend, how have you been? How long has it been since I've seen you?"

"Nearly six years, I think." He gave Vanya a hug and kiss.

"You've grown into quite a good-looking young man." He put his hands over Pavel's shoulders and smiled. "I can see Uncle has been taking good care of you?"

Pavel nodded, trying to hold back the tears. "Yes, he has. But I'm afraid I haven't been able to take very good care of him."

"Now, I don't want to hear any of that nonsense. You know this has nothing to do with you," he assured him. "*Dyadya* has been sick for years, probably longer than any of us ever knew. You know how he is…he never tells anyone the whole truth about what's going on with him." He reached in the back and grabbed his bag then they both walked inside the house.

"Tomi's down for his nap for the next hour or so. Alexeev comes in around three o'clock to get him up, and then they do some stretching exercises."

---

[151] *Dyadya Medved'*: Uncle Bear

"Well, I don't want to interrupt the routine." He looked around, then saw the staircase. "I think the last time I was here, Tomi had me in the second bedroom on the left upstairs…"

"Oh, yes, that would be fine," said Pavel. "In fact, Kirill put clean linens on the bed just yesterday. Tomi is napping in the front parlour, so you won't disturb him…Alexeev was hoping you would show up for Tomi's birthday…and here you are!"

Vanya gave Pavel another hug. "Yes, I'm glad I could make it. Sveta's sister is staying with her and the children while I'm gone."

"I'm sorry you had to come out here, just when you have a newborn to take care of."

"Now don't you worry about that," said Vanya with a slight chuckle. "When Sveta and her sister get together, they treat me like I don't even exist. They probably don't even know I'm gone."

Vanya went upstairs to put his bag away and Pavel put a pot of water on the stove to make tea. When Vanya came back downstairs, he peeked into the parlour for a moment to see if Tomi was still sleeping. He was still curled up on the settee with a blanket wrapped around him and his two feline protectors curled up beside him. They raised their heads to acknowledge Vanya but didn't move from their designated posts. The parlour seemed a little cold so Vanya put a few logs in the fireplace and built up the fire. He leaned down and kissed Tomi on the forehead then quietly shut the parlour door and joined Pavel in the kitchen.

"By the way, Pavel, Sveta sent a box of her homemade apple candy. I think it's something Tomi would like." He set the box on the counter and got out two cups for the tea. Pavel poured the water into the teapot.

"Well, I'm not sure he'll be able to have them. He still has a problem chewing his food," he said. "Let's see what Alexeev thinks when he gets back."

"I didn't realise it was that bad." Vanya got a few plates down from the cupboard and set them on the table. Then opened the box and took a few pieces of the apple candy and placed them on the plates. "Alexeev wrote and said Tomi had been sick, and he had another episode…"

"He hasn't been able to speak since it happened," said Pavel. "And he can't move his right side."

"Oh, I see…" Vanya sat down at the table. "How is Alexeev handling it? I mean…do you think he's going to stay?"

"Oh, of course," Pavel said with confidence. "I have never seen anyone so devoted as that man. He spends all his free time caring for Tomi…he gets him up and dresses him every morning, prepares his meals, bathes him and cleans up after him…I honestly don't know how he manages all that without breaking down."

"I'm glad Tomi has someone like Alexeev to care for him." The two of them sat for a while, drinking their tea and trying Sveta's apple candy and talking about Tomi.

Just as the clock struck three Alexeev came in through the kitchen door. "I thought that carriage looked familiar," he said. "I'm so glad you were able to make the trip."

Vanya stood up and they gave each other a big hug. "Thank you for letting me know about *Dyadya*. We live so far apart, sometimes I don't hear about things for several months. Tomi is not very good about keeping us informed about what is going on in his life. Until after it has already happened."

"Have you been in to see him yet?" asked Alexeev.

"I went in to see if he was still asleep, but I didn't wake him up. I did build up the fire though."

"Well, it's about time he got up," said Alexeev. "Give me a few minutes so I can sit him up and get him ready."

Alexeev went into the parlour and gently patted Tomi on the shoulder.

"Tomi, it's time to wake up," he whispered. "You have a visitor."

Tomi opened his eyes and reached out with his left hand. Misha and Mitya hopped down, acknowledging the end of their shift, and they ran out the parlour door.

"Are you ready to get up?" Alexeev helped him get to a sitting position, then took the blanket and folded it over Tomi's lap. "Before we visit, do you need to use the chamber pot?"

Tomi shook his head then reached out to Alexeev.

"Now, can't you just be surprised for once? Don't try to get me to tell you who's here…just be patient."

Tomi smiled then fussed with his shirt.

"Here, let me help you." Alexeev knelt down in front of Tomi and straightened his shirt, then took the brush from the end table and brushed Tomi's hair. "There…you look very nice."

Tomi smiled and cocked his head.

"Are you ready for your visitor?" Alexeev stood up, put his hands on his hips and looked Tomi over. "Yes, I think you are ready."

Tomi nodded.

Alexeev opened the parlour door, stuck his head out for a moment and motioned for Vanya and Pavel to come in. As Vanya came through the door Tomi reached out his left hand and tried to say something, but only a few grunts came out.

"*Dyadya Medved'*, it's good to see you!" He rushed to Tomi and gave him a hug. Then he sat next to him on the settee but kept his arm around him. "You're looking well. How do you feel?"

He was so happy to see his favourite nephew. Tomi mumbled a little, then rested his head on Vanya's shoulder.

"Uncle Lexee, I brought some apple candy…Sveta made it," said Vanya. "Do you think Tomi could have a piece?" Pavel handed a plate of the apple candies to Alexeev.

"Well, let's see…" Alexeev said as he took the plate. "Tomi, if you promise to eat slowly, you can have one piece now and maybe another piece after dinner. How's that?" He took one of the apple candies and handed it to Tomi. "After you finish this, would you like to show Vanya what you've accomplished?"

Tomi smiled and nodded as he took a bite of the candy.

"I'm afraid his vision is still a little blurry, but he knows who you are," said Alexeev. "When this happened four weeks ago, he couldn't move his right side at all. But we're working on it every day." He touched the side of Tomi's face then leaned over and kissed his cheek. Tomi could hear everything that was being said, but he couldn't see very clearly. Fortunately, he didn't see the tears in Vanya's eyes or the desperate look on Pavel's face. Tomi never wanted anyone to feel sorry for him and he didn't want to be a burden to those he loved. This whole episode was very hard for him and he was feeling more tired and worn out as the days went on. He was glad Vanya had come though, and for the next few days, he felt like things were going to get better.

After Tomi finished the candy, Alexeev put him through his exercise routine. First, he stretched his left arm above his head and bent at the waist to the right. Then Alexeev helped him lift his right arm up and he bent to the left. They repeated this stretch ten times. Then Alexeev stood in front of Tomi and removed the blanket. He held out his hands, palms up towards Tomi, who slowly raised his right hand and put it on top of Alexeev's, then raised his left hand and did the same. As Alexeev held on, Tomi slowly pulled himself to a standing position.

"Now come forward a few steps," said Alexeev as he backed up just slightly.

Tomi shuffled his feet towards Alexeev and took a few steps.

"Now turn around and go back to the settee," he said as he placed his hands around Tomi's waist.

Tomi turned back around and shuffled back to the settee, then sat down.

"That was wonderful!" cried Vanya.

"He can walk from one end of the house to the other if he holds on to me…but we haven't mastered the stairs yet."

Just as Tomi sat back down Misha and Mitya came scampering in through the open parlour door again. They immediately jumped up onto the settee next to Tomi and began meowing and butting their heads up against Tomi's chest and chin. Tomi smiled and started petting them.

"Vanya, I'd like to introduce you to Tomi's two nurses." He patted each one on the head. "This is nurse Mitya, and this is his brother, nurse Misha."

"Yes, we've met. They looked me over when I came in to build up the fire. I don't think they quite knew what to make of me at the time." Vanya chuckled then sat next to Tomi. He petted Mitya who then came over to him and sat across his lap to be indulged a little more. "*Dyadya*, I didn't know you had cats."

Tomi tried to get some words out, but they just sounded like mumbling again.

"He's had them for about six years now," said Pavel.

"Vanya, we usually read during the afternoon. Would you like to stay and join us?" asked Alexeev. "We've been reading the *Life of Alexander Nevsky.*"

"I'd love to stay and listen. I don't think I've ever read that book before."

Alexeev got the book from the shelf and he sat down on the other side of Tomi. It was a beautifully illustrated book with colourful intricate drawings in the margins, ornate lettering and gold-leaf added to many of the pages to enhance its beauty. It must have cost a small fortune, but Tomi loved his books. Alexeev opened the book carefully and started reading from where they had left off the day before. Tomi rested his head on Vanya's shoulder as Alexeev read and Misha and Mitya stretched out and relaxed on Tomi's and Vanya's laps. Pavel went about his routine for the rest of the afternoon and left the boys to enjoy their reading. He still had several things he wanted to take care of before Tomi's birthday and only a few hours left in the day to get everything done.

The afternoon went by quickly, and once their reading was done, Alexeev led Tomi into the bathing room for his daily hot bath. Alexeev believed these hot baths might bring back the feeling and control in Tomi's right leg and arm. But regardless of their effect on Tomi's mobility, they seemed to help with his aches and pains, and Alexeev enjoyed them too. He usually got in the tub with Tomi and massaged him or just let him lean back and rest his head on his chest. It was a way they could be together in intimacy, even though they weren't making love. They still kissed, caressed and cuddled, and even though Tomi couldn't get a controlled erection, he enjoyed watching his lover flex and pose and even masturbate. Then every night they would fall asleep in each other's arms.

Tonight was no different. After their hot bath, they had dinner, then sat and talked with Pavel and Vanya in the parlour, and finally Alexeev carried Tomi up the stairs to the bedroom. Tomi was nodding off even when they first went into the parlour. So, when the clock struck nine, Alexeev decided Tomi had stayed up long enough. Vanya and Pavel stayed up a few more hours and got caught up on each other's lives, but by eleven o'clock, they too were ready for a good night's sleep.

Chapter 26

The Birthday Party

This morning wasn't like any ordinary morning for Alexeev: it was his lover's birthday. Everything needed to go right and everyone needed to do exactly what they were told to do. Most of the time, Alexeev took things in stride and didn't let minor setbacks upset him. He understood most things had a way of correcting themselves. Today needed to be special though, it needed to be wonderful, and it needed to make Tomi happy. It was just over a month since his episode and there were very few signs of improvement, in fact each improvement was accompanied by a complication.

He could stand with Alexeev's help and take a few steps, but he was having difficulties balancing and got dizzy very easily, even when he was sitting down. He seemed to understand what was being said and what was going on around him, but he still couldn't speak and his vision seemed to be getting worse. He was able to chew his food with less difficulty, but couldn't keep things down, except for tea and the occasional broth. Yet Alexeev was still going through with the party and all its regalia. He hoped when Tomi was around his neighbours, former co-workers and the few family members who were able to travel, it might help him to recover a little quicker.

Alexeev got up and lit the fire, then kissed Tomi on the forehead and went to the door. As soon as he opened the bedroom door, Misha and Mitya came running in and hopped up onto the bed. By now, Alexeev realised there was nothing he could do to prevent their uncompromised devotion to their papa, so he allowed them to continue their morning routine. They didn't disturb Tomi but cautiously crept up and curled up next to him. Alexeev patted them both on the head. "Now you behave," he whispered. Then he continued back down the stairs. It was six o'clock but no one was up yet. *Don't they know it's Tomi's birthday?*

he thought. *I guess I'll have to start breakfast myself.* He filled the water pot and set it on the stove then got the fire started.

A few minutes later, Pavel came through the kitchen door with an armful of food from the cellar. "What are you doing down here? You should be upstairs with Tomi." Alexeev smiled and kissed him on the cheek then started back to the bedroom. "We can manage…Foka already has the menu planned for the whole day."

He met Vanya on the stairs, dressed and ready for the day. "Good morning Uncle Lexee. Did you and Tomi sleep well?"

"Yes, I think so…I'll bring Tomi down when he's ready to get up, but he doesn't usually get up this early."

He carefully opened the door and saw the three of them still curled up together on the bed, each of them purring. Alexeev chuckled to himself. "They are truly three of a kind." He lit the lamp on the dresser and got out a set of clothes for Tomi then poured some water into the pot he had hung in the fireplace. He sat quietly next to Tomi on the bed and started stroking his back. In just a few minutes, Tomi rolled over and looked up at him and smiled.

"I…love…you, *moy…general*," he said, half mumbling. The words were distinct enough for Alexeev to understand.

Alexeev wrapped his strong arms around Tomi and kissed him. "I love you too, *schast'ye moye*." He felt the tears starting to fill his eyes so he quickly started to wipe them away. But Tomi reached his left hand up to Alexeev's face and brushed one of the tears onto his finger, then brought it to his lips and kissed it. They both laughed and kissed as they held on to each other desperately and cuddled.

After a few minutes, Tomi sat up and pointed to the dresser. "T…tro…*trost'*[152]," he said with some difficulty. Alexeev saw the cane leaning up against the side of the dresser. Tomi had used it in the past when his rheumatism had become very painful, and also after his injury in the army. It sounded like he wanted to try to use it now. It wasn't easy for Tomi to submit to being carried wherever he went. Alexeev brought the cane to him and laid it on the bed beside him. "Let's get you dressed for breakfast."

Alexeev had picked out Tomi's best white silk shirt, his favourite burgundy robe lined in gold braid and his pink trousers. Tomi looked at him a little

[152] *trost'*: Cane or walking stick

confused about having to wear such fine clothes, but he didn't have the strength to argue or to form the words. After Tomi was dressed, Alexeev knelt down and pulled his stockings up under his trousers, then put on his good brown boots. "There, I think you're ready to face the day now."

The walk from the bedroom down the stairs and into the dining room was a slow struggle for Tomi, and an anxious several minutes for Alexeev, but he knew Tomi needed to do this on his own. He shook as he walked and nearly stumbled a few times, but he managed to make it all the way with the encouragement of his devoted lover. As they sat down at the table, Pavel brought in Tomi's porridge and a plate of *blini* and sausages for Alexeev.

"You're looking good this morning, master," he said. "You must have had a good night's sleep." Pavel leaned in and kissed Tomi's forehead and set the bowl in front of him.

Alexeev noticed the unintentional look of dissatisfaction on Tomi's face, and realised he must be getting tired of liquified food for every meal. Aside from Sveta's apple candy, he hadn't had any solid food for a month. He cut a few of his sausages into small pieces and placed them on a plate for Tomi, along with a few of the *blini*. "Now I want you to eat these slowly." He picked up Tomi's fork and placed it in his left hand. "You'll be eating like the rest of us in no time."

Tomi looked up at Alexeev and half-smiled then he forked a piece of sausage and put it in his mouth. He did fairly well, eating most of what Alexeev gave him, and he managed to eat some of the porridge as well. But he looked forward to the tea most of all. He had woken up with a headache and it was still lingering well into breakfast. Vanya joined the boys about halfway through breakfast and brought out another plate of Sveta's apple candy, but Alexeev insisted Tomi wasn't ready for more just yet.

Alexeev had several things he wanted to get done before friends and family started arriving in the afternoon, so he asked Vanya if he could help Tomi with his hot bath. Vanya was pleased to help out, so after breakfast he found Kirill who helped him fill and light the boiler for the hot water. While Tomi soaked and relaxed, Vanya read to him from some of Shakespeare's sonnets and ended with sonnet 126.

O thou, my lovely boy, who in thy power
Dost hold Time's fickle glass, his sickle, hour;
Who hast by waning grown, and therein show'st

Thy lovers withering as thy sweet self grow'st;
If Nature, sovereign mistress over wrack,
As thou goest onwards, still will pluck thee back,
She keeps thee to this purpose, that her skill
May time disgrace and wretched minutes kill.
Yet fear her, O thou minion of her pleasure!
She may detain, but not still keep, her treasure:
Her audit, though delay'd, answer'd must be,
And her quietus is to render thee.[153]

Tomi slumped down in the tub, as if maybe he realised this sonnet revealed that his youth had been overtaken and overrun by time, and death would soon be upon him. It was a terrifying idea that he may be on his way out of this world. He abandoned the religions of his youth, both the Christian and the Judaic, so the idea of an afterlife or an eternal soul was neither a recurring thought of dread or a fear. He had concluded one's existence was merely a flicker in time and we should make the most of every moment we are alive.

He treasured each day, each hour, each minute he spent with his beloved Alexeev, yet wondered what his lover would do or become once he no longer had this burdensome old man to care for. Simply living out each day became a challenge and bothersome, and many of his thoughts circled around ways to end his life peacefully: to put an end to his suffering, but mainly, to end the burden his lover had to endure. He wasn't ready to die though. He and his lover were together and that had to count for something.

Vanya helped him get out of the tub and helped dry him off. "It looks like Alexeev has left some scented oil for you." Tomi stepped into the trousers and pulled them up with one hand. Vanya tied the dark pink sash around Tomi's waist then handed him the silk shirt and burgundy robe. Tomi put a few droplets of the oil on his hand and rubbed it on his chest and neck, then finished getting dressed, and the two of them walked back out to the dining room. Pavel had cleared the table, so they continued on into the parlour and sat on the settee.

As soon as they sat down, Misha and Mitya spied from around the corner to see what was going on. Tomi mumbled, "*Idi sy...uda...lap...ochka*![154]" And his

---

[153] William Shakespeare (1564-1616), English poet and playwright, Sonnet #126 (*Public Domain*)

[154] *Idi syuda, lapochka*!: Come here, honey! (Literally, come here, little paw!)

two treasures quickly pranced up to the settee and hopped up onto his lap. As soon as he started petting them, they began to purr and knead his lap. The sight was almost comical to Vanya who had never had any animals as pets, though Sveta was always urging him to find a nice lapdog. He decided long ago that any animal he had would need to earn its keep, either by eggs, milk, cheese or the ultimate sacrifice: sausage! But Tomi saw the value of pets as companions. He didn't know how he would have coped these last six years if it hadn't been for his two feline friends.

Alexeev came back just before noon so he could make sure Foka and Pavel had things well underway for the festivities. Foka managed to bake everything in the outbuilding kitchen so Tomi wouldn't suspect a surprise was brewing. There were already a few arrivals from town and Pavel was able to divert them to the outbuilding so Tomi could be properly surprised.

The city treasurer, Rurik, and his wife Kapeka had arrived, along with councilmember Grigori and his wife and brother-in-law Polina and Arseni. Some of the neighbours had also arrived early: Melor and his wife and two daughters, Pasha and his wife and son, Yuriy and his wife, son, and three daughters, and Dmitry and his wife and four sons. Alexeev had also sent word to Alena, Gevorg and also Ludi since they were some of the closest and last friends and relatives they had seen along their trip home, but he knew the chances of any of them making the trip were slim.

Tomi would be happy if just the members of his own household were present, so Alexeev was hopeful the afternoon celebration would be a success. All of Tomi's servants would be attending the party, including the new recruits: Pavel, Kirill, Anton, Gugal, Viktor, Roman, Libor, Milan, Foka, Ivan, Nikita and Demyan. So far, the count was up to thirty-nine, and he was still expecting three more families in the neighbourhood, and three or four more businessmen and merchants from town. His tentative count, which included everyone who had given him a firm commitment, was sixty-seven, including the guest of honour.

By one o'clock, the last of the guests had arrived including several tag-alongs, which brought the count to seventy-eight. Tomi was getting hungry and looked like he was getting quite concerned that Alexeev seemed so distracted. But Vanya assured him lunch was being prepared, and Alexeev had some pressing engagements he needed to attend to in the meantime.

Finally, they could postpone the surprise no longer. All the food, drink and gifts were ready and waiting in the outbuilding, along with seventy-five anxious and hungry guests. Pavel quieted everyone down while Alexeev went back into the house to escort Tomi to the festivities.

"Tomi, I thought we might take a short walk before we eat," he said as he helped him get up from the settee. He handed him his cane and they walked outside. Vanya quickly walked out the kitchen door to join the crowd.

Tomi struggled to speak, "You work…too hard. You…should rest…more."

"Now, don't you start worrying about me. I get plenty of rest at night." They walked slowly down the front path, then turned to go towards the outbuilding. Fortunately, Viktor and Roman had directed all the guests to park their carriages on the far side of the outbuilding, well out of sight from the path they were taking. Many of Tomi's day lilies were in bloom, so the pathway was lined in pink, white and yellow blooms.

They stopped for a moment and bent down to take a better look at the beauties. Tomi hadn't told Alexeev the vision in his left eye was still blurry but Alexeev had his suspicions. He noticed how Tomi didn't react to people entering the room from his left until they were almost in front of him and he wasn't reading again on his own yet. "How are you feeling? Did the bath relax you this morning?"

Tomi nodded and slowly stood back up. He held the cane in his left hand and leaned against Alexeev. "Tired…so tired."

"We just have a little farther to go and then we can have some lunch." He put his arm around Tomi to help support him as he walked. As they came up to the door, Alexeev made sure he jiggled the handle to let everyone know they were coming in. He opened the door and the room was very dark. Tomi could smell fresh baked bread and roasted vegetables so he knew someone was inside. They took a few steps into the darkness and suddenly, he heard shouts of joy and congratulations, bells and whistles and noisemakers. Then little by little, the crowd started lighting candles and lamps and Tomi could see a host of friends and neighbours all smiling and laughing and wishing him well. The hugs and kisses went on for quite a while so everyone could wish their friend a happy birthday. Tomi looked at Alexeev and shook his head, but he half-smiled at the same time so Alexeev knew he approved of the festivities.

Finally, everyone gathered around the two long tables. Tomi and Alexeev sat side by side at the head of the first table and Vanya sat just to the left of Tomi. Foka, Ivan, Kirill, Viktor and Roman brought out five large earthen jugs of blackberry wine and filled everyone's goblet. Many of these goblets were part of the set given to Tomi and Alexeev by his *Tetushka*. They looked at each other and smiled, and Tomi thought he saw the start of a tear in Alexeev's eye.

Once all the goblets were filled, Vanya stood up and lifted his glass. "First of all, I would like to thank each and every one of you for taking the time to join us in celebrating our dear Tomi's birthday." Several in the crowd pounded the table as a sign of approval. "My *Dyadya Medved'* means so much to me, I can't even begin to say how much. He has been my second father and he has been my closest friend. He was there when I met my wife for the first time, and he was there when I married her. He was there when my first child was born. He also encouraged me to take over my father's business after his passing, and he helped comfort me while I mourned his death. I could have never asked for a better, more caring uncle than my dear friend Tomi."

Then he turned to Tomi. "May your life be filled with happiness and may the gods and fates bring you many more years to celebrate!" Everyone raised their goblets and cheered, then they all drank together. The food was passed around and everyone talked, and laughed, and ate, and drank for several hours. During the meal, each of the guests would take a turn at coming up to Tomi and giving him a gift. Many of the gifts were simple: a jar of homemade preserves, a plate of cookies, a box of candy, scented soaps, a scarf, a new set of handkerchiefs, a woollen cap and a bag containing four tulip bulbs imported from Holland given to him by Kapeka, the city treasurer's wife. She knew how much Tomi adored flowers of every kind, and these treasures from Holland were still used as currency in many areas in and around Holland.

By mid-afternoon, Tomi was feeling exhausted and Alexeev could see he was not going to last much longer without getting some rest. He told Vanya to make sure the guests continued to enjoy themselves as long as they desired. He picked up Tomi and carried him back into the house and up to the bedroom. Tomi was so tired he almost fell asleep in Alexeev's arms before they even got to the bedroom.

As Alexeev set Tomi down on the bed, he felt him start to shiver. "Are you cold, Tomi?" Tomi nodded and quickly tucked himself under the covers. Alexeev started a fire then took off his clothes and got under the covers with Tomi. He wrapped his arms around him to help transfer his heat to Tomi. Within minutes Tomi stopped shivering and drifted off into a calm sleep. Alexeev hadn't shut the door all the way, and soon Misha and Mitya came wandering in the bedroom.

They meowed softly from the floor, seeking permission to join in the slumber. "Yes, yes, you can both come up," Alexeev whispered. "But be careful not to wake him." They hopped up onto the bed. Misha snuggled in by Tomi's stomach and Mitya curled up on Alexeev's pillow just behind his head.

They had napped for less than an hour when Alexeev heard the sound of another carriage pulling in alongside the house. He could hear Vanya and Pavel talking, but he couldn't make out what was being said. Soon he heard footsteps coming up the stairs and then a gentle knock on the bedroom door. Alexeev carefully removed himself from the bed and pulled his shirt on over his head. He opened the door and to his surprise it was Ivan, Katia's son. He immediately put his finger up to his mouth, motioning Ivan to keep quiet, but then he grabbed him and gave him a big hug.

"It's good to see you," he whispered. "Are Katia and Alena here too?"

"Yes, Pavel took them out to the party to get something to eat." He patted Alexeev's shoulder, then examined his hand.

"Yes, everything healed very nicely." He smiled and gave Ivan another hug. "I am so glad you could make it." Then he realised he wasn't wearing any trousers. "Come in while I get dressed. Then I'll wake Tomi and see if he's ready to go back downstairs." Ivan sat on the bed while Alexeev got dressed. Mitya gingerly made his way over and sniffed Ivan's coat, then rubbed against his arm and started to purr. Tomi was still fast asleep.

Alexeev knew he could usually sleep through anything if he was tired enough. He went over to the bed and gently shook Tomi's shoulder. "Tomi, a few more guests have arrived. Would you like to get up and go downstairs again and visit for a while?" Tomi stretched his arm out and yawned. Then reached up and gave Alexeev a kiss and nodded his head. Alexeev motioned for Ivan to leave. "Let's see, it might get a little cold this evening, so I think you ought to wear something a little warmer. How about the blue robe with the sash? I think that one's a little heavier than the burgundy one. Then if we go back to the outbuilding you can wear your long coat."

"Who?" asked Tomi.

"Well, I guess you've already been sufficiently surprised for one day… Your niece, Alena, is here with Katia and Ivan."

Tomi got noticeably more excited. He looked around for his cane but didn't see it leaning up against the dresser like it usually was.

"I'm sorry, I think I left your cane in the hall…you can lean on me though." He helped Tomi to his feet then wrapped the robe around him and helped him get his arms in the sleeves. "Now let me put the sash around you." He wrapped the sash twice around Tomi's waist then tied it loosely. "How's that?" Tomi motioned for his hat. "Ah yes, we mustn't let those ears get cold." He handed Tomi his hat but Tomi tucked it under the sash.

"Brush…I need…to…my hair."

"Of course, I should have known." He reached for the brush on top of the dresser. "Would you like me to help?" Tomi nodded. There was a small bottle of lavender oil on the dresser next to the brush, so Alexeev handed the bottle to Tomi as he started to brush his hair (even though there wasn't much to brush). But Alexeev knew how important the routine was to Tomi's self-confidence. Tomi placed a few drops of the oil on his fingers, then reached up and rubbed it on Alexeev's neck. Alexeev stopped and smiled. He put the brush under Tomi's chin. "I'm supposed to be getting you ready, not the other way around." Tomi unbuttoned Alexeev's shirt and rubbed some of the oil on Alexeev's chest then smiled and started to laugh. "I love you so much, *schast'ye moye*," he said as he took the bottle from Tomi and placed it on the nightstand, then kissed him. They finished getting dressed and then Alexeev placed his arm around Tomi for support. "Are you ready?"

"Yes…*moy general*."

Off they went in their slow trek down the stairs and into the front parlour where Ivan was waiting patiently. As soon as Tomi saw Ivan, he reached out to greet him. Ivan rushed over and gave Tomi a hug and kiss, then the three of them headed on out to the party.

"There is plenty to eat, Ivan, so don't be shy. As soon as I get Tomi settled, I'll introduce you to some of our guests."

Once they got inside the outbuilding, Pavel and Alena immediately took Tomi and whisked him away, and Katia joined Alexeev and Ivan. They made their way through the crowd, and Alexeev proudly retold the amazing story of the roof repair and Ivan's bravery.

"Yes, he grabbed my arm just as I was thundering down the roof towards him…any other man would have moved aside for fear my momentum would take them down as well. But not our Ivan. He held on to me as I dangled over the edge of the roof. I was amazed at his incredible strength! He was obviously in pain too, but he sucked up the courage to maintain his grip. He would have gone down with me if I hadn't forced him to let me go." There were 'ooos' and 'aaaws' from the crowd as they listened to him recounting the details.

Polina reached out and put her tiny hands around Ivan's bicep as he flexed instinctively. Then she smiled at him and stroked his hair as he blushed. "That was very brave of you, my dear. Weren't you afraid you might fall?"

"The thought never even crossed his mind," interrupted Alexeev. "And I'm sure he saved my life in the process. If he hadn't grabbed my arm the way he did, I would have gone tumbling down at a terrible speed. But he held on to me and stopped the momentum." He put his hand on Ivan's shoulder. "And, as you can see, I'm perfectly all right now, thanks to this brave young man."

Ivan never forgot how Alexeev retold the story that day, making it sound like Ivan was the hero, and a muscular one at that. He admired Alexeev, and later in life he would think time and again how selfless Alexeev was to give all the credit to him rather than putting the focus on himself.

As the afternoon progressed, some of the men gathered in the back yard to play *svaika*[155], while the children got together and played *babki*[156]. The women brought Tomi out to watch the games. They set up several chairs and benches and Pavel brought out a few blankets for those who were feeling the chill. Each of the women rooted for their man as they had their turn, and Tomi cheered for Alexeev every time he threw the iron peg. Alexeev always seemed to surpass the skill of the other players, which was fine with Tomi, but it did seem to create some tension among the women. After a few rounds, Tomi motioned for Alexeev.

"Sit…with me?" he asked.

Alexeev immediately sat next to Tomi and put his arm around him. "I'm sorry, I shouldn't have neglected you. After all, this is your birthday." Tomi leaned up against Alexeev's chest and could smell the lavender oil mixed with his personal manly scent that Tomi adored. He unbuttoned one of Alexeev's shirt buttons. Alexeev grabbed Tomi's wrist. "Not here…not in front of everyone." Then Tomi relaxed and was content just being held by his lover.

Just after sundown, another carriage pulled in alongside the house. Pavel walked over to see who had arrived, then escorted the young man to where Tomi and Alexeev were seated. "He says he knows the two of you, but he wouldn't tell me his name."

---

[155] *Svaika*: A traditional Russian folk game played with iron pegs (also *Quoits*)

[156] *Babki*: A traditional Russian game played with the leg bones of cattle

The young man walked over in front of Tomi, knelt down before him and bowed his head. The hood from his cloak was covering his head so neither Tomi nor Alexeev knew who the fellow was. He took Tomi's hand and kissed it. "Ludi sends his love but regrets he cannot make this trip in person."

Alexeev sat up straight. "I recognise that voice…Timur, is it you?"

He kept his head bowed. "Yes, master. Forgive me for my failings when we last met and permit me to stay…I beg you." He sounded like he was nearly in tears.

There was something wrong but Alexeev didn't understand. He put his hand out and tried to lift Timur's head, but he jerked it back down. "Timur, what has happened?"

"Private…in private," whispered Tomi.

"Yes, let's go into the house where we can talk." Alexeev helped Tomi up from the chair and the three of them went into the house and into the parlour. "Now what's going on? Why would Ludi send you instead of Yuri?"

Timur finally pulled the hood back and lifted his head into the light. It was bruised and beaten and it looked like the bruises went down his neck as well. Alexeev pulled back Timur's shirt and he could see cuts and bruises all over his neck, chest, back and torso, and from the bloodstains on Timur's trousers, it was evident he had wounds all over his body.

"It was my own undoing," he said. Then he started to cry.

He told them the whole story. A week after Tomi and Alexeev had left Ludi's, he started boasting to his friends how he had been sexually aggressive with a man in a wrestling bout. He spread the story through the town and laughed whenever anyone would scold him or try to chastise him for his immoral actions. His father tried to take the strap to him, but he overpowered his father and threw the strap into the field. Timur kept up the boasting and continued to defy his father.

Then during the New Year's celebrations, he got drunk and struck his father in the face when he refused to allow him to continue working in the bakery. His father kicked him out of the house. Then he tried to stay with friends for a while, but he got thrown out of one house after the other because he couldn't keep his mouth shut about the wrestling incident. In April, a week before Easter, the men on the town council, along with many of the prominent men in the neighbourhood, decided they could not let Timur's sin go unpunished. They found him and dragged him into a field, surrounded him, then beat him with their fists, clubs and sticks. Timur managed to escape the mob and fled to Ludi's house where he hid out for the night. The next day, Ludi gave Timur his old carriage, a week's supply of food and precise directions to Storozhevsk and to Tomi's cottage. He made his escape that night, but feared he was being followed for several days after he started his journey. It wasn't until he reached *Ust-Sysolsk* that he knew he had made it safely away.

"Don't worry, Tomi, no one knows I hid out at Ludi's and I never told anyone where—"

"I think we understand," interrupted Alexeev. "I think you need to get cleaned up though…and I have some clean clothes you can wear." Alexeev took Timur into the bathing room. The water was still warm from earlier in the day. "You start cleaning up and I'll bring some clean clothes down for you to change into."

As Tomi sat alone in the parlour, he thought about what all this could mean, why these things were happening now. He contemplated what he should do and how he should react. He loved Alexeev but he also knew Alexeev had feelings for Timur. He didn't want to force Alexeev to stay, or to make him feel obligated to stay to take care of him, but he also did not want to create an opportunity for Alexeev to leave when it might not be necessary. He felt a hard knot in his stomach and then he felt the room starting to spin.

It wasn't quite the same feeling he had before though. This couldn't be happening again, he thought, not when he was finally making some progress. Then his left eyelid started to twitch and he felt the rest of his face twitching and then go slightly numb. His arms and legs began to shake uncontrollably and he lost his balance. He landed hard on the floor, splitting his lip on the corner of the table on the way down. He was fortunate he didn't catch his eye on the sharp corner, otherwise, he might have lost his sight. There was a helpless feeling of not being able to move or speak. He couldn't yell out or even reach for something to throw, anything that would make noise. He didn't know if the sound of him crashing to the floor had made any noise at all.

Everything was a blur and a whisper. His left arm was pinned between the couch and his body, and his left leg wasn't strong enough to push himself away from the couch. He could do nothing but lay there and wait for Alexeev to come in and discover his dilemma. He could hear the clock chiming in the background but he couldn't count the bongs. The pendulum seemed like it was ticking slower and slower. *Maybe this was what death is like?* he thought. Then complete darkness filled his mind and he lost consciousness.

Only a few moments later, Alexeev came back into the parlour to find Tomi trapped on the floor between the settee and the table. He quickly rushed to the window and threw it open and yelled for Alena. Then he pulled the table away and began tending to his broken lover. Tomi's body was still twitching like a fish thrown onto the shore of a pond and his muscles were tense and rigid. "I shouldn't have left you alone, I shouldn't have left you alone," he cried as he picked him up off the floor and set him on the settee. He saw the laceration on Tomi's lip and stopped the bleeding with a napkin that was on the table. Tomi's eyes opened slightly and Alexeev could see his eyes looked like they were rolling upwards. All he could see was the whites of his eyes. "You're going to be all right. Alena will know what to do and then we'll send for the doctor."

Alena and Katia came running through the kitchen door followed by Ivan, Pavel and several of the guests. "Ivan, keep everyone out of the parlour until I can find out what's wrong," said Alena as she stepped through the parlour door. "Pavel, I need fresh water and several clean cloths." She knelt down by Tomi and watched his breathing: erratic and shallow. She felt his skin for temperature: cold and damp. Then unbuttoned his shirt and pressed her ear to his chest to listen to his heart: rapid beat and irregular.

"The doctor said he had apoplexy before. Is that what this is? Has he had another episode?" Alexeev could barely get the words out, he was so concerned.

"I'm not sure. This doesn't seem like that kind of episode." Pavel brought in a pail of water and several cloths. She wiped his forehead and face then noticed Tomi's eyes. They looked like they were rolling back in their sockets. "I've seen this before…Alexeev, were you with Tomi when this happened?"

"No, I had left the room for a few minutes."

"Where did you find him?" There was a sense of urgency in her voice.

"He was on the floor between the settee and the table…he was shaking, more than he is now."

"Pavel, can you go get the doctor?" She escorted Pavel to the front door and instructed him exactly what to tell the doctor. Then she returned to Tomi. "I'm not positive, but I think his episode is what they call falling sickness. I have only seen it a few times though."

"I've heard of that before. I think one of the neighbour's children had that where I lived in Moscow." Alexeev thought for a moment. "But those episodes happen more frequently, don't they? And the little boy only lived to about eight years old…no, this couldn't be the same thing."

"Like I said, I don't know for sure." She looked around the room. "I don't think we should move him until the doctor gets here, but we need to get it warm in here so he doesn't catch a chill." Katia got up and started a fire in the fireplace and then brought over a blanket from the armchair.

Meanwhile, Timur had finished his bath and had changed into the clothes Alexeev had brought for him. He came into the dining room to find the crowd of guests pressed up against the parlour doors. "What's happening, did someone die?"

Several of the ladies turned around and shushed him. Then Kapeka said, "Tomi is the one who's dying! Now be quiet so we can hear what's happening." The shock was too much for Timur and it was probably exacerbated by his multiple wounds, lack of food and the fact he had never been around anyone who had died since he was a young child. Suddenly, his legs became weak, his face felt cold and he crumpled to the floor. One of Tomi's neighbours realised Timur had fainted, so he poured a glass of water on his face.

Timur woke up with only slight discomfort and humiliation. As soon as Timur regained his composure, he wiped off his face and made his way through the crowd to the parlour doors. He hesitated for a moment but then opened the doors and walked in, shutting them behind him. Misha and Mitya slipped in with him before he closed the door. Timur sat in the armchair at the far end of the parlour so he wouldn't disturb Alena's examination of Tomi. At first, the two cats started to approach the settee where Alexeev was cradling Tomi, but they quickly turned around and sat on the floor on either side of Timur.

Tomi started to regain consciousness and tried to sit up, but Alena held him down and whispered to him not to move. "Headache," he said as he pressed his hand against the right side of his head. Alexeev took a damp cloth and held it against the area Tomi had his hand over. Tomi's breathing sounded like it was forced or challenging for him.

"Do you know what happened?" asked Alena.

Tomi shook his head. But then he held his hand up and moved it in a circle. "Room…spinning."

"How do you feel now?" she asked. "Is the room still spinning?"

Tomi shook his head again but repeated, "Headache." Then he relaxed and started breathing more normally. He held Alexeev's hand and then shut his eyes.

"He should sleep until the doctor gets here. I don't think there's anything else we can do for him right now."

Alexeev nodded his head and leaned back on the settee with Tomi's head resting in his lap. Alena and Katia left the parlour so Tomi could rest a little easier. Of course, all the guests wanted to know how their host was doing, so she had quite a bit of explaining to do. She managed to calm the crowd and reassure them the doctor would need to examine Tomi before anything else could be done. Katia and Ivan helped migrate the guests back to the outbuilding and backyard to resume their conversations where they would not disturb Tomi's slumber. Many of them resumed their games, which also kept the children occupied. But Timur stayed in the parlour with Alexeev. They talked quietly while Tomi slept.

"Maybe I should leave," said Timur. "You don't need my presence complicating things when Tomi's health is waning."

"Don't be ridiculous. Tomi and I have already reconciled what happened at Ludi's. Besides, where would you go? You can't go back home with the townspeople wanting to kill you. And I know you don't have any other relatives to stay with…no, you need to stay here, at least until we can figure out what you're going to do and where you're going to go." Alexeev noticed he hadn't closed the window all the way but he didn't want to wake Tomi by getting up. He pointed to the window. "Would you mind closing the window and drawing the curtain?"

As Timur got up to closed the window, Misha and Mitya followed him closely. After he shut the window, he noticed Ludi's painting of Alexeev and Tomi hanging next to the painting of Alexeev in a flex-pose. "Ludi does beautiful work. I wish you could have seen the compilations he did combining some of your poses with mine." As he looked at Alexeev and watched him stroke Tomi's face while he gently held his sleeping body, he finally realised Alexeev wasn't in the relationship for mere physical satisfaction. Alexeev's part in this union was a sacrifice of his will, a setting aside of his desires. He knew the two of them had physical relations but he was now seeing a different aspect of their love. It reminded him of how his father had sacrificed himself his own needs so he could give him a better life. He would always buy new clothes for Timur before he bought new shoes for himself. Timur always got the biggest portion of meat and the most comfortable bed in the house. His father worked long hours so Timur could have a little more of everything. Now he feared he would have nothing.

Pavel returned within about an hour, but he didn't have the doctor with him. "Doctor Vasilyev is in *Ust-Sysolsk* delivering a baby and isn't expected back for at least a week."

"Then Alena will take care of him until the doctor returns or until Tomi gets better." Alexeev saw the look of dread on Pavel's face. "Now don't you worry about him. He is going to be all right. You heard Alena. She said this episode isn't like the last one."

Pavel knelt down beside Tomi and gently touched his forehead. "I don't know what I'd do without you."

Just then Tomi opened his eyes and looked around as if nothing had happened. He reached out and brushed a tear away from Pavel's cheek, "Going…to be…al…right." Then he sat up and felt the cut on his lip that was now slightly swollen.

"We think you must have passed out and hit your lip on the table on the way down."

Tomi looked at Pavel and smiled then shook his head. "*Ya neuklyujeyy!*[157]" He didn't want to give him anything more to worry about but Pavel wasn't convinced by Tomi's charade.

After Tomi regained his composure, he motioned for them all rejoin the party and asked Alexeev to help him make his way back out to continue watching the games. Earlier while they were eating, Kapeka had revealed that her husband had brought some fireworks from Cathay, and Tomi didn't want to miss the excitement. He had never seen fireworks before, but heard much about them from merchants who traded in the East. As they arrived in the backyard, the men were finishing their games for the evening. A few of them had already started a bonfire in Tomi's backyard firepit.

Foka and Ivan brought out sausages and skewered vegetables to roast over the fire and Libor and Milan brought out a large kettle of *Krupnik* to heat up. As the rest of the company joined the group around the fire, Anton, Gugal, Viktor, and Roman moved the benches and chairs closer to the firepit along with the blankets, and distributed them to those who wanted them. Alexeev sat Tomi down next to the firepit and wrapped a blanket around him. For a few hours, the company enjoyed eating the roasted sausages and vegetables, and especially the hot *Krupnik.*

---

[157] *Ya neuklyujeyy!*: I'm awkward!

Alexeev could tell Tomi was getting tired so he called out, "Rurik, how long are you going to make us wait? The host is getting impatient!"

"It sounds like the host is not the only one who is impatient," he replied. "But I won't make anyone wait any longer." He opened up the wooden box he had been sitting on and asked a few of the men to help him move it farther away from the crowd. It took them several minutes to set up the display, but they finally had everything ready. One by one, he lit the fireworks. Some of them resembled fiery fountains of red, yellow and orange. Some of them shot up into the sky over the crowds' heads, then exploded in whites, blues, greens and reds. The display was remarkable. A few of them were bright enough to make the backyard as bright as day for a few seconds. Everyone in the company was amazed and excited to see such a festive spectacle. Alexeev sat next to Tomi with his arm around him. He felt Tomi jerk every now and then from the sudden explosions or loud noises but Tomi smiled the entire time and thoroughly enjoyed the evening.

Once the last firework fizzled in the sky, and Tomi finished his last sip of *Krupnik*, Alexeev knew it was time to get him to bed. He stood up and thanked everyone for coming, for the gifts and especially for their support of their friend Tomi. Then he excused the two of them, and helped Tomi back into the house. Pavel made sure everyone knew they could stay as long as they liked, and even offered the cots and blankets in the outbuilding for anyone who wanted to spend the night. The ladies, of course, were welcomed to take the spare bedrooms in the house.

Tomi was so tired, Alexeev had to carry him up the stairs just like he had done six years earlier. He set him down on the bed and built a fire in the fireplace, then came over and helped Tomi finish getting undressed. "Did you have a good celebration, *schast'ye moye*?"

Tomi nodded and yawned, then tucked his frail worn-out body under the covers. Alexeev got undressed and joined Tomi in bed. "I…love you…*moy…general*." He leaned over and kissed Alexeev then rested his head on Alexeev's chest.

Chapter 27

Parterre De Broderie for Tomi

The rest of spring passed by too quickly for Alexeev. Vanya had left to go back home a week after Tomi's birthday party but promised to bring the entire family to visit over the next summer. Alena, Katia and Ivan also had to get back to their own business, so as soon as Doctor Vasilyev returned, they took their leave as well. Alexeev spent most of his afternoons working on the property with Timur, Libor, Milan and occasionally Viktor or Roman would help out as well. Timur had decided to stay on to help Alexeev, with Tomi's permission and blessing, as long as they needed him. The rest of the staff kept Tomi's business going and maintained the affairs of the estate.

Pavel, Ivan and Foka were getting ready for the largest blackberry harvest the estate had seen since it was established, which meant they would have both an excellent wine and cordial production as well as an abundance of blackberry jam. The summer started out warm, which helped to ensure the fruit would be large and flavourful. There would also be a plentiful honey harvest throughout the growing season, and Alexeev made sure he took advantage of planting as many of Galina's flower seeds as possible so they could be well established in the estate's gardens by mid-summer. He also planted many of the seeds around the cottage to help beautify Tomi's front yard as well.

As the months went on though, Tomi's health continued to decline. His eyesight continued to get worse. Since he was unable to read for himself, Alexeev and Pavel made sure they read to him every night before dinner. His headaches continued at a furious pace and the teas didn't seem to do much good anymore. The severity of the pain was so intense at times Tomi would need to be isolated in the bedroom with the shades drawn so the light from the window would not hurt his eyes. Even the doctor's prescription of laudanum didn't seem to do much good.

Misha and Mitya seemed to sense he was getting worse because they were continually by his side now, rubbing up against him or curling up beside him. They followed Alexeev whenever he would carry Tomi downstairs and throughout the house and would even follow them outside when Alexeev would take Tomi out to sit under a shade tree for a mid-morning picnic.

Tomi's speech had improved somewhat though, much to the delight of Alexeev and everyone else who needed to communicate with him. He spoke slowly and deliberately, but he no longer struggled to form or find the words to say. But his mind would sometimes wander, and Alexeev suspected part of his physical problems may be caused by something going on in his head. The doctor hadn't confirmed Alexeev's suspicions but didn't deny the possibility, and Alexeev remembered Doctor Leskov thought there could be a growth behind Tomi's eyes causing the headaches.

During the last week of July, Tomi asked Pavel to go into town and make an appointment with the Advocate for him. So, on the last day of July, Alexeev took Tomi into town to see Nikolai Volkov, who had been Tomi's advocate and business adviser since before he started his wine business. Tomi had told Alexeev he needed to speak with Nikolai about some of the legal matters of the business. In his heart, Alexeev knew he was trying to get his affairs in order though. He had observed a change in Tomi's focus, from living with hopes and dreams, to living with the need to finish neglected projects, make amends, and divvy up possessions.

Shortly after his birthday, he gave each of his servants a bonus of 5,000 rubles and also gave each of them a deed to a parcel of his property. When Alena and Katia left, he gave them the crystal set, and he sent his collection of porcelain jars and vases with Vanya. Tomi seemed to get a tremendous amount of joy each time he gave something away, so Alexeev decided to stay quiet and let him do what he thought he needed to do.

Since he would be with Nikolai most of the afternoon, Tomi asked Alexeev to visit the local cooper and purchase another four wine barrels for Ivan, since the harvest this year was expected to far exceed last year's. Two of the barrels had already been ordered so they brought the open-bed carriage to transport them back to the cottage.

Tomi also had a list of items for Alexeev to purchase from other merchants as well: copper tubing, 500 glass bottles, cork, sugar and yeast. Alexeev checked back at the advocate's office after he visited each merchant to make sure Tomi wasn't waiting, then picked up the last items on his list and waited outside the office until Tomi was finished. Nikolai escorted Tomi out to the carriage and handed Alexeev several sealed scrolls and instructed him to keep them in a safe place. Alexeev helped Tomi into the carriage and they made their way home.

It was a very quiet ride. Alexeev wanted to ask Tomi the specifics about the documents they were carrying, but he also respected Tomi's privacy. For Tomi's part, the afternoon was exhausting and he was overdue to take his afternoon nap. He leaned his head on Alexeev's shoulder and sighed, "I'm glad it's over." Then he shut his eyes.

Alexeev put his arm around him and didn't ask anything about the papers. He pulled in alongside the cottage and carried Tomi up to his bedroom, took off his boots and clothes, and placed him under the covers. Ivan took charge of the supplies and asked Viktor and Roman to help with the unloading. Tomi stayed in bed through dinner and told Alexeev his stomach wasn't feeling well, so he slept until morning. Pavel and Alexeev both noticed Tomi had not been eating as he should, and he had lost a considerable amount of weight since his return from Moscow. Vanya and some of the guests at the birthday party even commented on how thin Tomi looked, but Tomi would just shrug and thank them for noticing.

The summer was getting warmer and warmer, so Pavel brought Tomi outside in the back yard every morning after Alexeev would leave. Tomi sat for hours in the shade under the tall pines that lined the back of the cottage. He would listen to the birds singing in the trees, and smell the fresh scents of the trees, grass and flowers. His lilies and chamomile gave off a strong sweet scent and every once in a while, he could smell the roses blooming in his neighbour's yard as well.

Many of the flowers Alexeev had planted from among Galina's seeds were also blooming: many colours and varieties of daisies, chrysanthemums and carnations. Misha and Mitya would sit patiently on the ground beside Tomi's chair or one would hop up onto his lap while the other would wedge himself between his leg and the arm of the chair. He would always make room to accommodate his treasures.

Often, he would have only a vague recollection of time, yet there were other occasions when he would count the seconds and try to endure the tedious humdrum of his existence. Although he longed for the day when he could again give and receive physical pleasure with Alexeev, there was a dark feeling deep inside him that was unrelenting, which mocked him and told him he would never have or give that kind of happiness again. But each afternoon, Alexeev would return from his work on the new lodge.

Each time he would kiss him and hug him and tell him how much he loved him, and each and every day he would affirm that Tomi was *schast'ye moye*. Sometimes it made Tomi cry because he wanted to be more to his lover, not a burden who had to be carried everywhere. He couldn't eat without assistance now, he couldn't get dressed without someone finding and handing him his clothes, he couldn't bathe by himself, nor could he clean up after himself. But Alexeev never complained. It even seemed sometimes as if he enjoyed taking care of him, though Tomi thought otherwise.

The hours he spent away from Tomi were hard on Alexeev. By mid-August, Tomi was eating no more than a few bites of food each meal and he was only taking a few sips of tea mixed with his regular dose of laudanum. When he would try to eat or drink more, his body would reject it and cause him to vomit. His mind was also fading fast. Most of the day, he would sit silently with Misha and Mitya and not respond to anyone else around him. He seemed to recognise Alexeev and Pavel, but everyone else seemed to be strangers to him.

Often, he would simply stare off into the distance, oblivious to the happenings around him. Doctor Vasilyev came by on the third Sunday in August but had no encouraging words for Alexeev. Instead, he suggested that Alexeev make a visit to the priest before the end of the week to make arrangements for Tomi's final services. He also advised him to immediately notify any of Tomi's family members who might want to see him before his passing. The next morning, Alexeev sent a courier to Moscow—with specific stops along the way—with the doctor's message and his own personal invitation to stay at the cottage if they chose to come.

Less than two weeks after the doctor's visit, Tomi woke up early one morning with surprising clarity of thought and understanding. He rolled over to Alexeev and put his hand on his shoulder, "*Moy general*, I want to see the progress on your lodge today." His voice was weak and soft but his words were clear and understandable.

Alexeev was startled by the request. "I don't think it would be wise to take you that far across the estate. You need to rest."

Tomi placed his hand over Alexeev's mouth, "I need to see what I'll be missing."

Alexeev sat up and got dressed then he helped Tomi get dressed. He carried him down to the kitchen where Pavel was already cooking the porridge for Tomi, and blini and sausage for everyone else. "I think Master Tomi can have *blini* and *tvorog* this morning instead of porridge." He set Tomi down in his chair next to the head of the table, then he sat down at the head and tucked an embroidered napkin under Tomi's chin. "And we'll use the good china this morning, Pavel." Tomi couldn't see the tears as they rolled down Alexeev's and Pavel's faces and they did their best to make Tomi feel like nothing was different.

Tomi finished half of his blini and took a few sips of his tea, then his eyes wandered back and forth. "Is there any blackberry jam or honey?" The question almost sounded like a final plea.

"Of course!" Pavel passed him the jam and Alexeev passed the honey. "Would you like me to put some on your blini?" Tomi nodded his head and half smiled. He took a small bite with a little jam then another small bite with a little honey and he was done.

"Pavel, Tomi and I will be going out to the other side of the property this morning and I think I'd like to take Misha and Mitya with us." Then he whispered to Pavel to gather the servants and have them join them on the grounds by the lodge. "Tomi wants to see how everything is progressing." He reached over and wiped Tomi's face with the napkin then he smiled and kissed Tomi's hand. "I think we'll bring some of your blackberry wine to celebrate."

Pavel immediately nodded in acknowledgement and went down to the cellar to get a case of the finest wine. Then he packed fourteen silver chalices. While Alexeev got Tomi ready for the trip across the grounds, Pavel ran out to the servants' quarters and instructed them to meet on the far side of the estate immediately. He gave the case of wine and the chalices to Foka and Ivan so he could go back and get Misha and Mitya. When he got back to the cottage, he called for the kitties to come to him. The two treasures seemed to know instinctively what was happening, and they jumped into Pavel's carrying basket without any hesitation.

Alexeev didn't want to use the carriage because he thought the bumps and jolts from the road would be too uncomfortable for Tomi, so he decided to carry him across the estate and Pavel walked alongside them with the furry companions. Tomi wrapped his arm around Alexeev's neck and was asleep within a few minutes of leaving the house but as soon as they arrived at the site where the lodge was going to be, he woke up.

Pavel had not yet seen the work site and he gasped with amazement as it came into sight. Instead of working on building the lodge, Alexeev, Milan, Libor, Viktor, Roman and Timur had been creating Tomi's *Parterre de Broderie*[158] garden. It was magnificent. In the centre, there were four sets of stone stairs leading to the top of a raised mound with a large stone firepit surrounded by four beautiful stone benches. Each bench was made with a different kind of stone, and the seat of each bench was carved out of a single flat stone with ornate scrolls, flowers, birds and animals engraved on the surface. The paths throughout the garden were cobbled with multi-coloured smooth pebbles gathered from the local riverbanks.

The gardens themselves were laid out in patterns of scrolls, circles and *Fleur-de-Lis*[159]. The bushes and shrubs were trimmed in the patterns of different animals and shapes, and most of the flowers were in full bloom. The waves of colour shifted gently from yellows to oranges to reds to violets to blues and then to pinks and whites. It was an amazing display and a brilliant use of patterns and colours, and a spectacular view from the benches on top of the mound.

Alexeev sat Tomi down on one of the stone benches and Pavel set down his basket on the ground. The two cats jumped out and up onto the bench next to their master. Tomi smiled and gazed out at the amazing floral display. He took a deep breath. "I knew you could do it." He looked up at Alexeev and smiled.

Alexeev sat down next to Tomi and placed his strong arm around Tomi. "You are my inspiration and my only love, *schast'ye moye*."

In a few minutes, Foka and Ivan and the rest of the servants joined them around the firepit. Foka unpacked the wine and Ivan passed out the silver chalices to each in the company: Kirill, Anton, Gugal, Viktor, Roman, Libor, Milan, Foka, Nikita, Demyan, Timur, Pavel, Alexeev and finally himself. Tomi and Alexeev would share a chalice. Foka followed him with several bottles of the finest blackberry wine and filled each goblet. Alexeev raised his goblet, but emotions overtook him and he couldn't speak. Then Tomi put his hand over Alexeev's hand on his goblet. "There are no finer boys on this earth than the ones standing before me now. I love you all dearly." With that, they all raised the goblets in agreement and drank.

---

[158] *Parterre de Broderie* (French): (Literally, embroidery floor) A garden characterised by the division of paths and beds to form an embroidery-like pattern

[159] *Fleur-de-Lis*: A design representing a flower whose three petals are joined together at the bottom. A conventionalised iris in artistic design and heraldry

Tomi moved the goblet to Alexeev's lips so he could drink, then Tomi took one sip of the wine and suddenly felt a strange sensation, like warm water pouring over his body. He set the goblet on the bench next to him and held on tight to Alexeev's hand, interlacing the fingers of their right hands. Alexeev felt their rings touch and for a moment he thought their lives would be intertwined like their fingers—forever. Then he looked into Tomi's eyes and immediately knew his end was near.

"I don't want to die, *moy general,*" Tomi said softly, his voice quivering as he spoke.

Alexeev brushed a tear from Tomi's cheek, then put his finger to his mouth and kissed the tear. "I'll never leave you, *schast'ye moye*." He leaned down and drew Tomi's face closer to his, then he kissed him on the lips. As he held the frail body in his arms, Alexeev felt Tomi's last breath leave his body. He hugged him and kissed his face and neck and held Tomi close to his chest.

The tears flowed from Alexeev's eyes as he rocked Tomi's body back and forth. Mitya and Misha sat on either side of him and rubbed their heads up against his arms. Then they gazed into his tear-swollen eyes. He reached out and petted each one to comfort them. Pavel had already fallen to his knees and was also weeping. Then, as the company realised what had transpired, they gathered around and knelt on the cobbled walkway in front of Alexeev and Tomi.

It seemed like time stood still for a while. The birds in the trees stopped singing and the leaves in the trees stopped rustling, yet there was a gentle cool breeze flowing through the garden. *It would have been a perfect day for a picnic*, Alexeev thought. *And Tomi would have loved having a picnic in his own special garden.*

As the afternoon went on, the men walked back to their quarters, two by two, with their arms around one another, or holding hands, or comforting each other with gentle words. Eventually, Timur and Pavel had to help Alexeev to his feet. Misha and Mitya hopped back into the basket as if they knew it was time to return home, and Alexeev held Tomi's body tight and close to his heart as he walked back to the cottage.

"I will never stop loving you, *schast'ye moye*."

Appendix

Russian Words and Phrases, Foreign Words and Other Words and Phrases of Interest

A

Ahelo-Pirgas: Burgas, Bulgaria

Akh, kak khorosho!: Oh, how wonderful!

The Apples of Youth and of Living Water: A traditional Russian fairy tale

B

Baba Yaga: A famous Russian fairy tale character, Baba Yaga is a wild witch of the east

Babki or knucklebones: A traditional Russian game played with the leg bones of cattle

Babulya i dedushka: Granny and grandpa

Bäckerei: (German) Bakery, bake shop

Bilious fever: A medical diagnosis often used for any fever that exhibited the symptom of nausea or vomiting in addition to an increase in internal body temperature and strong diarrhea.

Blini: Russian pancakes that are thin and flat like crepes

Blini cake: Stacked *blini* with custard or cream filling separating each layer. Topped with custard cream sauce and fresh fruit

Bol'shoye spasibo: Thank you very much

Borscht: A popular soup in Eastern Europe, usual made with beets, cabbage and potatoes

Bozhe moy!: Oh my God!

Buterbrody: Sandwiches or bread served with butter

C

Challah: A traditional Jewish braided bread

Chalka: A soft, sweet Polish bread

Chemú byt', togó ne minovát': What must be, must be. (literal) Which have not been avoided

Cheremsha: Pickled wild garlic

Chtoby vse horoshee iz starogo goda pereshlo v novy: To carry the best from the old year to the new or To all the good things of the old year was transferred to a new

Chuvstvennyy: Sensual, erotic

Chyorniy khleb: Russian rye bread or black bread

D

Da, pozhaluysta: Yes, please

Dam kusok piroga, Da kuvshin moloka: I will give you a piece of cake, and a jug of milk.

Davay!: Come on! (an enthusiastic interjection)

Dedushka: Grandpa

Desyatnik: Sargent

Do smerti: Until death

Dobroye utro: Good morning

Dorogoy: Dear, darling, sweetheart

Dostatochno!: Enough!

Draughts: Traditional Russian board game similar to parcheesi

Dushen'ka: Darling

Dvoryanin: nobleman

Dyadya Medved': Uncle Bear

E

Escargot: (French) A French delicacy, cooked land snails

F

Farshirovannyy sladkiy perets: Stuffed sweet bell peppers

Fleur-de-Lis: A design representing a flower whose three petals are joined together at the bottom. A conventionalised iris in artistic design and heraldry

Fröhliches Hanukkah, grüss gott: (German) Happy Hanukkah, good day

G

Glubzhe! Glubzhe!: Deeper! Deeper!

Gnav: A traditional card game

Gospodin: Lord, master, gentleman, mister, sir, monsieur

Gustera: White Bream (fish)

Guten Morgen: (German) Good morning

H

Halupki: Stuffed Cabbage

Herr: (German) Mister

Houska: (Czech) Bohemian sweet bread

I

Idi syuda, lapochka!: Come here, honey! (Literally, come here, little paw!)

Ikra: Caviar

Ilya Muromets: A folk hero of ancient Kievan Rus', a knight errant

J

K

Kabak: A public ale house, bar or tavern

Karnöffel: A traditional card game

Kartoshnik: Potato cakes

Ketubah: (Hebrew) Written thing. A traditional Jewish prenuptial agreement, part of the marriage ritual

Khoroshe vo otdykha moye schast'ye: Rest well, my dear (Literally, my happiness)

Khorovod: Traditional Russian and Slavic dance. Derived from old Russian, *khorovod* means "moving around the sun"

Kirschenmichel: (German) A traditional bread pudding made with cherries, cinnamon, almonds, and chocolate

Khlynov: former name of Kirov, Kirov Oblast.

Kotya, koten'ka, kotok: Kitty, kitten, little cat

Koshenya: (Ukrainian) Kitten

Kozyain: Hostler or stableman

Krupnik: (Polish) Hot honey-spiced Vodka drink

Kulich: A traditional Russian and Ukrainian Easter cake

L

La Città del Sole, written in 1602, a socialistic work by Tomasso Campanella (1568-1639) in which he attempts to reconcile humanism with Roman Catholic theology

Lapta: A traditional Russian bat and ball game

The Lay of the Twelve Dreams of Emperor Shakhaishi: 14th century Russian literature of unknown source, possibly Tibetan in origin

Lyubimyy: Darling

Lyubimyy moy: My love, my lover

M

Mamen'kin synok: Sissy boy

Medovik: Multi-layered Russian honey cake

Medovuhka: A Slavic honey-based alcoholic beverage

Medved': Bear

Milyy: Dear, or sweetheart

Mors: A sweet, non-fermented juice made from foxberries

Moy drug: My friend

Moy general: My leader, my master

Moy golyy general: My naked general

Moy khoroshiy: Literally, my good—referring to complete satisfaction

Moy robkiy drug: My timid friend

Moy malen'kiy chelovek: My little man

Moy muzh: Husband

Moye Schast'ye: My happiness, my joy

Moy sladkiy: My sweetie, my sweet

N

Nareznoy baton: A popular Russian wheat bread

Ne khorosho byt' cheloveku odnomu: It is not good for man to be alone

Nyen: Current city of St. Petersburg. The town of Nyen was a wealthy Sweedish trading centre until 1702 when it was conquered by Peter the Great and renamed Sankt Piter-Burkh

O

O, bog!: Oh god!

O Bozhe! Divnyy!: Oh my God! Marvellous!

Odin yedinstvennyy: One and only

Olad'i: Similar to traditional American pancakes, but usually smaller in size and thicker

P

Parterre de Broderie: (French) (Literally, embroidery floor) A garden characterised by the division of paths and beds to form an embroidery-like pattern

Partesny: (Partesny singing) A style of polyphonic singing, based on the Western European system of harmony and counterpoint, which arose in the early 17th century in the Ukraine and in the mid-17th century, spread to Muscovite Russia. (Reference – Orthodox Church of the Mother of God, *Joy of all the Sorrowful* – Mays Landing, NJ. churchmotherofgod.org)

The Passionate Shepherd to His Love: By Christopher Marlowe (1564-93) English poet and playwright, *Public Domain*

Pastila: (Pastels) A Russian candy similar to Turkish Delight

Pedik: Fag, queer

Pekarnya: Bakery, bake shop

Pelmeni: Russian dumplings

Pfeffernüsse: A traditional holiday spice cookie, originating in Germany, Denmark and the Netherlands

Pirozhki: Fried buns stuffed with a variety of fillings

Pozdravlayu: Congratulations

Pryaniki: A Russian spice cookie or honey bread

Pyatidesyatnik: Lieutenant

Q

Quoits and svaika: A traditional Russian folk game played with iron pegs

R

Romovaya Baba: Yeast cake saturated in syrup made with rum

Rozhdestvo Khristovo: Nativity

Rugalach: A Jewish crescent-shaped pastry

S

Sankt Piter-Burkh: Former name of St. Petersburg

Sbiten: Hot drink made from spices and herbs with honey or sugar

Sehr gut: (German) Very good

Schast'ye moye: My sweetheart

Schast'ye Zhdet: Happiness waits

Shall I Compare Thee to a Summer's Day: William Shakespeare (1564-1616) English poet and playwright, Sonnet #18, *Public Domain*

Shoynaty: (also known as Storozhevsk) is a small village about 96 kilometres northeast of Syktyvkar in the Komi Republic, Russia, on the banks of the Vychedga River

Sonya: Sleepyhead (literally, dormouse)

Spasibo, spasibo!: Thank you, thank you!

Spyashchiy medved': Sleeping (hibernating) bear

Streltsy: Soldiers

Svaika: See *Quoits*

Svinopas: Swineherd, a person who tends pigs

Syrniki: Fried cheese cakes

T

Tablier or Draughts: Traditional Russian board game similar to parcheesi

Tetushka: Auntie

Trost': Cane or walking stick

Tselovalnik: Literally, kisser. A tavern keeper, who was allegiant to the tsar

Tsvetok: Flower

Tvorog: A traditional Russian cheese, similar to farmer's or cottage cheese

U

Ubiraysya k chertu!: Get the hell out!

Ushchipnut' ikh!: Pinch them!

Ust-Sysolsk: former name of Syktyvkar

V

Vatrushka: Sweet rolls with a creamy cheese filling

Vinegret Salad: A Russian salad made with diced cooked vegetables (beetroots, potatoes, carrots), chopped onions, as well as sauerkraut and/or brined pickles

Voskhititel'no: Delectable, delicious

W

William Shakespeare: (1564–1616), English poet and playwright, Sonnet #126 (*Public Domain*)

X

Y

Ya neuklyujeyy!: I'm awkward!

Ya sobirayus' vzorvat'sya vnutri tebya: I'm going to explode inside you

Yeshcho'! Yeshcho'!: More! More!

Z

Za lyubov' i schast'ye!: For love and happiness!

Zdravstvuyte: Hello or good day